THE

Garretson Chronicle

To burn the bones of the king of Edom for lime, seems no irrational ferity; but to drink of the ashes of dead relations, a passionate prodigality.—Thomas Browne

THE

Garretson Chronicle

A NOVEL

BY GERALD WARNER BRACE

W · W · NORTON & COMPANY · INC · New York

Book Design by John Woodlock

PRINTED IN THE UNITED STATES OF AMERICA
FOR THE PUBLISHERS BY THE VAIL-BALLOU PRESS

CHAPTER 1

My FATHER's hair must have been ruddy gold long ago; I can recollect the pinkish bloom of it, like reflected glow on spun silk. But reality demands a pure white, a wave blown back from the high forehead and merging with the surrounding radiance. He always stood straight and fairly tall; he walked with the fine stride of a pedestrian, carried a stick, and surveyed mankind and nature with shining benevolence.

In Compton, his town, he moved about with the confidence of a proprietor—often hatless, so that his head was a familiar light among the tree shadows; he wore country-squire clothes —wool shirts, rough tweeds, an enveloping cape, even knit stockings and knickerbockers—all in a day when suburban gentlemen dressed in dark serge and high starched collars. He spoke with all sorts of men and neighbors, not heartily, not in shouts, but rather with cool, knowing philosophy, with certainty of good taste and ironic wisdom. When he considered the village green, the great elms, the Unitarian Church, the war memorial, the green wastepaper cans, any of the town properties, he did so with the amused modesty of one who had all such matters in charge, who knew how things ought to be and how things really were and was making the necessary allowances.

More than anyone, he made Compton aware of itself; he steered it out of the gilded age, restored it to a colonial self-

5

esteem, and actually became himself a sort of embodiment
of the esthetic and moral virtue of the classic past his vision
had created.

In a life like mine, the present is a constant assertion of the
past. The same is true for others, but I write it with the conviction of personal and harsh discovery. I emancipated myself
from things past, and abandoned them, but more and more I
have been bound and made captive by them. I find such binding an essential to continuing life. In a godless world nothing
endures but the past.

I, Ralph Garretson, happened to belong to a generation
that tried to abandon not only the past but nearly all belief.
Most of us got only a little way in the direction of abandon-
ment—some got a long way, and wrote of it in many books.
It was said to be a result of war, that lostness; but it came
from more than war, more than a few young men reveling in
disillusion. "It is through the malice of this earthly air," wrote
Melville, nearly a hundred years ago, "that only by being
guilty of Folly does mortal man arrive at the perception of
Sense." We advanced from faith into reason, and inevitably
reason has led us to unreason, and so in time we shall come
round to faith again.

My father was not the sort of country dweller who recorded
temperature and rainfall and barometric pressure, but he did
hold himself responsible for such affairs; morning and evening
he stepped out and breathed appreciatively, as though he were
tasting the firmament. To him, as to others before him, this
earthly air was charged with benevolence. If rain fell for a
week, or if snows piled up or intensest cold lay on the land, he
felt that divine poetry was expressing itself and he explicated
to the rest of us—a sort of technical, half-humorous gloss on
the text of creation. It gratified him that Compton was
recognized to be the coldest town in the county, but actually
any event of weather, cold or hot, gratified him.

I suppose his way of life was Emersonian. His face expressed it almost self-consciously in its lines of thought, in its abstractedness, in a fine sort of light that radiated from it. Yet he considered himself a failure—and for a long time I did too. It was part of my purpose to record that failure, to point to his retreat from life, his holding to illusion, his ultimate ineffectiveness. I intended to say that Randall Garretson, his people, his way, his beliefs, were humanly anachronistic. At one time I held him to blame for my own ills and ineptitudes, and accused him of educating me for a transcendental dream-world that had no existence beyond his own study walls. He represented the sort of complacent benevolence that we war-taught moderns have rejected: his inherited property, his belief in God, his grace of manners, his respect for family, his sensibility—we condemned them all. Our world had no place in it for an untimely gentleman and philosopher.

Yet judgments about life have grown less and less simple. Twenty years ago the Brahmin remnants were fair game—and Ralph Garretson joined the hunt. Now I believe a humility has come upon us. It is not so easy to blame our failures on our fathers. They and we together make up a great fact, a truth that has never yet been embodied in words.

And all my past—and my father's past—comes crowding round me, and I want to embrace it with words. It is an area, a region with all dimensions of space and time, as real as anything mapped with instruments, yet except it be somehow caught in this common stock of words it has no being. When a man's father dies, the loss is in some curious sense geographical. One stands suddenly on a little hill and looks back at the settled region of his life, the secure homestead, the safety of property, the old order—an order of comforting authority and loyalties. Always in the long struggle against fear, that homestead has stood, not necessarily prosperous or materially splendid, but simply there, like love or faith. It is where, when you have to go, they have to take you in. Usually you never have to go, but *when* you do . . . Perhaps there are strong souls who need no comfort like this, and there are many waifs who know nothing of it, but for me the region over which my father presided was a steady reassurance, like a quiet harbor somewhere down to leeward. And then death, and the physical and legal dissolution. Debts, taxes, fees, confusions. Property to be sold and lost. Books to divide. Lamps, china, silver, kitchenware, junk. Great-grandmother's two spool beds. The bird's-eye desk. The Persian rug with the hole. No father any more, no grandfathers—no grand any-body—only Aunt Liddie in Boston (who wanted one maple rocker, if no one minded). And of course mother out in San Francisco who refused to return—she had got clear once and intended to stay so. And all the confusion of brothers and sisters and half brothers and half sisters. But I think to each of us survivors came separately a fatal sense of lostness. We stood each on his achieved vantage point looking back at the vestiges of our father's estate and saw it vanish like an airy nothing. We had to go from there along into the future, without refuge.

Fathers must all die—and simple as the fact is, no one is ever quite reconciled to it. But in these times of ours there seems to be a vaster fact, a death that touches mankind. My generation has lost more than its earthly father—and the circumstance has given us much pride. We have relished our lostness with peculiar vanity, as though no young folk had ever before been so magnificently abandoned; we have pitied ourselves for being simply men on earth. Cause or no cause, we have made more fuss about living than any folk ever known.

My father's father bought the house in Compton—and there is a small irony in the fact. He was a moderately success-ful writer of novels and essays, and could scarcely afford the modern house he desired. The best he could buy was the plain, square, unimproved relic which later turned out to be one of the colonial beauties of the village. My grandfather would have preferred turrets and golden oak, as suitable to real literary success.

Grandfather used to stand before the fire, tall and black-suited and bearded like a prophet, his hands clasped behind under his coat in such a way that he could flip the tails up and down. I'm not sure what type of coat it actually was—not a Prince Albert, I think, since the tails were cut back like the hind feathers of a junco; it was black or dark gray and thick, and may have had a velvet collar—and there were high collars and cuffs and a general starchiness to go with it, and grandfather always flipped his tails and told stories about himself. Even now two phrases echo in my memory like refrains: "And I said to him"—a marvelous line when intoned richly, with solid weight on the *I* and a meaning inflection on the *him*, and a shake of the head to drive it home; then, secondly, or rather finally, since it invariably came in at the finish, "Well, of course—heh, heh—he was very much chagrined." No one had ever told me what "chagrined" meant and the first time or two I may have wondered, but after a while there was no doubt. Grandfather usually rocked upon his toes when he said it and gave his tails a great flip, and then repeated it with another chuckle. Sometimes, rarely, the effect seemed to demand a third repetition, done with a gust of chuckles and only the lightest articulation.

His beard still confuses my judgment, as all beards do; it flowed in heavenly ripples down over his necktie and in some mysterious way removed him from mortality. A man becomes a part of his beard; he is what it is, as an actor is what his costume and lines are. Devil, doctor, moneylender, retired colonel, rabbi, prophet, sea captain, hayseed, God—by their beards we have known them since time was. The changeless qualities of wisdom, benevolence, pride, diabolism, faith are embodied in beards, with flesh and brain merely incidental. I still think of my grandfather as a great gentleman mainly because he had that kind of beard. I was only twelve when he died, but I still recollect the bewilderment of wondering what would result if the cataract of whiskers were removed. I was convinced—and still am—that the man behind the whiskers was a minor mortal we knew nothing of.

Naturally, I took him for granted, as children take for granted the only world they know. His dark and starchy clothes were as inevitable to existence as the vestments of the Catholic priests or the brass buttons and helmets of the Boston policemen. Nor did I question the formalities of our living, the calls and the cards and the best parlor and the awful moral stringencies. I remember seeing my own friends insulted and driven off like vermin, yet it was not till years later that any indignation generated itself. I simply assumed that the rules of existence were as arbitrary as those of cops and robbers and all the other games we played.

I was brought up ostensibly in a tradition of liberality and democracy, and actually in an atmosphere of class distinction. My people, the Garretsons and Randalls and Boylstons, had been a ruling caste for a long time—which in Massachusetts meant that they had been scholars, ministers of the church, and property holders. Grandfather had gone into the ministry himself, had held a church in Framingham (Congregational, though he later inclined to the Episcopal), and retired only when he decided he could make a better living by writing didactic novels, which he always considered a part of his ministry. I think he returned to his father's village of Compton partly because it seemed native to him, and partly because next to Concord it had the best of literary reputations. The great historian Theodore Brattle lived two houses from ours, and was of course a close friend of grandfather's—long before my time. Carver Hollis—known to the village as Mr. Plato— lived in the gray farmhouse on the Waltham road, and though he had nothing to do with the Garretsons, he did widen the fame of Compton. And there were others—my father has spoken of them at every occasion: Harriet Sunderland, whose *Village Romance* is a small New England classic—and Compton to the life; Henry Livingston Mayo, who retired from Harvard to Compton to devote himself wholly to his Dante; Charles Edward Mayo, the poet—I find myself falling naturally into my father's phrases: dear old Charles Edward with his Father Time beard (I never saw him, of course; he died in '82, but he exists in my memory as clearly as my grandfather himself); dear lovely Harriet Sunderland, and her cousin Franklin Gray whose book on the North American birds is the poetry of great science.

In the two years I spent at college I was taught to despise all of these—all except Carver Hollis, whose ferocious Platonism had turned out to be an expression of revolutionary communism. I never took seriously anything that happened in college, not even my expulsion, but it was the intellectual fashion then to treat all the American classics as though they were written by boys and girls of an upcountry high school. That was in the twenties, of course. Now in the forties the humility of God has entered our souls. Only last year one of our really unpopular critics—Eliot or Wilson, I think—published forty pages called "The Native Divinity of Charles Edward Mayo." It seems that the old boy was spiritually akin to Dante, and in the end succeeded in resolving the tragic duality of American matter and spirit—contrasting in this respect with the notable failures of Melville and Whitman. Dear old Father Mayo, you wouldn't be surprised at all; you always did consider yourself a better man than Melville or Whitman, and you certainly did resolve your matter and spirit—to you it was all as natural as play to a child, and no more profound. You lived in Compton, Massachusetts, in a day when God and nature were one, and all things progressed in a beautiful, peaceful, Grecian simplicity, and men found a divine pleasure in their evident duties. Let's play life, your poems say; let's dig and plow and sow and cut and reap, lets build and make, and weep and laugh and lawfully love—do all things in the divine innocence vouchsafed to children. You don't quite know you are saying that, but there it is, all in the golden light of your pretty verse.

I think my grandfather was a bit blind to that golden light. It is hard for me to create his character fully, because a child's view is peculiar. It is only since I have read his books and letters and talked with father and Uncle Richard that I have created a man in my mind. His books are in many ways antihuman, by which I mean that they condemn most normal human impulses. The novels, written between 1860 and 1885 or so, are moral tracts for the times, advocating temperance, continence, aristocracy (always in democratic guise), and the status quo. But they attack better than they advocate: they attack drink with a violence almost pathological—and while drink never appeared in our house, I cannot recollect any talk about it, or any implication or emotion. I rather think he attacked it with such virulence simply as a matter of policy: his readers expected it. In the same manner he attacked any sort of extreme pleasure. I remember one promising young character who came to a bad end because he loved games and wasted his energies in riotous athletics. Another fell in with bohemian musicians and artists and barely escaped to the sanctuary of a law office. And so it went. He hewed to a line of traditional puritanism, conservative, materialistic, suspicious of any sort of individual peculiarity or independence. Success meant inevitably money and social position —there were no other possibilities.

Yet—Theodore Garretson doesn't fit into that nutshell, not all of him. He was devoted—and I think passionately is not too strong an adverb, or too absurd—to trout fishing. And that one senseless, joyous vice made him a true citizen of Compton, in spite of his broadcloth and inappropriate books. For Compton in the old days was a pretty human sort of place. The Mayos were great scholars and gentlemen, but they lived happily, they did actually practice what Charles Edward so innocently preached—country living and country religion. They loved their lives; they did truly saunter to their tasks surrounded by a wide halo of ease and leisure—I think those are Thoreau's words—and they did what they loved best. It pleases me to remember that old Byzantine Brattle was a sheep shearer—there's a huge red afghan on my couch right now made out of his wool, carded and spun by his wife and crocheted by my grandmother. And the Mayos always had fun with their haying: those haymaking poems of Charles Edward's are the real thing, not simply a pastoral convention; in fact, he was so proud of his power with the scythe that at the age of seventy-two he killed himself by mowing too much —saving Time the trouble, as he said at the end. At least, that's what my father says he said; I've never seen it written anywhere. And then there was Franklin Gray, Miss Sunderland's cousin, who came to know more about birds than any man who ever lived, not for the sake of science, or his rank at Harvard, or his conscience, but simply because he loved his life. It isn't enough to say he loved birds—and that makes a sentimental untruth, anyway: people who say they love birds are simply fooling themselves. Franklin Gray never did a day's work, so he often said; life to him was one increasing delight, from his childhood in the woods and fields of Compton to his adventurous old age in the same place. I can just remember him (thank God), an old, thin gentleman with three pairs of glasses and a face shining like a light, like truth itself. In Compton he always wore farmer's clothes and an old hayseed hat, as though he had got himself up for a comic song, and the village kids trailed along after him not so much to laugh as to love. Every thicket and frog hole he passed through turned into pure white magic—rather I should call them outposts of paradise, for Franklin Gray saw all things ordered by the mind of God; every incredible bug, every aimless wiggler in the swamps of creation, seemed to him as divinely appropriate as his own immortal brain. And while he was with us, his hand on our still shoulders, his long finger pointing at the miracles of creation, we could see, too—not only the sign of life, but the portent. We saw in ways none of us will forget, and perhaps since then our eyes have been quicker, but many and many a time I've gone back through the same thickets and swamps, and better ones, and have seen nothing but the usual meaningless swarm.

CHAPTER 2

IN COMPTON the three of us Garretson kids played with any-one we liked. My sister Jean was three years older than I and grew up fast, but she kept playing boys' games until our step-mother made her stop because she showed her legs too much —and naturally there was an everlasting row about it; but that occurred later. Steve, fourteen months younger, stuck pretty close to me all through the early years—in fact, the three of us took refuge together from the virtue of our grand-father and the terrible uprightness of our stepmother. Jean is like me in several ways—big and plain and unfashionable and sort of homemade in all her arrangements, but there's no doubt that she is the best of us. It does surprise me to hear other men call her beautiful; Dana Wakeling still looks at her with the same sort of ageless worship we give to classic marbles—and it makes me proud that he does; but sisters and brothers can't see each other that way. I have always loved Jean exactly as I have loved life, with enduring thanksgiving, with thoughtless acceptance, with easy fatalism, with all sorts of instinctive delight and hope, but without much clear realization. The kid brother Steve has grown far apart from us; he looks upon Jean and me as earthy old domestics and is embarrassed that I am a carpenter and always speaks as though my painting was my chief business in life—whereas actually it is the minor amusement of holidays. But in the old days Steve lived in our shadow—always a little weaker, more fragile, more fearful, more charming.

Except for the Mayos, who were all one with us, my own best friends lived down across the tracks. Whenever I see that phrase, the geography of Compton flashes into my mind; in fact, I am sure Compton started the tradition. The main street ran uphill from southeast to northwest, and about a third of the way up the long slope the B and M tracks crossed the street, following the contour line of the hill. Just above the crossing were the stores, five or six, not counting the post office and town hall, with a strip of green, a Civil War statue, and the most magnificent elms in all creation. Farther up, partly along the main road, partly on the side streets, stood the best houses, some very old and lovely, like ours, some newer and dingier; many of them led backward to sheds and barns and so to mowings and pastures beyond. Just below the tracks were two factories: one made wooden boxes, and later closed; the other, much larger, made what we have come to call notions. And scattered below the factory buildings and down the road to the curve at the bottom were the houses of the laborers. There were smells and dirt and some disease down there, and also a solid human sort of immediacy that I have found essential to living. In our house the past counted most; down across the tracks they lived from one day to another.

Next to the Mayos, my best friends in Compton were three brothers, Tom, Dick, and Terry Madigan. They lived in back of a stable about a quarter of a mile below the crossing—I say in back, and mean it literally. Their dwelling was actually the rear end of the stable itself, two rooms downstairs, and one upstairs. Terry runs it as a garage still, but lives in a new six-room house a hundred yards or so farther behind—and rents those three same rooms to a family named Karshis. Mr. Madigan used to be what my grandfather liked to refer to as his coachman—and in truth we kept a horse and carriage in our barn long ago, and Patrick Madigan wore a flat-topped derby hat and drove for us; but that glory passed when I was only five or six. Patrick worked in our garden after that, then to my astonishment became a constable—without a uniform, but with a silver badge he kept in his hip pocket, then finally he borrowed a thousand dollars from Rutherford Mayo (so gossip had it, at least) and took over the stable.

Old Patrick had many vices and one virtue—one that I remember. He could be the grumpiest man on earth, a sour, profane, compressed body of sorrow, but through all his grief he remained just. He even recognized and cultivated his virtue, and preserved it in spite of his racial temper. "There's no man blacker hearted than an Irishman," he used to say in the depth of his native grief. "Don't ever you trust a one of 'em, Ralph, me boy; they're not able to trust themselves. I believe the devil has their number, he's got a grip inside their hearts." He used to close his leathery right hand when he said that and stare dourly at the fist; his mouth clamped shut with the stupid precision of a beak, leaving a remnant of tobacco stain from corner to chin. I feared him almost as much as his sons did, but I could see the way justice worked within him like leaven; I could see the struggle and the coming victory. "Since I was a young boy," he said once, "I been workin' for your folks, and for old lady Brattle and the whole tribe of Mayos, and there's not a one of 'em has done any wrong by me, and many's the extra help I've had in time of need. I couldn't do no better than to treat them as fair and square as they treated me, but, boy, I'm tellin' you once and for all—" I remember how he checked, looked round furtively, shook his head— "There ain't a day of the year goes by I don't have to fight the old 'un. You couldn't know, Ralph, boy, there's none o' this black old blood in ye."

Grandfather treated Patrick fairly enough, but expected him to be the humblest of servants. Relations between them assumed a glazed formality.

"Patrick, the robe."

"Yes, sir. Will that be right, sir?"

A stiff nod. "The post office first; then the station. And look sharp, Patrick."

"Yes, sir."

They both liked it. They seemed to know that as long as they could go on that way, all was well with mankind. But to me it was evil and I think the cause of my earliest revolt against order. I often accuse my grandfather of lacking a sense of humor —a heavy accusation, but the suspicion trickles in now and then that the lack was mine too. I never could be amused at the little act they chose to put on, and even now I should grow ridiculous with wrath—however much I chuckle in retrospect.

My father could be amused at all these comedies. He took over Patrick of course, not as a coachman in a square-topped hat, but as an occasional driver and handy man. The livery stable had flourished in its day, then declined again, and Patrick returned to odd jobs. My father treated him as a sort of crotchety old terrier, but Patrick never responded. "Yer grand-dad, Ralph, there was a great gentleman—I always recollect them whiskers. A just man, me boy; I owe a debt to him."

Mrs. Madigan improved all of us. Old Patrick took no part in improvement, nor did he concern himself in the least with the coming of tomorrow, nor with the fate of his family or him-self. He did what he was told, even to being a constable and keeping a stable. I truly believe that his only conscious concern in life was to be just. But not Mrs. Madigan. Just she may have been, up to the limit of her prejudices, but ambition was a greater force—ambition without means. She was the sort of naturally stout woman who keeps herself lean with work and black tea. I want to define her as a witch because her features had a deep-lined and shadowy effect, yet as I think back I realize she lived in a state of simplehearted anxiety. She handled her four men as though they were cattle—drove, pushed, washed, fed, and cursed them. And while old Patrick grew morose, and at last retired into the whisky he had always craved

and fought off, the three boys have done her proud, and she
rests in peace.

I used to be down there half the time. It smelled of everything foul, the kitchen was like an indoor dump, the yard was
all cinders and cans, but a boy could live with the freedom of a
buccaneer—at least, I thought so. The horses, the smithy in the
lane, the teamsters, the Polish-Irish-Yankee cussing, the fights,
the bets, the pick-up ball games anywhere and anytime—without all those how may a boy grow wise? If it weren't for the
Madigans' yard I should never know what a bare fist feels like,
the sickening shock of it on the jaw or nose; I shouldn't know
how to speak to a half-drunk man, or a three-quarters drunk
man; I shouldn't know the fierce language of fighting, and how
much of it is bluff and how much is deadly. More than all this,
I shouldn't know the measures of common life, the basic cycle
of work, rest, food, work again, and how all things, fighting,
loving, playing, are fitted into the everlasting cycle. Perhaps
one learns those things sooner or later, but for me the fundamental learning occurred right there round about the stable.

What I am saying here seems to me the clearest of truths, so
much so that it needs no rhetoric to make it evident, yet my
father never really perceived it. He read about simple toil and
was devoted to the ideals of craftsmanship as reflected in Mayo's
poems, but Mike Doonan's forge belonged to a world he feared.

There were other youngsters down there, but I liked the
Madigans best. Mrs. Madigan had bullied them into the paths
of decency, by which I mean they were more loyal and more just
than most boys—more just, for example, than Steve and I
usually were. "Ye'll tell the truth and take the consequences if
I have to beat the britches off ye," she said almost every day,
and sometimes acted as she threatened. But not often: they
took their consequences.

Terry was, and is now, my general size and age—thinner but
tougher. Yet not tough by nature or even by speech. A quiet,

brown, slow-talking boy, always steady like a well-trained retriever, always faithful, the best garageman in the world, the best friend. What old Patrick used to say about the black-hearted Irish never did include Terry, though his mother always harried him as unmercifully as she harried the others. I should add, by the way, that she treated me like a visiting prince, no matter what I failed to do to deserve it: "Why, Ralph, child o' grace, I can't believe ye'd be into any such business. It's that Terry and Tom and the likes o' them that don't know no better. Whatever would your grandad say if he knew the truth of the friends ye've got?" But Terry never did the wrong. Tom or Dick, possibly, or more likely one of the Noonans or the Krakowskis, or even myself, but never Terry.

Terry and I didn't always hang round the cinders of the Madigans' yard, we ranged the hills like Indian scouts, we fished and swam and chased foxes and climbed the West Compton Rocks looking for hawks' eggs. We loved the great wheel of the seasons with a pure happiness that we both clearly understood.

"Terry."

"Huh?"

"What do you like most?"

"Well, gee—coasting over on MacGregor's hill, you know when it's all quiet and no wind, and then maybe comin' along home hitchin' behind Grant's team. 'Member how Harvey's rope breaks every time and he has to run and run?"

"Terry, next winter lets us take our sleds and just go and go— let's just go way back where all those hills are beyond Osterman's farm and just go all day."

"Sure. Yeah, sure, we could take a lunch, maybe roast a couple of dogs—"

"There's nice places over there, Terry. That big hill beyond Osterman's, and all down to the river there—"

"Tell you, Ralph."

"Huh?"

"I guess it's more fun goin' after chestnuts."

"Gee, the way everything is in the fall—the way it all smells and feels. Terry, suppose we had to live where some guys do, like Boston or down south where it's all dust. Suppose we just couldn't go out and swipe a few apples and some o' those grapes up to Kingsley's, or go after perch and shiners over in Spring Pond, or shoot crows and stuff like that."

Silence.

"Terry."

"Huh?"

"Let's go swimming."

"Where?"

"The pool in Sandy Brook."

"Spring Pond's better."

"Sure. Let's go to Spring Pond."

"O.K., boy. I'm with you."

The others came too, Tom and Dick and Harvey Mayo and my brother Steve, but most of the time Terry and I made a unit among them, and it was understood by everybody that no matter what happened we two were pals. Not that we ever put such stuff into words—at least, not many words.

"Me an' you, huh, Ralph?"

"Me an' you, Terry."

It was a warm flame in our hearts, a steady joyful glow that made all life quick and full of spirit. Day after day I used to set off down the line of elms thinking of being with Terry, of the wondrous satisfaction of fooling round with him, of sitting on a fence, of tossing a baseball, or throwing rocks at the telephone poles, or watching Mike Doonan at the forge, or scuffing round the fields and thickets, or counting freight cars, or doing nothing at all. And often enough he'd be halfway up to my house, leaning up against an elm trunk or maybe lying on his stomach on Doc Jewett's terrace wall, and then everything was all right and the warm flame burned strongly inside us.

"Hey, Marquard won another."

"Gee, that's fifteen, is it?"

"Yuh, fifteen."

"Who was it, the Cubs?"

"Naw—gee, I dunno. The Pirates, I guess."

"Say, Terry."

"Huh?"

"If we ever got those bikes maybe we could ride clear in to Braves Field some day. We could go to a game, hey?"

"Sure we could do it, except we'd have to have money, we'd have to buy a ticket."

"Well, gee, we could go over the fence, couldn't we?"

"Naw, they don't have fences, not like they do at the fair. Tom says it's all like a lot of buildin's; you know, the stands all built up all around like big buildin's, and even kids has got to pay."

"How much?"

"Well, half a dollar or so. You ask Tom—he says some folks pays a dollar to get in. It makes pop sore to hear about it."

My father didn't care about baseball either, so our interest in it was a sort of conspiracy—one of the many conspiracies we had to carry on in order to live. The dream of bicycles was another. I had a dollar and seventy cents in a tobacco tin on a certain ledge in the barn loft, and Terry had only sixty-four cents—he kept that in our barn too, on another ledge. Soon afterward Terry began earning as much as fifteen cents an hour, but it was a long time before he had a bicycle.

Of the lot of us, Tom Madigan was the real ball player. His four extra years put him infinitely ahead in all sorts of ways, and in time he cut loose entirely and was what we called a big guy. But he was a better ball player anyway. We called him a natural and for years after used him as a standard when the question arose as to who was or wasn't a natural ball player. It is a question that about fifty million Americans regularly discuss, and each one has a clear image in mind of some youngster like Tom Madigan.

It still seems a distortion of the truth to describe Tom as he actually is, small, pudgy, rather oily—the type of mortal sales-man that American business produces in quantity. Not exactly loud-mouthed, but easy-mouthed, full of the oil of human kind-ness—a natural. His ways are not calculated; he considers him-self as honest as noonday, and every acquaintance is the true friend of his youth; yet two minutes after a warmhearted part-ing, with handclasp and arm on the shoulder, he has winked my way and tipped a head outward: "That guy is just a bale of hooks and eyes; he'd sell his father's bones for old ivory."

But when we played ball and swam and fished and fought and ran hare-and-hounds, Tom Madigan stood by us. He possessed infinite good humor and good nature, and an intense zeal for seeing that all was well. He refereed, coached, encour-aged, laid plans, all with tireless delight. He dug up the necessary equipment, improvised bats, hockey sticks, fishing poles, raided the dumps, persuaded, bargained, knew all about premiums and coupons and the ways of mail-order houses. He got us out of trouble, or into it and then out again; he gave evidence, true or false as needed; he taught us some of the evil he knew, then cursed us for listening to it and advised us to do good and grow up to be great men like Mr. Garretson and Mr. Mayo. The word "natural" keeps coming back as I think of Tom. When he was drafted for the first World War, and came back from France a sergeant with a medal, we knew exactly how it was; we could see him taking care of his men just as he took care of us—like a busy collie with a flock of sheep, not with any recognition of duty or principle, but with a natural instinct for making every-thing as jolly as possible.

Afterward he went forth to sell, beginning with brushes and ending with automobiles, and has risen and fallen on the wheel of business. Tom's is not the face that advertises the American citizen; he has grown flabby and loose round the mouth and chin, his head is partly bald, he wears a paunch; but he represents more Americans than anyone I know. When times are good, he is up; when they are bad, he is down; when averages of any sort are computed, I am sure Tom fits to a decimal. Whatever most Americans do, Tom does: he lives upstairs in a two-family house in Watertown; he has a wife three years younger and three children (if it were possible to have two and whatever fraction the average is, he would have them); he drives a Chevrolet and trades it every two years whether he can afford to or not; he buys all the best gadgets— always on a time-payment system; he drives to see his relatives on Sundays and to the beaches on holidays; he hated the New Deal, is full of cruel gossip, but voted twice for Roosevelt, and always votes democratic in state elections. The list could make a volume. Yet Tom is a natural, an unconscious, untrained enthusiast for the ways of life he has grown up with, and I am forever in his debt, not because he gets things for me wholesale, or knows the boys in the city hall (as of course he does), but because he goes along with life and has taken me part way along with him.

"Lookit, Ralph, lookit here, you choke your bat just a couple inches, like this, see? Now look, you watch me, look, you stand like this—see where my feet are? Now, boy, you watch that ball, you watch it like a hawk, like a *neagle*, don't you ever stop watchin' it, and when she comes you keep awatchin' it, and then you step right out toward it—see, Ralph, boy? Don't you step back, that's no good, you couldn't hit a pumpkin that way —you gotta step out toward it and you watch it just like a *neagle*, see? And swing easy—don't try to murder it, boy, don't worry about homers, just crack it easy and square. And *watch* it—half you guys don't watch it when you swing." And then likely as not he would screw his face into a wink, wiggle his tail a little, and swing as though he were playing golf, and set us off into snorts of mirth. He always swore more than the rest of us, with a natural fluency that made it as easy as breathing, and somehow it sounded like good clean cussing, but when any of us tried to do the same—as we constantly did—it sounded all wrong. "Fer Chri' sake, Ralph, cut out that filthy talk. Yer old man'll whale hell out of you if he hears it—an' that goes for all o' you bastards." And Tom made it funny enough to set us roaring again, but we felt silly about the filthy talk and left most of it to him.

I don't recollect ever once hearing any man of my family swear or use intemperate speech of any sort, so of course it didn't come natural to me. But being a worker with my hands, I have to do some swearing—no man who hammers his thumb or drops a piece of four by four on his toe can do otherwise; yet I can still hear Tom Madigan's derision of my efforts. Yes, he was a natural; he has gone through life the way a river runs downhill, fast and slow, frothy and sluggish, surviving without effort, coming through war, drought, depression—I'm afraid Emerson could never have approved of Tom, nor could any of the high-minded gentry of old Compton, but there he is, as much a part of nature as anything covered with fur.

When Mrs. Madigan died back in the thirties, Tom was getting along pretty prosperously as floor salesman for one of the big motor companies on Commonwealth Avenue, and Mrs. Madigan was filled with the pride that the Irish alone are capable of. But even so her chief joy was Dick, for Dick had turned himself into a scholar, and therefore a gentleman. I saw only last week that Richard Madigan had been appointed principal of the East Roxbury High School, and I am sure his mother has spread the news over all the back fences of whatever heaven she dwells in.

Dick, in a family that owned only one book, read more than I did. He said later that he had read every book in the village library, but I think it would be nearer right to say every bad book. He loved literary tripe, as I did, and no one interfered with his feast—except that old Patrick despised any sort of reading. But Mrs. Madigan had an ambition, and she made Patrick see it her way: Dick was cut out for a priest. Let him read, let him have glasses to help him, let him have time and a chair under the light, let him be—no matter what he read, as long as they were printed books. So Tom did the errands and odd jobs and Terry swept the steps and "cleaned up the yard" and Dick read Elinor Glyn and Zane Grey in preparation for the priesthood.

We came to accept the fact that Dick could never be trusted beyond our sight. Old Patrick's training only clung to his visible surfaces; he played fair out of natural deference to authority. His ways involved a subtle and charming calculation of opportunity. I remember how he always came out of Steele's big general store with a handful of something—nuts or hard candy or cookies or nails or buckshot, and we agreed it was wrong, and I felt the wrong down inside and so did Terry, and Tom always had a lot to say about it and how Dick had better cut it out or he'd tell pop, but in the end we couldn't seem to be sore at Dick at all, and took whatever share of the loot he offered. He made it seem so obvious: he simply took what he wanted, and that was that. No trouble, no fights, no prick of conscience, nothing to lose, except the immediate stake. And Dick managed so that he never lost anything.

His life success follows. The schools liked him, the church backed him and saw him through its college. Good jobs came to him. So far as I know he suffered only one setback—a temporary one. Harvard refused to grant him the master of arts degree that he wanted and it was characteristic of Dick that he understood why. "They expected me to work for it," he told me. "It's a damned outrage. I'm not accustomed to working like that and I'm too old to begin. From now on I'll stay where I'm appreciated." But he would have enjoyed adding the Harvard letters to his name. "If I had that, maybe your old grandad wouldn't throw me out of the yard—provided he ever caught me in his yard again."

Though my grandfather remained the head of the house up to the instant of his last breath, he paid little attention to the details of my life. If wrongs were thrust upon his notice, he spoke out, like Jehovah. "Randall, I will not suffer these children to eat like canines. Sit up, sir! Close your mouth and masticate quietly! Do I make myself clear?"

"Yuh."

"Why, Ralph!" This from the mater.

"Yes, Grandfather."

General complacence among the elders, and a few moments of truce. Then a new blast. "And while I think of it, Lucy, there was a most egregious clatter in the front hall this morning." When grandfather used a word like "egregious" it was meant to be humorous, and he articulated it with droll distinctness. "You had gone to market, I believe, but I'm sure you would appreciate knowing that these children were apparently engaged in rolling cannon balls down the stairs."

"We dropped the baseball," I said. "By mistake."

"For years," grandfather proceeded, "I have labored to obtain a decent peace and quiet during working hours, and now at last a baseball is rolled down the front stairs."

My stepmother, whom the three of us called "Mater" with as much austerity as we could, spoke out with perfect reasonableness. "The children do try to be quiet, Father. I'm sure it was an accident. Chew quietly, Ralph—please try to remember."

"I'm not referring to their chewing, Lucy. I'm referring to their throwing baseballs down the stairs. Also to loud voices and other commotions outside my study door."

It was still the general and sacred assumption of the household that grandfather devoted his mornings to writing. At this time he was nearly eighty and had published nothing for a dozen years—nothing, that is, except the letters to the editor of the *Transcript* which he cut out and filed in a manila envelope, and also a few book reviews in the *Christian World*. But nonetheless he caused it to be known that for four hours each morning he wrote, and that not only the household but the whole community must pay some sort of respect to that distinguished fact. The house conducted itself like a hospital, tradesmen stepped silently to the back door, visitors tiptoed and whispered hoarsely. The only approved noises were the snorts and harrumphs that issued from the sanctum itself. I remember coal wagons being severely turned away and told to come in the afternoon—not before three-thirty, however, for grandfather rested after lunch. I remember the ignorant man who started to mow the lawn in the morning (Patrick knew better, of course). I remember the organ grinder on a bright June morning.

"Ralph!"

"Huh?"

The study door had flung itself open and solid footsteps had crossed to the living room, where I was wasting life in a book.

"Ralph, tell that creature to go away. Tell him it's a perfect outrage, it's an indecent disturbance, it's—why, I never in my life heard such an outlandish racket!" He turned like the embodiment of Wrath, then stopped.

"Ralph!"

"Yes, sir."

"I want that man to go away. Is that clear?"

"Yuh, sure. I mean—sure—"

The steps recrossed and the door closed like fate. Meanwhile "The Wearing of the Green" poured through the house.

A boy of eleven can only laugh when nothing is at stake. I walked down the path like a reluctant martyr. The swarthy face smiled and bowed and the ready hat came forward in the left hand.

"Go away," I said.

A shadow of doubt. Another bow and half smile. The hat agitated. I pointed and gestured. "Go away. You are bothering grandfather."

The shadow suddenly black; the menacing shrug of shoulder; the hat planted on the head like Custer's flag. The sort of compressed noises a besieged cat makes sounded above the torrent of "The Wearing of the Green."

"Grandfather—" I tried again, and suddenly decided to retreat. I knew the whole business was exactly like grandfather, but I returned up the path even more reluctantly. "The Soldiers' Chorus" followed me through the door.

"I thought I instructed you," a great voice began, but I spoke up with unexpected manliness.

"He won't go, Grandfather. He got mad. I told him you said to cut it out, but he won't." I had stuck my head into the sanctum and could see grandfather registering astonishment and shock. His whiskers helped immensely.

"Ralph," he said finally, taking full command, "I want you to call a constable—at once, do you hear? Tell the operator you require a constable, and at once. This is an emergency—make that clear." He rose, selected the knobbiest of his canes, threw back his aged shoulders, and marched through the door as though I weren't there. "A disturbance such as this is a serious outrage and I don't intend to submit weakly. This is not a trifling matter, sir, I can assure you of that!" Whether he addressed this last to me or to the editor of the *Transcript* I am not certain.

I dashed for the telephone in the back hall, dragging a chair along to stand on. The whole household by now had mobilized itself, and I crashed solidly into Abbie emerging from the kitchen. But I rang up central and told her to get Patrick quick, there was a big fight out in the street—and I realized as I said it that half the town would be there inside of ten minutes. Then I dashed back to watch grandfather.

"The Soldiers' Chorus" had ceased. A sweet June silence filled the hall, the porch, the whole world.

"He can't abide them hand organs," Abbie was explaining to my sister Jean.

"What's happening now?" I called, and rushed past them and down the path.

But the show was mysteriously ended. My stepmother had taken grandfather's arm and they were walking back. I saw the organ trundling down the shady street.

"A public outrage," he was saying, but quietly. "I question if such men have a legal right to disturb the peace—" They passed me without noticing me.

"I called for the police, Grandfather."

"The police?" He looked back and down at me from a considerable distance. "Just tell them we no longer need their assistance." His tone suggested the appearance of a uniformed platoon.

"If Patrick comes," my stepmother said, "tell him I'd like to see him. He should have had the corn planted last week."

So grandfather retired, shutting the door against us.

"What on earth happened?" Jean asked with quiet innocence, as though the whole affair could be translated into a few words.

"Did he take the cane to him?" Abbie wanted eagerly to know. "I come out to lend a hand myself, but it's all over and no blood spilled at all."

My stepmother looked earnestly from one to another. "Why, nothing happened. I gave the Italian ten cents and he went on. That's all they expect. If you give them twenty-five cents they come back again."

I remember how reasonable her face was, and how it drooped with solemn certainty like the old sheep's in *Through the Looking Glass*. Not that she could have been very old then, but she seemed so, and I realize now that there had never been any youth in her. She was far too reasonable.

"Mr. Garretson," she explained to Abbie, "gets very excited. I'm afraid it isn't good for him."

Yet I stood and looked at her with astonishment. It may seem naïve of me, but the essential fact of the ten cents had not before occurred to me and in one flash I perceived a great and obvious truth. The Italian played his organ for money—

and naturally, *naturally*— Well, there lay the world clear before me. I heard "The Wearing of the Green" come rippling from the distance, a lovely, happy sound, like a June morning in Compton.

"Is it always ten cents, Mater?"

"Oh, no. Most people give him pennies."

"But you thought he'd go quicker for a dime, is that it?"

"Yes, that's it."

We had all been whispering, half in and out of the open front door. I glanced in at the closed door of the study and fixed up a question.

"Why couldn't grandfather—?" But I didn't finish. What was the use? We all knew that grandfather was like that.

The kids were there then, Ellen and Ted, with their fists in their mouths, and mater began shushing them all off. And I saw people coming up the street in a hurry, and my young brother Steve running ahead. I edged off the porch, round the house, and cut for the barn. I have been pretty innocent about a great many things in life, but I could see no profit in being grandfather's goat any longer. I hoped he'd have to do his own explaining.

He didn't, of course. And never while I lived in Compton did I escape the ridicule that followed the story. Not that I minded—in fact, it made people like me and served as a sort of initiation to the cracker-box gang down at Steele's. They knew my grandfather was like that too.

I regret in a way that this chronicle is not the confession of an artist as a young man, or of a sensitive child misunderstood by common folk. It would make a much sharper drama. But the tragedy of vulgar persecution was not mine. If anything, I thrived on it. As I mentioned earlier, I paint pictures, for the fun of it, to use the vaguest of phrases to describe the most complex of emotions; and my greatest triumph on earth so far has come through the agency of the Compton Better Business Club, which last year arranged an exhibition for me—in the

Town Hall of all places. The whole thing had no connection with art as apprehended by the best critics. Most of those who so enthusiastically shook my hand never looked twice at the pictures—not even Terry Madigan, who surreptitiously bought one of them and had a "sold" label stuck on it so effectively that three others followed. As I say, it turned into a triumph and was reported in the papers as a local-boy-makes-good story.

If Compton resembles all American towns—and I am certain it does—then two common superstitions need airing: one that artists are despised, the other that gossip slays. We Americans despise the affectations of artists—more, for example, than we do those of politicians or sportsmen; but we look with reverence upon the talent that translates a canvas into the forms and colors of mysterious life. From Steele's counter boy to tottery old Mike Doonan, the folk of Compton honored me for what they innocently conceived to be a talent.

"Ralph, me son," Mike said after he had shuffled in and waited for his wheezing to quiet, "it's God has given you the power to do miracles. I little thought in the old days when I threw you out of the shop that ye'd come to do famous work like this."

The fact that Mike had spoken before looking at the pictures at all was characteristic; in fact, half of the enthusiasm came from folk who never went to the exhibition.

Perhaps it has not always been so. Pioneering, like war, may eliminate the arts of peace. But I give you my experience as a modern American.

⤎§ CHAPTER 3 §⤏

WHAT MY grandfather did to us kids should by all literary canons have led to retribution, but so far as I know my own heart bears the only marks of it. It happened late in the same summer as the organ-grinder affair. A wondrous summer, not only in the flow of memory long after, but right in the current fact of it. Boyhood reaches a peak where freedom seems absolute and time has no end. A time for revelations comes, like the revelation of the organ grinder and the ten cents; life takes shape with marvelous rapidity, and one believes in divine logic. The summer of my eleventh year came just right for me, and for Harvey Mayo and Terry Madigan. We feared nothing, doubted nothing, and the long days floated us from one revelation to another like magic carpets. From the first splash of sun on the painted pine floor to the last sigh of oblivion in the sweet darkness I lived like a boyish Adam in the divine garden. I think the others did too. We created a sort of unity of emotion; we swam and played ball and followed the haying and fixed up a cabin in the woods, all with a single impulse and single joy. Tom worked with his father at the stable and Dick had a few lawns to do, but they kept time for us too—it was Tom who engineered the cabin in the edge of the woodlot beyond the pasture way out behind the stable.

We had to do a lot of fighting over that cabin, too, but even the fighting seemed part of the divine harmony. We borrowed or stole all the available wooden boxes in town and lugged them out there one by one, and the house looked like what a child builds with blocks. We made ourselves unpopular with all citizens who had usable building materials; the owner of the woods, old Ebeneezer Grant, turned crabby and had to be pacified—it seemed fantastic that he should expect us to set fire to his woodlot; but our chief battles were with the kids from the other side of the tracks—a bunch of micks, as Tom called them. If they had organized into a gang, they might have destroyed us, house and all, but they had no such leader as Tom. There was a big slob named Schloss who plotted evil against us, and a little fighter named Bill Keeney who could lick anything his own age including me. Not too easily; I could wrestle him down, but I couldn't stand up to his fists. We respected Bill Keeney; we perceived that he passionately loved to fight, whatever the outcome, and that he attacked openly and joyfully. The others in that crowd were smaller and trailed along and threw stones from a distance. And in the end Tom won over Bill Keeney, and he got along better with us than he ever did with the others. But Schloss—we always called him Schlob—was as near pure evil as anyone I ever knew.

Villainy is another overused device. But Herman Schloss, so far as we knew, never consciously did a decent thing. It might be as accurate to say he never consciously did anything, for he drifted round like a too-fat carrion bird, as though all the world were a garbage dump. We were afraid at first; he seemed nauseatingly big, like a piece of bad meat. I remember how Terry and Harvey and I came to the cabin one morning and found him methodically busting holes in the walls with a piece of birch cordwood. There was no sense in it; he simply kept swinging the birch log like a battering ram, without any expression on his face or any apparent delight in what he was doing.

"Hey, cut it out, will ya?"

Crash!

"Hey, Schloss, what's the idea?"

Crash!

We were afraid of him. He was big and old and he seemed deadly. Terry went off like a shot across the fields to get Tom. Harvey and I started throwing rocks, and Schloss calmly kicked the door open and went inside. And we were helpless—or thought so.

"Gee, Ralph, he'll wreck it now."

"Yuh."

The crashing continued.

And then Tom, like Galahad against the giant. The vision will be clear as long as I have a mind: Tom charging over the wall, his round face intent, his compact body electric with purpose; Tom assailing the portals without a breath's pause, Tom brandishing the sword of righteousness—no, he had nothing but fists, but as he went through the door he was arrayed as a champion should be. We capered and yelled in ecstasy; we rushed in to cheer at the death—and if Schloss had been then and there slain in hot blood, we should have yelled ourselves into madness.

But not so Tom. He did right with a deadly efficiency. He peppered the brute with straight rights and lefts as though he were exercising on a dummy; in two minutes Schloss became a sniveling punching bag, smeared in the face and bloody at the nose. Tom drove him out the door and told him to get, and I remember how his fat legs and hams hustled fearfully off toward the wall.

And how we roared and danced and pounded each other! It was one of the high peaks of existence, an undimmed glory, a triumph more fantastic than anything in the chivalric books. And there stood the champion himself, compact, round-faced, homely Tom in his stable overalls, grinning like a comic full moon—good old Tom, you fixed him, boy, you polished his apple off, you whaled the sawdust out o' him, the slob, the hunk o' sauerkraut, the fat end of a porker—he won't come suckin' round here any more—by God, did you see that right to the schnozzle, did you see that smacko right on the beezer? The words are thin things without the music of our joy, the whooping and cussing and war-dancing and demonstrations of rights and lefts and fancy footwork.

"Call me if you need me, fellers. I gotta get back to the horse manure." So spoke the hero. He nodded in the direction of the slob's retreat and made noises with his mouth. We all made noises and yelled all the names we could think up, and then Tom went off, and we fixed the place up for a while, but we were still too excited to do much work, and wanted to get back where we could tell people about what had happened.

We learned more about Schloss after that. We learned that any two of us smaller kids could handle him, and that his evil was simply a mindless, flabby boredom. He wouldn't work, and drifted around with nothing in the world to do, with no friends, no purpose, no hope. For a time we hated and hounded him like jackals; then in the end he became one of the many properties of village life. He eventually took over his father's junk business and turned crafty enough to buy and sell. But in my fancies he remains the ogre with the bulbous club, the giant of all evil, and Tom, bustling, pudgy, talkative Tom, is still the knight caparisoned in silver.

After we got tired of the cabin in the woods we floated to other adventures—there were caves in the West Compton rocks, and crows to be hunted, and an old boat on Spring Pond, and then my sister Jean got a puppy and we spent a lot of time rolling round the lawn with him. Jean always liked animals and children, but up to this time she hadn't been allowed a dog because of the three younger kids. Our stepmother felt that the household was complicated enough with grandfather at one end and three babies at the other, though she didn't put it that way. But when Uncle Richard came to visit in August he brought a basket with a red setter puppy in it for Jean, and of course we kept it. Mater agreed that a dog would be educational for all the children, and grandfather admired his pedigree. Jean underwent an instant and visible transformation; she became a mother, not in anxious ostentation, but in pure joy. She has never laughed aloud at many things, but the young always strike her as infinitely funny, and the first glimpse of Pete set her chuckling—and years later I have seen her laugh the same way at her babies.

The rest of us caused her much trouble by interfering with her training system. We spoiled the puppy with irresponsible love, we fed him the wrong food, we treated him too roughly —though in the end he grew to be a success. But as I said, we spent a number of days playing round the yard and the barn, and one afternoon we took a notion to build a tree house in the maple near the corner of the barn. Our barn faced the road as the house did, but stood to the left and farther back; the front corner of the barn nearly touched the back corner of the kitchen ell of the house—and since then father has connected them by a covered passage. We did most of our playing in the area in front of the barn and at the left side of the house. It didn't matter how much we scuffed up the driveways, and the patches of lawn near the woodshed and kitchen were less valuable than those directly in front of the house. And near the left corner of the barn stood an ancient huge maple, not so tall as the elms along the edge of the street, but greater in girth.

We had been loafing round in the half shade, Terry and Steve and Pete the dog and I, and along came Tom and Bill Keeney with gloves and a ball.

"I told Dick to get Sid Steele and we'd have a game. Sid's got a good bat." Tom flung himself on the warm grass.

Bill Keeney stood and thumped the ball into his glove. He was always restless like that.

"Nobody's down in the school field," Tom said. "We can have a good game." He chirruped to Pete and began rubbing his neck and rolling him over. Tom liked animals too and could talk to them. "We better get Harvey, huh?" He looked round at all of us and then grinned at Steve. "You ooze over to Harvey's and if he ain't there get his mit."

We all roared because Tom said "ooze" the way he did, and for a minute or so nothing happened because we were yelling "ooze" at one another and wiggling round on the grass, but I knew Steve wouldn't go because he hated to be laughed at. He just lay still with a set mouth.

"Come on, kid," Tom said. "Drip yourself along."

And then we roared and screamed some more—all but Steve, who smiled a little.

Tom was not one to get sore at a thing like that. He seemed to know how kids like Steve felt. But I could see Bill Keeney's dark face peering at Steve. Bill laughed when he had to, but he took life hard and if he thought things weren't right he went into action like a packet of firecrackers. So I was just beginning to get sore at Steve myself to get in ahead of Bill when Dick and Sid Steele came along.

But Sid's bat had got busted, and we talked that over for quite a while. I had a kid's bat, but Tom said it stung the hands off you—and it did. Harvey's brother Ted had a real Louisville Slugger that he used when he played at Harvard, but none of us dared take it. Sid had got his from his father's store, and we thought he ought to have another, but the more we talked the lazier we got—all except Bill Keeney, who got Dick to have a catch with him.

And then Tom, who had been lying on his back staring up at the maple, said why didn't we get together and make us a house up there. He explained that a tree house was the most fun of anything in the world, and anyone who had a tree house would be safe no matter what happened; it was a good thing to have in case of a flood and even of a forest fire because a big maple like that wouldn't burn, but of course it was specially safe from robbers and enemies because you could pull your ladder up and shut your trap door and be as snug as the man in the moon.

Whenever Tom got started that way the rest of us made a sort of chorus that filled out the pauses.

"It's like the natives in Borneo or Africa . . ."

"And we'd haul messages up in a basket . . ."

"And a rope ladder . . ."

Tom only half believed any of it, but he loved to create the idea. It is what he does when he sells something and makes it a point of honor to carry his audience and play out his part with an actor's integrity. "And boy, you got the best damned old tree in town, I tell you. I been lookin' for just the right tree—you see, you gotta have a wide crotch just like that and not too many little piddly branches to get in the way, and its gotta be just right to reach with a ladder and so you can pull up your ladder—"

And pretty soon we had got the fifteen-foot ladder out of the barn and were all going up the maple like monkeys and yelling about where to put the floor beams and trap door and windows and Terry went way up as high as he could get to find a place for a lookout, and then almost before I knew what was happening Tom and Dick and Bill Keeney were lugging out a lot of old boards that had been stored in the empty chicken house behind the barn. I realized then that things weren't going right—in fact, I realized several facts, chief of which was that the tree house never would be built. Of all the star-strewn dreams of boyhood so few ever come true, so many grow ignominious, that most of us run close to an edge of despair. I realized, too, that the Madigans were the kind of boys who routed out ladders and boards that didn't belong to them, and that our front yard wasn't the right place for such goings on anyway. But above this layer of doubt the great enthusiasm still waxed, and I was persuaded to get hammers and nails and a saw, and before long everything swept ahead on the full flood. Tom had us organized—and I know that for him it was all a great pretense because he had me rig a tackle to haul up material when it was easier simply to pass things up by hand, and Tom knew it and I did too, only very dimly, but we went ahead anyway with ropes and slings and a lot of sheer confusion.

Then into the midst of this activity came grandfather. He had been walking, with cane, straw hat, and usual clerical habit, and now we looked up and saw him.

I suppose a boy takes his own folk as normal and conceives others to be odd because they differ. Most of my comment on the quality of the Garretsons is a long, long afterthought; I did at the time find my grandfather difficult, but so were other standard things such as weather and bodily ill. I remember that when I looked up and saw him pacing the driveway I realized instantly that as far as the Garretsons were concerned I was doing wrong and that he, grandfather, stood for strict Garretson virtue; but at the same instant I realized that we had all been happy out there, that my friends were filled with warmth and good will, that building a tree house was still a brilliant adventure.

"Ralph," he said, "what is all this?"

The next two or three minutes include the sort of catastrophe that seems incredible in time of peace. Life had been running securely and pleasantly for ages and ages, and especially all this summer when our diurnal affairs revolved with an almost cosmic harmony.

"We are building a house in the tree, Grandfather."

"Nonsense. See that all this—this equipment—is put back exactly where you found it."

Absolute motionless silence. Tom and Terry astride the great limb ten feet above ground, Sid Steele above them frozen in the act of stretching for a high branch, Dick and Bill Keeney and I down among the boards and ropes.

"Yuh, we'll put it back."

So far all was understandable. The sober, awful solemnity, the authoritative disapproval, the instant show of obedience —all this ran true to custom. We many times ran afoul of the elders, and not only Garretson elders; Mrs. Madigan, and Pat himself, and Mr. Steele—they all got after us. Yes, sir, we'll fix it, we'll put it back right away, we didn't mean any harm, we're sorry about it. In these sober crises certain responses had proved dependable. And so now. Perhaps that pile of old boards had some mysterious value, perhaps they were rare cherry wood, or ancestral pine, or something beyond the knowledge of boys. Things often turned out that way.

"We'll put 'em away, sir," Tom called in his best Horatio Alger voice. "We'll tidy it all up clean as a wistle." That's what Tom always said to his mother about their yard. Every day for ten years he promised to tidy it all up clean as a wistle.

But grandfather by ill chance had fixed his gaze on Bill Keeney and Dick Madigan. Conceive of him as he appeared before us, larger than life, with formal clothing and stick and whiskers and deep eyes and frowning brow.

"Ralph, who are these?"

His tone said, "What are these?"

"Why, that's Bill and that's Dick. You know who Dick is, Grandfather."

But suddenly I was seeing them with his eyes. Bill Keeney was without doubt a mick. His patched britches had been recut from some his father must have worn out, his shoes gapped, his work shirt was ripped at each arm—I hadn't ever before actually seen those clothes; but it wasn't really the clothes that made Bill a mick, it was the dark snarl of his face, the thin, ratlike hunger of it.

"Bill?—and Dick?"

That tone created a grandfather I had never known. My heart despaired.

"Sure. Bill Keeney. And you've seen Dick lots of times." And as I spoke I realized about Dick too. He was another mick. Not so flagrantly as Bill; Mrs. Madigan kept her boys cleaner and better sewed. But—well, we all knew Dick was shifty—he knew it too—and we somehow allowed for it, and no matter what happened he had always been one of us. Now suddenly I could see the shiftiness like a sordid garment. Grandfather saw it, of course, and Dick himself seemed to become more and more that way. His eyes slid furtively, his skinny body twisted into guilty shapes. I tried to will him back to the Dick I knew, to give him some sort of quick signal that would restore him to honorable life, but grandfather's eye exposed him beyond redemption.

"When you boys have put back all this lumber, you will leave the place at once. I will not allow boys of this sort to play here. Do you understand?"

Silence.

"Is that clear, Ralph?"

Silence.

"Ralph!"

My throat may have rattled. I stood there risking the lightning.

It was Tom who broke the death spell. "Yes, sir, we'll clean it up, sir. You needn't give it a thought. Come on down out o' there, Sid." Smooth as butter, that voice. Tom moved along the limb with a comforting little bustle.

But grandfather's cold eyes still held us. "I have allowed the Madigan boys to play with you here, Ralph, but that is enough. We can't have these—these others here." The hand said what the words omitted.

In the years since, the scene has grown more and more portentous. At the time I couldn't understand it, beyond the fact that I was being exposed to ignominy before my friends. Though the glory and harmony of our afternoon's enterprise were cruelly destroyed, I still presumed that grandfather knew what he was about and that he acted with respectable adult wisdom. I spoke with the desperate logic that children cling to through all crises.

"But that's Dick Madigan, Grandfather. That's Tom's brother."

I must have had a notion that Tom was the safe one—Tom who always slid through our troubles as though he were on runners. And from his tone of voice I realized that he had diagnosed and understood the whole business already.

Grandfather glanced at Dick again, and for an instant I supposed that my logic would carry the day. It was as good as logic ever could be. But there before us stood Dick openly accusing himself of all the vices of poverty, vulgarity, meanness, and general disreputability. And grandfather turned away and walked toward the front door.

"Come on, fellers," Tom snapped out. "Get this stuff put away." He and Terry began collecting it.

I glanced fearfully at Bill Keeney, wondering if he would fight now or later and planning how I'd duck in under his fists and get him round the middle. I was scared of Bill and was trying to make ready for the worst. But he picked up a board and threw it on the pile. "I guess the old geezer's sore," he said. "Come on, you Steve—grab an end of this." And Steve did it, and they went off round the barn. One sour old geezer more or less meant nothing to Bill.

"The old gent's all right," Tom was saying. "We shoulda known not to go messin' up a nice place like this—it's lucky pop didn't catch us, he'd tan our tails for it." Then he nodded off toward the barn. "That Keeney's just a damn mick. He's a good kid, all right, but he oughta stay off this end o' town." I can still hear Tom's confident tones, and can still see the world he lived in where everything is the way it is and always will be. "You see," he went on, "I figgered on us all playin' ball down on the school diamond—that's where we oughta be." He made a funny noise with his mouth, hoping we'd all laugh.

Terry said nothing and never has mentioned it to this day.

Ordinarily he spoke little anyway, but just then I could feel his silence. It was a month before I got him back on the place again.

But Dick has never been back. He stood still slouchy and furtive, staring narrowly off toward the door of the house, and I noticed to my surprise that he looked white, or rather a grimy yellowish color, with spots of red. For years I have read of characters in books turning red and white and other inter- mediate shades, but I am always surprised when it happens— and so far as I remember this was the first time I had ever actually seen a face pale with emotion. His eyes flashed an intense cold little light at me, but there was no cynical smile to go with it, no conspirator's shrug. Among all us kids, Dick Madigan was the most knowing and most perceptive and the least emotional; he could shrug his way out of almost any- thing. But now I could see murderous anger in him. It was like looking at a snake; my heart seemed to shrink inside a closing coil. When he turned and walked away out of the yard, not even Tom called after him.

My grandfather lived for about seven months after this event, and then was struck with a fatal paralysis. Until that moment, he never relaxed his grip on himself or his house- hold. He did not speak to me again about my choice of friends, but one evening after dinner I heard him talking about it. We had had supper earlier in the kitchen, as we always did when guests came for dinner, and I was upstairs getting ready for bed and crossing the hall to the bathroom at the top of the stairs. Grandfather's voice came rolling up from the living room, and I knew he was standing before the mantelpiece with his hands under his coattails.

"Riffraff and micky boys," he was saying. "I simply had to draw the line. One or two of them are no doubt decent enough—we mustn't be snobbish about this sort of thing— but I decided I had to draw the line somewhere. So in the end I told them—" I listened in electric tension. There it all was again, the whole business, only larger, deeper, darker than it had been; I knew it was growing, and I'd never get clear of it. I heard him chuckle, the gust of satisfied chuckles that signaled the end, and I waited for the last words.

"Well, of course, they were all very much chagrined."

[◆]§ CHAPTER 4 ﻝ◆

MY FATHER's story may not be told as one remembered. Jean, being three years older than I, might come nearer to it; my mother and my stepmother could each give a version, or an apology; perhaps Uncle Richard and Aunt Liddie see the whole more clearly, but I never think of them as articulate enough to find the right words for it. Aunt Liddie does not speak of what is unpleasant, nor does she see or hear it; for seventy years she has lived in a little cloud and wherever she moves, the cloud moves too. A sweet cloud, a sweet lady— and not simply because she is old. Uncle Richard, my father's older brother, is every inch an eminent citizen, a great legal mind, as the universities phrase it when they bestow doctorates on him, but I find it difficult to talk with him. There are echoes in his voice that I am too familiar with, echoes from my grandfather's mantelpiece. He never got along well with grandfather, which accounts in part for his success.

I do know surely that my father possessed more charm than any of the Garretsons—and I notice that my brother Steve is learning the same arts as he grows older, though with less ease. And that charm of my father's may correctly be described as fatal—fatal to himself. On the face of it, and considered in the clinical light we moderns are accustomed to, his life is a sort of object lesson in failure and decadence. I perceive that conclusion of the valedictorians, but when one knows a man as well as I knew my father, one jumps less readily through the hoop of a fixed idea. He lived in a cloud too, like Aunt Liddie, but a large and splendid cloud, a fair world of cloud, and he knew no other world. To others, his realities may seem most impalpable vapors; but not so to him.

His first marriage took place in 1895. The fact is noted in his journal of that period—just barely noted. Most of the journal deals with nature and books in a sort of Emersonian fashion, with no space for the humbler facts of marriage and birth. He walked zealously through the Compton seasons, noting his encounters with flowers and birds and famous men. He dwelt among happy ideas. He remarked to Franklin Gray that nothing short of God could have conceived of a dragonfly, and Gray was pleased to agree. He walked round Spring Pond with Theodore Brattle and debated whether the ancients loved the earth or feared it. He challenged Henry Mayo to justify the ways of Dante as a Christian. He recorded discovery of a yellow lady slipper. But of hint of a devotion to Miss Alice Hollister, or to any woman, there is no word.

It is to be understood, of course, that his journal was a bit of window dressing, not so much for public display as for the delight of his own soul. He felt himself a worthy disciple of the great. As I read the flourishing hand I can understand quite simply his dreams of philosophical grandeur and his transparent hope that the phrases will undergo the alchemy of immortality. There are echoes, thin and far and nearly always too sweet, like true sounds destroyed and translated by distance. "Today I saw our first bluebird," he wrote on April 3, 1889, "and fancied the icy sky of winter had softened and been reborn and taken heart again."

No one but Jean and me has read the journal through. Steve has dipped into it as a sort of cultural reassurance. But sometimes Jean and I talk about father, and if the time is right Jean talks quite a lot. "All that nature, Ralph—how did father ever get that way? And why? He never cared so much about it later, when he got old, but here's this ecstasy about seeds and blossoms, and all so terribly sentimental. 'This evening God opened the western gate of heaven'—things like that. It's as though he weren't living in this world at all—I mean this modern world. Not that I'm trying to be hard-boiled, Ralph. I'm sentimental enough about nature, and so are you, but father acted as though he had drunk too much of it."

Randall—I call him that to make the narrative simpler, though the name comes unnaturally to my pen—like Pip was brought up by hand, his father's hand, of course. I can't say much about his mother because she disappeared long ago—I think of her as fading off gradually like an anxious Cheshire cat and at last happily vanishing into well-earned oblivion. I remember how startled I was at grandfather's funeral to see the marble stone with his name carved in it, the final date still fatefully blank, and below it his beloved wife, Beatrice Randall Garretson, 1839–1887. That she had lived, breathed, borne four children, and suffered as any woman must have suffered under grandfather's rod, all so long ago, back in the dim middle of another century, seemed to me a mere fiction, a fanciful tale for a tombstone. And the fact that father himself seldom spoke of her increases the impression Jean and I have that somehow she never lived at all. But we do know she played the piano beautifully as a girl and gave it up after Bronson, her fourth child, died.

That death shaped Randall's fate more than he knew, for it made him the precious survivor. If little Bronson had lived, my grandfather might have continued his propagation without much attention to the results, but the accident of death and injury to his wife led him to take precautions. It would be necessary, he felt, to bring up Randall by hand.

I suppose Liddie, being a girl, just grew—and I hope she was a solace to her mother. I think of them as similar. But apparently from earliest times Richard, the eldest, resolved on his own courses, handwork or no handwork. It is astounding to anyone who knows the Garretson tradition to realize that

Richard graduated from Princeton, class of '83. And once off to that remote college, he hardly ever lived in Compton again.

Randall in his early youth surrendered himself to his home. I picture him as tending to be frail in both character and body. One would recognize him instantly as a nice boy. If you will reread Dr. Holmes's careful analysis of the Brahmin caste in the first chapter of *Elsie Venner* you will perceive the reflected figure of Randall Garretson—paler and more attenuated than the original, withdrawn from the struggle by the grace of one generation, but nonetheless marked as a thoroughbred. And his father perceived him that way too. Not that Theodore Garretson ever accepted Holmes's psychological nonsense—he called it irresponsible heresy—but he did recognize the same cultural heritage, the same aristocracy of brains and character. He gave his younger son the training of a scholar-prince.

Young Randall went to Compton grade schools, but in addition his father personally taught him Greek, Latin, and Christianity. Scientific studies had to shift for themselves. By the time he was sixteen and ready for Harvard he had read all of Plato's Dialogues, and, as he confessed many years later, he never read any Plato again. He did acquire a touch of science from his walks with Franklin Gray, and always fancied himself as an ornithologist, but it was a pretty transcendental fancy. In later years he was secretary of the Middlesex Wild Bird Society, and a famous leader of bird walks. It is true that he admired the elder Holmes, but with a worshipful admiration that took little account of Holmes's temper of mind.

Early in life he conceived of himself as a writer. One sees it in the journal, where he took pen in hand as though he were presiding at a literary reception. There were many poems, essays, an unfinished novel—I have the handwritten scripts still, a nine-inch pile of papers, and wonder what to do with them. It is the essence of a life and time, that pile of writing, graceful in every line, sensitive, sweet, not with any vulgar saturation, but with the delicacy of sweet fern. At least three of the poems were published in magazines, and there were some reviews in the *Transcript*—just enough to give Randall a professional rating. And his reference to himself all through life as "one of the minor writers" was touched with the half-humorous charm so typical of him. Whenever I filled out one of the questionnaires where "father's occupation" is called for I always hesitated long enough for the whole span of his life to flash into thought, and then wrote the single word "writer."

Naturally the high school in Compton was considered unsuitable for Garretsons, and for anyone who could afford better. The best of anything in those times was to be acquired only by private purchase: the public schools, like all the other public conveniences, were created only for those who had to use them. As I have already pointed out, Theodore Garretson leaned more and more to an aristocracy that was Anglican in quality, and he naturally sent his boys off to the Lincoln Rectory to be trained as Spartans, classicists, and English gentlemen.

Since then the Rectory has become one of the great Gold Coast private schools with famous neo-Gothic imitations of Winchester. My brother Steve teaches there and dwells in a lovely air-conditioned sacristy with a fan-vaulted ceiling. But back in the late seventies the school occupied a three-storied mansard dwelling and was made up of one head, one usher (afterward called master), and about fifteen boys. And of course the head, the famous and reverend Cadwallader Hooke, always called the rector, ruled like a king of Sparta. Hardly an uttered word or a drawn breath escaped his awful scrutiny. In the early years he taught all the classes, played all the games, and every morning took an ice-cold tub in full view of all his pupils. He wore gaiters, said prayers in a stentorian voice, taught Greek like a sergeant drilling a squad of hayseeds, and

out of his student body of fifteen produced a football team
that never lost a game. These are legends still cherished at
Lincoln Rectory. The old man died of apoplexy in the autumn
of '19 when his team beat Saint Luke's in the last second of
play, and since then every Lincoln team has known its duty.
There's even a song about killing off the rector.

Uncle Richard grew strong on such training, but my father
considered himself a bit delicate ever after. He always chuckled
at the memory of cold water, cold rooms, cold food, and hot
sport, but confessed that it was all too strenuous for him.
There was no place for the sensibilities in *that* life, he used to
say, but he sent Steve and me there just the same. He felt that
it was a splendid tradition, and realized that our sensibilities
were probably stouter than his.

When he went on to Harvard in the autumn of '83 he found
the ways made smooth for him. Up to that time I think of
him as a rather anxious youth, too thin, too tight, too apprehensive. His orbit centered on his home; he worshiped God
in the guise of his father, or his father's vicar, the rector. His
intellectual and moral diet lacked greenery. In Cambridge he
began to discover the pleasures as well as the duties of the
imagination, and he learned a geography of esthetics unheard
of in the chill Rectory. His early journal, begun in his sopho-
more year when he roomed in Holworthy, records a few names
rather strange to his generation: Ruskin, Morris, Pater, even
Swinburne. "The effect of wine," he writes in a spirit of
exploration, "is almost identical with the effect of this mad
poet, Swinburne. It appals me that one of God's rational creatures should be capable of abandoning himself so wholly to
emotional intoxication, but I find the sheer beauty of it irresistible."

So far, Randall had been trained for either the ministry or
scholarship. He has told me that his father expected him to
become a clergyman; he himself, he said, rather fancied the
classics, and at Harvard pointed himself in that direction—

reserving a private vision of added success as poet and essayist. He saw a career like Lowell's or Norton's, not in any arrogant conceit, but in such dreams as all young men have. And Harvard welcomed him and encouraged him: who more likely than Randall Garretson as candidate for the great office of scholar and gentleman of letters? He had read Plato in the original, he was anointed by Cadwallader Hooke, he addressed the great Mayo as Uncle Henry and dined with the Eliots.

But his stream shoaled and widened, grew sparkling to the sight and melodious to the ear. He learned to talk, and so indulged himself 'ever after. He took up Brahms and Wagner and French impressionism. He drank tea at Shady Hill and told stories of Whistler. He sang in the earliest Gilbert and Sullivan and wore his hair in a wave and sent to London for his boots, though he realized the affectation of it. "I was so anxious for to shine in the high aesthetic line as a man of culture rare." He never could quote Gilbert without a lilt of Sullivan too, and often as not once started he couldn't stop. But always he referred to those days as his happiest. "When I lay upon the daisies and talked in novel phrases of my compli-cated state of mind—Ralph, is there purer happiness this side of heaven? Why, boy, it was all a golden river of dreams. I suppose you've felt it too, I suppose all youth does some time, but back then we were drunk with beauty. Everything we lived for could be put into one word: beauty, only beauty. The pure gemlike flame. For a year or two I forgot Compton and my stern parent and the rector, I abandoned everything for that young man's dream and went off to dwell forever in the garden of Proserpine. And I—we, the chosen of the goddess, felt that we alone had found the true secret of eternity. You can't con-ceive of such fanatical ecstasy—and what insufferable snobs, what deluded asses we must have been. But, Ralph, we loved, we loved with an unearthly vegetable love; we forsook body and bone and common clay and we followed Beauty up to the very bars of heaven. It seems a naïve way of sowing one's oats,

I suppose, but of all delusions that was unquestionably the happiest."

He spoke often of those days. He liked to compare my own follies with his, and for a year or two when I played round with some young communists he kept watching to see how much of an ass I made of myself. "But you don't get so much fun out of it, Ralph. Even your follies are grim." And once when we were talking of this he reflected in silence for quite a while and then said, "You may be wiser. You know that ballad of Keats', the knight at arms alone and palely loitering—well—" when he paused again I realized that his mask was no longer there. I looked straight at the thin bones of his face, and for the instant time and life turned bitter for us both. "It is the saddest I know. Its beauty makes it nice; like love music—it has the dying fall, but the truth has haunted me. I tell you, son, when you need verses for my stone, take those." Gradually the mask came again, the twist of ironic smile, the bland lift of brow. He nodded to me and quoted:

> And I awoke and found me here,
> On the cold hill's side.

"There you have me in words of one syllable, in clearest amber. That goddess of ours—" He shook his head for the humor of it.

Randall was graduated in '87 with honors not of the highest, but with splendid festivity and congratulation. His sponsors forgave his minor failures in consideration of youth and charm, and there was a vague assumption that he would buckle soberly to his classics and turn scholar. But no persuasions were held out, no scholarships or assistantships. He declined an offer from a newly endowed academy in western Massachusetts —it seemed far away from the sources of his life. And he felt no compulsion. In the eighties time and tide waited for a gentleman. His fancy was occupied by his trip abroad with the best of his friends, Livingston Mayo and Charlie Ives—the happiest prospect of his life.

But chance played a few cards. His mother declined, grew sick, approached her death. Randall canceled his passage—the famous three graces of the class of '87 were never together again. And with this melancholy summer in Compton, Randall seems to have undergone a reversion. His star-crowned goddess, his blessed pure Beauty appareled in celestial dreams, turned once more into the demure spirit of the Compton meadows. From Sappho and Swinburne he came home to his own flowering fields. And his journal settles down to a faithful reflection of his spirit's adventures and his many travels in Compton. He read Virgil and Walton and Gilbert White and finally Thoreau.

Very little was ever said of his mother, or of her death in the first autumn weather. Several days later his journal takes the theme of death and life, but the desperate sentimentality of it seems to both Jean and me like the sweet scent applied to smother the stink of decomposition. In that respect he is wholly Tennysonian. There's no esthetic delight in oblivion here; rather a tearful resolution to look upon the bright side of immortality. "All we know of the divine order," he writes, "is inconceivably wondrous. The Beauty and the Good of Nature lie about us in infinite richness, and even to us of little faith every bird sings an angel's song and every flower lifts an angel's face. Here before us is God's plan, yet men still deny what their eyes may see. Here in our hearts is God's hope, in our minds his reason, yet we fear like children in a dark room." He must have been reading *In Memoriam*, though he doesn't say so. And it seems odd that he seldom referred to his mother as an actual person. It was more as if he himself had died, and was reminding God to supply the promised life everlasting.

So he settled in the good home he never escaped. Richard came for the formalities of death, then returned to life. Liddie filled her mother's place without alterations. Grandfather Garretson gave the law. And Randall wrote his verses and little essays, read a few pages of Latin each day, walked abroad, and remembered how in due time both Milton and Hawthorne had risen and shone among the constellations. He might also have remembered how both these great ones were tempered of a sort of puritanical steel.

Another play of chance, and he found himself sailing for Liverpool. Instead of the gay company of Garretson, Mayo, and Ives, there are three rather earnest Garretsons. A heavy father chaperoning his daughter and son on the grand tour, with full equipment of Baedekers, foreign phrases, and cultural reading for the evening. A first-class tour, with all the flatteries and complacencies, all the illusions of a world designed for the rich and free. Grandfather Garretson was doing well in those times, and after a few weeks in London his state became almost ducal.

England in spring, Scotland in summer, the lakes, and so southward with autumn, Brittany in the bright weather. Paris, much Paris, much wondrous Gothic, and, I fear, some stained-glass attitudes, then southward again and at last Italy, the garden of ruins, the paradise of old statues, the grand finale complete with scene, costume, music, and quaint Popish blessing.

If this were all, it would be worth little particular notice in a Garretson chronicle. The nice people of two or three generations ago did the same. But Randall fell in love, not entirely in a vegetable way. The course of his true love merged with that of his travels, and he and she and all of them behaved for a time exactly like the people in the novels of one of the nicest of nice Americans, Henry James.

◆§ CHAPTER 5 §◆

In London, the Ascot House catered to Bostonians. The management seemed to recognize the degrees of respect to which the Lowells and Cabots were accustomed. The best Americans, it was understood, were quite as good as the best anybody, and check-suited fellows from beyond the Hudson were received coldly.

Naturally the Garretsons stopped here, and Mr. Garretson by virtue of two previous visits was made to feel like an honored patron. And there were nice people, friends, neighbors, and cousins. The elder Boylstons lived there, and so did Mrs. Pierce Newbury and her daughter Hortense, and every summer the professors came and went, the Brattles and the Dunsters and of course the great Warrener and his lovely daughter Eileen.

In their travels that summer, the Garretsons and Warreners had crossed and recrossed one another's tracks, but always at slight distance, without formal connection. Propriety forbade even the exchange of glances. But Randall kept discreet watch for them, and as their travels progressed he grew more and more eager at the sight of Eileen's pert little figure. She and her father together made a charming pair: both small, eagerly alert, very tidily turned out, like well-plumed sparrows. They toured with vigor, and seemed to admire ruins and churches and famous scenery with a special sort of intelligence. But until they all met correctly at last in London, Miss Warrener apparently had no inkling that a respectable family of Garretsons existed. Mutual friends introduced them.

"Not Theodore Garretson?" Professor Warrener's voice was quick and bright, like his face, and pitched to carry well in a drawing room. "Well, upon my word, you must be Minnie Boylston's cousin—and of cawss, of *cawss*, your books! Why, this is delightful. Eileen, my dear, these are the Garretsons we've been seeing all about the country—how perfectly stupid of us not to have known!" When he spoke he leaned back and lifted the point of his dark beard to the horizontal and smiled with fierce brightness.

Miss Warrener extended a gloved hand with regal assurance, yet prettily. "Really, Mr. Garretson, I have several times been on the verge of taking propriety by the forelock and introducing myself. And to think you were from our dear Compton all the time—why, I used to visit the Brattles long ago. I have no doubt we are fourth cousins at least."

And then a sweet recognition of mouselike Liddie, and at last a cool smile for Randall.

Not tall or pale or divinely fair, not long of neck or consumptive in the fashion of the time, but rather exquisite in every vital detail. Randall had had many dreams, and conceived of his love as a willowy, tragic creature with blue-black hair who wandered forlorn in the meads, but the dreams vanished before this cool little mistress of life and manners. He had come to know her well in his watchings. Her clothes, for example, were always perfect as a picture, whether she were dining at the Royal Arms in Edinburgh or walking up the Helvellyn path with boots and a stick; her speech, her gestures, tastes, conformed to the best patterns, not in any conscious imitation, but in thoroughbred certainty. Detractors used harsh words against her, chief of which was "intellectual," and failed to perceive that Miss Warrener represented the new woman.

The age of blessed damosels seems to have been drawing to a close. For a long time the pale Gothic ladies had been growing paler, as well as thinner and more sickly and more unutterably tragic and, from the look of them, more bored. Randall was bored too, and so were the poets and painters who had invented the whole business. Miss Warrener would in present times be set down as competent and admirable, but in the late eighties she shone with conspicuous brilliance, much as though Clara Middleton had stepped from *The Egoist* straight into actual sitting rooms of the Ascot House.

After he met her, Randall abandoned Pater and Swinburne and took up Browning and Meredith.

And so began one of those charming journeys where the adventures of the road and the facts of legend and art are combined with the piquant fiction of courtship.

They met at Amiens and again at Rouen, and the learned, talkative, ever active Professor Warrener took charge of their goings forth. "My dear man, don't go near that church without me." This to the dignity of Theodore Garretson. "I know more about that church than anyone in the *wü-u-ld*." (It need hardly be said that Mr. Warrener never pronounced his *r*'s in such words but it is impossible to transcribe the shrill noise he made.) "I could give you the intimate story of every stone in it, but I shall forbear, I shall forbear, indeed. I assure you, my dear fellow, that whatever I may say will be charming as well as instructive." Here the bright smile and the beard leveled like a thrust finger.

Liddie, and even Randall, found this charm somewhat conspicuous. Mr. Warrener played his part as though the world's stage contained only himself and his satellites. If they encountered him in the market place he began speaking a hundred feet off in a voice pitched to carry a quarter of a mile. "Ah, there you are at last, idling away your priceless youth!" He might as well have burst into a tenor solo. "These buxom country folk are so delicious, do you see the one with the wood shoes? Fragrant too, by Jove. And such fat melons. There's a girl with a goose somewhere—too ridiculous for *words!*"

And sometimes Eileen smiled and tried to quiet him. "Father, dear, they can hear you for blocks."

"Ah, yes, so they can, but be comforted, my dear; they can't comprehend a word."

He addressed all lesser folk with supreme and joyous confidence, and assumed that their only concern was to serve him. He delighted particularly in the office of *concierge*, and sent for that individual at every turn.

"My good man, I assume your water is poisonous. What have you got here that's safe to drink?"

"My good soul, your hostelry is the most delightful in the whole republic and I shall be glad to testify to the same on oath, but will you have the kindness to send your cooks and scullery maids to bed before two in the morning."

These as likely as not shrilled across a crowded lobby.

Food, drink, blankets, bathtubs, laundry, trains, cabs, alley cats—he discussed all with similar charm and verve.

"When you have been about as much as I have," he explained to the provincial Garretsons, "you'll learn how to deal with these creatures. They expect it, of cawss. The continental servant is simply a bandit in livery and will strip you naked if you give him the least opportunity."

At that time DeForest Warrener was the foremost American authority on art, and quite conscious of his unique distinction. "Ten years ago America had never heard of art," he said to Randall. "And when they did hear of it they considered it a sinister foreign wickedness. You should have seen some of those muttonchop puritans when I proposed a course in Italian painting; they looked at me as though I had horns and a tail. 'A course in *pictures*, Mr. Warrener? You mean that our students will actually examine such things as—ah—

Titian?' A filthy habit, puritanism. And this at Harvard, mind you. If I had proposed such a thing anywhere else in America they'd simply have shot me."

But art had grown fashionable in spite of the puritans and practical folk. Ruskin gave it sanction and reconciled it, some of it, with virtue. Pater had followers. Whistler grew notorious. The mystery of esthetics took on glamor. And DeForest Warrener became the apostle of the new culture. He wrote, lectured, attended dinners and drawing rooms, advised museums, appraised collections, patronized young painters, and all the time played his part like an actor who had stolen the show. His outthrust point of beard, his bristling sparrowlike figure, his white smile, had become an international caricature; his far-carrying tones were familiar in the public places of a half dozen countries. "My dear Whistler—" so the cultural bray in the fogs of Pall Mall. "My dear Howells—" across the spaces of St. Marks. My dear George, or Leslie, or Aubrey, or James, my dear Sir Edward, or my dear Marquis—so the password among the knowing, and so you may still find it in Warrener's memoirs, *Arts and the Man* (his original title was *Beauty and the Beasts*—so my father said—but the publishers made him change it).

It annoys me to read what he says about Theodore Garretson, though it be gospel itself. The trip down through France and on to Rome fills a page or so: apparently he was chiefly concerned with a theory of the pagan origins of Gothic art, but in passing he refers to my grandfather as a cold, stuffed evangelist. I see what he meant, of course, and if I had said it first there'd be more truth than humor in it. But Warrener intended his wit to slay not in a cause of truth but in defense of his famous ego.

Randall and Liddie each have a line: he the sprout of Young Harvard, charming though virtuous; she the nun unrecognized even in heaven. "Eileen," he said, "found them restful."

I doubt if he could have admitted love to his mature reckon-

lings. I notice that as men grow brilliant they find love either
contemptible or comic, or they fail to perceive it at all. Yet
he may have known more of Eileen's feelings than I am willing to believe. Like so many of his words, "restful" is calculated
to hurt.

But for those few weeks Randall flew on wings of ecstatic
hope. He loved art, he loved Eileen, she loved art, she loved—
Randall? Why not? They worshiped together at the feet of
many a Venus. They also worshiped virgins and fauns, nymphs
and cherubim.

"Dear Miss Warrener, can you conceive what it means to
me to be coming into the presence of the Venus of Milo for
the first time—and with you?"

"Every time is the first time, Mr. Garretson. Custom cannot
stale, nor—well, whatever it is—" A quick girlish giggle may
have broken the limpid surface of reverence, but only for an
instant. In the year of our Lord 1887, the most sacred object
on earth—as far as the nice people were concerned—was the
Venus of Milo, nor could even a worldly Warrener deny her.
They came into the presence, as Randall properly expressed it,
and remained there speechless for sixty minutes by the watch.

"There are no words," he said afterward.

"No," she agreed. "That is all ye need to know."

They returned another day with Liddie and sat for fifty-
three minutes, and Liddie dozed a little.

And so with prayers and thanksgiving they did the master-
pieces. Forty minutes, I believe, for Mona Lisa, thirty minutes
for a Raphael, and so on down to queer little primitives. It
required faith and moral resolution, but in those qualities our
Victorian elders surpassed us.

At that time, as I understand it, nice people looked upon all
art as either old and good or new and bad. The new academy
stuff had reached the colored postcard level, Pre-Raphaelitism
had dwindled and grown scandalous, and impressionism was
rather weird—I use the same anxious phrase my father used

for all new things. But the old masters—the names spoken in a hush of reverence, like the sacred prophets, like the very archangels! I was nearly man grown before I knew for sure that Raphael and Michael Angelo were mortal men, and even now the mists of divinity hover about them; I see splendor and wings and diadems and the white clouds of God and the angel Raphael dipping brush in the gold and azure of heaven; I perceive a time when men mounted a flight of broad alabaster straight to the shining city and walked there among the martyrs and saints and saw the Virgin on her throne.

Mr. Warrener professed a cold and skeptical wit, but behind his bristlings lay the soft body of sentiment. He loved the Gothic for its mysteries, but he refused to accept Ruskin's moral denunciations of all else; he loved the glitter of Rome too, he loved high altars and golden cloth and well-fed angels; he loved all things old and splendid and masterful. And of course Eileen, behind her intellectual certainties, expressed the same feelings.

"I worship beauty, Mr. Garretson," she said during a late afternoon in Florence. "And of course God. I believe that one is to be found most truly in the other."

It was dusky along the river, and they had grown solemn by degrees.

"Beauty," she said, "is most purely a moral thing."

He considered.

"Couldn't you manage to call me Randall?" he said.

"I simply don't agree with these new critics who are denying that art is moral and implying that virtue is nothing but a wet old blanket smothering life's flame—and I'm sure it wasn't Pater's idea, either."

There are moments when the heart speaks out directly. "Eileen," he said. "Do you mind if I call you Eileen?"

She knew, of course. But no creature on earth at that instant could have been more crystal cool than Miss Warrener. "Why, of course not. You should have called me that from the start.

But this person Wilde—do you read him? He finds lies more charming than truth, and therefore more desirable. The good is simply his own pleasure . . ."

Here Eileen Warrener stood in Florentine dusk, listening to the first remote mutters of an imminent love; here a young girl stood, sweet of body, heart thumping under soft breast, blood flushing the creamy skin and singing round the brain.

"I suppose we can all agree that beauty *is* truth, but the difficulty is in saying what truth is. It really isn't easy, Mr. Garretson—" She did falter just there. The icy raiment softened and melting flame spread outward from her heart. "I'm sorry. I meant to say Randall." In the half dark no deepening blush showed. Her words were still like little crystals. "It's really much nicer—Randall, I mean." So the lady, the untouchable, cleaving only to the highest. "Truth is too general, I think, but untruth is much easier to grasp . . ."

Randall plunged. "It is the loveliest of all names—Eileen. I have called you that from the start—you don't really mind? I've thought of you as Eileen. It has a sort of—of Celtic poetry. Eileen—I love to say it."

"Well, my grandmother came from Dublin."

"Was she Eileen too?"

"Yes. Eileen O'More, and she married Noah Stebbins and they lived on a farm near Bellows Falls, Vermont."

"It's specially nice with Warrener; it's really lovely, you know. Only I—I've been thinking—how would it—"

"She was a Protestant," Eileen slipped in without a tremor. "Isn't that odd? Her father edited a paper in Brattleboro—they had nearly starved in Ireland. And then she turned into a Stebbins—that's odder still, don't you think?"

"It's lovely—why, it's a perfect dream. The sweet Irish Eileen and the stern Deacon Stebbins—flame and steel—he was a deacon, surely? Aren't all Vermont Stebbinses deacons?"

"Oh, of course!" Her father's voice, then, pitched a little high.

"And quite severe, with white whiskers?"

"Yes, indeed. Something like Mr. Garretson's."

"Ah." Randall had sensitive ears. "Splendid old tradition, after all. And beautiful Eileen O'More—"

"But no one said that, you know. She really smoked a clay pipe and drank poteen and swore horribly."

Randall flushed and looked down along the dark river. "Eileens are always beautiful," he muttered.

Her gloved hand slipped under his coat sleeve and when he looked back he saw that she was smiling. "It's getting chilly, I think. We ought to be back for tea." She moved him along faster, her step light on the stones and her eyes bright. "We must look at the Giotto again tomorrow. Father says Americans can't understand primitives—we are still too close to the Indians. What do you think?"

"Too Protestant, rather," he replied dutifully. Eileen smiled with feminine pleasure and touched his sleeve more firmly. He reflected and said, "Too many Deacon Stebbinses. Too many fathers and grandfathers."

She nodded. "You may be right. We do lack so many appreciations in our country—why even in Boston there's so little true understanding. Don't you think so, Randall?"

He answered with perfect seriousness. "Yes, even in Boston."

A few days later they traveled to Rome, where they reread *The Marble Faun* and *Daisy Miller*. "All Americans are struck with superstitious awe," Mr. Warrener said, "not by the Rome they see—they look upon that with a touch of contempt—but by what they think underlies it. The surfaces are so small and dreary that Americans are baffled. They expect grandeur, and behold, there are squalid alleys and beggars and stinks." Mr. Warrener spat out his words. "Look at your Mark Twain, turning the relics of all history into a comic stage—poor, bewildered creature, laughing in his dismal ignorance; I suppose the fifth-century Huns did the same, except that Huns are humorless beasts. But, mark you—behind all that is the fear, the conviction of things unseen. Both Hawthorne and Mr. James have minds of infinite and tender subtlety—more so, I believe, than any other Americans—but they look upon Rome with positive superstition. *The Marble Faun* is simply a ghost story superimposed on a guidebook, and as for *Daisy Miller*—dear, dear!" What Mr. Warrener meant was not quite clear, but his words were so charged with conviction that they seemed brilliant.

Grandfather Garretson often listened to these discourses with a show of respect, though it was evident that he attended to none of their finer points. His desire, of course, was to take the floor himself, but his breeding required that it be done by proper rule. "Well, for my part I quite agree with you, Warrener; there is a good deal of superstitious nonsense in Hawthorne, and this Mark Twain—as you say, a poor creature indeed, though his success is amazing; but I particularly view with alarm the moral temporizing, if I may call it so, in the younger men like James. There are certain truths which should be held inviolable; these speculations and rationalizings by responsible writers can lead to incalculable harm." The rest, of course, follows obviously and has nothing to do with anyone except Grandfather Garretson. But I think the Warreners by this time had grown restive.

There were many worldly folk in Rome, and Eileen seemed to know them all. Randall had thought she was his, but now he saw her attended by uniforms and titles. Would she visit the Vatican with him? Well, yes, of course, but not tomorrow, nor Tuesday, nor Wednesday—say tentatively, Thursday? But on Thursday the nice Tudor-Smiths arrived from Mentone and on Friday they all visited the Campagna and had a jolly time digging up building stones and bits of pottery. Eileen loved nice people; she sparkled and glowed among them and became their center and source of life; she planned their goings and comings, inspired their laughter and set a pace for their wit, directed their taste in art and food and deportment.

To Randall she seemed hedged about with divinity.

"Eileen, I humbly petition for two hours. It is much to ask, but for the sake of old times I beg you to grant it."

"Why, Randall!" Her bright eyes expressed all things from triumph to silly anxiety. "Why, of course we'll have two hours —three, if you say so. It's too absurd, all these plans and people—but fun, don't you think? Aren't you having fun, Randall? I'm sure all the nice people in the world are coming to Rome this winter."

"I had more fun in Florence." Pathos in his voice.

"Well, yes—I know. Just the five of us, and the heavenly paintings. Rome is so busy and worldly."

"The two of us, you mean," he said feelingly.

But her smile made light of it.

Randall despaired. Her brightness was a pure glaze without a seam, an armor of diamond; yet underneath it he could believe a warm and mortal heart lay delightfully beating.

The time came—a long morning in heaven. Only there was no length for Randall. He brought his lady to the immortal marbles; they breathed the pure, serene and contemplated divinity; they whispered of beauty and truth, and became one with time and the gods.

"If Phidias had seen you, Eileen." The thought sustained itself in the incorruptible air.

"You think he'd admire my—costume?"

But Randall was above frivolity. "I think he would perceive only your soul."

Elsewhere he might have blushed and she might have laughed. But here they both simply stared at the soul of Aphrodite.

They walked at last across the square in front of St. Peter's and he asked her to be his.

⊷§ CHAPTER 6 §⊷

WHEN MY father returned to Compton after his grand tour, he felt that life owed him an explanation. The only explanation he had succeeded in getting from Eileen Warrener was that he was a nice boy—a very nice boy. But he had known that himself; he always knew that, even to the end of his days. Yet something was wrong. The lovely creature would not be his, though he perceived in her the body and soul of his dreams; his supreme niceness had not sufficed.

He agreed with himself that he must work and do good in the world. His father felt the same, but with him it was a matter of common morality. Good men worked, even good rich men. New England morality. Concerning his son's personal doubts he had no curiosity.

At all events, Randall Garretson went to Boston every day and studied architecture. I notice that in feminine fiction, the best heroes are architects. Randall's choice was made for the same reasons. The architect combines business with culture; he turns art to profit and cultivates a sensitive taste with practical results; he affects the tweed jacket, the soft shirt, the pipe; he talks like an art critic, works like an engineer, and reaps good commercial rewards. No lady could ask for more.

It wasn't his fault that he undertook the career in the one period of modern history when the art had reached its ebb. But it may be considered his fault that it took him thirty years to recognize what had happened. The esthetic mist that hovered over his times gave a rosy glow even to its chocolate-cream architecture.

"It was Ruskin," he explained when I asked him about it. I had said that the houses of the eighties seemed to me an insoluble mystery—as they must to everyone who looks at them clearly. "You don't realize how persuasive that man was. We must create houses in the image of our aspirations the way monks created Melrose or Tintern; we must never, never, never accept a standardized form. It is easy now to see that the results are, as you point out, incredible; if those are truly our aspirations, God help us—and I gather from the gleam in your eye that I have stated your thought. You think evil of the Gilded Age, the vulgarity and the ostentation—more pathetic now than evil, I suppose. Yes, I find it hard to make a defense. Even the best of us didn't quite see—any more than Ruskin himself saw. He was surely right about the ideal, but he didn't see the direction of our aspirations. He thought in terms of a medieval Christianity; he failed to see that in building his little dams against the flood of mechanization he was actually trying to stem the new sea of faith. Yes, my boy, the whole thing was an anachronism. I suppose it is no wonder that those houses seem unbelievable. Gothic dreams subjected to commercial requirements . . ."

I remember the speculative look in my father's eye when he said this, and then the twinkle as he looked at me. "You know, that's rather good. It would make an article. The new sea of faith—" He shook his head with a quaint sigh. "That's not for me after all—it's for a younger fellow. But it's rather good just the same. Personally I don't care for the god of the machine, the divinity of pure mechanics; I can't worship stainless steel, no matter how immortal it is said to be."

Actually he had come to worship the colonial house. It was more than the shrine, more than simply the temple of the most high; it was in fact the manifestation. All he ever knew

about the divine abstractions—the truth, the beauty, the holy
spirit itself—appeared literally in the white pine boards of
his house. The front door, the fan light, the fluted pilasters,
represented the ultimate for him, the miracle of common
substance translated into pure spirit, unique and infinite. That
house, he might have said, is all ye need to know on earth,
but be sure ye know it truly; every molding, every rectangle,
means good, the one and only good, immortal and unchanged.
In his late years he lived wholly in the service of his house;
his habits of dress, speech, deportment, were shaped by the
house; his judgment of men and nations was directed by the
house; he became its counterpart in flesh.

But this faith came later in his life, like an unlooked-for
Indian summer. He searched the world rather vaguely for truth
and in the end found all he needed at home.

In 1890 he worked in an architect's office on Bromfield Street
and went to a school of drawing. He learned how to reproduce
the classic orders and to draw the elevations of Gothic vault-
ing. He was instructed in imitations. Architects at that time
were humble men, as I understand it; they looked upon the
three great periods of the past much as a common wayfarer
might look at the peaks of the Himalayas. There, on equal
terms with heaven itself, stood the pure and shining classic,
the Parthenon indistinguishable from celestial snows; and
there, too, the aspiring Gothic, the farthest heavenward shaft
ever shot by man; and there the domed Italian, man's own
pomp and pride somehow equated with God's. In the shadow
of such grandeur, the modern man on earth could do no
other than worship. He made a phrase for it—the Great Tradition—and appointed himself its keeper; he established the
orders and preserved the codes. He imitated not in ignorance
but in patient wisdom and learned respect. His memorial halls
and public libraries expressed only one faith: that the past was
forever glorious and the present was contemptible. The
mountainpeaks were for other men in other times; here we

lived in the valley and the shadow, looking always back and up.

For some years Randall Garretson earned a little salary and conducted himself like a professional man. I think his work had mostly to do with decorations; he was known as a man of taste, with a knack for cupboards and mantelpieces. He did delicate pencil sketches and could conjure delightful effects out of nowhere with a grace that was both well-bred and humorous. Jean always calls it his "Ah, dear lady" manner, but the phrase has to be done with gestures as well as voice. And the tweed jacket, the soft shirt, the careless waving hair —they were notable eccentricities in a time when gentlefolk set themselves off in starch and black. He grew conspicuous in a nice way and was an asset to the firm of Peabody and Peabody.

It was a good time for him. The memory of Miss Warrener remained sweet and sad, an emotional overtone of the most delicate timber. When she married an English gentleman, Randall's heart may have ached for a time more than was pleasant—but less for his own loss than for another man's gain. No man, he felt, excepting himself, should be permitted so exquisite a virgin—the thought of it filled him with a very common sort of masculine nausea. But beyond that he admitted that an English gentleman was probably very suitable for her, and in time he forgot that his heart was pierced. She tended to a worldliness not for him—he knew it and could sigh for his loss most pleasantly. Furthermore, he had new friends, a whole Bostonian world of friends. He dined and called and found himself a social success, especially among mothers and daughters.

He found the warmest of welcomes at a brown house on Marlborough Street in the Back Bay, where Mrs. Vernon Hollister lived with three daughters and a cousin. The cousin, named Ada, was poor and anxious, had a little room on the third floor, and did all the sewing—they called her dear Ada. The others, Mrs. Hollister and Alice and May and Caroline, called one another darling: Mother, darling, Alice, darling, and so on. They lived in a flutter of affection and feminine good will, like four expectant heroines. They played musical instruments and went to the Friday-afternoon symphony; they did charity work among the poor and were eager in support of their church; they spent six weeks of the midsummer at the Asticou House at Northeast Harbor, and the month of early autumn at the Ravine House in the White Mountains, leaving dear Ada to see that the servants were well taken care of at home. Of course, they urged Ada to come with them—this was discussed every June: Ada, dear, *do* come—it's such fun, you've no idea, and such nice people and picnics and young men—really, I mean awfully *nice*—you'd love it, Ada. But Ada said she hated summer hotels. Once she said she hated nice people, but the remark caused such a flutter that she never ventured to repeat it. Poor dear Ada, they felt she was beyond help.

The Hollisters themselves were exceptionally nice people. Mrs. Hollister was a Bradstreet; Mr. Hollister was dead, but had been wealthy. In Boston at that time the sources of wealth were not questioned, and it wasn't until after his marriage that Randall learned that Mrs. Hollister received forty thousand dollars a year from the rents on South End properties. Of course, she knew next to nothing about all that; the trust people managed it very competently. She realized that wealth was a responsibility, and she hoped her darling girls would understand their position in the world—it was really gratifying to see them take hold in church work and the Girl's Friendly. We mustn't let the Bradstreet traditions fail, she said. And she noted that Alice was particularly eager to do her part in the world. Alice had a lovely nature—she seemed exceptionally sensitive and liberal.

To Randall, the house on Marlborough Street was a castle of lovely indolence. He dwelt in it without care. Lunch or tea or dinner was always waiting—even a room and breakfast if he breathed a desire; and three maidens to laugh and sing and flatter him with eager, innocent love. "Dear Randall," Mrs. Hollister used to say, "it's so nice to see you here—you're our boy, you know, and you must consider this a second home, a refuge from the cares of the great world. And you do remind me so of your dear mother—she had a really artistic nature, and I'm sure she'd be very proud of you. Architecture is such a *fine* profession for a young man. Alice always says if she were only a man she'd be an architect—Alice is the most gifted of my girls, I think—though May does beautifully on the violin, and darling Caroline is coming along so well, it makes me really proud . . ."

The girls consulted him about drapes and covers for furniture, and even about hats and clothes. He had really marvelous taste, they said, though they giggled and fluttered and made great mystery of their feminine arrangements. No charge of immodesty could be brought against a Hollister— though possibly Alice was a little daring, and she certainly prided herself on being modern. The others thought she went too far when she made Randall decide between two evening gowns sent on approval—quite low cut, too, and there she stood turning round and round like a model all smiles and perfume. But it all seemed part of the family, as Mrs. Hollister rightly said.

For a time he loved all three. Others did too. Affection and esteem surrounded them like spring fragrance. But Randall belonged more securely than anyone. He met without dismay the young Eliots and Endicotts and cousin Charles Pierce and dear Francis Harding, and stayed on for supper or the night, and in the evening sang with them or read aloud or played anagrams. He admired Alice particularly, and treated her with defensive respect; she seemed to expect more brilliance from him than the others did. He loved May as a sister—as more than a sister; she the steady, the ever sweet, the quiet doer of deeds, the one who saw to fresh sheets for his bed and counted the lamb chops and hung away his coat and hat and reminded him to wear rubbers, who played with steady grace the "Air for the G String" because it was his favorite. But he truly loved Caroline, the young and pure, the white blossom, the innocent—always just too young to be fully alive, always behind, sheltered, kept from the full truth, but fair as a white rose, or as new snow.

Caroline had always been called a big girl—such a big girl, and so round and smooth and pure. Her skin was too white for the touch of sun, her eyes too wide and blue to look at the world's dazzle. All she had learned in her eighteen years was innocence. She was the perfect product of the education given to all young ladies in that innocent age. She knew by implication that life outside her cloister was evil; the street was evil, and the poor and the shops and flats—in fact, all men. But she knew that all evil was impotent against her veil of purity; she knew that she lived as safely and cleanly as an alabaster figurine in a glass case. She never thought of evil, or reckoned with it, any more than one in a garden shade reckons with the mortal glare of a desert sun. Innocence was not her duty, it was her all.

Of the three, she was the fairest. She was the queen's youngest daughter, snow white and flaxen haired, carved of ivory, unstained by touch of earth. And yet somehow charming in her felicity of sweetness and light, like a myth come true. Even Randall knew that she was a little stupid and never thought for herself and had to be taken care of like a child, but her innocence was a mystery in itself. He conspired with the others to protect her, in a state of mind that could only be called religious.

For a year or so after Randall attached himself to the Hollisters, Caroline remained a little girl. No one was expected to notice that she was three inches taller than her mother and a fully developed female. She wore high black shoes, black-ribbed cotton stockings, and short skirts that hung about eight inches below her knees. Her hair fell in a hempen braid down her back, and her sisters—and Randall—were proud that she could sit on the end of it. She went to Miss Newton's School, of course, and was being encouraged to read Scott. She was nearly eighteen, very quiet and sweet, walked lightly on her feet, and always smelled of castile soap. Randall particularly loved her freshness. She had the air of one who has just at that moment been created complete.

May "came out" that season—not that she cared about it at all, but she knew how much it meant to her mother. Alice was already out—miles out, she said, deprecating her continued maidenhood. May went through the motions calmly enough, was greatly admired and refused two formal offers— a triumph mitigated by May's talent for modesty. "It's only that they think I'm perfectly safe," she explained to Alice. "They don't detect any signs of a brain in my head, and their mothers all tell them how well I can darn socks and order groceries—in fact, I'm sure Francis was simply quoting his mother when he popped the question."

Caroline was not included in these worldly confidences, nor was she allowed to go to the full-dress evening affairs, but she did timidly appear at the informals—still uniformed as a child and closely guarded. The eligible men passed her by, the eligible maidens were all sweet to her, and only the married and the very young had any words for her—with one exception. Randall Garretson appointed himself her protector, with family sanction. He waltzed with her—she a bubble of ice in his hands. He brought refreshment. He took her home at discreet hours, driven by Timothy in the carriage. "It is sweet of you, Randall," May said. "I wish you treated me like that."

"You mean, like a little girl?"

"No—like a little princess."

"But think of all the princes in your train."

They were sitting at tea, just the two of them in the second-floor library. May lifted an expressive hand. "Yes, just think of them. Who am I to be dissatisfied?"

Something unexpected in her tone, a compressed, half-choked sound, a faint tremble.

But Randall smiled at her humor. "You—dissatisfied? You can't pretend that, you know." He looked appreciatively at her calm face, her clear plain features—not really plain, but very simple and unadorned, and just now touched with light.

"Yes, it's silly," she said. "I have everything. Yet I complain."

"Too much attention, I'm afraid." He nodded wisely. "You should be a little less successful—content yourself with one prince instead of a dozen."

"And which one would you suggest?"

"Well—" he went blithely on as though nothing were at stake—"There's good old Francis, always dependable, plenty of property—no shining armor, I suppose, no chivalry, but after all, in the long run—" He stopped. May was sitting up and looking at him with frightened eyes.

"Randall, you—you're so *stupid!*" she almost shouted it, then clapped a handkerchief to her face and scurried from the room.

He blushed unseen, and settled himself with a few sips of tea. May must be terribly tired, he thought, and renewed his belief in the mystery of woman. She had always been as self-possessed as—as a household priestess, a regular Agnes Wickfield, calm as a May morning; they laughed at her because of it, and she laughed at herself because they did. Never a tantrum—until now. Randall brushed back his flowing hair and tried to think what he could have done.

"Oh, tea already?" Caroline came in like a bright cloud. For some reason she had wound her blond braid round her head to make a crown.

"Ah, the princess." Randall stood and bowed. There was no irony in his action.

"Aren't the others coming?"

His eyes were doglike. "Caroline, couldn't you find it in your heart to smile and say, 'How pleasant—how nice this is'?"

"Well, I just thought May was down here."

"No pleasure without May?"

She smiled timidly, but with radiance. "Why, it isn't that—" The effort of realization brought a wash of color to her clear cheeks. "It's always pleasant here—"

"No, no, Caroline." The loving patience made an effort. "The point is that I am happy to be with you—here or anywhere else—and I hoped that you felt the same."

"Why, yes, of course"—faintly

He shook his head. "You speak in icicles. Do you realize that you have no right to be as beautiful as you are, with that spun-gold coronet, with eyes like spring sky—and then to behave as though I were your governess? Why, you know I'd rather be here with you than be the king of the Golden River—" He spoke with impatience, as though he were shaking her, and she looked at him open-eyed, and a little openmouthed. He smiled ruefully. "It's all right. I am your slave, that's all; but you don't seem to grasp the fact. I wanted to make it clear. You don't seem to realize that you are as beautiful as—as the fair Elaine—" His voice ended in a tremble.

"Don't be foolish, Randall." Her words were uncertain and small, but dutiful. She took cup and saucer, poured the tea with well-trained hands. "Will you—are you ready for more?" The loveliest timidity in her voice, like tender little droplets of spring water.

He gulped the cold remains and handed her the cup. "Let it be a symbol." He spoke darkly, and she busied herself without paying much attention. "But mark my words, I shall someday expect more from those white hands—more than very good tea. You are still sleeping—in a palace of glass on top of a glass mountain—"

"One lump and cream—all right?"

"And if you call me foolish then—well, you'll be sorry, that's all."

She handed cup and saucer back with the smile of one who is doing well.

"I can hear the ice tinkling in your veins—a delightful little music, really. It's one of your fascinations." He put his tea on a small table and noted the warmer flush of pink on her cheeks. He was strangely aware of his voice continuing. "Caroline, I do probably sound foolish, or presumptuous—your mother would disapprove, I'm sure; but you are so unbearably beautiful, and so good and perfect—I—well, you see, I am falling in love with you—I have fallen, rather. I shouldn't be speaking of it—not yet—you'll have to sort of pretend—" He made a choked sound and paused.

Caroline sat still as a stone, back straight, eyes fixed on him.

"Next year," he stumbled on, "it will be different—I mean, you'll be all grown up. Just please forget what I—that is, I didn't intend to say it." He seized his cup, rattled spoon and saucer, spilled tea, gulped it, burned his throat. "All right," he muttered. "It's just hot. Is yours too?"

"Not very." She lifted steady cup and sipped. "You must have swallowed too much at once."

"Yes, I did indeed. Nervous of me, wasn't it?"

Her final yes was like a duty done.

She turned her head. "I think Alice is coming."

"Well, children!" Alice made an entrance.

Randall popped to his feet.

"Having a tête-à-tête, are you? Where's May? I'm simply dying for a cup. Been on the go since morn." A whole new feminine atmosphere fluttered in with her, a whirl of scarfs, ribbons, long gloves, bangles, skirts, and delicate scent.

"You didn't start out till eleven," Caroline explained.

"A cup of strong tea, my child, and don't be so literal." Alice smiled for Randall. "She ruins my best effects, poor

sweet innocent. But really I am bristling with virtue; I refuse
to be deprived of it."

"Babies again?" Caroline asked.

"Not really babies—but the darlingest, most awful children,
like filthy cherubim screaming murder at you. Randall, something ought to be *done* about it. Truly, if I were a man, if I
could only get up in the legislature and tell them what's going
on in this fair city— Thank you, darling. Any cakes or food?
I'm starved. It was a sort of milk clinic down at the Settlement
House—milk and crackers, and I must say it took my appetite
away—really and truly you couldn't believe what they're like
—Italians and Greeks and I don't know what, but I'm just
ravenous now. Go ask Nora for some of those crusty things
with raisins—and more water, while you're at it. Mother'll
be along in a minute."

Randall's eyes followed Caroline as she floated away with
the kettle.

"Too absurd, putting her hair up like that. Of course, it'll
have to go up soon enough, but that braid makes her look like
an early Greek—and so childish. She's going to be a beauty,
that girl—woe is me! I always wanted to be a beauty, and now
I'm in the clutches of jealousy. If the darling child weren't
so innocent I'd be in a fury with her. Randall, the places
those poor creatures have to *live* in—it haunts one. It's a job
for you architects, not just building houses but arranging for
a whole new city and getting rid of those unspeakable match-
boxes. There's the queerest book—I must get it for you; Janie
Lee has it now—it's called *Looking Backward*. Have you seen
it? All about what we'll be like in a hundred years, and really
it's too thrilling—it makes you see how *stupid* we are.
Mother'd have a fit if she knew I was a socialist—don't betray
me, Randall; but you must read it. Some of those slum children are perfectly darling and they get to be such fiends, and
all so filthy."

Alice seemed to rustle as she spoke, as though she lived in

a complicated silk pavilion. She tended to be plump, and her features were soft, like a too-ripe peach. When she flushed, her nose turned pink and the rest of her face became a patchwork of red and white—so absurd, like a kitchen tablecloth, she said. Sometimes yellow, too—that's the worst.

"Here's mother," she said, and Randall popped to his feet. "Hello, darling; Caroline's getting cakes and water—we're all famished. Such a day, I was just telling Randall—"

Mrs. Hollister fluttered and bustled even more than Alice. "Well, this is jolly," she was saying, not listening to Alice. "Do sit down, Randall. Where *are* the girls? Really, I've had the most exasperating time with those cleaners; they refuse to do a thing about my watered silk, and it's just ruined— we've been fighting the entire afternoon. Randall, it's lovely to see you. How is your dear father these days? You must bring dear little Liddie in to see us—it's such ages. Child, Randall would like more tea—where in the world is the kettle?"

"Mother, darling, I was just saying to Randall that he really ought to come down to the Settlement House with me— don't you think he should? I mean, being an architect, and seeing what might be done, and those tenements are so dreadful—he just ought to *see*. Don't you think so, Mother?"

"Indeed I do, darling. I don't think you ought to go down there alone at all. She will do it, you know—" turning to Randall—"She considers it her duty and won't listen to a word I say. But it isn't only a question of courage, I tell her; it's a question of wisdom, of doing what is wisest in the *long run*." Mrs. Hollister got up and imperiously rang the bell. "Where can Nora be? Oh, Caroline—at last. Darling, you shouldn't try to carry so much, you must let Nora."

Randall was on his feet again, and he hastened to transfer a plate from Caroline's hand to a table. Then they all settled down.

"Alice is perfectly devoted—it is splendid, but I'm not sure it is quite wise. Do tell us what you think, Randall—from the point of view of a man of the world, I mean. You see, it is right in the slums, and the most awful men, really I can't describe it with Caroline here, and of course Alice works with the children and mothers, but there are so many—" her voice dropped to a stage whisper—" so many saloons everywhere, it is too dreadful. Now, really, Randall, I'd just like to know how you feel about it—a lovely girl like Alice, and so precious to us all—don't you dare blush, Randall; I've known for a long time, and I admire you for it—no, let me finish." She waved a left hand. "This is a very serious matter, and I want Randall's opinion. Caroline, darling, do see where May is— she's probably forgotten all about the time; she reads so much—too much, I sometimes think, but she has always had an unusual mind—it won't be long before all my girls are far ahead of their old mother—and Caroline, ask Nora to tell Bridget not to make mint sauce, we'll just have the plain lamb gravy—dear me, is that the front-door bell? Caroline, tell Nora if it's Mrs. Bellows I'll see her in the drawing room; if it's Charlie Pierce, send him up, of course. I did hope Agatha Bellows wouldn't come today—Nora will have to bring in tea for her, I suppose. Is Ada in? She and Agatha always get on so well together, and she could fix up the extra tea tray." Mrs. Hollister rustled nervously, then rose—bringing Randall with her. "I'd just better see. Caroline isn't always very quick." She swept away.

Alice smiled in confidence. "I'm so glad mother talks more than I do. It would be too tiresome hearing myself go on all the time."

"What am I to say to her?"

"Oh, she'll have forgotten all about it. Just say you'll come down with me and look things over—but it isn't on my account, Randall. Gracious, what a fuss about nothing! No, I think you ought to take an interest in things like that—as a rising young architect, of course."

"Well, of course!" He tried to be hearty, and smiled so that she felt successful. "Just say when you'd care to do it— any afternoon is fine for me."

"Why, Thursday is my day."

"Good." He uncrossed his legs and started to rise. Then seeing Caroline he stood up quickly, waited for her to settle into the corner of a divan, and sat down again, watching her with half-veiled eyes. "Right after lunch, I suppose?"

"No—come to lunch at the Settlement. Twelve-thirty. They'll be thrilled to have a gentleman."

"Someday I'd like to go, Alice," Caroline said.

"You'd hate it, darling. It isn't very nice."

"Well, someday."

"Perhaps," Randall said, "I might someday be permitted to escort you—after my own initiation, of course."

CHAPTER 7

A YEAR later in March, Randall and Alice were married. Trinity Church and the bishop, the Bradstreet veil, bridesmaids in tears, carriages, awnings, red carpets, silk hats, the Eliots, the Mayos, the Brattles, Rector Hooke, and flowers like summer. No man could recount the preparations. Dear Ada did the sewing and darling May arranged the catering—she was marvelous—and of course mother attended to the invitations, a tremendous task, and Caroline addressed most of them—they didn't have to hire anyone; Caroline was an angel about doing anything you asked. But above the actualities hovered the ecstasy. The ancient passion of epithalamium electrified the house; the very air, the heavy twilight of dark halls, the gloom of walnut rooms, sang for this once the harmonies of marriage—not the love, but the pure exalted ceremony, the miraculous social fulfillment, the triumph of the maiden's life.

Clothes became the vestments of ritual, down to the least ribbon and stitch. All bodily functions grew mystic and portentous—the sleeping and dreaming, the eating, the bathing and hair washing, the quivers of temper and distemper. The ringing of bells, the step of the postmen, the whispers by doors ajar, the shouts downstairs, the infinite, thrilling complication of decision and indecision, the exhaustion from the fateful choosing, the sighs and debates by night and by day over patterns, colors, monograms, quality and quantity—it seemed to them that the whole city waited in tension for each wondrous detail, all the stores, all the clerks, milliners, caterers, officials great and small, the hierarchy of church and state, the men and women passing up and down Marlborough Street.

For a month no life existed apart from the event. Mrs. Hollister told Nora to tell Bridget to send up a few cold scraps—it didn't matter; no one was hungry anyway. And from basement to roof the house was turned inside out with cleaners and polishers and window washers and the men to whitewash the ceilings and other men to fix the wobbly banisters, and men carrying in new rugs and carrying out old ones, and the decorator discussing the new drawing-room furniture, and the seamstress helping Ada upstairs, and a regular parade of delivery boys ringing the basement bell.

The women grew bright-eyed and taut and eternally alert, like folk at war. They campaigned through the city shops by day and studied their spoils by night. They argued to the edge of fury and despair.

"But, darling, Caroline isn't out yet—she's still a child, don't you see?"

"That's perfect nonsense, Alice." May's level voice had iron in it. "She's putting her hair up for keeps now—it's stupid to go on calling her a child. Mother was married at her age."

"That's nothing to do with it. She's just a baby, and you know it. I don't care if she does wear corsets and everything —she simply isn't *out* yet, can't you see that?"

"Well, what in the world has being out got to do with it? I never knew you to be such a stick-in-the-mud, Alice. You're worse than mother."

"Listen, darling; this is *my* wedding. Do you understand that? I've asked you to be my maid of honor. That is all there is to it. I never in my life heard of such a crazy idea as having two maids of honor—and I refuse to have Caroline standing up there beside you, and I refuse to have her alone. If you won't do it I might as well not have the wedding. I think you're just beastly, that's all."

When Alice burst into tears she dissolved like a squeezed tomato. May furnished some handkerchiefs, and cried more quietly.

"All right, it's your wedding, but I don't want to do it. Do stop blubbering, darling."

"Well, you act so *queer*, May. It's almost as though you didn't want me to—to—*have* a wedding."

More blubbering. And May took a long breath, not crying any more but staring at the picture on Alice's bureau. Her face had its plain look—her mouth straight and thin, her cheeks gray.

"I'm sorry, Alice. I don't intend to be like that. I want everything to be wonderful for you. We're all so tired, and I just had the feeling that Caroline ought to—well, I don't know what I thought. She'd be so stunning in that pale blue —I've been seeing her standing up there in it looking divine, and it doesn't go with me nearly as well—"

"Oh, stop!" Alice's overripe face came out of the handkerchiefs. "You're being perfectly idiotic. You look lovely in blue, and you know it, and anyway a bride has some rights— do you think I want the whole church staring at Caroline all through? It would go to her head, too—she's much too young."

Caroline and Liddie were among the six bridesmaids, and it may be that the church stared at Caroline even so, for she walked in a mist of unearthly beauty, like a maid of paradise. The groom himself stared at her as he stood waiting beside his brother, but of the hundreds there, only two saw where his eyes were or divined the emotion that made his expression that of one facing appointed death. When Richard jogged him forward to his destiny he stepped without volition, like a sleeper.

"Too absurd," whispered Aunt Alice Bradstreet to Mrs. Hollister. "Grooms always behave like sacrificial calves."

But Mrs. Hollister was beyond any hearing. She stood in an ecstasy.

Uncle Lyman Hollister gave away the bride. It was agreed that Alice behaved with marvelous assurance. Her color remained just right—no kitchen-tablecloth effect, no crushed tomato: she even smiled with infinite tender sweetness, and then and there visibly took charge of Randall—but charmingly, in good wifely taste.

Mrs. Hollister audibly gasped with the joy of it. It was above perfection; it was magnificently right. Her Alice in the Bradstreet veil carrying all before her with triumph, with unparalleled fitness of detail. Not a flaw, she thought, not cause for a lifted eyebrow in all Boston; her destiny on earth was being fulfilled in the way she had dreamed of—and darling Alice the very embodiment of her life's work, and Caroline the nicest child anyone had ever seen, and dear gentle May—they were *hers*, created and directed by her own hand, led forth to their duties and destinies with more than royal success. May's turn next, and very soon—

Mrs. Hollister glanced at May. The girl was like a scrap of paper, bloodless and swaying with a helpless inanimate sort of flutter. No one seemed to see her. The bride was saying "I, Alice—" and the church listened breathless for her tones.

Mrs. Hollister started out—it was only ten feet from her to May—then hung at the pew's edge. Perfect up to now— every detail in harmony, every note, every last nuance of the faultless wedding—and May on the verge of fainting. She looked impulsively for assistance, then discreetly. After all, May of all people—

The bishop's voice rising: "Those whom God hath joined, let no man . . ."

"May, May, darling!"

Only three turned heads. Richard looked, and slipped a hand under her elbow. The great bouquet stopped fluttering. May gasped air as though she were drinking it, bowed her head to touch her hand, then straightened. A twist of her pale lips reassured him, and she glanced forlornly back at her mother.

The ceremony drew to its end. Mrs. Hollister re-entered her ecstasy, and presently tears flowed warm on her cheeks. It was all right. Everything was done. Tears were next. Aunt Alice was crying, so was Liddie—but not Caroline, she as serene as heaven, and not May, white and taut like stretched cloth.

The slow recession toward the daylight, and then as the great organ quieted the release from ritual, and the wildfire of excitement.

"Too lovely, darling!"

"Alice a perfect dream—really. I never saw anyone so . . ."

"Pale and so distinguished, like a poet . . ."

"And the way she said 'I, Alice—' well, I thought I'd simply die!"

"Poor dear, did you see her face? I really was terrified—she was practically in a dead faint. I suppose you realize she has done the whole thing—she's the brains of the family, and she just *slaves* for them. You know how Mrs. H. is—no more sense than a hen, and Alice exactly like her—what they'd do without May I can't imagine, and there the child stood swaying like a *leaf*."

"But, my dear, did you *see* her? Why, really, you could have knocked me over with a straw—that child, that babe in pigtails, blossoming out like the queen of Sheba—well, pretty enough, I must admit; she certainly outshines her sisters—or will when they give her a chance—but it gave me a shock to see her there, and poor little Liddie like a wraith beside her . . ."

Garretsons and Hollisters shook hands and smiled and

blinked and made little speeches, and all rode in carriages to Marlborough Street: first the bride and groom and the best man and maid—still in the clutch of ceremony, still tight with the sense of duty and destiny beyond control; then the elders and parents, like royalty, in purple and silk, with all plumes of pride and wings of vanity.

"It's so—so *appropriate*," Mrs. Hollister struggled to say to Mr. Garretson. "The dear children have so much in common. I sensed it from the very first—their artistic natures, very sensitive as you well know, but more than that: it is what dear President Eliot calls moral good taste, a sense of—of duty—"

Mrs. Hollister floundered briefly; Mr. Garretson bowed. "Indeed, as you say, dear lady—"

"It was really the Settlement project that forged the bond between them." She picked up speed again. "You have no idea how my girl has devoted herself—without stint, my dear Theodore, regardless of her mother's warnings and her own well-being, without any consideration of her own social position—it has been a revelation to me, I can tell you, it has made me both proud and humble—very humble, I assure you. And I saw at once that Randall recognized the beauty of her devotion and wanted to share it. The dear boy insisted on seeing it all for himself—it was so interesting to see their— shall I say their destinies—merging and becoming one. I simply gave them a doting mother's blessing—really, it was too perfect."

Mr. Garretson bowed approval again.

"I think May looks a bit run down," Uncle Lyman Hollister remarked abruptly. "Better send her up to the farm this spring —bit of country air, eh?"

"Run down!" Aunt Alice produced a resonant snort. "She's practically dead. Annie makes a slave out of her."

"Why, Alice! What a thing to say! It's outrageous—you know May has always had these headaches, and she is simply devoted to darling Alice—no two sisters could be closer. Naturally, it has been a strain—it has for all of us. I shall be a perfect wreck for months."

Mr. Garretson sat up a fraction straighter and issued a preliminary clearing noise. "Let me say, dear lady, that you have in this respect, as indeed in many others, outshone—I say outshone—your charming daughters."

Mrs. Hollister spread herself with delight. "What absurd flattery, Theodore. You shouldn't take advantage of an old woman."

They rolled up to the door in a bright cloud of self-esteem.

CHAPTER 8

"Randall, dear, you ought to be in town, you know. You need the associations—I'm sure Mr. Peabody would say so too; but—well, of course, a woman's notion may not be worth much—but I do have a very strong *conviction* about the future. I seem awfully featherheaded to you, and really in some ways I am—after all, women are given a child's education—but, Randall, can't you see the way this city could be rebuilt—I don't mean marble pillars and all that, I just mean honest, clean dwelling houses with decent yards and plumbing and—well, you know what they could be like."

He sighed, then taking thought smiled. Her round face had run to reddish patches and her soft and glistening mouth opened slightly with the earnestness of what she was saying.

"Well," he said, with half-humorous charm, "I am torn between two convictions. On the one hand is the city of the future, as you visualize it, full of sanitation and light; on the other is the country—not only of the future, but of the present."

He spoke so mildly that she went on in a rush. "And, Randall, I haven't said anything about it before, but I do want to go on with my Settlement work—there's so much to be done, you know, and Miss Fowler says I'm being very useful. It's sort of like a Cause, isn't it—and it is one of the things we have in common, you and I; and of course I'd want to be as near as possible—do you see, Randall?

"Do you mean you want to work there?"

"Well, not really. I just want to sort of keep on with the work—you know, help them as much as I can. And I thought it would mean something to you—and your career, I mean."

"My career," he said, "consists mainly in designing pantry cupboards."

"Please, Randall—I really am serious."

"You can't be serious in summer, not in the city. Just wait till I can show you Compton."

Her eyes brightened. "And Maine too—we'll have a long time there, won't we? Did you know the whole Harding family are going for August—isn't that too marvelous? I do think May ought to marry Francis, don't you? It would make it so nice."

The career was put off till autumn, at least. They returned from the month in Virginia, stayed another month at the Hollisters' house in town, then went to Compton. Randall kept in touch with his firm, as he called it, and during June commuted from Compton. He designed some pantry cupboards and went on to stairways and mantelpieces, though his best work was done with a bit of loose paper and pencil in pleasant consultation with clients.

But the Compton mood came upon him again strongly, not only the security in his father's house, but the transcendent peace. He once more assumed the halo of ease and leisure. He walked with Franklin Gray again and took notes on the doings of birds and flowers; he saw much of the Mayos and helped them with their haying—in memory of Charles Edward Mayo and his poems. He wrote a few things of his own, verses and essays, and one or two were modestly published. When he took Alice to call on Harriet Sunderland she welcomed him as a fellow author and sweetly observed that the Compton tradition was in good hands.

"You see, my dear," he said later, "what we conveniently

refer to as civilization exists in its most perfect state in Compton, Massachusetts."

"But, darling, it is so quiet here."

Randall paused at that. He studied her.

"Do you mean that you find quietness unsatisfactory?"

"Oh, well, of course, it's nice—but, darling, I just meant that nobody seems to do anything."

"You don't consider Franklin Gray's *Birds of America* anything?"

"Don't be huffy, Randall. I think Mr. Gray and Miss Sunderland are marvelous, but, goodness, they're as old as the hills. It's all very well for you to go off talking about birds and philosophy with them, but where does that leave ordinary creatures like me?"

His face expressed an astonishment so fixed that she rushed ahead recklessly.

"Well, darling, I really am an ordinary creature—you needn't make faces about it. But I want to do what's best for you—it isn't only me I'm thinking of, even though it may seem so. The main thing is our future together, and I feel we simply must keep in touch with things—and I do think an architect especially has to be right in the main stream. There's so much to *do*, Randall—you just ought to read some of the things I read last winter, and talk with people like Janie Lee's father, and we really must get to the Copley Forum and the Lowell Lectures."

She had to get breath and cool her flushed cheeks. Randall looked down at her, his own face pale and remote.

"Yes," she said with a quick nod, "I suppose I do sound sort of half-witted to you, but I don't care."

"I think," he said, "that you don't quite see what Compton means. In the city everything is faulty—worse than that, it is ugly. Not just the streets and houses, but the way people live— the rich acting rich and the poor acting poor, without human ideals. But the life here is whole and beautiful. You can write an ode in the morning, pitch hay in the afternoon, discuss Dante in the evening, and you are neither rich nor poor, gentle nor vulgar, but simply a man—and a man free to do your best. But more than that, you live here in harmony with the only source of beauty—the very fountain, I suppose. The groves are not merely God's first temples—they are His only true ones."

Randall was addressing God and the future.

Alice seemed a little bewildered. She looked out at the quiet dust of the empty street. "I suppose I can't talk philosophy with you," she said as though he were taking unfair advantage. "I do love you to writes odes, though—I think it is wonderful of you; but Randall, darling, that isn't the same as being an architect and doing great buildings. You see, I'm just looking at it practically."

He nodded without clearly hearing her.

"Ideally," he went on, "it is the city which should come to us. The notion that the secret of civilization lies in the city is absurd."

"Well, I know it's dreadful, Randall. But we can't just abandon them, can we? I mean—all those children fighting in the streets and growing up to be bad people—if we could do just a little for them it would be such a help. And cities don't have to be so dreadful—think how nice places like—well, Geneva and—well, they *could* be so much better."

He looked down at her. "Missionary work!"

She flushed again with uncertainty. Her great-aunt Marian was a missionary in India and was admired among the Bradstreets. "I really didn't know you felt like that, Randall."

"You'll understand better," he said, "after you have lived longer in Compton."

In July they went to Mount Desert by night boat, and most of the Hollisters and Hardings were there too. May had gone abroad with her aunt Alice—a pity because May was a marvelous sailor and got up all the picnics and knew where to go and how to make coffee on the rocks and all about cream and eggs and such matters. Caroline was no good at that sort of thing at all and simply trailed along and did what she was told. So it was up to Alice to organize things, and with Francis Harding's help they got along very happily. And of all the dreams of felicity, a Mount Desert summer in the old days was the sweetest. Of course, Bar Harbor on the other side of the mountains was fantastically rich and fashionable, and people of taste already looked upon it with amused contempt, but Northeast Harbor was the paradise of Nice People, the true haven of all gentle delight. Forests and mountains and cliffs and islands seemed to have been arranged by a master designer for the special use of a few good Boston families and their friends, and there they lived in the bliss of old clothes, comfortable philosophy, humor, affection, and incredible beauty of mountains and sea.

Randall had come to it dubiously, as to an idle resort. The hub of his particular cosmos centered in Compton, and the thought of people going off to Maine to seek pleasure seemed absurd. He had been taught that pleasure was not to be had by seeking, that it came only as the unsought reward of serious living. But a day or two in paradise changed his views. The very first morning he met Mr. Eliot on the road to the village; at lunch he sat across from Dr. Byers, the man who had discovered that Troy never existed at all; and the old dodderer with the beard and the white canvas hat who rowed round Sutton's Island every day was none other than Josiah Belcher, the close friend of Darwin. But even better than the old and great were the young and friendly, the girls willing to climb steep trails or get wet in salt spray, the boys in old flannels showing him how to sail. They liked him, and his wit and charm prospered. Alice regarded him with pride.

"You just seem to belong," she said, giving him the summit of honor. "It is too nice."

And she herself forgot her city ways. Most of the drapes and bangles and feminine anxieties disappeared, and she grew healthy and red-faced and full of joy.

But of course there was Caroline—always Caroline, like a sea nymph, a golden northern goddess, more beautiful here in the sun and wind than ever in the city shadows. Randall followed her with an almost mystic devotion. Their speech kept to the trifles, but if he called to her on an upward climb that they were "almost there" and she turned smiling with a "yes, almost" he felt that the mountain spirit had voiced itself. And she did seem to waft herself upward with bodiless ease while mortals like Alice puffed and streamed with sweat. She stayed cool when others were hot, and warm when others shook in the sea wind, and early or late, wet or dry, she remained a beautiful lady.

A well-attended lady. The hair was up, the skirts down to floor or boot-top as occasion required, and suddenly all the mysteries of ladyhood surrounded her. Her legs had disappeared forever, her middle was encased in fascinating steel, her bust seemed to be built up formidably, and no man could treat her with other than full chivalric ritual. Doors flew open before her, chairs sprang under her, arms offered themselves, handkerchiefs even dusted immaculate granite ledges for her to sit upon as she faced the sea. Bitter, bitter to the man who was only her brother-in-law, who could no longer even claim her as a minor under his protection.

Sad, a fate like that, yet beautiful and poignant. He didn't turn away from it; rather, took it with delicate relish. Simply to watch her facing the wind, framed in blue, was like having special glimpses of Artemis, goddess of the world's beauty. He knew that no one else could have the same vision. To others she was a lovely woman, clothed and shaped in proper fashion.

No concern there with Career or Future—no world seemed to exist beyond the silver horizons. They lived like children, each day golden.

But then September, the end of a season, the return to the harsher world. In Compton, with the strong harvest fragrance in the air and inside the house, they consulted soberly; it was very serious Garretson business, first opened by Randall and his father, then taking in Alice and at last, when all was settled, Liddie.

"Well, Randall, my boy, I suppose you'll go back to those Peabodys again?"

"Why, yes, certainly, Father. You haven't any objection to them, have you?"

"Oh, no indeed, no—not at all. Very decent people, I'm sure. Of course, architecture—" He waved a hand. "One gets a taste for that sort of thing abroad—cathedrals and castles, very fine, of course. An excellent profession. But—well, to be frank, Randall, it doesn't seem to me that it suits your talents—or perhaps I should express myself in the past tense. I very much hope you are making a success of it—we shouldn't entertain thought of failure, of course. At one time, as you know, I had expected you to go into the ministry—a devout wish, I may say, and a very grave disappointment. Man merely proposes, of course; the disposal is in other hands—doubtless better hands."

He smiled a little at his philosophical self, and Randall laughed gently.

"I hope so too, Father."

The conversation had suddenly grown affectionate. It was a fact that of the Garretsons, these two got on best together. Randall always felt that his father was a great man. They apparently had nothing else in common.

"But regardless of the direction of your ambitions, I hope— rather I should say I expect—" he smiled to show his intention —"I *expect* that you will make your home here. I recognize clearly that our house is far from modern; doubtless to an architect it seems very plain, but in the course of a generation it has become dear to us—some of us, that is." The name of Richard remained unspoken; even then Richard was posted a deserter. "And far too ample for Liddie and myself. It would mean much to me—to both Liddie and me, I should say, to have you with us—you and Alice, of course."

Randall nodded with full understanding. It was nice of his father to suggest it, and it was true that this would always be home. Of course, Alice would have to be consulted.

The matter of finances could be easily arranged. "We are by no means wealthy, but your mother's property has been left in trust for you children—and naturally we live economically here. Even though your salary is very modest, we shall have ample—we can very well afford another maid and eventually a nurse. And I have already arranged for a modern heating system—my boy, you will be astonished when you see what we are doing—it will make all the difference, I assure you. Even the back wing is to have steam pipes."

Randall's astonished look came over his face. "You don't mean steam heat? Why, I thought you felt—" He broke off. "That is, do you consider it safe?"

"Oh, entirely. I have talked it over with one of their chief engineers in town, and they guarantee every detail. I may add that I have done this especially for your benefit, Randall—though of course I shall share in the pleasures—that is, I should say, your benefit and Alice's."

Those were the opening arrangements. And after a few days of settling and adjustment, Randall donned his town clothes and went in to the office. And even as he walked through the smoke of the old North Station and up toward the cobblestones of Haymarket he bore with him a little cloud of his summer's serenity, so that the crash of the carts, the whirls of autumn dust, the throngs on the walks and spilling into the cobbled streets, all seemed removed from him. He believed in none of those realities. He walked along in a sort of country innocence and about ten o'clock arrived at the offices of Peabody and Peabody.

As he climbed the stairs he sighed, and his feet went

slower. The little cloud dispersed and left him staring at the dingy prison house of his career. The small outer office lacked air; Miss Wilkins gave him a thin vinegary greeting and said at once that Mr. Peabody would like to see him. He stood for a moment thinking she might have more to say, and in the silence a chill settled over him.

"How are things, Miss Wilkins?"

"Quite well, Mr. Garretson."

He brushed back the right wing of his hair and went on to the inner office.

"Ah, Garretson, back again."

A bulgy man, untidy in tweeds and small nose glasses with black ribbon, full of energy and conscience and devotion to his career. "Bad news for you, I'm afraid. Might as well plunge into it at once—sit down, won't you? Have a good summer? —I can see that you did. Family well, I hope—wife, of course —good, very good. Well, you see, as a matter of fact the Senior has felt the need of certain changes—retrenchments, perhaps, at least for a time—we have consulted pretty seriously and of course my own conclusion agrees with his—very astute man, the Senior, as you know, though he is no longer active here—" He came close to stuttering, and paused. "We have three younger men—no need to explain that, naturally—but just now things are a bit light for us, and to be frank—you understand my position naturally—to be frank, there's not much of the sort of thing you can do—that is—" He stumbled again, took off and put on his glasses, and went on. "Gregory and Johnson have worked in very usefully—good construction men, both of them—they've been about most of the summer, and Johnson has been working up steel construction—practical engineering, you understand—and we need that kind of man. And Gregory—he's very keen on commercial developments—I'd like you to see some of the new designs he's getting up—stores and offices—not quite the thing for esthetes like you and me, ha?—but necessary, my boy, very necessary."

He whirled toward his desk, arranged some papers, and whirled back again.

"Well, it may be a shock to you for the moment. Believe me, we are reluctant—it seems unkind, of course—but your talent is unmistakable, don't for a moment be discouraged—in matters of decoration, interior design, you are far ahead of most of us." He wiped his face with a very large white cotton handkerchief. "I'll be glad to say a word on your behalf whenever—yes, don't hesitate to call on me; there's plenty of work to be done in the country too—residences—more in your line, I should judge. Of course, we're giving you a month's salary—seems very little, under the circumstances, but I'm carrying out the Senior's instructions. You understand, I am sure, that personally I deeply regret the necessity . . ."

When Randall returned to the streets he felt at first as though nothing had happened. The whole scene had occurred like something on a stage. He walked along in the same cloud of ideas, conscious of himself as an entity and dismissing the whole surrounding city as an accident without significance. From Mr. Peabody down, they were all simply men on earth, while he was Randall Garretson of Compton, philosopher and associate of nature and God. No arrogance in this—rather a consistent and simple illusion. In a way, Mr. Peabody had released him and returned him more safely to himself.

His talent, Peabody has said. Not the talent for materials, for steel and plate glass, but nonetheless a talent. Randall may have held the thought too close and warm, frailty that it was. A talent—for country living. Henry Thoreau had had the same. He knew that Peabody's phrase was simply a bit of syrup intended to sweeten the bitter taste of failure, and as far as Peabody was concerned nothing counted but the failure. The word esthete had slipped in cruelly. But, Peabody or no, those "talents" remained the articles of his faith. Stop any one of these men, rich or poor, on the walks of Boston Common

and ask him to render an account of his existence on earth—
you'd get hardly more than a financial statement.

Certainly this material life could not be considered God's
primary idea. Not, of course, that he fell back into any pious
dependence on "God's will"—he hardly framed the word
"God" to himself at all, the way childish folk did; but in his
mind a picture clearly formed, a picture marvelously and simply
including the whole cycle of country harmony, the rising and
setting, the seed and harvest, the song of bird and bloom of
flower, the roll of seasons and the serenity of man living close
to all this vast benevolence—man wise and sweet with pure
understanding: he saw all this precisely as one whole picture,
not as many, and the wholeness of it was simply God. There,
in the mind's eye, existed truth itself—not a phrase or a formula,
not any sort of creed or doctrine or difficult explanation but a
vision, a thing seen. He might have seized brushes and paints
and then and there thrown it on a canvas—a big George Inness
sort of canvas, with all the kaleidoscopic rich country colors
and mysteries and the vast design that made one purposeful
fact of heaven and earth and the final focus of man.

So, back to Compton forever—back on an afternoon train
in mid-September when the sweet pungence of smoke and
harvest filled the cooling air. He took the long draft of freedom and sauntered homeward under the gold-glinting elms.
Tomorrow there'd be time for contemplation and the beginning of his own harvest, the seasonal essays that would catch
the immortal harmonies of Compton. He could almost feel
the words flowing with his blood as he walked along, the little
miracles of language that would make truth as evident as snow
crystals, so that readers for all time could have the very ecstasy
of spirit and body that he now felt this autumn afternoon.
Tomorrow, at last, he would saunter forth in ease and leisure
like the wise and happy of yore.

⋖ঙ CHAPTER 9 ঙ⋗

"RANDALL, do you mean you—you—?"

"Yes, my dear, just that."

"But I don't understand. What has happened?"

Her round mouth and eyes released an anger in him. "I am an esthete, my dear. You should have realized that."

"Please, Randall. It's just that I don't understand."

"Well, there's nothing obscure. I assure you. Messrs. Peabody and Peabody have informed me that they no longer need a man to design pantry cupboards and mantelpieces."

"But, Randall—" Her face grew soft with woe.

"Instead they demand men of steel and concrete. The New Jerusalem requires chiefly offices and department stores—" He checked himself. "No, Alice, the truth is that I am out of touch with modern progress. I am not one to build a new world. And I very much fear that you have been misled—I mean—well, your husband isn't quite the man you hoped he was."

"Oh, Randall, don't be absurd! I married you because—because I loved you." She collapsed into a welter of tears.

He reviewed his life hastily and patted her on the shoulder. For a moment he couldn't think of anything worth saying.

They were in their bedroom upstairs, and early dusk had already begun. Randall looked out at the still bright fields and tried to recover the certainties he had felt an hour before.

"I have ideas, Alice. It seems like failure now, but in the end it won't."

She sat up and spoke through a white handkerchief. "Tell me *exactly* what he said—I mean everything."

He did so, but soothingly.

"Randall, I *know* you have a talent—*of course* you do. You're so s-s-sensitive—" She waited a moment. "I can't help crying; it's just silly, and I'll stop in a minute, but it was a shock, just as though you had taken the f-f-floor away—" She cried freely, then stopped and straightened again. "Now don't feel badly about it, darling. Just because old Peabody doesn't understand what your special abilities are—I mean actually he doesn't, and all he cares about, of course, is the commercial side of it; and things like good taste and lovely design and—well, they don't interest him, and really this will give you a wonderful chance to do the sort of thing you—don't you *see*, Randall? Now you can find just the right opportunity and it will mean so much more in the end than just designing p-p-pantry cupboards!" She blubbered again, and he patted her hair and shoulder.

"Good girl, Alice. You sound just like your mother."

"Well, why shouldn't I?"

"Why not, indeed!"

She shot a glance under wet lashes and managed a little pout. "I don't see why you go making fun of us. After all, it's no time to—to—"

"No, my dear, it is no time to. I was only thinking what a good loyal wife you are. Here, use my handkerchief."

"Did Mr. Peabody—did he—?"

"No, he didn't suggest anything else."

"Well, you'd better start right away tomorrow—and if I were you I'd go and talk to Judge Higginson first thing; he's a cousin, of course, and trustee of the Museum and he knows simply everybody and he's wonderful. Mother always asks him about everything. He could introduce you to people, and he'd really *know*."

She put tears behind her and sat up eagerly. "Randall, don't

tell people about it yet—I mean your father and—well—
mother and the girls would worry, don't you think? If you told
them after you had decided what you were going to do, then
it would be all settled and—"

"Yes." He nodded. "Excellent strategy. It would look as
though I planned it that way."

"Well, sort of." She giggled, then sobered. "It's just that
people get to talking—they don't mean to, but you know how
mother is, she just talks like a house afire and never thinks what
she's saying—the way I do—sometimes."

Randall looked out at the fading brightness in the trees.
"Let me tell you what I think, and what I hope to do."

"Oh, yes, do tell me. And, Randall, I want to go in with you
tomorrow—may I? I get sort of lonely here—without you, I
mean. Of course, Liddie is as sweet as she can be, but I feel so
useless, and I'd like to be with you as much as possible and
there's some shopping I ought to do." She glanced up. "Yes,
please tell me just what you think, Randall."

"Well, I don't think I'll go to town tomorrow. In fact, I
don't ever want to go to town again, though I'm not making
any such resolution, of course. But, Alice, this break with
Peabody is a profound relief to me. You see, I have planned a
lot of things—some essays, a book, even some poems. And at
last this is my chance to do it. I am full of desire—I almost said
inspiration, but that sounds pretentious—but the purpose is
very strong within me. Perhaps I could call it a faith—"

He developed his motive again in words, walking back and
forth near the window and keeping watch on the thickening
dusk. The words came less beautifully than the images that had
preceded them, they missed the wondrous shining peaks of his
dreams, but he knew that words were stubborn articles. He
developed only a primitive first draft, experimental, subject to
infinite improvement.

"And, of course, this is the place to do it—here in this tradition and atmosphere. Compton itself is the work of art that

must be translated into the world's language and made to shine forth in its own glory."

Silence.

"What are you thinking, my dear?"

"Why, I don't know, Randall. I guess I don't understand very well. Do you mean that you have decided to give up your career?"

"My career—" His expression returned to its defensive humor. "I have just outlined a most glorious career."

"Oh, you know what I mean. Gracious, you don't need to be so superior!"

"It's only that I have just been trying to explain myself and apparently with so little success—" He sighed. "As to my work as an architect—a rising young architect, I should say—my conclusions are first, that I shall make a better author, and second, that if, as Mr. Peabody says, I have a talent, it is one that will flourish more happily in Compton than it ever would in a metropolis." He considered some of his ideals. "There are certainly possibilities—"

It may have been at this moment that he first suspected the possibilities of the house he had lived half a life in. He paused on the word, and seemed to stare as if transfixed at the fireplace, the mantel, the paneling across the whole wall that included the closet door on the left and the door into the hallway on the right. It was all painted white and except for the essential moldings was as simple as the carpenter had been able to make it.

"Yes, I must certainly consider. The stone farms of Brittany are very beautiful, but these simple wooden dwellings of ours— You know, Alice, I believe we have been worshiping idols. The John Ruskin Gothic has no place in this life; it is simply false to us, and so is all the desperate Byzantine and Romanesque, and this frosted classic we are doing—Corinthian false fronts and gasworks like Roman baths." He paced the floor again. "I must do an article, a series. Why, this very house, this plainness, this sacred simplicity—it expresses us exactly. It is beautiful, Alice!" He stretched a hand toward the white mantel. "Do you see it? Truth itself, before our very eyes. And so few have seen it. We live so blindly—even I, though I have tried to see, though it has been my chief concern, my career, I suppose."

"Randall."

"Yes, my dear?"

"Would you please tell me in plain words what you are talking about? I understand that you are not going to town tomorrow—and if you don't mind I think I'd like to go anyway; I really must begin to look at winter coats, and I've got to see Miss Fowler and make some sort of plan. Now just where are we?"

"Right here." He waved an eager hand. "This is home, thank God!"

"Forever?"

"Well, I don't know about infinity. It would be nice forever."

"You mean this room, I suppose."

"This room?" He glanced at her and saw that her face had gone red and white like a kitchen tablecloth. He caught his breath. "Why, this room, and house, and the whole place—"

"And where do your father and sister live?"

"They live here too, of course. But, Alice—"

"Your wife will pay board, I assume; and will be permitted to use the sitting room at certain times."

"Good heavens!"

"When she has visitors, perhaps—that would be very seldom. The rest of the time she would remain in this—this lovely rat-trap of a room. This would be considered her very own, of course."

"Alice, you mustn't feel that way. Why, father and Liddie have both—"

"Randall, you stupid fool!" She suddenly screamed the words, and her face turned white and damp. "You fool, you sickening fool, you—you think I'm just a chattel, a tame pigeon —you're simply too selfish to understand! You—you aren't human, you aren't even a man, you haven't one grain of heart or sympathy or—or anything—and they all told me I was so lucky and everything was so wonderful—and here we are—here —look at us—stuck in a dingy bedroom forever!" Her voice screamed again. "Forever!"

"Don't shout so, Alice."

"I will too shout!" She spat the words, and the moisture glistened on her chin. "And don't you start any of that fancy talking either—all those big words that don't mean a living thing, and you look so disgustingly pleased with your noble self." She began to shake all over, and her voice choked and gurgled. "I don't care—I've tried my best to understand and be patient—what on earth did you get married for? It's all so —so stupid! If you wanted to sulk away here in the country, in your father's house, why didn't you just do it, instead of dragging me into it? You knew perfectly well what I was like and—and—well, maybe you didn't, maybe you are really and truly a fool—you certainly don't know anything about women. And maybe you think I'm crazy, screeching away like this, but I'm nothing but a woman and you haven't got the wits to understand it."

She began gasping, and a mortal agony of sobbing seized her. She flung herself on the bed half strangled and doubled up in pain.

Randall stood, white and motionless.

She made little sound, but he could feel the tearing release of the sobs.

Nothing else happened for several minutes.

"And it's no good saying 'there, there,' as though I were a hurt b-b-baby," she managed between gasps. And again her body was caught on the rack.

Shadow darkened in the room. The world outside was a gray blur.

Randall moved to light a lamp.

"I had such wonderful hopes," she said, with curious quietness. "I guess I was a fool too. Up to now I kept trying to pretend." Very quiet, but jerky and choked. "All that h-h-hope—" Silence again.

Then without warning an onslaught of sobs, a fury of wet tears. The tempo changed, and she cried without ceasing, a snuffling little-girl cry.

"And the babies, Randall—I just can't *bear* it!"

It was a broken heart. His own eyes grew wet and breath shuddered.

"Alice, I—you mustn't—" Futile noises.

It ran to exhaustion. Dark outside now, and Alice limp cloth on the bed. Randall sat with hand brushing her damp hair.

"Tell them I have a sick headache," she whispered. He felt a last sob begin to make itself up inside her, then dwindle away. "I just wasn't ready for this sort of disappointment. I'm sorry I made a scene; I guess it was stupid—I should have known what was coming. We live in such a silly storybook dream, and —and—" Her sigh was pure weariness. "Don't talk now—just tell them I'm asleep." She stroked his hand, then turned over and buried her head and lay still.

He hovered near her for a moment, patted her again, fixed his hair and tie, and tiptoed out and downstairs. Not quite time for supper yet. He slipped away for a walk in the dark— up the road with determined briskness and back again more slowly. His blood flowed again in its veins; appetite asserted itself; but the shock remained. For once he felt no comfort in trees and night sky, though he expected it and lifted his eyes to seek it. His active mind stayed numb. Pictures of his wedding flashed through, and all the ceremony of clothes and forms and properties, and the weeping and laughing, and his golden Caroline like the pure serene of heaven. Alice's dream was silly indeed, but his moved him like the chords of great music, like the celestial glow of old masters. As he turned at the end of his outward walk he felt the salt of tears on his lips. Nothing now but to muddle ahead.

He returned, brushed back his hair, straightened himself, and appeared before his father and Liddie with smiling face.

"Alice wants to be excused—she's gone to bed with a headache."

Mr. Garretson frowned. "Ought not to miss supper. Surely you could explain to her—"

"Explain what, Father? Don't go up, Liddie; she's asleep—all tired out, I fear."

"She should not give in to these trifles. Mark my words, son, when a woman begins to have headaches you are a lost man. There's no end to it." He got up and walked to the mantelpiece. "You'd better run up and see, Liddie. You can tell what to do."

Liddie gathered herself timidly, glancing at Randall.

"No, Liddie, I'd rather you didn't."

Mr. Garretson's eyes lifted quickly. "I tell you, Randall, we've got to put our foot down right now. Life is not easy for most of us, but we go through with it whether we like it or not. We don't go to bed and feel sorry for ourselves. We—"

"Quite true, Father. But right now Alice is asleep, and I don't want to disturb her."

"Nonsense!"

Liddie stirred, but remained.

A silence of several seconds, then Randall's voice, unnaturally solemn. "You have asked us to make this our home, and naturally we are enormously pleased." Another pause. Mr. Garretson cleared his throat, but Randall spoke again. "It makes a problem for Alice, however. I suppose any woman—any wife, that is—wants a home that she can call her own. If we are to live here, Father, as I hope we may, we must somehow make Alice feel secure in her position."

Mr. Garretson waved a hand as though brushing a fly.

"Naturally, naturally—you need not lecture your father, Randall. My reference concerned an attitude toward health and duty—quite another matter."

"No, Father. The point is that you can't order her about as though she were your child. By rights, she should be giving the orders."

Randall held his breath at what he had said, but his father merely brushed another fly. "Nonsense—no one is giving any orders. Liddie, just run up and see if you can be of use to—ah—Alice. She may feel like coming down after all."

This time Randall felt the blood hot in his face. "No one is going upstairs to bother Alice. If she wants to go to bed, she has a right to without interference. Otherwise we had better live somewhere else." His voice shook on the last phrase.

Mr. Garretson's hand closed tight. "Randall, recollect yourself. You are making an issue without justification—it is not like you, I must say. Now, let us say no more about it. The matter is closed. Liddie, see if our supper is ready; it is time, I believe."

But Liddie still hesitated. Her thin face had grown anxious. "Father," she said, "what Randall says is really true. Alice's position will be very difficult unless we all somehow—do what we can—to—to—"

"Oh, of course, of course!" He looked down impatiently at the thin face. "Naturally, we will do what we can—much more than that, I am sure. No need of making such a to-do!"

Liddie turned to her brother. "If Alice will take charge of the housekeeping I'll do what I can to—to—make it easy for her."

"Nonsense, Liddie!" Mr. Garretson exploded with force. "You've been doing it for years, and all this talk is preposterous. Now run along and tell the cook we are waiting."

She glanced helplessly at Randall and went out.

Later on Randall slipped upstairs with a dish of soup and found Alice sitting in bed reading. She spoke coolly.

"I suppose I'd better take some. Have you all finished?"

"Yes. We always have supper at night—country fashion. Maybe you'd like to have it your way—dinner at night."

She drew slow breath. "It doesn't matter."

He said nothing.

"Your father wouldn't want change." This had an edge to it.

"Well, you can't be sure." He hesitated, and plunged. "Alice, it is hard for you at first. I know how it is. But give yourself time. We all want you to feel as though this were your home, and you can make it the way you want it—"

She shrugged coldly. "It doesn't matter, Randall. The way I want things is entirely unimportant. Just don't discuss it."

He retreated. He went down to the sitting room, fixed the lamp, picked up the Howells he had begun earlier, and settled to read. His father had retired to his study, as he always did. Liddie was off in back somewhere. The peace of the house was a pleasant thing at last; security returned to him, and he looked round at the old room in comfort. He could live his life well, so long as Alice didn't make a fuss, so long as this peace remained, and the books and the fire and the ideas and the purpose. He noted the paneling and the mantel—a Doric design, but so delicate in proportion that you hardly thought of it as imitation. Its measurements were certainly not taken from Vitruvius—the effect was more slim and pure, and the very plain leaf motif carved across the frieze gave it a life of its own. Randall reflected on the question of originality and what it was that transmuted imitation into art, what elixir could change the most banal of designs into this unexampled simplicity. There you had it, wood and paint affirming the evident presence of God.

"Is Alice feeling better?" Liddie stood in the door.

"Oh—yes, she's reading."

Liddie melted into the hall shadow. The stairs creaked faintly.

The room was crowded with incongruities. He began to see

the stuff he had grown up with, the pink lamp globes, the marble Sophocles on top of the glass-fronted walnut bookcase, the white bas-relief of pastoral folk leading a heifer toward an altar, the Sistine Madonna in an oval gilt frame, the huge Landseer above the fireplace, the scrollwork chairs with horsehair seats, the great round table in the middle with its chocolate-colored cloth hanging in tassels almost to the floor. A trained architect, he reflected, ought to be outraged—but the general effect seemed very comforting. Classic and cultural reminders mixed in with a brown plushy homeliness and set in the white colonial—perhaps someday he could rearrange it all, but meanwhile it did well, it reassured the troubled spirit.

Randall's thoughts encompassed the Great Tradition as he sat there. In one vast sweep he gathered in the immemorial quest for the true and the beautiful from the most ancient glories down through all the grandeurs and magnanimities of time, like white Alps mingling with God's blue, from ancient Sophocles, mantled in the pure sun of Greece, to the angelic Raphael and all those who made manifest the divine destinies of man. And Randall, as he swept up this immense vision with a single flicker of his imagination, also perceived that he himself was one appointed to carry forward the same work, that he stood as an outpost of the same tradition and belonged in the company of the truly great.

"Randall." Liddie spoke again, and he realized that the evening had passed. "I'm going in with Alice tomorrow."

"Oh, did you see her?"

"She said you aren't going back to the Peabodys."

"No. No, I'm going to do some writing."

"Oh." She paused. "That's nice, Randall. I think you write beautifully."

"Well, I—I hope so. I want to try, at least."

She lifted her eyes respectfully. "Randall, I hope Alice will be happy here."

"Why, I hope so too."

"I—that is, we had a little talk—and I tried to tell her that I—hoped that she—we—well, you see, all this is so different for her, and being in the country—and father sometimes seems a little difficult, though once she understands him—I mean, he's really so fond of us all— Do you know, Randall, she said that what she had always wanted most in the world was children of her own, and I think that's so—so lovely—" Suddenly Liddie seemed to recollect herself. The words dried up entirely.

"It's nice of you, Liddie."

"Oh, no! I haven't done anything, really. But I think Alice is so wonderful and full of energy, and she has so many interests."

Randall considered. "Yes, you're very good, Liddie. I think between us we can see that Alice is happy."

≈§ CHAPTER 10 §≈

JEAN AND Ralph and Stephen. A first baby, Randall explained to his elder son many years later, creates insuperable difficulties and anxieties; a second baby normally triples those same difficulties and anxieties; a third baby—he waved a hand to indicate the infinity of the sum total.

"If you ever hear a mother lamenting the troubles brought by one child," he said, "you can be sure she knows nothing of trouble."

His own habit was conscientious. When Jean lost weight, he did; when Ralph caught cold, he did also. He heard cries in the night and walked cold floors and sat up waiting for the doctor. He held himself responsible for protecting his father from all trace or suspicion of babies. Of course, the nurse helped, and so did Liddie and Alice, but Randall kept watch like a sentry.

It had been his plan to write steadily every morning, like Walter Scott and others—in fact, like his father. He fixed up a little room in the upstairs part of the wing, right over the cook's room. The new heating plant failed to keep it much above sixty degrees in winter, but otherwise it did well as a study. The household was instructed to observe his habits solemnly, and for a year or so all went serenely. It seemed that for most of this period he did more reading than writing, since he felt a need for a solid foundation of ideas. First Spenser and

Milton—he read them with puritanic devotion, as one studying
the gospels. They made duty beautiful, he said, and vice versa.
The highest morality coincided with the highest romance, and
the very good were very happy. He read carefully, made pencil
notes in the margins, and looked up the difficult words and
references. Long, slow work—and solitary. His father never
bothered with the poets, and of course Liddie and Alice were
not accustomed to ideas and had never read beyond Milton's
minor poems. So Randall plunged along, hour after hour in
the forests of allegory, with a blanket over his knees and a
woollen shawl over his shoulders.

Yet never quite out of range of nursery troubles. Squalls
penetrated his solitude, and the anguish and despairs of mortal
life.

"Randall, he just howls and howls."

"Let him, my dear. You spoil him with all that coddling."

"But he's just wasting away; he howls himself down to the
bone, and then won't eat. I wish you'd look at him—even
Liddie can't do a thing."

The same Alice still, but marked deeply by the anxieties of
martyrdom. His own worries he kept concealed under the fine
countenance of gentleman and scholar, but Alice had become
a visible and helpless worry. Her body clutched itself together as a sort of temporary expedient, her motions were
little fits and starts of indecision, her face had half dissolved in
tears.

"Don't take it so hard, my dear. The more you agonize, the
more your babies do."

"I know, Randall. I'm just doing everything wrong—the
more I try the worse it is."

He often inspected the howler, gave advice, even walked the
floor and made his voice deep for soothing noises.

"There—you see—he's all right, he's just tired. You're tired
too—we're all tired. All we need is sleep enough."

But always at the first peep in the night she was out of bed and into the nursery. "But they'll wake your father. You know what he said this morning—*his* children never carried on like that. Oh, no—even if his wife had to die for it, *they* were quiet, *they* were little angels. I wonder she didn't throttle them—perhaps she did, perhaps that accounts for Bronson—at least that's one way of doing it!"

"Good heavens, Alice!"

So it went. The nurse always left after two weeks and they had to break in a new one. And the colds, the ears, noses, throats, chests, and all the other maladies—

"I expect it's the steam heat," Father Garretson observed. "Luxury brings weakness of the flesh—doubtless of the spirit too." He had come to disapprove wholly of his son's wife, and mentioned the heat with uncharitable irony.

But what of the literary dreams—the poems and delicate essays, the little journeys through the Compton seasons? The cold record lists a few poems published and many book reviews —some of them almost literary essays. But the burden of his thought never reached print. The fact is that as he grew serious he grew heavily literary and didactic. The grace of his well-bred style is unfailing, but behind that is the too evident preacher, the down-talker, who takes the common folk to task for all their common follies. They live in cities, with dust and heat; they compete bitterly for sordid prizes, such as money and property and position; above all, they fail in delicacy and taste. With this invariable prelude, he develops his Compton motif, his song of transcendent harmony and simplicity. The philosopher walks among the supreme luxuries of God, the sun-clean meadows and forest where sound the immortal melodies of all life from wondrous birth to wondrous death. "The music of the spheres," he writes, "finds its fitting lyre in the throat of the hermit thrush." One realizes that he had no notion of what a lyre sounds like, but mentioned it for its cultural eminence.

In all this there is no hint of the rending tensions of an unhappy household. But he did attribute his temporary failures to that atmosphere. "I simply can't work seriously," he said to Alice, "with all these interruptions."

At first she tried to help him out. His literary career seemed to her a mysterious possibility, at least, and she had a strong sense of duty. If her wifely destiny required martyrdom, she would do her best. His convictions and rhetoric were beyond her range, but she had been trained to be respectful toward men of culture and learning. So with pressed lips and flushed anxiety she did her job. But time changed her.

"If you can't work here, you'd better go somewhere else. You picked this place out, I didn't."

He said, "I wish you weren't so bitter, Alice."

"No one ever called me bitter before—all this. I used to be known for my foolish enthusiasms."

He sighed and tried to think what to do. "I thought you'd like having the children—you always used to say you'd like babies."

"Randall, I didn't know anything in those days. I was a silly child, full of dreams and hopes and nice little visions of a happy home and plenty of love and laughter and all those things you read about."

"And aren't they satisfactory children?" he asked coldly. "Did you expect better ones?"

"No, they are lovely children, I can see that. But I've got so I almost hate the sight of them. I feel as though I haven't had a night's sleep for five years. And as for love and laughter—does anyone laugh in this house? 'Hush, child, you'll disturb grandfather! Ralph, don't run in the hall! Jean, go up on your toes—you shake the house!' There it is, day and night. I tell you, Randall, I can't stand it much longer."

Love, she had said. He patted her shoulder and said "there, there." He treated her kindly and shared the task of keeping the children quiet. He said nothing more about interruptions. But his writing failed. The *Atlantic* returned his essays always with a personal note.

When Steve outgrew his worst babyhood, Alice began going more often to town. Her sister May, still unmarried, did many good works, and Alice tried to revive some of the old enthusiasm. The Settlement House would take too much time, but she could serve on committees, go to meetings, organize benefits, and talk. Of all things, talk was best, the lovely ecstatic chatter: My dear, it was too killing; you simply won't believe it but I heard it with these very ears—and really I couldn't resist telling her—

May had taken up woman's suffrage, and Alice joined in with vocal delight. But the fact was not mentioned in Compton. She led a double life. Grandfather Garretson would naturally have disapproved of all such works, and since the notion of woman's suffrage infuriated him it was never referred to. He assumed that Alice went off for innocent social purposes, and for the most part Randall did too. She grew happier for a time, yet even more distracted. Her clothes billowed and dangled more than ever, her hair looked like an abandoned bird's nest, and her breath came in gasps and puffs so that her talk grew sputtery. She hurried without ceasing, and suffered from being forever late.

"Alice, darling," May said, "you aren't at all well. I think you need change and rest."

"Don't be fantastic, May. I'm the mother of three—among other things."

"Well, I think it is perfectly stupid that you don't come back to Asticou for the summers at least. You could take a house there so easily, and think what fun it would be, and so good for you."

"You just don't understand Compton, darling. The Garretsons' Compton, that is."

"Oh, nonsense! There was some point in staying there when they were all babies, but there's no reason now why you shouldn't go."

"Well, it's something about philosophy—I really don't know

what. It's one of Randall's theories and I'm sure he'd be delighted to explain it to you. All I know is that he is outraged that I never seem to grasp it, and it means so much to him that I don't ever mention it any more." Alice said this with several puffs, and panted a little. "I tell you what, May. You tackle him about Maine. He thinks you have more sense than any of us."

"All right. I'll tackle him." She thought a moment. "Get Caroline to, why don't you?"

"But, darling, Caroline hasn't any sense."

May sighed. "Alice, I never expected to hear you talk like that. He certainly thinks she's a paragon of sense—and if he knew that she and Francis are planning to build down near the Eliots—Alice, why not get him to build something too? You could find a lovely place—"

"We aren't rich like the Hardings, darling."

"Oh, well, ask mother—she'll lend you enough."

Sometimes after talks like these Alice grew young again and her old cherublike smiles came back, but more often she went home and wept. She pounded her pillow in foolish despair and turned against herself for her own selfish indulgence in grief. She knew she had passed all barriers of reason and had lost herself forever in failure.

May came out for a Sunday—her first visit in more than a year.

"It's dreadful to stay away so much," she said to them. "Here the children grow so, and I hardly know them." She had become a little plainer, according to common fashion, yet more beautiful. The bone structure of her face stood out clearly, and you could see all her life there. You saw that the beauty would grow with age.

"Some day," Alice had said, "you'll look like one of the Founders of the Republic, while I'll get to look like an old pincushion."

After the heavy dinner, with the five-rib roast, May and

Randall and little Jean went walking into the late-winter countryside.

"I wish you came out often," Randall said. "You'd like our country."

"You love it more than anything, don't you, Randall?"

"Not more than anything, May. To me it is everything. We all exist within it."

"Like—like God, Randall?"

"Why, yes—yes, that's just it. Do you see it that way too?"

"In a way I do. I understand what you mean, at least."

He looked at her. It was the first time he had ever looked at her.

"I believe you really do. Not that it's so obscure—actually it's as simple as—as light—as the white radiance itself. It is simply a great whole, like a circle of which everything we see is part of the circumference, and if you see it truly—I mean each finite detail—you see where it belongs in the infinite circumference."

He perceived that she nodded calmly, with a quirk in the corners of her mouth that seemed sympathetic.

"And it is the sort of sight—or vision, perhaps—that makes the world universally beautiful, because every slightest fact, every flake and twig and breath, has its essential part and contributes to the marvelous whole."

She nodded without confusion, and Randall spoke further. Little Jean trotted ahead and splashed the puddles with her rubbers.

"I can't get Alice to follow me," he said. "It makes life such an adventure, but she seems unable to see it. Don't you think so? Don't you see it that way?"

"Not quite that way."

"Oh. Well, what do you mean?"

"Do you expect me to be a philosopher, Randall?"

He looked at her again. His sweet smile returned and the grace of his speech. "I'm sure you are a very wise girl, May."

She dropped her glance, and very slowly the color glowed up into her face—so slowly that he didn't observe it. He did observe that she was good to look at.

She lifted her head. "Well, I'll try to tell you." Her words had a humorous precision, and were quiet and cool. "You think of nature as being everything. When you think of truth and beauty you see it in images of trees or snow or clouds. Am I right so far?"

He agreed cautiously. "Not necessarily just trees or—or clouds—but—" He waved a hand to include infinity.

"I'm not much of a debater, Randall, but I'll go on, just to see. I think that you would say that your nature includes humanity. We are all the children of earth, like the birds and beasts." Again the clipped humorous enunciation. "But actually you leave out humanity—or you make it equal with other lesser kinds of life. In a way, you are more delighted with the sight of a bluebird than you are with—with Jean, there."

He shook his head. "Oh, no—you mustn't say that, May."

She smiled and went on.

"You take her for granted as a very familiar sort of—of object, rather annoying at times, and of course nice and lovable at other times, but you don't really include her in your general thinking. To you, nature is best when people are left out of it— I don't mean just Jean, of course, or Alice, or anyone in particular, but mankind, the idea of humanity."

"No, indeed, May! Really, you don't understand. You see, every man—every being—fulfills himself by living with nature. It is the source of whatever wisdom and happiness he has. You imply that my belief is—well, inhuman, but actually it is pretty familiar Christianity—only in a way more inclusive and rational. 'I will lift up mine eyes unto the hills . . .' —that's all it is, May."

She smiled again, but shook her head. "Not real Christianity. There's mighty little about hills in the New Testament, and there's a lot more about neighbors and children and love. The trouble with religion is that it gets to be a system for personal salvation. What must I do—I personally—to be saved and rewarded? How may I fulfill myself?"

"Not I alone—all men."

"But, Randall, it amounts to you alone. You and the solitudes."

"Yet I seek to make it apparent to all. It is not my private property—it is free and open."

"Open to some gentlemen of leisure, perhaps," she said— and then added quickly. "Oh, I understand, Randall. But your vision to me is a cold one. The thought of God alone, or nature alone, without mankind, without Jean and you and Alice and Caroline, is to me frightening. If I were condemned to live forever alone in this charming countryside, without sound of human voice, I should prefer death."

Instead of splashing on ahead, Jean dragged heavy feet through the puddles behind. She had fallen back, and when they waited they saw that she was crying. She did it quietly, as though nothing would come of it.

"Jean, darling, are you tired?"

She nuzzled in against May's skirt, and leaned there.

"Do you want to go home?"

Jean nodded.

"Why, we've just started," Randall said, looking on up the road. "If we keep on we can come round the other way."

Jean lifted round brown eyes to May's face.

"You like home better, don't you, Jean?"

Jean moved her head down and then up. After a reflection she said, "I like you."

"Only you wish I didn't talk so much, is that it?"

Jean buried herself in the skirt again. "Talk to me," she said.

"All right. I'll talk to you." She took Jean's hand and started back along the road. "Do you see that big tree? That's a maple tree. Can you say 'maple,' Jean?"

"Maple!" Jean shouted, and laughed.

"Good for you! Your father loves maples trees—remember that, Jean."

"I love you," Jean said.

"I'm glad you do. I love you too. Now, do you see that very big tree? That's called an elm tree—"

"I love you—" Jean struggled and tried again. "I love Aunt Liddie."

"Yes, of course you do."

"And Sandy M'ree and Brownie and Piggy-wiggy and Annie—" She held her voice as if she were going on.

"And mother—and father—" May went on with it.

Jean looked at her as though she were thinking hard. "I love you best." She thought again. "I love Aunt Liddie best too."

"You see how essential you are," Randall said with careful detachment. "You'll have to come and visit us very often."

"Randall, forgive me if I seem to be interfering, but Alice seems to be terribly run down—don't you think so?"

He considered his response. "Yes, I agree with you. She is run down."

"Couldn't you get her away for a change?"

He turned suddenly toward her. "May, I really don't understand. We have done everything for her—from the very first we have tried to arrange things to make her comfortable. No one could do more than Liddie has done. And a lot of the time we had a nurse to help out. And yet—well, as you say—" He waved a hand.

"Can't you tell what the matter is, Randall?"

"Not really. I can see small difficulties, but not any one great matter."

"Well, it just isn't her home—her own, I mean. Most women would feel that way, but Alice is more so—she always had a tremendous sentiment about things like that."

"But she could *make* it her own. That's what both Liddie and I have tried to get her to do. And the children too."

"Then if I were you, I'd try something else."

"What do you mean?"

"I'd take her and the children and move into another house."

The idea astonished him. "We couldn't do that," he said sharply. "That wouldn't be possible."

"Why not, Randall?"

"Why—it would seem so senseless. Do you mean here—in Compton?"

"Perhaps. But Alice would be happier in town."

"But, my dear May, you couldn't expect me to live in town!"

"Possibly not, Randall. But that's how you can save Alice."

"Save her?"

"Yes."

"Surely it isn't a question of salvation!"

"Well, I think it is."

"And further," he went on rapidly, "we could never afford any such arrangement. My own income is pretty meager— I'm far from a popular writing man, as you know." He smiled blandly. "We can just manage to live comfortably the way we do."

May said nothing.

"Moving would be out of the question," Randall repeated.

The silence seemed to bother him. "I am just getting my writing into shape—these last five or six years have not been easy for a writing man. I haven't mentioned it to anyone yet, but I am working on a novel—it will be a long task, of course." He smiled a little. "I try not to have illusions about myself, May. I am hardly a great writer, but having once undertaken it as a—a career, I feel bound to labor at it seriously."

She stopped to see if Jean was all right.

"Maple tree," Jean said, pointing at a white birch.

"Not tired any more, are you, Jean?"

"Going home!" Jean said.

May squeezed the little hand and straightened.

"And this place is really the source of all my being," he went on. "If I left, I should become an exile, an expatriate—"

"You know, Randall, I used to think there was no one in the world like you. To me you had every charm a man could have —every virtue and every grace, as the old poem has it." She saw him flush and felt herself do the same. "It is outrageous of me to be speaking such words, but I am desperately worried about my sister. And I begin to think you have no heart—or not enough heart. Alice lives on affection. She needs love the way other people need air. And really, it wouldn't matter where she lived if only she were sure of love—I don't mean the romantic storybook sort, but just lots of affection. You don't really care about people, Randall. You were brought up to be good, and you care about ideas and ideals, but you live in a sort of human vacuum. I think Alice is dying because of it."

Randall at first tightened his mouth and drew himself up. "The whole truth," he began, "isn't nearly as simple, May. I'm sorry you are so disappointed in me—" Then he paused. "Really, I shouldn't start talking like a prig, should I? You are quite right in what you say. Alice needs affection. I can only say that we have tried. We can try harder. But, May, temperament simply can't be manipulated beyond a certain point."

"Temperament—yes. It's just that I thought you might see the possibility of a different atmosphere. You had better give Alice a summer in Maine, at least. I'm sure that would agree with her temperament."

Her sharp words seemed to carry no rancor. He nodded agreement. "I'm sure you are right, May. You always are."

She looked at him. "No, not always. Sometimes I'm quite wrong."

⊰§ CHAPTER 11 §⊱

BEFORE SUMMER Alice fell ill. It came inexorably, but she persisted in denial that anything was wrong. She slept badly, ate little, suffered from day-long weariness, and little by little collapsed. She continued all her activities—seemed, in fact, to increase them.

Then the sudden fever, the dread presence of disease.

"I want to go home," she said almost at once.

Dr. Jewett smiled gently. "That's where you are, my dear."

"I want mother," she said.

"She'll come. Now just stay quiet."

"I can't stay quiet here."

Suddenly she was out of bed, bare feet on the floor. "I'll just get dressed and go. It won't take a minute. Have them get a carriage. I'm going to be sick a long time. If I stay, I'll die. Mother will know what to do."

Dr. Jewett's kind hands were very strong and he put her back like a child.

"You don't understand." Her voice was full of thin terror. "I'll die here."

"We'll arrange it, Alice. Please relax for a few minutes." He held her still and spoke to wide-eyed Liddie. "I think the hospital would be best for her. Just ask Randall—"

"No." Alice's voice was pitched a little higher. "Either I go home or I die. You think I'm hysterical, but I know what I

124

mean. Randall will know too." Her head and shoulders flopped back. "I guess I don't much care which it is."

Dr. Jewett suddenly nodded. "All right, Alice. I'll speak to Randall. Now take these with a bit of water."

"Not till I know I'm going." Her face had gone all mottled, and she breathed hard with mouth open.

Dr. Jewett laid a hand on her forehead and pushed up some of the loose hair. "Alice, I promise it. I shall go in with you myself and see that you are safe in your mother's charge. Now be a good girl and take the tablets."

Tears flooded across both cheeks; her mouth shook like a small child's. "You—you—you—" She choked.

"There, my dear. Don't try to talk."

She sobbed in a helpless despair.

"Doctor, you don't know—you—you mustn't be kind like that. It hurts so. I did it all wrong—being a mother and wife— nothing came out the way I—"

He held her up and put the glass of water to her lips. "Stop talking and drink all you can."

"There's nothing left now but hate. He thinks I've ruined his life, only he's too polite to ever speak the truth. And they have destroyed me—I can never come back to this house, I can never live here again. Doctor Jewett, what can we do with those children? Do you think I am sinful—I mean do you— do you? It's too late now, isn't it—everything is too late and here's death all of a sudden. They are sweet children and if I could only take them away and live in peace and begin again without all that trouble, and I wouldn't be unkind—I really wouldn't, Doctor. I never knew what a disgusting woman I could be till all those years I didn't sleep. Am I going home now, Doctor?"

"Yes, very soon." He brushed her hair up from the hot face. "If you would rest—lie back and close your eyes—"

"Tell Liddie," she mumbled, "tell her—please—just—" She lost track of her words and lay silent.

Dr. Jewett had to explain to Randall. "I promised her," he added. "And she must go at once."

"Father won't like it," Randall said. "It will seem very strange."

"It is a matter of saving her life. I have already sent for an ambulance. You can make your peace with your father and the neighbors later."

The words were quiet enough. No one had ever heard Dr. Jewett raise his voice or speak inaccurately.

"I understand," Randall said.

"I believe you do. It is not a question now of blame or justification, but simply of doing what is necessary. She has a fixed idea and it could very easily be the death of her. I needn't explain her temperament to you."

When Grandfather Garretson returned from his afternoon walk he heard the news with dignity.

"You say Jewett ordered it?"

"At her insistence, Father."

"Well, I must say, it seems—"

"She is desperately ill, Father."

"Ah." He nodded, and the motion of the beard somehow made the gesture portentous.

So they carried her away. And when Randall had seen her settled, less than conscious, in her old room and bed, and had been gently elbowed out of her existence by the overwhelming ministrations of her mother and sister, he wandered emptily downstairs with the feeling that a seven-year journey through the great forests of life had unaccountably returned to its starting point. There were the carpeted halls and carved walnut banisters exactly as they used to be, but his steps came heavily down and his head nodded under an ache of weariness.

And there in the library sat the golden Caroline, the beautiful Mrs. Francis Harding.

"I came right over," she said. "How is she?"

If May had said the words, or almost any woman, Randall

would have answered straightaway, but it occurred to him that Caroline spoke exactly as one might expect a china doll to speak. She hardly seemed to require an answer. "I am very sorry she is so ill," she said.

He looked at her sharply. She had taken off her monstrous hat and was sitting up with divine grace—not a young Boston matron at all, but Artemis herself with the glow and shimmer of the source of all beauty.

"Is it pneumonia?" Her flat little voice broke silence again.

"Yes—some sort of pneumonia."

"There's lots of sickness this spring. Mrs. Harding, my mother-in-law, has had the grippe. Several other people we know have had it."

"You look well, Caroline."

"I am very well, thank you."

"How is Francis?"

"He has had a bad cold, but is better. He works in a very drafty part of the city, you know, and I'm sure it affects his health."

"Drafty?"

"Yes—down there beyond the South Station, you know. It is very damp. All the offices of the woollen business are there. I often urge him to move up closer to other businesses, but he says he can't possibly. I'm sure it is very unhealthy down there."

A thick silence followed this remark. Nothing sounded on the dusty air but the respectful ticking of the mantelpiece clock. Randall sat thinking of death—not so much because Alice lay close to it upstairs as because their hopeful ventures into life had returned forlorn, with nothing to show but weariness and age and broken hearts.

"What do you hope for in life, Caroline?"

"Hope for? Why—why, I don't know. What do you mean?"

"What do you want most?"

"Oh. Well—we've always wanted a house at Northeast Harbor, and it is actually nearly finished."

"And then you'll want nothing more?"

"Oh, of course—but I don't know just what you mean, Randall."

"Well, don't bother. The less you want the better."

"We are very lucky, of course," she said. "We have so many nice things."

He looked at her with appraising eye. Her beauty was a wondrous thing. It would shine through a man's life with a golden radiance no matter what other darkness crowded round. Suppose, Randall thought, one could hang an Andrea del Sarto Madonna on his own wall and live forever in its splendor; it would be a pure and certain relationship, with no ache of human heart, no great expectation and disaster. But his eye grew hostile. That innocence of hers was craven and stupid, without even the excuse of wildness and natural fear. She lived like a hand-fed rabbit. He remembered now that always, ever since he had known her, he had been exasperated with her.

"Do you think I could be of use, Randall?"

"No," he said.

She got up. "I'll just speak to mother. It wouldn't be wise, of course, to risk carrying home any germs with me—my little Frank is quite susceptible—but I'll just see mother a minute."

He waited in the silence.

He saw Cousin Ada hurry past the hall door.

Later she came back again and looked in. "Have you had any supper, Randall?" Her figure and face and voice expressed the awful anxieties of a family crisis.

"Why—it doesn't matter, Ada. I don't feel like it at all."

"Then I suppose Dr. Jewett hasn't had any either." Here a distinct note of disapproval.

"Oh—no, I guess not. Could you give him something—tea and toast, say?"

"He'll need more than that."

Her small black eyes explored him. She said nothing for a

moment, but he thought he knew what she meant. The whole cycle of his life among the Hollisters became an image in his mind and he felt that Ada saw it too—had seen it from the first. She didn't seem to approve of him. He wanted to tell her that he agreed, that he knew. In those days he had been a fool indeed, ignorant of hearts, obsessed with conceits and dreams.

"Tell the doctor it will be ready in the dining room when he comes down. Shall you be staying here tonight?"

"No." He spoke with the gravity of a judge, as though his decision were above personal control. "I shall return with Dr. Jewett." It seemed like the word of destiny, and he heard it spoken with astonishment.

Ada turned away without comment.

Mrs. Hollister came downstairs with Caroline, and they whispered in the hall; then Caroline went on down.

"Randall, there's not a thing we can do now. Your doctor is such a dear—and to think he came all the way in with her— he'll be downstairs in a minute and of course I've sent for Dr. Wendell and they can consult together. It's so characteristic of her to insist on coming home here, and darling May is the best nurse in the world—I'm sure it will be all for the best. Is Ada getting something for you, do you know? Ada is such a comfort at a time like this. Now, Randall, I'm putting you in the other little room on the top floor—you won't mind where you are, I'm sure—"

"I'm going back with Dr. Jewett."

"Oh—are you? Well, I—I just supposed—"

"I'll have to keep an eye on the children."

"Yes, of course. You are so conscientious—it is lovely of you. And you mustn't worry one bit—just remember that she is in the hands of her mother, and there's really nothing you could do if you did stay—I mean, of course, that you are more than welcome and if you want to stay now or later we should love having you and—well, you just do whatever you think best. It was so lovely of Caroline to stop in this evening, with all her responsibilities—and I think dear Francis is waiting for her in the carriage; I do hope he hasn't caught cold—there's Dr. Jewett coming down, and I know he must be starving. Now Randall, just don't worry. This is hard for all of us, but I have great faith and I'm *sure* it will all turn out for the best."

Dr. Jewett and Randall returned to Compton by train and for most of the trip spoke not at all. As they walked up Compton's silent street toward the doctor's house a brief conversation took place.

"You realize, Randall, that this illness is a serious physical collapse. I believe, however, that its cause is spiritual failure."

"Yes, I know."

"Ah—you know it?"

"I think Alice will never want to come back here to live."

"It would not be advisable," Dr. Jewett said. "I give that simply as medical advice."

"I need spiritual advice too."

"You think I am competent to give it?"

"Yes, I do."

The old doctor shook his head slightly. Then he smiled. "It is always proper for a doctor to recommend a change of climate. I suggest California."

"Do you mean for me too—and the children?"

"Yes, I mean it very definitely."

"But—" Randall's voice failed at the enormity.

"First this, Randall: California will give you new life in every sense of that overworked phrase. New work—everything is still to be done there—new health, new spirit—" He paused a moment. "New beauty, too."

Now they had come to the doctor's gate. Elm trunks reached upward above them and the branches crossed and recrossed the stars. It was cool spring still, both soft and chilly; a few peepers sounded from the marshes, as though the air had taken voice.

"But this—this is my life."

"It will be a choice, of course."

"This very spring, this northern air—everything."

"Yes, I understand. There are other lives and other ways of life. Good night, Randall." He went up his path and steps. "Of course, our first task is to see that she pulls through."

"Good night!"

The key clicked against the lock.

Randall walked on home. The doctor's words remained in his mind only—on the outer edge of his mind. One might as well talk of the moon as of California—the other side of the moon, which no man had seen. Randall's heart categorically denied existence to either place.

But all through the spring the thought bored into him like an irrepressible insect. It persisted through his country walks, and he found himself staring at his native properties much as a man might take a last look at sweet sunlight and blue before stumbling up to the scaffold. He felt the tremor of spine and the tight stomach even while his conscious mind rejected the whole fantastic notion. He woke with it in the night and felt the lump of it below his throat. It loomed over him like fate, like death—California and its white eternal sun, its glare of space, its terrible emptiness.

He knew precisely what the old doctor meant. He followed the logic to its end, and his conscience persecuted him. But Compton persisted in his heart, the only true love he had ever known.

When Alice began to recover strength in June, Randall paid her a visit. He had seen her frequently since her collapse, but this time he recognized that the issue had to be put into words. He would rather have avoided it. He preferred to let the forces of his destiny push him around in polite silence.

She sat up now, even walked about the house. It unsettled him to find her so pretty—the last thing he expected. It sent him back suddenly to the summer in Maine when he first kissed her—she had been pretty then, and serene and confident, as now. The illness had made her thinner, but color had come back evenly into her cheeks. Her round face had grown quiet and a little remote. Someone—was it May?—had brushed and tidied her and eliminated the superfluous flutters.

He spoke with almost a choke of embarrassment. "They're all fine now, at last. But I'm afraid the measles have come to town. Ted Mayo has them and Harvey has been exposed, of course."

"How is Liddie?"

"Oh, she's the same as ever. And the new girl, Jennie, has turned out very well—we hope she'll stay. Steve has been having colds right along, but these warm days have pretty well cured him."

Nothing in her face changed. It all seemed commonplace. He said, "The weather stayed cold very late this spring."

Then it came: "Randall, what do you think we should do?"

He couldn't speak.

Her tone grew cold. "Mother wants me to go to California."

"You mean, to live there?"

The slow red seemed to mottle her face against her will. He realized that she was fighting tears, but they spilled out and ran down one by one. She wiped them and sat silent.

Randall took a great breath. "Alice," he said with supreme gentleness, "Alice, suppose we all go to California—you and I and the children."

"You mean, to live there?"

He looked away at the bar of afternoon sun cutting the dust motes. "Yes, I mean to live there." Then he hurried on into the silence. "We have wholly failed here—even I have failed so far as a writer, as the sort of writer I hoped to be. I think I am growing wiser—perhaps in time I shall do something. But meanwhile it would be best for us to go where we can begin to live all over again, and they say the climate is wonderfully healthy, of course, and you would have you own house."

"And you would be willing to leave Compton?"

"Yes." His face had gone paper-white.

"Forever?"

"Yes—forever."

"What would we live on?"

"I think I could find work to do. Perhaps in architecture—they say great things are being done out there—"

She waited, staring at him uncertainly. "I don't quite understand why you are proposing this."

"Well, you—" He paused in a sort of dismay. "If we are going to keep on together, it is the only way."

"Why should we keep on together?"

"Because we are married, of course."

He saw the red come back to her face again, an ominous beet color.

"And the children," he added hastily.

But she didn't cry again; she turned angry.

"Don't throw those children at me, Randall. I realize that they exist just as well as you do."

"I'm not throwing them; I'm simply saying that we can give them a home—"

"A home without love—what's the good of that?" She shouted the words. "You haven't once got it through your head—you just can't *see* that nothing is any good without love!" She gulped at the word. "You're so—so complacent and cold and—and—oh, I don't know, Randall. It's no use, that's all. You've never loved me really, and I—just—never knew what I was doing. I know I was a fool, and I was taught to be a fool—all girls are—but even so it might have worked out. If I had a lot of character, like May, I could have done it—and why in heaven's name you didn't marry her I don't see—you simply don't know anything about women, and you never will. You let me live in that house knowing perfectly well I couldn't survive it—if I had only conveniently died everything would be settled. Only it's too late to get May; I don't think she'd have you."

"Well, what do you suggest?"

"There you are—always reasonable and cool. You let me talk myself into fits and then come out with something like that. Why don't you get mad for a change? Why don't you tell me what you really think of me? Good God, Randall, you come in here with a nice little scheme for going out west and when I ask what for, you say coldly, 'Because we are married.' I'm surprised you didn't insert 'legally.' "

She did some mopping and snuffling.

"I'm surprised you haven't told me not to get excited. Everyone does. I guess that's all I'm good for—to get excited."

"Alice, I really meant that we could be happy together. It isn't fair of you to twist my meanings the way you do. I thought if you had a house of your own and a free hand and the children there—"

She peered at him so strangely that he paused.

"Randall, while I can, let me say this: you are a good man. I may not appreciate your ideas, but I do know that you stick to your principles. When you said you were willing to go and live in the west—to leave Compton—I knew what that meant to you. I expect you've been lying awake nights trying to think it out—and Randall, please believe me when I say I understand. I get so bitter and say such nasty things, and I mean them in one way, but not literally, and I realize that your point of view is so different from mine. So much of all this is my fault, from the start. While I was sick I thought about it a lot."

She settled back in her chair, a quiet and dignified Alice, and the colors of anger and grief receded. She spoke almost as though she had prepared a short lecture on the role women must play in the new century. Randall bowed his head gravely while she pointed to the tragic ineptitudes of man-made society. She quoted a Mrs. Fincke and a Miss Kidder. She sketched the sort of sanitary and socialistic community that women might create, given half a chance: "Just half a chance—that's all, instead of a hundredth of a chance as it is now. That's what Miss

Kidder says—she's perfectly splendid, and she could explain all this far better than I do."

Alice's eyes brightened at these thoughts. "It's really thrilling, going round organizing clubs and getting up things and working—and Mrs. Fincke and Miss Kidder say I am very good at it. Really, Randall, I think you'd be surprised at—at—well, at how much we do. Of course, I'm just a beginner—some day, perhaps, I'll make speeches the way they do. Miss Kidder is just wonderful—I know you'd be impressed."

A twinkle expressed itself in the politeness of his face. "No doubt," he said. Then gravity once more. "I see that you have decided very firmly. From now on our marriage is at an end."

Silence.

"Is that a fact, Alice?"

"Randall!" She broke suddenly into sobs.

He hesitated in a sort of dismay. "Well, we've got to have it clear, you know."

"I know—of course I know!" She blubbered. "I'm just acting like a f-f-fool again. But when you said that—what you just said—it sounded so simply awful that I—I—well, I just—" She gathered herself in with an effort. "You act like such an iceberg—my goodness! You'd think a marriage at—at an end—you'd think it happened every day." A few sobs escaped. "All right, Randall. That's the way it is. You made your offer—you did your best. I decline. Now you can return to Compton, all safe forever—and for God's sake go now, go quick, don't say anything—please just go!"

He would have argued again, but she pointed wildly. Her hand and arm seemed to push him out of the room.

He heard the collapse behind him and the long sobs tearing the inside out of her.

But May said "go" too, not by word but in motion of head and eyes. She had been waiting to catch him in the hall. "Alice still needs a lot of rest; you can't count on anything she says now, but she has to say it just the same."

The quiet and the simple logic almost startled him, and he looked stupidly at her.

"I've persuaded mother to take her away—they are going to visit Uncle James out in Berkeley."

Randall went on home. During the trip by car and train his mind turned vaguely from one thing to another. The dust and clatter oppressed him. A sort of emotional bewilderment took charge of him. Life seemed a roily pool, and he drifting blindly in it.

Then, at last, the walk homeward in the June evening. The quiet of elms and dark-leaved maples, the last shine of green-gold radiance on the upper branches, the steady fiddle of insects and the rich rolling aria of wood thrushes, and the whole shimmer and scent and immortal mystery of June—June in Compton, his now and forever. Father and wife and children, duty and sorrow, sick hearts, lost hope, all the turbid whirl, the vexations, the black waters—all receded, quieted, grew clear, translucent like the lovely soft light slanting across the evening hills, drenching the tall elms in golden radiance, bringing down the peace of heaven to the touch and reach of a man's hand.

CHAPTER 12

WHEN I refer to my father as Randall and re-create the scenes of his life which no man witnessed, I feel far away—not so much from the impulses of his heart and mind as from the physical apparatus of his life, the literal world he lived in. And on the other hand the dominion of blood is great; I confess myself a sort of mountebank in pretending candor which nature itself abhors. If I am a true Garretson I am false to myself, and vice versa.

My actual memories do not clearly include my mother. She went to California when I was four, and I remember they said she was sick and had gone away to get well. The truth gradually became a euphemism. She never came back. We may have asked a few questions, but both Aunt Liddie and my father were convinced that truth was a danger to children. Poor dear Alice couldn't possibly stand this Boston climate; the doctors insisted on California.

But in the course of time a legal divorce did occur and though no mention of it ever directly reached us, we realized that terrible and tragic emotions were at large. Doors stayed shut more than usual, and the language of passion escaped through cracks and keyholes.

Grandfather's voice, never wholly subdued: "I say it is unthinkable, it is monstrous, Randall! That you should for a single moment consider—"

I had never heard words so charged. The voice seemed to issue under incalculable pressure.

And Liddie's face fixed on worse than death. Her expressions were always simple ones: little smiles, little gasps—all legible to children; and when the unspeakable scandal came to our house, she showed it tragically. She crept along the halls like an eternal penitent. She turned the place into a ward of sorrows, not in any righteous ecstasy, but unconsciously and simply, as though we had all been stricken with the plague and were doomed. She contrived to send us to bed earlier, to omit desserts and other pleasures, and to enforce a mourners' silence through the day. Grandfather must have it quiet; he was not well; he was resting or writing or thinking, or perhaps conferring in long mumbling sittings with Randall.

"But, Randall, it was a *reporter!*" I remember that last word whispered like a jet of steam as she leaned over the stair railing and spoke down to him. I was in the bathroom, neither seen nor heard, peering out with eyes like buttons. I knew that the end was near. My father groaned. A reporter, I felt, must be more terrible than a burglar, who until then had stood for terror at its worst. If Liddie had breathed the word assassin, it would have sounded no more awful.

So the whole evil of divorce became torture to the Garretsons. The newspapers did mention it, not at all with brasses and drums, but with more than decent curiosity. Randall was the son of the well-known author; the social connections were notable; particularly it was remarked that Mrs. Garretson, the former Miss Hollister, was active in the cause of woman's suffrage. That detail stood out above all others and seemed to give the case national importance. Poor dear Alice, indeed. She became for a time a symbol of the unsoundness of feminism —at least in the more conservative end of the country. I think California at that time was of a broader mind.

Randall made a working truce with his father, but they tacitly agreed to live thereafter more austerely. The household was conducted with military severity; no frivolity could be tolerated—not, at least, within range of adult ears. I remember the three of us one day in the meadow down behind the orchard screaming and screeching with every childish fiber—for no other reason than the joy of free noise. But even that didn't work. The law caught up with us. Lectures and deprivations followed. A great deal used to be said about propriety, about gentlemen and ladies and the respect due to all things grave and reverent. That was Aunt Liddie's duty—the interpreting of the code, and she worked at it with selfless devotion. Left to herself, she would have chosen the ways of resignation and innocence, but for those few years she trained herself in Garretson service—partly out of simple love for her brother and mostly out of elementary fear of her father. I regret to say that we children came to regard her as one of the enemy, not so much in fear as in impatient contempt. Her decisions seemed to have no connection with life's realities as we saw them, and we protested not that she was strict but that she was stupid.

I think now that one competent woman could have vitalized that whole household. May Hollister could have done it. Grandfather Garretson was exactly the sort of bear that some women can tame with flattery, wit, and straight feminine command. And my father—let it be said that he always meant well. His intention was forever kindly, rational, peaceable, but only somewhat touched with inhumanity. His greatest desire in life was that there should be no evident trouble. As to Aunt Liddie, she has always been the most innocent of spinsters and likes nothing better than being told what to do.

More than mere competence, though: the true essential was love. All along it has troubled me that love has played so small a part. I consult my heart pretty anxiously to see if the fault lies there, if any lack in me has transferred itself to my record of the family. Consider the outline: Randall Garretson fell in love with Eileen, then with Caroline; he married Alice; May loved him. Material for classic passion—yet so far as the love goes, it all gives way to time and disappears. Even May, who could never have given her heart lightly, recovered enough to be surprised at her own illusion. The only heavy catastrophe involved the marriage, in which love itself played a minor role. I think love could easily have conquered all—not only the evident love of man and woman, but all the quiet, unrecorded loves that hearts are capable of.

How could a mother leave her children the way mine did? How could children grow up without that strong blood tie? And under the broad Compton roof, could life go on with so little pure affection, with none of the tumult and nonsense of family love?

My mother was capable of enduring sentiment, and even great love, but the problem of existence terrified her. She fled. I think she came to resent her own basic innocence, which partly explains her devotion to the cause of women's rights. She had been carefully brought up to know nothing, and was full of sensibility and hope and a feeling that life was simply a tale told by Hans Andersen with annotations by George Eliot. And when she began to see the full possibilities of failure and sorrow, not only touching the poor and foreign, but enveloping her own charmed life, she instinctively did what she did. In the end she lived quite happily, contrary to all accepted sentiment. She became that figure of universal comedy, a woman's club leader, and devoted herself enthusiastically to meetings, committees, conventions, and all good feminine works. I am sure that California is a better place because of her.

What seems to me less easy to recount is my father's second marriage. The record demands it, but it lacks the makings of a good story—at least to me. I felt always, and still feel, that it was a dreary affair—and now that I think of it I realize that it was a case of excessive competence.

She was Miss Lucy Brattle and a graduate of Smith College. She had lived most of her life in Compton, was a grandniece of Theodore Brattle (the author of *The Decline of the Spanish*

Empire), but being nine years younger than Randall took very little part in his early affairs. She was a devoted botanist and a devoted Unitarian. She wrote a book on Unitarianism in Central Europe, and she assisted Franklin Gray with his later revisions and indexing. Without irony, it may be said that she was a very intellectual young woman.

Like Alice, she believed that women should play a great and serious part in the coming age, but she had little use for clubs and teas and all the flutter of benevolent feminine enterprise. She believed, rather, in stern self-discipline, in the power of knowledge. If it hadn't been for her partly paralytic mother, she would have gone back to Smith and led a scholar's single life, and up to the time of her marriage she so intended. What caused her to marry instead—well, who can tell what longings stir the heart of a lady scholar? She lived always with perfect correctness, as though she were modeling, not clothes or manners, but true culture. She was simply too good to be true. I knew her under the most pitiless of human conditions, from the time she took charge of three sullen stepchildren to the time I left home fifteen years later, and I never knew her to do wrong. She behaved with the calm and uncanny certainty of a Delphic oracle.

But—never a sign of an abandoned heart, never a flush or tremor of passion. She bore three children, but to think of her giving in to the primitive indulgence (ecstasy being out of the question) is hardly reasonable. Actually it is indelicate—the thought, I mean—and leads to the source of all ribaldry, the incongruities of tyrannical body and pretentious soul bound up in the same hide. Yet I don't seem to be making her marriage any clearer. I know that she felt a duty toward us children, that she and Randall were full of literary and philosophical ambition, that she fitted the Compton pattern and came to embody it more and more as time went on. Perhaps it began simply as a marriage of true minds.

For Randall there was certainly good reason. He craved a

companion for his thoughts. Solitude was all very well as subject for a transcendental essay, but in practice it led to melancholy and a sense of defeat. These became Randall's hardest, saddest years, when he began to see that the shape of his life had fixed itself and that past and future were now visible in one mold. Not that he repined; he flattered himself with much thought of his felicities, and envied few men. But still—no Works, no recognition, no true embodiment of his philosophic dream.

He walked with Lucy, and they traversed the subjects of bugs and birds and beauty. She was a straight, very fine girl, tall but small boned, with features cut from white marble. With the aid of desire or the arts of fashion she would have been purely beautiful and a heroine for old romance; but the beauty and poise of her features seemed so incidental as to be pathetic. The sweet lips and glowing brown eyes never dallied an instant with heart's frivolities, never laughed or wept at mortal folly. Rather, she talked with bladelike precision on all matters animal and vegetable and on her view of God as the supreme mathematician.

It caught Randall at a period of special austerity. His Gothic days were past, the dreams of mystic beauty lay shattered. Now instead came a classic purity, and Lucy's fine little head was a vision of clear, sweet reason. At the time he had little thought for the rest of her.

Her mother died, and Lucy married. She took charge of us with terrible competence, not as a cruel stepmother or a jealous second wife, but as a woman who knew every answer. I have never known anyone as coldly just and steadily high-minded as she. She lived herself, and caused us to live, as though she held an open manual of good conduct—not the picayune conduct of surface etiquette, but the Way of Life which she conceived with learned conviction. We were trained systematically in true culture.

I remember the sound of her voice, like a small and articulate silver flute. The wine-dark sea and the rosy-fingered dawn, clear-eyed Athene and wise Odysseus—I can still hear her precise, passionless phrases administered to us like doses of cold water. We sat under Homer and Virgil and Milton and Spenser for an hour between supper and bed. She felt that Ovid was too frivolous and she avoided Chaucer, but she guided us through the epics with systematic care, pointing out the wisdom, the beauty, the allegorical meanings, not with learned righteousness, but with simple devotion to truth. She did us good, no doubt. But for a long time great literature seemed to me like the skies of winter, and without touch of sun.

So also the house itself. Her discipline gave us a cold security. We learned the conditions of survival, and obeyed and were safe, but we shivered too easily.

One of the conditions I specially remember had to do with church. During his transcendental period, my father had given up church. Alice was, of course, a solid Episcopalian, and she and Liddie and grandfather went off together every Sunday morning, walking in pretty stiff array. It was the only thing they had in common. But Randall worshiped in the groves—not ostentatiously, of course, but with quiet devotion to the solitudes. And it may seem surprising that we children were let alone. Grandfather preferred to walk to church without the risk and annoyance of our company, but made up the deficiency by conducting prayers and scripture reading in the parlor after supper. But many of these ways changed after Lucy—or mater, as I must henceforth call her—came to direct us.

For one, she made a Unitarian of Randall. He had never taken to the Episcopal church, of course, partly because it was a stuffy little gray-stone Gothic affair with dark woodwork and dark colored-glass windows. He would have enjoyed a good Gothic imitation, but the Compton church is oppressive to a man of taste. But the Unitarians occupied the old white-painted beauty on the green—originally built for the Congregational Society, later taken over by the party of revolt which called itself Unitarian. The building is more plain than many: there is no pillared portico, no spire, no fine Georgian decoration, but the white rectangles are lovely with elm shadows. During the Victorian baroque it existed without much honor, and the interior was given plush and mustard decoration to improve its gentility; but the colonial revival saved it and later restored it to a beauty it had probably never known. In a way, it stands now as a monument to Randall Garretson. His church and his love.

Lucy got us all there—all but grandfather, of course. About the time I was nine, a new minister came—he was Lucy's discovery and represented all that was new in Unitarianism—told funny stories, played baseball, had taken his doctor's degree under William James. For all I knew, his sermons may have been lectures in pragmatism. Randall approved of him, took him to walk in the sacred woods and made him agree with his views on the higher pantheism. And all went well, except for the behavior of one Ralph Garretson.

From my point of view, I am not one to revolt. I behave with clear good reason. But my record might suggest a cantankerousness more than normal. I remember clearly how I hated Mr. Arthur Dunne, the new minister. He came to the house often, and Jean fell in love with him—her first love. A fine, chesty figure he had, head thrown back and ruddy face shining with moral health.

"Ah, little man, we need you!" His hand fell fraternally on my head with the weight of a boot.

"You do? What for?"

"And you need me. We must work together—you and I together."

"What work?"

"God's work, my lad!" He laughed his humorist's laugh. "Good work, that's what."

"Why doesn't God do it?"

"Ha, Randall, your boy is a philosopher." He squatted down

and laid a heavy arm on my shoulders. "Well, you see, Randall my lad, God thinks that people—good people, like you and me and your father and mother—would enjoy helping him. It gives us a share in life—makes us all work together. Do you see?"

"My name is Ralph."

"Why, of course it is. Didn't I say Ralph?"

"You said Randall."

"Oh, surely not. I—"

"You did too!"

"Never mind, Ralph." This from father.

Mr. Dunne laughed briskly and stood up. "Spirited little man, aren't we!"

"Well, let go of me, will you?"

This time the shock electrified us all.

Then I felt my ear seized firmly. It was mater, calm as ice, and deadly. She marched me off the stage, and I was terrified.

"Up to your room—and stay there."

"Yes, Mater."

And afterward came the lecture, as reasonable as a knife blade. I took it like a condemned victim, and later wept. But I don't know just why. Mater did me no harm, but I was afraid.

Yet from then on church was what I hated. It now strikes me that Unitarianism is the most reasonable and well-intended of all human professions, but between my ninth and twenty-ninth years I despised it and every other Sunday institution, with all the dreary display of piety and beatific bootlicking. I hated the smell of a church and the holy whine and sob of an organ; I hated the minister's black clothes and the godly face he put on and most of all the slick prayerful tones of his voice like so much nauseous sweet oil; I hated the women, the pride and pomp of their silk and feathers, and the way they prayed and responded like God's special pets. To me Sunday was a day touched with death. The sun shone down in utter stillness and the world lay abandoned like wide stagnant water.

"Mater, can I stay home from church today?"

"No, Ralph. I want you all to go."

"Well, I feel sort of rotten—"

"Rotten?"

"I mean—sick, sort of. Stomach-ache, I think."

"Oh, that's nothing, Ralph. The walk will be good for you."

"Well, I'm pretty weak, Mater. Dizzy, sort of."

"You may need castor oil. I'm sure that will fix you up. Suppose you lie down for five minutes and if it still aches I'll give you a good dose."

"Yes, Mater."

I suppose other kids would have known how to handle her, but I certainly didn't. She checkmated me without half trying, almost as though she hadn't even noticed what I was up to. It got so I had to wear Sunday clothes for the whole day—blue coat and pants, black stockings, high black shoes, and the humiliating device called an Eton collar. The purpose of the costume was to display gentility and incidentally to break my spirit. In the afternoon we walked abroad at a funereal pace, and often paid calls and sat stiffly on the edge of horsehair seats in houses where on other days I might have been having cider and molasses cookies on the back steps. And if I spied a Madigan or Sid Steele I shriveled in my soul—I, who walked and breathed like a boy, who could spit and wrestle and catch behind the bat, now revealed in white starch and patent leather.

Good for me, said grandfather. Discipline, decency, self-respect—all the heartless virtues. But other Compton families were less rigorous. The Garretsons, I realized, made a public spectacle of themselves.

Jean, I noted with uneasiness, thrived on virtue. On Sundays she rose far above me and grew as pious and starchy and complacent as all the other women—more so, because she had openly given her pure heart to Mr. Dunne and behaved like a self-appointed saint. That was just on Sundays, I'm glad to say: on other days she was her whole self again. But young

Steve was harder to figure. I knew he was against Sunday virtue, just as I was. He co-operated with me in sending the pious elders to unspeakable corners of hell; we arranged a wordless language of blasphemy and signaled to each other across the laps of the godly. An upward-pointing finger, slowly agitated, nearly choked us with obscene mirth, though Steve's self-control was far more skillful than mine. He had and still has a gift for innocence. But what bothered me was his perfect acquiescence. I remember his brisk little voice, his "Yes, Mater; right away, Mater," and his slick obedience. He conformed, but my own controlling impulse was nonconformity. I was against everything, and I naturally assumed that other kids were too.

When my grandfather was struck at last with mortal illness, he lay helpless for many days, then recovered speech and a little strength. He sent for me. It was a Saturday morning in March and yellow sunlight poured across rugs and blankets; everything in the room was bright, and remains so in my memory— the splash of light on the floor and walls, the mahogany bedstead, the white spread, and most of all the old man lying still against his pillows like a figure of stone. I was nine years old and had begun to read Howard Pyle, and it seemed to me that I was looking at a bearded king of Britain, ancient Uther Pendragon lying in state on his bed of death. I tiptoed in and stood transfixed. I remember the high white brow and the fine cloud of silvery hair against the black skull cap, and I can still see the curving nose, strong and thin, and most of all the kingly beard, the very character of royalty. I had come in fear, partly of death and mostly of the old man. For several months his room had been a center of mystery; I had had one glimpse of his paralysis that had cut straight into my bowels like a knife point. No one explained it to me. I simply looked at death itself for the first time, and have never forgotten it. But now that he lay there in his own dignity again I remembered his character and was afraid.

"Ah, Ralph. Sit down here." The voice was very quiet and full of a remote and gentle austerity. I was deeply moved by his dignity, and my fear changed to reverence.

"Ralph, don't let it trouble you that I am old and ill. No matter what comes, I shall be comfortable."

I perched on an edge of chair and stared at him. He did not smile or soften the grave lines of his mouth and eyes.

"Do you hear me, Ralph?"

"Yes, Grandfather."

"We may not be able to talk together again—not in this life." He lay motionless for several breaths. "One must always regret an end and a parting, but faith can transcend all regret."

The voice seemed to come quietly from a great distance. I can remember the clear articulation, though I understood nothing of what he said.

"Your name, Ralph, is honorable. In terms of character and devotion to the best, no name on earth is more honorable— remember that, my boy. In time to come you will meet those who deny and even despise the ideal which your name embodies. The philistines are spreading like rats. I want you to promise me, Ralph—" He turned to look at me. His old eyes had sunk under their brows and showed nothing but a pale gleam. "Do you understand what I say?"

"Not very well, Grandfather."

"I forget you are a child. But I must tell you, even if you don't quite understand. You will some day be the eldest to carry the family name. I want you to carry it proudly, Ralph; but more than that I want you to respect the ideals that have made it a good name. It is our belief that intellectual and moral excellence is more to be desired than all the kingdoms of earth. Let me tell you, my boy, that the conditions of peace and freedom and moral good exist only because a few people strive to maintain them. You will fight the good fight, Ralph. It is your heritage and your very great privilege."

The old blustery pride had gone out of his voice entirely;

instead his tones were quiet and rather remote, as though his God were speaking prophecies through him. I may have understood nothing literally, but I have never forgotten the tone, the accent, the stillness of his carved face and beard, the presence of ancient wisdom. To me he had already died and was speaking in his immortal capacity. Ever since then I have seen him as two distinct persons: one the enemy of all youth; the other the prophet speaking his last quiet words in the presence of his God.

"You will save men not by exhortation, Ralph, but by strong devotion to wisdom and honor. You will be simply yourself."

He nodded with finality. I said, "Yes, Grandfather." And when he spoke no more I said, "Well—good-by," and tiptoed out, looking back to be sure he was permitting me to go. The sun made a brightness round his head.

I never saw him again.

⤳§ CHAPTER 13 §⤳

IN COMPTON before the first war the seeds of rebellion were hardly planted. We lived as though all things were everlasting. I think of the ladies and their long gloves and hats and veils and all their trailing garments, and especially their supreme certainty. Perhaps I judge my mater, whose knowledge approached the absolute. She never put on a show of manners, she played no part, adopted no accent. Not that she spoke the same language to low and high; she knew an occasion when she saw it, and could speak formalities. She delighted in the great folk who came to town, and her mind sharpened and brightened in the presence of her peers. But to her and all ladies then the laws of conduct had passed from mere code and theory into the very blood stream of life.

So it was with me too. After grandfather died, we all lived in peace. We learned deportment and began Latin and French, and on Saturdays escaped into a boy's world—a wakeful world of streams and green fields and abundant life. Tom Madigan had a gun—a six gun; and I remember the winter day we went off over the frozen marshes and set up slabs of clear ice to shoot at, and the one time we all took turns at a slab propped up in a bush, and I shot last—one immortal shot, for when I opened my eyes again there was a round hole dead in the center. I can see it now—the gray-white day, silent swamp, bare trees and bushes, and the white shield of ice and the hole dead center.

Tom swore, they all swore. I'll never forget it. But of course that was contraband, and when old Patrick found out about the gun we had to lie low for a long time. Yet whatever happened, the sense of everlasting peace was ours; time stretched away behind and before like a road through quiet country, forever safe.

Germany, they said, might go to war, but Tom knew that England could lick Germany. It was like sport talk, matching weight and speed. Dreadnaughts was the word, and Tom spoke it with relish in the same tone he used for Jim Jeffries, Jim Thorpe, and the New York Giants. "Hoch the Kaiser!" we sometimes yelled when we heard that Smokey Joe Wood had won another.

Boys are like that forever, come war or peace. But the peace of those days beguiled all men. The world, my father said, couldn't afford to go to war; peace was too precious to break, civilization too solid. You wouldn't settle family disputes by burning down the house. All good men said it, not my father alone.

But more than rumor of war, more than prize fighting or even baseball, we loved automobiles. The old names are like melodies in my ear even now: Pope Hartford, Stevens Duryea, Stanley Steamer, Chalmers Detroit, Mercedes, Panhard. They used to come into Mike Doonan's blacksmith shop like ships of old romance, and when word spread we ran down to see, to touch the very brass and iron, sometimes to slip into the driver's seat and grip the wheel. Boys know all those things now, and speed and the magic of power are familiar; but then the automobiles came out of nowhere, as though the Creator had suddenly passed a miracle. And the vast mystery, the very inexact science of it, fascinated us. The way Mike Doonan used to stand back and tip his cap up and shake his head reminded us that the machine possessed a wayward spirit: she would or she wouldn't, and no man could tell; and when she wouldn't she turned into a demon, with smoke and noise and the powers of hell. "Stand away back out o' there!" he shouted when things went wrong and we all made a circle of fear and hope.

I remember the epic race around the world. We never knew where they went, or how, but day after day the reports came in from far points, from Alaska and Asia and places no motorcar had ever been before, and my hopes were all with the Stutz —but I think she failed me in the end; and Tom—who was always right about sport and war—bet on the Thomas Flyer with such certainty that we knew there was a connection; and in the end it was our impression that the Thomas Flyer won. Perhaps Tom arranged it so. It is all a dream now. But none of us ever yelled "Get a horse!"—I'm sure of that. The machine was our hero always; when it broke down we suffered with it and never lost hope.

My father, of course, felt that the motorcars were among the evils of progress. He denounced them, not with moral indignation the way grandfather did—on behalf of God; rather, he noted the smoke and noise and the ugly metal, and smiled at the folly of bumping through lovely country at twenty miles an hour. He even sold the old horse too, and taught us that it was beautiful to walk.

This period turned him into the Squire of Compton. His life under his father's reign had to be conducted in upstairs rooms, with secrecy and solitude, but now he could walk forth in freedom. His hair slowly whitened and he let it grow into the fine plume of the artist and scholar; he wore English tweeds and flannel shirts, always carried a stick, and in cold weather wore a cape. His face shone with benignity and philosophy, almost like Emerson's, and though he gave up his writing entirely Compton began to be proud of him. He became a public figure, was appointed to the Village Improvement Society and the governing board of the church. Though he always stressed our poverty, mater and he between them controlled a large property. His pretending was part of the role he had conceived for himself—the colonial squire living in stern but philosophical simplicity. He kept two servants and a gardener, but not in the feudal manner of old; rather he adopted a cheery communal habit and wandered in and out of the kitchen door and helped himself to doughnuts in the pantry and peered into the pots on the stove. I think he had Brook Farm in mind, and was trying to live a pastoral life. He did more gardening than he ever had before, and Patrick lost all respect for him.

Except that he knew he had failed, he lived happily. I think that as time went on his failure seemed to be part of an earlier, separate character. He beguiled himself almost entirely by his new role, his delightful squireship, his tweeds and cape and colonial properties, his perfect taste and natural affinity with poets and prophets. Only rarely did he let himself see through the illusion.

As for mater, she fitted his scheme perfectly. Tweeds and homespun became her. She regarded philosophy and housekeeping, science and cookery, with the same clear intelligence. The household became a system, revolving on a yearly schedule: the canning and preserving, the dressmaking, the papering and painting, all the rituals of the four seasons, the observances of ceremony and holiday—in fact all the things on the human calendar were taken care of with sidereal precision. In time she grew lean and a little grim; the fine mouth tightened and turned down at the corners, the skin stretched itself into many small lines as though the energy of her mind were too intense for its housing. She remained quiet and sure, but the habit of command grew until all the life under her charge became a solemn discipline. Never mean or senseless, never hateful, her regime lacked only one element: love. It was as though we were an institution.

It will be hard in this chronicle to speak fairly about myself, but if I am to go on with it I cannot keep putting the issue off. As we—the century and I—entered our teens, it became evident that something was wrong with both of us. All things were arranged forever, all the values were sorted and settled and agreed upon by intelligent folk, and the future lay fair and straight before us. Any deviation could be nothing but cussed perversity. Revolt seemed to have no sanction whatever, yet look what happened. The century, of course, has had many apologists, but what of Ralph Garretson?

In my early teens I grew too fast. I had a big head anyway, and a lot of obnoxious curly hair, and my awkward body turned me into a puppy of the worst sort. There may have been innocence and charm to the first ten or twelve years—as long as a kid is happy he is all right—but after that, after the happy days, comes the shadow life of adolescence. For some it may pass easily; it may even be a straight, clear passage like any other time of life; but for me it turned into a long confusion, partly happy enough, and partly dark and shameful.

First I grew too big. At fourteen I was a shambling, rather flabby hulk of a hundred and sixty pounds; and with size I developed the habit of godless laziness that infuriates all grown-up folk. I never washed, changed, picked up, or put away—unless so ordered, and then grudgingly. I used no grain of sense about anything—I went coatless in the cold and hatless in the rain, and hated rubbers and sweaters and all other nuisances; I read books in a poor light, lying on the back of my neck with my feet on the best pillows; I wanted no food as much as chocolate candy; I would have stayed up half the night if Steve hadn't constantly squealed on me. I contracted colds and pimples and all the diseases of youth. And more and more as age gave me power I enjoyed perversity: I argued, contradicted, sneered; I despised all the habits of gentility, all ladies and gentlemen, all things nice and godly.

The others always carried on their living quietly. Jean was a good girl; Steve had an instinct for secrecy. The three little ones operated like clockwork. Ralph was the misfit.

It was mater, of course, who symbolized the opposition. Liddie had gone away by then, gone to the solitude of Boston, and mater concentrated all authority in herself. As far as family affairs went, Randall was pretty well out of it; he walked about the house like benevolent royalty, smiling at childish antics and patting curly heads. But mater enforced the law.

I often wondered at my contrariness. I perceived the good intentions, the comfort of property, the peace; I even acknowledged mater's integrity; but I harbored a devil under my chest, a little physical devil that prodded and gnawed and drove me steadily toward rebellion.

I remember the end of my fourteenth summer when the cares of autumn began to bind our free spirits. In the three golden months we had lived like pampered vagabonds. The roads and fields were open, and clear waters for swimming and fishing, and long evenings for late baseball and sprawling on the grass with Harvey and Terry and trying out corncob pipes way down behind the Mayos' sheep barn. But then came September and the blight of school and church and the seasonal evils of music and dancing lessons.

The Madigans all went to Compton High, and so did Sid Steele and all normal folk. But Ralph was required to take a train to Waltham and go to the Bronson Alcott School for Boys in that town. I wore a suit and white collar and tie and a priggish blue cap—a serge thing built like a pancake, and every morning I walked to the station I ran the gauntlet of the high-school gang. Whistles and yowls and grins and echoes of derision: "Oh, you Bronson Al-cott!" I can hear that falsetto now, nearly thirty years after—and I know it wasn't wicked or mean. I did actually look like a well-brushed poodle and what they said was all right, but I wished I was over there saying it.

For a time I was the only boy in Compton who went to that school. But there was a girls' branch of it—called Louisa May; and Jean went to it, and several other girls all starched and prissy and decorated with big ribbons—particularly the very rich Cadwallader girls who drove up to the station in a black Locomobile with a chauffeur. I had to keep clear of the girls and watch which end of the train they got on and then stroll non-chalantly up to the other and swing aboard just as the train started. Jean paid no attention to me—she always sat with Susie Brattle anyway, and when we got to Waltham I could hop off and be halfway to school before the girls started. But it was humiliating. I always seemed to hear those giggles following after, and I acted like a fool—but I couldn't help it. The Cadwalladers had no character—we all knew it; they were made out of ivory and wax and milk; they wore starched petticoats with lace edges; they never laughed; when they walked they wavered like grass in the wind—yet they made me feel like a mongrel. My suit was too small, my wrists stuck out, my tie slipped down, and I hated those clean waxy girls and their starched petticoats.

I hated the Bronson Alcott School too. Of course, we all hated school in those days as a matter of principle, but I was specially convinced that Bronson Alcott was a shameful place. At that time I was the biggest boy there, but not the brightest. It was run in a vague feminine fashion, with lots of art and culture and religion, and no sports—nothing but what they called recreation, which meant tag and relay races in the yard. I remember that I never finished anything; if I began a drawing, it got smudged and rubbed and turned into a mess; if I began fair and clean with an algebra problem it got all crowded into the corners of the paper and came out wrong; whatever I did dwindled off into nothing, and no one there could do anything about it. They were too polite and vague, and urged me to do better next time, but there was always a general sadness in the air, a helplessness in the face of adolescent stupidity. "Dear, dear, Ralph—you do make such a smudge of things."

Every Friday we had dancing class. It was an extra. I carried patent-leather pumps in a cloth bag—and Dick Madigan found out and never let it alone: "Now, girls"—in a high falsetto—"All together: *slide, slide, and a one-two-three!*" And he pranced all over Main Street sticking his behind out like a bustle. The pumps reduced me to misery. Mater made me bring them home because I might need them, and on Fridays she always fixed me up in a special clean shirt and fancy tie, so that Dick couldn't possibly overlook me.

Miss Mifflin used to clap her hands and walk out on the floor with a little mincing hen walk, then turn with a sweep of skirt and a hand held beautifully aloft. We called her the Prune; the girls called her Piffle. "Girls—young ladies! You will please take seats along the wall. The gentlemen will stand at the other side. Quiet, please! When the music begins, the gentlemen will—quiet, please! There will be no pushing and no running. Now, when the music begins, you will walk to the lady opposite and—"

Shuffles and elbowings and profane breathings. "Keep your hands off Gladys, you rat!" "Who gets Myrtle this time, huh? I'm damned if I'll take her again." "Ralph, you big ox, you gotta take the Beanpole—"

"Quiet, boys! All ready now—music, please!" And hand graciously aloft, the Prune minced down the floor as the piano broke out with a two-step.

So I had the Beanpole. I hated it all so much I didn't care— yet I remember the ferocity that built up among us, like a pressure of steam, and mostly because of Gladys. She had whatever it is that drives little boys and grown men crazy—and even a big ox like Ralph Garretson. She smelled and felt like rose petals, she moved like a bit of fluff, and her white starched petticoat made boys desperate. Beyond that I know nothing about her. I realized that my substance was too coarse and left her to the slick ones like Otis Weatherby—though I loved her fully as much and dreamed at night of saving her from bandits and escaping to a happy land. All the passions were bred among us there under the eye of the Prune, and the fine arts of bribery and corruption and gang rule. The next day none of it mattered, but during the decorous hour we were charged with desires as strong as murder and rape. I saw the dark eyes of Otis Weatherby turn cruel as a snake's, his lean head thrust out toward a red-faced Dicky Powers. "Just come out back with me, will you? I dare you to. Two minutes is all I need to beat the guts out of you."

"No talking, boys! Take your places now for the next number—"

We bowed from the waist; the girls curtseyed.

"C'nav this dance?"

The Beanpole's smile fixed itself carefully.

Ta-tum, ta-tum, ta-tee . . . Shuffle of feet and the shrill voice of the Prune. "*One*-two-three, *one*-two-three—not so fast, boys!"

I grew hot and sticky. She remained cold and smooth. I shuffled and bobbed and breathed aloud and worked our arms like pump handles and stumbled on her toes; and she, at arm's length, followed as gracefully as a hatrack.

The wags grinned and whispered as they went by. "Ice water, huh, Ralph?" "Keep trying, boy; you'll melt her down." "Look at ole Ralph turnin' on the heat."

I was the only one tall enough for her. The Prune forced the others to take her now and then, but the sight of little red Dicky Powers pushing the unbending icicle round the floor led to riots of laughter. Five feet eight, she was—and twelve years old, and pale and grim, with blotchy skin. Not that she was the only oddity among us; from the Prune down, we all shared our humanity pretty equally—all but Gladys and Otis Weatherby who were flawless. But the Beanpole stood out as a separate and conspicuous specimen. And naturally since she was thrust upon me I had to hate her.

I remember her clothes—very sweet and feminine, with frills and ruffles and ribbons—patent-leather slippers, white lisle stockings, skirts cloud-white and crisp as petals, a general Alice-in-Wonderland effect of straw-pale hair and ribbons; and yet underneath all that the stiff and silent Beanpole, an unhappy arrangement of angles and bones. It seemed to me indecent, and in some obscure fashion I was sorry for her—as one must be for all the gaunt creatures on earth who are required to decorate themselves like women. I realized that she had been turned out by an ambitious parent, even as I had, and that perhaps she also suffered in silence under these plumes of vanity. But I despised her too for not being soft and creamy like Gladys, and for not dancing like the others and smiling and giggling and signaling with demure eyes.

Mostly we never spoke a word. Once I said, "Where do you live, Beanpole?"

She kept silent, and I couldn't read her face.

"I said, where do you live? Here in Waltham?"

She nodded, and then a tear rolled down beside her nose.

"Gosh, what's the matter, Beanpole? I didn't say anything, did I?"

She looked more incongruous than ever, and I was afraid.

She slowed and I stumbled over her slippers. Then she turned and walked fast into the room where we left our coats. The dances were in the boys' gymnasium, and there wasn't much of anywhere for the girls to go—unless they went back across the street to Louisa May.

The Prune was down the floor and didn't see, but everyone else did. Girls winked; boys looked with round eyes and mouths. "Nice goin', Ralph. How'd'ja do it?"

I shrugged and gestured with palms up the way we did, then followed her. The Prune was talking into the pianist's ear.

Beanpole was standing at a window with both hands pushing a handkerchief against her face. She didn't turn when she heard me, but made a frantic little effort to look normal. We waited through a vast silence of ten seconds.

"I'm sorry—Christina. Is anything the matter?" I recited the words the way we all did, as though it were a formula for making everything right. "You mustn't—I mean, do you want me to call Miss Mifflin?"

I had read about maidens in distress, but this was different.

She stared at me with steady glowering dislike and said nothing.

Boys up to fourteen or so have no idea what a girl really looks like. She is nice or she isn't, she captivates or she doesn't —he knows not why; he is unacquainted with her architecture, with the cut of her nose or chin; he knows no classic standards for judging a lovely mouth. But we had talked enough about the Beanpole to convince ourselves that she was a scarecrow.

The silence there grew intense.

"Well, can't you talk?"

It was as though she had been caught without clothes on. She stared at me, not with active hatred, but with a kind of desperation and self-abasement. I remember her face clearly, the blotchy skin, the mouth clamped in a straight line, the staring gray-green eyes—the eyes most of all. I tried to feel sorry, and to say something. Those pretty clothes of hers— white frills and big blue sash round her skinny waist and long, long stockings—and her big shoes—they all seemed in some way detached from the creature underneath. The staring eyes belonged to an organism I hadn't up to then perceived.

"What is it? What's the matter with you?"

She shook her head in stubborn sorrow.

"Look—is it just because you are tall—is that it?"

Eyes fixed and still.

"Why, gosh, Christina—all these little runts—they haven't grown up yet." I spoke with extraordinary chivalry and self-approval; the idea of doing good appealed strongly to me. "They're just peanuts," I went on grandly; "they'll grow up sometime. You got a head start, that's all. You ought to feel good being a decent size like that. Why, I tell you, Beanpole, those kids, they don't amount to—to *that*." I snapped a finger with a gesture.

But she didn't brighten at all. A sullen, damp, baby look came over her face. She drooped without pride, like a self-appointed victim. I knew the look because my brother Steve used it when his affairs weren't going right—and it made me angry.

"Cut it out, will you? You're just acting like a dope, Beanpole."

She turned and grabbed a coat from a pile on a chair. And then a curious thing happened. When she turned, her skirt swung with her, and the cascade of straw-colored hair moved on her shoulders, and as I looked at her back I felt a little tremor in me—like fear. I lifted hands to her shoulders, bridged and crossed the chasm between body and body; I turned her, stared into her miserable eyes—

Then inevitably the Prune came briskly in. "Children, what *are* you doing?" Her eyes like steel, her head tossed back—she knew she had caught us, and was frightened and thrilled. "Ralph, this is perfectly disgraceful—I never should have believed it. And Christina—you ought to be *ashamed!*"

Black clouds of scandal hung about us. The Prune's hair bristled, her eyes flashed, she licked her lips, she almost vibrated. "We must see Mr. Comstock—really, I don't know *what* we can do! The idea of coming in here behind my back—I've never been so shocked—and nice children too!"

She talked that way, and we seemed to expect it. A monkey head peered round the door and fingers waggled at us. Animal noises from without.

The Prune went on. What would our nice mothers say? What would everybody say? How could we hold our head up? What would people think of her?

Suddenly a voice yelled, "Shut your nasty old mouth!" It cracked into a desperate soprano. "Who cares what anyone says? Who do you think you are—talking to a nice girl that way? You'll go to Comstock, will you? Well, try it—just try it!" The room was filled with a wild passion. The voice went on like a crazy alarm, like the chatter of a frightened squirrel.

"Here's a girl sick and miserable and you come busting in with all this about shame and what will mama say—I tell you mama'll say a lot when she hears about it."

My voice, screeching—but I scarcely heard it. I was red and hot and in an ecstasy. I snatched a felt hat, flung it on the floor, and stamped on it—it was Otis Weatherby's and an elegant one; he didn't speak of my behavior until ten years later. I threw coats right and left, seized mine, thrust right arm into left sleeve, and stamped out the side door. "See if I come to your old classes again—you Prune you!" I remember the entranced faces clustered at the other door, and Beanpole and the Prune standing in petrified attitudes. I slammed the door with the noise of a cannon shot.

"But, Ralph," mater said in the aftermath, "you mustn't ever speak like that to a lady."

Her austere face expressed disapproval, but she spoke with control. She said that my behavior was a constant puzzle to her. Jean and Steve were such nice and reasonable children—at least they got along happily and quietly, and they always tried to reason things out; but I seemed so un-co-operative. She looked at me keenly: wasn't I happy? was anything wrong?

I stirred restlessly, muttering. "Why, I don't know—nothing wrong—"

"What are you saying, Ralph? Speak clearly; I can't hear you."

"Nothing's wrong, Mater." My voice rang out foolishly in the silence.

She studied me earnestly, as though I were a problem in physiology. A lecture began to take shape in her mind, a careful and reasoned statement analyzing my failures.

"It's just all these women," I said suddenly.

"What did you say, Ralph?"

"Women," I shouted. "Sunday school, dancing school—that old Mifflin, she doesn't know anything, she goes strutting around like an old hen—and that woman in art class, she's—"

"Ralph, don't talk that way."

"Well, I don't care. I'm sick of women. They all say don't do this and don't do that and don't talk that way—and these clothes I got to wear—and all this Sunday-school stuff . . ."

One thing about mater—she stayed reasonable. She also stayed firm. "Women are part of life, Ralph. So are clothes—"

"Sure, but gosh—talk about being reasonable! Do you call the old Mifflin reasonable?"

"I didn't say that," she snapped back. "You seem to think the world should be made to order for you. You are furious when things don't suit you. It is unintelligent of you, Ralph; you start fuming and fussing before you really understand the nature of things."

Well, we let it go for a while. I couldn't answer her any more. I was supposed to apologize to the Prune, but I turned into a stubborn mule and refused—and I felt notable and heroic for a few days. Then everybody forgot about it—except the Beanpole. I didn't see her for quite a while, since I no longer went to dancing class; but we met in the street. She went by as stiff as a pole indeed.

"Hey, Christina, what you mad about?"

No answer for three steps. Then, "I prefer not to speak to you, that's all."

I felt a rush of heat upward. "Well, for gosh sakes! You got me into this mess, and now you talk that way. You sound just like the Prune—"

"If you could ever mind your own business, there wouldn't be any mess." She walked on stiffly, nose up.

I yelled after her, "The whole lot of you can go to hell!" I was trembling and anger pounded in my head. "Beanpole!" I yelled. "Damned old hatrack!"

❧ CHAPTER 14 ☙

ABOUT A mile northwest of Compton on the back road to Sudbury lay the Kingsley farm. The road branched away from the main street just beyond our house, ran along the Mayos' fields and up over a ridge of oak and pine, then pitched down pretty steeply among ledges and juniper—a remote little spot, always green and quiet and wild—then opened up the basin that had been the Kingsleys' farm for a hundred years. The road cut the basin east and west, from rim to rim. A brook made a little valley in the north and looped down through pastures and mowing to a pond under the south rim, then spilled down into a gully and so out to the larger stream that followed the valley south of Compton. It is all a small sort of country, and not even rich in forest. Motorists whisk past it now with eyes set for larger prospects. But its design is as sound as design can be, with clean ledge and juniper for detail, ups and downs for variety and added dimension, and enough grass for space.

The farm opens up like a little Eden. In summer especially bells tinkle and cows make quiet woodwind sounds, and the sunlight pours over green meadow and growing fruit, and the forested rim circles it all like the walls of paradise. Near the eastern gate, where the entering road curves out to a level, stands an old, old house, a salt-box house, with roof slanting almost to the ground on the north side; and beyond that, farther out on the flat of the valley, are the barns and silo and a modern dwelling house—the only ugly object visible in the whole square mile of territory. There are big trees—elms and maples round the houses, and a row of maples following along beside the road, and down in the open by the brook one lofty wineglass elm all alone.

For a long time the Kingsleys were our enemies. We raided their orchards and arbors; they lay in wait with dogs and threats —an arrangement that had probably been going on for generations. It was a Compton tradition. A boy's first adventure into the great world occurred when he trailed along after a scouting party over the ridges to Kingsleys', when he squirmed from tree to tree to the very edge of the orchard and at last made off with shirt and pockets stuffed full of windfall apples. The echo of threats afar across the fields, the angry voices of dogs, the panting run up the ridge and away, the scratched faces and torn trouser-legs, the wild laughter and boasts—I can make the tremor of it still run up my spine.

A grim lot, those Kingsleys, like a clan of highlanders. Big Marvin Kingsley, with a beard like General Grant's, and his son Jim who looked just like him without the beard—they came to Steele's often enough, and we knew they were dangerous. We kept a little away from them and watched intently, though they spoke little and saw us not at all. But the one we most feared was Seth Kingsley, who lived in the old salt-box. He said even less than the others, but his face was lean and fierce as a hawk's and he had a mustache that curved downward each side of his mouth like a western gunman's. We knew he had been pioneering out to Nevada and Arizona, had driven stages and punched cows and played poker with gimlet-eyed desperadoes—even now we could almost see a Colt on each lean thigh; we said he could shoot the eye out of a crow with his rifle. We said a lot of things about Seth and the others, and not much of what we said had any truth to it.

One Saturday in March—I was going on fifteen then—mater sent me out there to get some eggs. Steele's had none and we needed them for Sunday. The Kingsleys had no telephone, so mater told me to go and see what I could find. She gave me a dollar in change and a flimsy basket.

It seemed strange to be actually going to the Kingsleys'. For years I had scouted and spied on them; I knew the lay of their land and the strength of their defenses; but I had never walked straight in on a peaceful mission. There were dogs. There was the old hostility. My spine tingled as I walked down the curve and saw the houses all bare in the winter light. A cold northwest gale was blowing that day, with massed clouds dark in the sky and spits of snow and now and then pale flashes of sun. The road had frozen to jagged flint. In the Kingsley valley the wind swooped fiercely, whipping the dust from frozen plowed land, and as I pushed out of the woods to the open flat the place seemed hostile.

For some reason I stopped at Seth's house. The big dogs belonged over at the other, and the kitchen door on the east side of the house seemed sheltered—and I walked up and knocked. A woman's face at a window, then the click of an inner latch, a step and the door opened a little inward. Then it swung quickly.

"Come in first and do your talking later."

That is one of the moments a boy remembers to the end of life. Nothing much had happened—just a face in the doorway looking at me, an old face under a knot of gray hair, pale bluish eyes, white skin with the seams and blemishes of a hard life, but I felt a spread of warmth in my cold body and I grinned idiotically. Those wide-set eyes had looked at me with love. I didn't really know it, and it didn't make sense—I have thought about it many times since and all I can say is that it was simply and truly love at first sight.

I walked into a white kitchen, the doors clicked behind me, and there I was.

"Froze anything?" she said sharply.

I pulled off cap and mittens, wiggled my fingers and rubbed

my chin. "I'm Ralph Garretson," I mumbled through stiff lips.

"I expect you are." Her voice had a little crackle that made me grin.

"My mother wants some eggs—she thought maybe I could buy some out here."

"Take your coat off—you'll stay warmer without it. And try that old rocker. We'll have a cup of hot tea in about two minutes."

She hung my mackinaw on a peg on the back wall. I sat down in the rocker and put my feet up on the ledge of the firebox of the wood-burning stove. Then I looked at everything.

It wasn't only that it was all as clean as soap and paint—our house in Compton was too. I have tried to get the right metaphor for it, the one phrase that will speak the truth of Mrs. Kingsley's kitchen, and the only possible terms are religious. The place was clearly a sanctuary. Outside, the winter gale bent the stiff trees and whipped dry snow round the corners and back against the south windows; inside, the serenity was like the end of all searching, the mortal dreams at last seen clear and true. The big stove made a little murmuring noise, and the black iron and nickel shone with ancient virtue. A little sigh of steam escaped from the spout and cover of the kettle, a breathy sound almost unheard in the quiet. I didn't realize it then, but the warm moisture in the air wrapped itself around me like a garment of comfort; that old wooden rocker with the tall slat back was like the soft clouds of dreamland, and then and ever after I sank into it with the peace of heaven.

The two south windows facing the road were full of plants, ivy and geranium, I think, and the table between was covered with yellow oilcloth; on that dour winter afternoon, with purple clouds massed low across the whole sky, the plants and the yellow cloth seemed to generate a little light of their own. The other end of the kitchen, where the coat pegs were and a low door into a cold pantry, was already full of night shadow.

"I know some of your folks better than you do," she said. "How's your father now? Grippe all gone?"

"He still stays in, but I guess he's all right." I spoke a little hesitantly because I was trying to think if I had ever heard of Mrs. Kingsley before. Up to then I had felt that all Kingsleys must be outside the Compton pale—though I suddenly realized that my notion of them was only a foolish boys' notion and part of the game we used to play. "Why don't I know you folks?" I said boldly.

"Because you're a Garretson," she snapped.

"Can't help that, can I?"

"I guess you can help anything you want, if you want to badly enough."

She spoke then and always with a grim thrust of her stony jaw—something like George Washington's—and a quick energy of words that snapped out aggressively like little bullets. I found in time that the whole Kingsley family quailed before her; yet for some obscure reason I loved that deadly attack. I came to know the quirks in the corners of her straight mouth and the blue softness in her steady eyes.

"I always stole your apples and grapes," I said. "If the Kingsleys ever caught me they'd murder me."

"They'd roast you alive, I expect. That's what they always do to the boys they catch. Next time you crave any fruit, you better just stop in here with a basket. You must be fifteen now."

I nodded.

"Six foot yet?"

"No—not yet."

"Big as all get-out though. I expect you don't remember your mother."

"No, hardly any. Did you know her?"

"I did. I knew you too—didn't suppose you'd ever grow up big like this. Your mother had a new nursemaid every two weeks, and I was one of 'em."

"You?"

"There isn't much I don't know about you, that's a fact."
She didn't actually grin, but the twist of her mouth expressed
sardonic glee.

"You mean all the bad things, I suppose."

"Bad—and good. Both ways." She studied me. "I know more
about folks in this town than anyone you can name, but don't
you dare to call me a gossip. I like well enough to talk about
folks, but not to anyone's harm. They're welcome enough to
talk about me."

She made tea in a brown china pot, got out two big white
cups, milk, sugar, and molasses cookies. She worked like a
conjuror. Suddenly out of nothing appeared the steaming cup
and cookies.

"I shouldn't drink it so much as I do, but I believe it keeps
the weight off me. Makes me ugly too, I expect. That's what
Mr. K. says and he's most always right. When Martha comes
in she'll scold, you'll see—here it's only but an hour to supper.
But it's what you need to get home on—I don't s'pose you ever
get filled up now, boy of fifteen big as you are. I'll bet that old
Irish cook of yours don't do more than load you up with
potatoes. I tell you I never expected to see Lucy Brattle tending
a house and six young ones, though if anyone could stand up
to your grandfather she could—and I've seen her do it too; but
that isn't dressing and feeding a bunch of young heathens.
She don't know who I am, of course, though I spent half my
life not a quarter of a mile from her old place—that's the
trouble with you Brattle and Garretson folks, you don't know
what's under your noses, unless it's something pretty to put in
a book. Nice folks, most of you, but you miss a lot of fun. I
used to see Lucy go off with her nose up looking for birds and
butterflies and such like, and taggin' along after old Franklin
Gray with little notebooks and opera glasses and all . . ."

That voice, sharp and hard and buoyant with unexpressed
humor—it went on forever, it goes on in my memory—on and
on, and the whole of Compton flows with it, all the life and

times, early and late; not the Compton of scholars and poets—not only that—but of men and women and their children's children. "And Abbie's father, he was a sharpshooter in the war—they tell about once he could have shot that General Lee right through the heart dead, but he said he was such a fine-looking man—and a sight better man than Grant, if you want my opinion, with all that whisky—well, what I mean about Abbie's father is he was a mason, built chimneys and such like, none better, they said—he rebuilt the chimneys in your grandfather's house, and times when he didn't have any work out this way he'd go clear to Cambridge, and mind you he'd walk it. Three hours in and three hours out, often as not with a bag of tools—and an honest day's work in between. I used to see him with that canvas bag over his back, and he wasn't but a small man, but he set a pace, I can tell you. His legs used to open up like a pair of shears and he'd move along fast as some folks could run. They used to tell how he walked his way clear back from the south after the war—wouldn't wait for anything, but just lit out. He was powerful fond of his family, I tell you—and Abbie's the spit'n image of him . . ."

She sat on a high wooden stool so fixed that she could lean on the sink counter with her left elbow, hold the teacup in her right hand, and command both east and south windows at a glance.

"You don't miss anything that goes by," I said.

"Not a thing."

"Bet you wish more folks went by."

"After you've lived in a place twenty-five years you take it the way it is. From my point of view this right here is the center of all creation. If I lived some other place, I'd feel the same about that. Most folks do. Makes it comfortable, long as you don't get to boasting about it and starting ructions, the way my cousin does. He comes from Maine, an island up there—though he gets mad when I say up 'stead of down—well, to hear him talk . . ."

Clock ticked slow and quiet on a shelf over my head; kettle sighed and faintly rattled; wood moved and flamed in the stove; I drank the bitter milky tea and listened. Dusk fell slowly. I don't know what made us sit and talk that way; we said nothing of great consequence, expressed no intense emotion—but we forgot about the eggs and no lamp was lit until Martha came in.

"Here's Ralph Garretson," Mrs. Kingsley said before the door was well shut.

A big collie had slipped in and was sniffing me and pacing round behind the stove and under the sink and banging his tail against things. I recognized him as one of the fierce watchdogs whose voice I used to hear echoing in the hills. He lay down with a heavy thump in front of the stove and looked at us with kingly benevolence.

Martha nodded, smiled, and deftly lit two lamps. "Hello," she said to me in the new light. "Don't you want any light here?"

She stood in the center of the floor holding one of the lamps. Her wool plaid jacket was open, the big collar still partly framing her face; her hair, pale brown and fine, had blown into untidy streamers. She seemed big and clean and full of country health. "What a spring day!" she said. "Ground like flint. Aunt Ag says no church for her tomorrow—she feels a spell coming. I don't believe any of 'em will go if she don't."

"Ralph here come after eggs," Mrs. Kingsley said. "Have we got more than a few?"

"No, but Aunt Ag has lots. I'll pop back over and get some." She set the lamp on a shelf over the sink. "How many? Two dozen?" Her gray eyes watched me with a straight wide steadiness.

"Yes, sure—I'll go over with you, shall I?"

"All right." She lifted the collar and belted in her jacket. "Dad's awful late."

We were out in the wind, pushing across to the other house.

We met more Kingsleys, got the eggs, came back. It wasn't dark out there under the clouds, but the wind roared loud. I remember all those details and the way Martha swung along beside me. I thought she was the finest girl I had ever seen and I was proud to be walking beside her and carrying the eggs she had got for me. She seemed free and steady and strong; she wore no hat in the winter gale, and her cheeks were bright with color and her lips smiling—full soft lips that made you feel good because they looked so natural and frank.

"Dad's home," she said as we passed the window.

I followed her in, knowing I ought to be going along; but she hadn't stopped. The kitchen closed round me again with all the warmth of heaven.

Seth Kingsley was hanging coat and hat in the dark end of the kitchen, and he turned and looked at me. He nodded very slightly. Then he stooped with fierce concentration of hawk-like face and took off his rubbers.

"We've got supper in the pot for you," Mrs. Kingsley said. "We should like it if you'll stay."

Martha was setting a fourth place at the table between the front windows—she did it with swift and happy silence, smiling a little at something I didn't know about.

"I got to go," I muttered. "Thank you very much, but—" My mouth stayed open foolishly. "Gosh, they wanted these eggs. I forgot. I better hustle, I guess."

"Come again," Mrs. Kingsley said. Martha ranged up beside her, arm round her waist. They were as different as could be, but for some reason they both liked me. I could see it in their eyes.

"I sure will," I said.

Seth Kingsley said nothing. I last saw him circling the women to reach the sink, and he paid no attention to anything else.

So I went. The night outside seemed at first dark and terrible. I stumbled along awkwardly with the basket. But then my eyes got used to the dark, and everything grew luminous and the road lay clear even up through the woods. I ran. I panted up over the ridge and loped carefully along down the slope toward home, keeping to the grassy edges where the footing was smoother.

I came home in a glow. But home was a drab place. Nora grumbled about the late eggs and mater asked where on earth I had been. I said I had just been talking with the Kingsleys, but I said it with indifference as though nothing had happened at all.

ఆక్ష CHAPTER 15 ౩ూ

My FATHER kept himself extremely busy; for a time he spoke humorously of having a nervous breakdown, and on doctor's orders he took a nap in the afternoon and various tonics before meals. He delighted in medicines of all sorts and made collections of them—pills and capsules and powders and liquids: whatever he heard of he bought. If mater had some of her own or Jean or any visitor or neighbor or Patrick Madigan or the postman, father sampled it eagerly. I can see him tipping his head with a turkeylike motion, then waiting for the sensation, smiling ironically at his own whim. "One never knows what may happen," he said. "And you have no idea what strange tastes there are. I could have been an alchemist, I believe, and sought life everlasting in a bottle."

He did constantly hope for some sort of magic that would re-create him. He waited—he spent all his life waiting, but not with certainty. He bided his time by taking things out of bottles, and by adopting the routines of a country gentleman. His habits became duties, then burdens. Every Tuesday, for example, he journeyed to Boston to work in the Athenaeum. He put on city clothes—not the dark starchy things that commercial folk wore, but rather a tweedy and scholarly kind, of English cut and quality; he carried a stick and a cowhide brief case; he made his duties and obligations evident to all. He found it necessary to consult records, to "run down certain data," to verify and correlate. He visited the Historical Society and the Public Library. All Compton knew when he went and returned and the general outline of his scholarly activities, but no one ever knew what actual work he may have performed. I can see him coming home with the other commuters, chatting and nodding, walking up the street with that fine and humorous pride of his. "A tiring day, Ralph, my boy, a tiring day. Be thankful you don't have to labor in the city as the rest of us do." And you couldn't tell whether he was mocking himself or not. His irony protected him.

He "collected material." It was impossible in his later years to get a direct answer from him. His business was complex and urbane and amusing and metaphorical, but never plain; and it was only through hints and conjectures that we understood that he wanted to write a book on the architecture of Massachusetts—not a simple history so much as a study in colonial esthetics. This was the era of his house-worship, a dream that stood by him better than any other. "Purity of heart, Ralph," he said once, "purity of mind, purity of line." His gesture of arm encircled our house and our past.

But affairs pressed hard upon him. The property made everlasting demands—the flowers, the vegetables, the paint, the shingles: on the surface he tended them with loving good humor, but there were dark anxieties underneath. Roses were winter killed, the furnace caused dry rot in the floor timbers, the barn sagged in the northeast corner, pipes froze in the new bathroom, plagues and pests descended—all, I suppose, the normal wear and tear of existence; but to father it meant eternal vigilance and unrest.

And his public duties were hard. He became secretary, then president, of the Village Improvement Society; he bore all responsibility for the upkeep of the church; he was always involved in the erection of memorials, and the year after the Armistice got himself into a furious civic row over the question of a war monument on the green.

It is only fair, too, to recollect that there were six children to be commanded. And even mater's competence had limits. The work that men do is not the tough part of their lives; it is the mere living, the keeping afloat on the waters of existence, the long days of breathing and eating and wearily sleeping, the everlasting thinking, the brain racking the body and hounding the heart, the talk and countertalk, the surrounding fears like eyes in the night. If my father had spent eight hours a day working in a Boston office, as other men did, his life would have been much easier. I always remember how happy he was when he got the grippe and carried a pile of books up to his bed and sank into forgetfulness.

That's where he was when I returned from the Kingsleys, and I stopped in his room after I had washed up for supper. We had electric lights then and he was reading *Clayhanger*—I remember how he and mater used to speak that name, and how absurd it sounded.

"Very drab," he said. "Drab but fascinating. We learn all about the masses. Wages and work and food and clothes and thousands of little facts. And nothing comes of anything. Life is a treadmill, round and round forever." He spoke with remote amusement. "Your mater thought I ought to read it."

"How are you feeling tonight?"

"I feel like a cat by the fire, but don't tell the others. It is disgraceful to enjoy poor health this way."

"I guess they know it," I said. "They hear you purring."

He looked at me sharply. I must have been grinning with the notion of my own devastating wit, for the humor suddenly vanished from his face.

"When you get to be as old as I am, Ralph," he said with gentle sadness, "you will know what weariness is. Have you been out this bitter day?"

"I went over to the Kingsleys to get eggs." I hadn't intended to say more, but more came. "And they're wonderful, really—

do you know them? Have you been there? I had some tea with Mrs. Kingsley—that's the first house, the old one—"

"The salt-box."

"Yes, sure—and she said she was our nurse once—"

"I have no doubt of it. Did you see the sitting room?"

"Well, no—I was just in the kitchen."

"They ruined that, of course. They took away all the paneling and bricked up the fireplace—there's a fireplace and brick oven all across that inner wall, all plastered over now. The sitting-room fireplace is filled in too, but the paneling and mantel are still there, and there's nothing better in Compton. Really, it's a pity the house can't be restored by someone who understands it."

"Haven't they always lived there?"

"Yes, I believe so. And they built the ugly thing beyond that looks like a gigantic birdhouse. It is a curious thing, Ralph, that ordinary people a hundred years ago seemed to be made of better stuff than they are now."

I felt a sudden welling up of fury. Anger always hits me when I least expect it, and before I can think or speak the blood is pounding in my face.

There he lay serenely, light streaming softly over blankets and pillows, touching his silvery plume of hair and his thoughtful face. He wore a dark blue Shaker-knit sweater, with roll collar and buttons down the front—he loved thick wool of all kinds. "If I could I'd buy it," he was saying. "It would be a sound investment. I don't believe Seth has the least notion of its value, even though he is a carpenter and ought to know better."

I struggled with passionate speech. I wanted to tell him he was nothing but a snob, but I couldn't think of the word or any other way of saying it. I couldn't quite understand what was wrong, and I stood there inarticulate.

"If you go again, ask them to show you the front hall and the sitting room—it would be worth a trip. No doubt the old kitchen woodwork was long ago burnt in the stove."

Mater came in lightly with a tray of supper.

After that I hardly spoke of the Kingsleys at all. I did ask Jean if she knew Martha Kingsley, and Jean said no, Martha was a good deal older—in fact, she had a notion that Martha was married, but she wasn't sure—there had been rumors.

"No, she isn't," I said abruptly.

"Oh, how do you know?"

"Why, she—she—well, I didn't see any wedding ring."

But Jean said there was probably something funny about it. She spoke indifferently, as though Martha didn't matter much.

"You'd like her, Jean—and Mrs. Kingsley too. Come on out with me and see them sometime." I spoke with controlled feeling and extreme generosity. Even then it seemed strange to me that the meeting with those two women had created so much passion inside me. I could think of nothing else, and I was angry with my family for not understanding.

"Why, I'd love to," Jean said. "I like farms—if I were a boy I'd work on one every summer. I'd like to marry a farmer."

"Me too!" I said. "I mean be a farmer . . ." It was the first time I had ever thought of it. But Jean didn't laugh. She smiled wisely, like an older sister, but without desire to hurt. At that time Jean had pretty much become a lady and was plunging into grown-up affairs, and though I despised ladies and all their habits I still felt that Jean was all right. She stayed plain and natural no matter what happened; she skated with us, and even took a hand at hockey when needed, and didn't display how female she was. She was so far from frivolity that she could have ranged herself among the ancient goddesses without much alteration, though no such notion would ever have occurred to her.

For a time I said nothing at all to Steve, though later I told him about the farm. He and I lived in the same room, yet in many ways were as separate as two planets. He did not go to the Bronson Alcott because it was assumed that he was better off away from me; of the two of us, I was the bad influence and the "problem." Steve did everything with quiet care; he behaved himself, got good marks, never made a fuss, was always right. If I ever imply that his behavior is obnoxious, it is the result of my own renegade confusions. His destiny appointed him to be a gentleman and he looked upon me as a willful barbarian.

On the Monday following my trip for the eggs I came back from school on the three-twelve, stopped at the house to put on old clothes, and headed for the Kingsleys. I actually felt the pull of a strong force, and I yielded to it with secret and intense delight. I was a young man in love, and all the driving ecstasy of first love impelled me. I hustled in a sort of trance, yet with instincts for secrecy. I slipped in and out in dread of questions and delay, and I cut across lots to avoid encounters. Then the road up to the wooded ridge, now wet with standing water and mud—I remember the brightness of the March sun pouring against my face and the enormous shining blue overhead. In the lee and sun the air lay as still as summer heat, but in the open the west wind whipped by in gusts of winter. It would freeze again by night, but just then the sunny ground was alive with silver trickles. The cedars and junipers on the ridge already glowed with fresher greens, and I noticed the burnish of red on the young twigs in the bushes. Then and later I noticed many things along that little stretch of country road; whenever I have to think of a season, a time, a bit of country at any point in the solar cycle, I think of that road over the ridge to the Kingsleys.

Voices sounded from the farm, then a crackle of fire. Wood smoke sweetened the air. I paused on the edge of the flat to see what went on, and the dogs suddenly set up a blood-curdling roar and came for me like death itself. Voices yelled, but the three beasts were hurtling at me in a savage frenzy. I tried to call, but I think no other sound came out of me but the wild beating of my heart. I mustn't run, mustn't show fear—I simply stood in a trance of terror and hoped the end would be quick.

They always did that—those beasts. Their white fangs slavered, their voices screamed hate and instant death, they charged with greyhound speed, but I am alive to write it. Maybe it was Martha who saved me. She shouted and ran after them, and instead of tearing me to pieces they made a circle of passionate barking round me. When she came up to me, they trotted back quietly to the farmyard, golden tails waving aloft like plumes.

"We can't seem to stop them," she said, "but they really won't eat you. Their idea is just to frighten you to death, but I guess you don't frighten so easy."

I took a breath and moved a little to see whether I could. I felt as weak as jelly, but her words did something to my spine. I straightened, filled my lungs, and tried a bit of speech.

"Gosh," I said. "Don't people keep dying of heart failure out here?" My voice quavered and I hoped she hadn't noticed. We walked along and I tried not to tremble. "What's going on here?"

"Oh—Uncle Marvin's boiling sap. Come on over. We don't usually get much, and some years it's no use even trying, but this spell of weather is just right. Yesterday it ran pretty well, and today it's wonderful. Come on over and help us collect it —can you stay a while?"

They were all there—big Marvin stoking the fire under an iron cauldron, and Jim coming up with a pail in each hand, and their wives—Gran and Maud—standing close enough to keep warm, and a bunch of young kids cavorting round, and all full of loud joviality.

"Here's manpower," old Marvin shouted lustily. "Can't get these women to lift a hand—they just come out here to keep 'emselves warm."

"Lift a hand!" Gran spoke with deep resonance. "You know I came out on purpose to tend this fire—me and Maud can do it good as you can. But will you leave it be? All you figger on is keepin' warm yourself." She was a fierce-looking, twisted woman, and ordinarily I should have avoided her, but out here in the March day her harsh voice was full of power and humor. I laughed aloud.

"Laugh, do ye?" old Marvin growled. "Don't respect your elders, hey?" His stubborn beard thrust itself in my direction.

I grinned uncertainly.

"He's just the same as the dogs," Gran said briskly. "Goes for to scare you."

Except for Martha, they were a shaggy, uncouth crew—and even Martha was big enough to stand up beside them. They talked in shouts.

"We don't do this like they do up in the country," Gran shouted. "Some of my folks up there in Windham County, that's up in Vermont—why they make three-four hundred gallons. They think its plumb funny to see us piddlin' round here with a pot in the yard like this."

"Biggest waste o' time the hull year round," roared Marvin. "You boil her a-larrupin' all day, burn up half a cord, and by nightfall you're lucky to get a couple gallons out of it—and all smoke and ashes in it. I only do it to humor the women."

"I suppose you eat it to humor us too." This was Jim's wife, Maud, and her voice almost shrieked with delight. She was as tall as Martha and twice as fat, with a face like a ripe peach and streamers of brown hair blowing all round it. "You and Jim— you'd finish up a gallon at a meal if we ever let you."

Marvin straightened his bulk and looked aloft at the vast blue of March. "Reckon we all got a taste for sweet. How's she runnin', boy?"

"Good," said Jim.

"You want I should come and lug it?"

"That means he don't intend to," Gran said.

"Ralph and I will," said Martha.

And so we did. We took pails and trudged off across the wet

ground, and along the line of maples by the road, and collected sap from all the cans and jars and lard pails. Of all the Kingsleys Jim was the most silent, and he went about his business as though he were alone on earth; but Martha and I kept together and talked and drank some of the sap—and tried to think it was better than it was. We lugged in several pailfuls, and the sun touched the trees on the western ridge and frost and shadow settled on us. The cauldron stayed full, and Marvin said they'd be boiling till all hours—but there was nothing more to do except stoke it and watch it didn't boil over when it began to thicken. When we turned back toward the other house he called, "Come again, boy!" And I was surprised to see a smile behind the gray beard.

In the great events of life, a visit to a farm on a bright March afternoon hardly counts; but I remember every detail of those first Kingsley days. The harsh voices still ring in my ears, the free speech, Marvin and Gran yelling the truth at each other; I see their faces plain as earth, twisted and furrowed and stubborn, and yet fertile with life; behind them I see the weather of March, wind and space, and the dark buildings of the farm, barn and silo, wagons and fences. Only a mile from Compton, from the gentle Garretson household, yet I seemed to be translated suddenly into a pioneer region, a far west or a great north where men lived by courage and will, unprotected by society. It felt enormously colder and wilder out there, and the dark forest on the circling ridge seemed like the edges of wilderness.

I walked beside Martha with a buoyant singing happiness. I walked like a creature in love, relishing each step, each breath, each flicker of my senses. The half-frozen springy ground delighted my feet; I tapped a shoe on the mushy crust of ice in a puddle. The wind had quieted, and the sky shone with dark translucent blue. I breathed it all deep into my chest and held it—all the cold and quiet, the enormous blessing of the moment in time and space.

"I hope they'll boil again tomorrow," Martha was saying. "You'd better come out and help—see, there's ice on the ground already."

"Might be able to," I grunted, with beating heart.

"Come in and see mom," she said.

"Ought to go—must be nearly six," I grunted again.

But in a moment I was in that old kitchen, grinning at the way Mrs. Kingsley's sharp eyes searched me. "Well, you came back, did you? Want eggs so soon again?"

"No, I just came."

"I had to drag him in to see you, Mom."

"I bet you did. Here, take your jacket off and sit down. You'll eat with us this time sure. Seth's just round—I hear his steps. Now sit down and don't bother us."

Being late at home wouldn't do, but there I sat like one hypnotized. The women served out biscuits and potatoes and thick gravy and cold beef and apple sauce. And Mrs. Kingsley looked at me with a sort of grim relish. "You just tell your stepmother I kept you," she said.

"Well—she won't like it."

"Ought to be glad to have one less to feed. Martha, tell him to get along in here." The "him" was spoken as though it were a name.

Martha called out into the shed, and presently Seth came with quiet long steps, bowing his head under the door frame. He went about his tasks of hanging up coat and hat, washing and drying hands, as though no one else were in the room, and I felt conspicuous. He sat down opposite me, folding long legs into place, and reached for the potatoes.

"Here's Ralph Garretson come for a square meal," Mrs. Kingsley said.

Seth's dour face turned my way for a second. "So?" he said. His eyes seemed impenetrable. I looked at him respectfully, saying nothing, wondering how a man so cold and hard could be tolerated in this sanctuary. He began his eating with intentness, and for a moment no one said anything; then he glanced at me sharply. "High school?" he said.

"Well, not exactly; I go to a school in Waltham."

"A higher school, I presume." He said it so quietly that I waited a moment to be sure he had said it at all. No smile showed under his desperado mustache.

"It's that Bronson Alcott School," Mrs. Kingsley added cheerily. "You know those Channing folks—they used to live over on the edge of Concord and started the school out there. and all that ever came to it was their own children."

"No money in that," Seth said.

"Well, they must be doing well enough now—what I hear, anyway. She has the girls and he has the boys, and quite a good number of 'em."

"Little men and little women," Seth said.

"Well, I can't help it," I said suddenly, not with passion but with a fear of being misjudged. "I just get sent there."

This time Seth looked me over with interest. "You take your schooling under protest, is that it?"

"Well, sure—I mean—" I spoke up boldly. "I don't like it there."

"You'd prefer to be ignorant, no doubt."

The cold eyes watched me a moment, and I squirmed. "I'd prefer a better sort of school," I said with dignity.

"Any other school but the one you're in?"

By then I had stopped eating and was sitting in misery and early anger. Seth kept looking at me as though I were a specimen on a pin. I knew I was turning into a fool, and they all seemed to be watching and saying nothing. Martha was sitting next to me with an expression of knowing delight on her rosy face.

"Maybe," Seth went on quietly, "you prefer not to be a great man—like some of those old folks. Maybe some of us are ashamed of greatness—is that it?"

"Greatness!" I said it stupidly.

"Oh, I was just asking. You ought to have more opportunities than most. Good folks, good school—what else does a young one need?"

The curve of his mustache silenced me. I wanted to be angry but I could only watch with a curious suspension of feeling.

"Don't let him fuss you," Mrs. Kingsley said. "He talks that way. You just tend to your meal there."

Martha still smiled as though we were all happy together, and it hurt my feelings. I felt the choke of grief in my throat, and for the moment I dreaded the disgrace of tears. I took a firm bite of biscuit and chewed busily.

Seth looked at me sternly and spoke.

"You don't speak up for yourself. Boy like you—what is it, sixteen?"

"Fifteen."

"I suppose," he said with an odd sharpening of tone, "you've decided on a career for yourself?"

Career was what he said. I laughed. "Lord, no—haven't any idea."

"Minister, maybe?"

"No, that's the last thing."

"Doctor?"

"Not me."

"Well, nothing? Nothing at all?"

Nothing I could put into words. If I tried to say "writer" it would sound childish—I knew already that the less said about writing the better.

He prodded me about school. Did I enjoy Latin? No. Greek? That came later, but I didn't expect any enjoyment. French might be all right, but the man was a fool—in my opinion all French teachers were fools.

"How many have you had?" he asked.

"One," I said, and had the grace to grin.

But I did like English, except for grammar and such stuff, and history wasn't bad.

I had felt uncomfortable again under the questioning, but Seth nodded abruptly as though it were all over and began to catch up with his eating.

"He never got enough schooling to suit him," Mrs. Kingsley said, using the pronoun as though it were a proper name.

"He had quite a time out west," Martha said. "Didn't you, Pop?"

He nodded gravely as he chewed. "I learned how to throw a diamond hitch," he said.

Somehow the balance had got itself right again. The clock ticked, the kettle sputtered, forks clicked pleasantly on china.

CHAPTER 16

"Ralph."

"Yes?"

"You ought to say 'Yes, Mater,' Ralph."

"Well, mater is a funny sort of name."

"Funny?"

"Yes, sort of—I mean, it's queer, I guess."

"What name would you prefer?"

"Oh—I don't know. Mater's as good as any. They're all funny."

"You must call people by a name, Ralph. It doesn't do to say 'you' all the time, or 'she.' "

"I suppose so."

"Perhaps you'd prefer to call me Lucy."

"Why, gosh—I don't know—"

"After all, it would be simple and reasonable."

"You mean, all of us too?"

"Why not?" She smiled at my astonishment.

"Well, it wouldn't sound right."

"If something is right, Ralph, then it sounds right."

I committed myself no further and waited for what she had meant to say.

"You seem to be visiting the Kingsleys a great deal."

Something flared up inside me. I got ready for danger.

"I've been out there a few times," I said.

187

"You mustn't impose on them, Ralph."

"Oh, no. They—" I clutched the vast miracle close to me. They loved me; I loved them. Nothing else. "They ask me to come. And I can help them a good deal—" I jumped ahead. "Maybe this summer I can really work for them—I mean with haying and crops and stuff like that."

"You mean work for pay?"

"Oh, gosh no—" I felt that mater had said something foolish, yet I still feared her probing logic. "I can learn about a farm," I said. "Horses and cows—I've always wanted to. They teach me all sorts of things, like harnessing a team and even plowing."

She nodded reasonably. "You like that?"

"You bet!"

"I thought Seth Kingsley was a carpenter. Does he farm too?"

"Oh, sure. Mostly it's Marvin and Jim—"

"They're nice people," she said. "I used to know Seth's wife quite well—ages ago, that was, and she's probably forgotten—"

"She thinks you have forgotten her," I couldn't help saying.

"Oh, but I never forget anything." She said it quickly, with a quiet pride that surprised me. "I remember the whole Kingsley family—not well, of course, but I remember how much Uncle Franklin liked them and he often stopped there when I was with him and we had drinks of water or cider—old James Kingsley was alive then, one of the only Democrats in town in those days, and Uncle Franklin loved to talk with him—he used to say old James was the stubbornest man in the county. They lived in the old house, of course. I remember when they built the new one—the early Sears-Roebuck, your father calls it. But they are fine people, Ralph—I'm glad you like them."

I was astonished and even slightly disappointed. The Kingsleys had been my own idea entirely, and I had prepared to defend it bitterly. "Yes," I said weakly, "I guess they are."

"But, Ralph—farmers are poor and they work hard. Don't be a nuisance."

"No, I won't."

"Don't impose on them."

"No, of course not, Mater."

She couldn't know the realm of feeling behind little words like those. She simply nodded and went off and left me in the center of my dream.

But I must have been a nuisance too.

I remember one Saturday in April I came on Seth sawing up cordwood in the yard.

"Can I split some for you?"

He dragged his sawbuck well away from the chopping block and nodded briefly.

It was birch and maple and beech, all hard and clean. I went at it with power and fury, and chips flew and the chunks bounced on the big block. "Gosh, is the ax sharp!" I breathed, and ran a thumb along the blade. The edge was honed like a razor and I looked stupidly down at the blood welling up into the white cleft in my thumb.

"I always shave with that ax," Seth remarked, and continued to saw.

I sucked foolishly at the cut, wrapped a handkerchief round it and took up the ax again. And once more I laid into the good wood with all the force I had.

"At that rate," Seth said after a few minutes, "you'd keep nice and warm all winter."

"Hot work," I agreed, breathing hard.

"Did you ever use an ax before?"

"Oh—some, not much, I guess."

He stood looking at me. "Well, let's see a minute." He took the ax, set a chunk of maple on end, and tapped it—at least it seemed merely a tap after my homeric blows. The chunk fell into splinterless halves. He took a half in his left hand and the ax in his right; two strokes made three stove-size pieces. But he shook his head warily. "It's a question how much you value your thumb there. I been doing it like that so many years I can grow a new thumb pretty quick now."

So I went at it again keeping both hands safe on the ax handle. "That takes care of your thumbs," Seth said, "but toes go almost as quick."

I spent two hours there and built up a nice pile of ragged stove wood. Seth kept on sawing and most of the time we didn't say much. Sometimes he spoke reflectively, not expecting me to answer. He said a man who cut all his own wood got heated six times over—it seemed hardly sensible, though the longer he lived the less sense he could find in anything. Men worked and suffered sixfold—he knew that much—but all it did was to keep them alive so they could work and suffer again. Anyway, he appreciated my help in reducing some of the suffering.

His ironies seemed nonsensical to me, and I let him go on. The April day was like a fresh sea swept with northern air; I could feel the cool of it in my throat and lungs. I swung the ax watchfully, hoping each stroke would fall as true as a surgeon's —though it generally fell inches out of the way; and I tried to keep steadily going like a man at work, even when my back ached from the bending and the skin broke in my hands. Nothing had ever seemed better than this working with a sharp ax in the Kingsleys' yard. I began to think I was doing well.

"You aren't accustomed to work, I imagine," Seth remarked as he tossed his final chunk on the high pile he had made.

I reviewed my life and drew breath. "No—but why did you say that? Because I chop so badly?"

"Well, a feller that works saves his strength. He hates to bend if he can stand straight. He does all he can with one motion—you watch a good ditchdigger some time, he don't hardly move at all, but if you look for him an hour later he's dug himself out of sight. Now you go to work like a windmill —you've been a regular perpetual motion there, stooping and swinging and chasing round after pieces."

Seth always made me think before I spoke. If anyone at home had used those words I'd have answered angrily, but here I nodded and grinned. "I'll watch you next time." I still felt good.

"I suppose a boy has extra power in him—he has to use it or waste it. If there was some way of harnessing all the energy of all the boys in the world the rest of us could afford to be idle."

I saw myself a marvel of strength and endurance. I seized the bucksaw and went at a four-foot length of birch—conserving my motions as advised, but whipping the thin blade through the log with fine vibrant screeches. My muscles enjoyed the new motion; back and shoulders pumped up and down irresistibly. This, I felt, was what I needed, this manly work with tools, this mastery of the essentials. If a man could live like a pioneer, with earth under his feet and a good ax or saw in his hands, if he could rely on his own sinews and his skill—well, it was absurd, I suppose: the blade began to run hard, the fine screeches grew hoarse and slow, presently it jammed. I pumped and grunted and used up my muscles, and then it stuck as tight as a wedge.

Seth had gone—he had a way of moving with catlike silence (it was one of his methods of saving strength), so I was free to that extent, at least. I worked the saw loose, set it back in the cut and tried again. It jammed again, harder. Anyone who has operated a bucksaw knows all this, and I record it not as an episode of rare barnyard drama but because it happened to be a turning point in my life. I wrenched the blade out of the cut, rolled the log over, and furiously assailed its other side. My arms ached with fatigue, but I made the dust spurt and the blade screech. Then inexorably the friction, the hard pull and push, the grim, spiteful resistance of that cursed piece of cordwood. I yanked out the blade, picked up the log and smashed it against the chopping block. I snatched up the ax and belabored the still unseparated wood and the blade did bounce crazily and slanted down into the dirt two inches from my left foot. It had gone like a flash, and buried itself in the soft earth. I found myself trembling in a sort of electric fright and disgust, and I tried to swear, but nothing came of it. As I laid the ax behind me on the ground I could feel the sinews and flesh of my foot—not tingling, exactly, but reminding me that they were there.

I finally broke the birch log with a mighty smash against the edge of the block, but the loose foot-long chunk flew across to where the saw was leaning against the sawbuck. Another smash, and the wooden frame of the saw lay twisted and cracked.

That ended the act.

I expected trouble from Seth. The ax, I noticed, was nicked, the saw was forever busted—and tools, I realized dimly, were the emblem of Seth's life. But when I called him and he looked at the wreckage, he nodded as though he had just missed a draw to an inside straight. He seemed almost to have expected it. "You didn't cut yourself in two, anyway—or did you?"

"No—but, gosh, I'm sorry! Can I—I mean, where do you get a saw like that? I'll get a new one as soon as I can." I spoke tremulously, partly because I had no notion of the expense involved. There'd be so much explaining to do at home.

Seth was handling the pieces. "I don't care much for new tools," he said. "You get accustomed to certain ones—now I never had a nicer blade than that one, and I got it filed and set just right."

I thought I had begun to learn how to read his face, but I missed his intention entirely. I apologized harder than ever.

He looked at me anxiously. "Why, son, this doesn't do any hurt. You don't need to trouble yourself—just a hickory end piece here, or birch would do. Why half a farmer's job is fixing —the last thing we do round here is to buy new store goods."

I followed him into his shop, which occupied most of the wing beside the kitchen. Now, in the afternoon, there was no sunlight in it, but there were windows on the north and south sides and he swung open the big wooden door on the east side, remarking that it was milder out than in. The place seemed as old as creation, with smoky rafters up above and all sorts of ancient gear stowed away and a scarred and blackened bench from end to end of the north wall; but it was full of new-cut wood too, fragrant boards and shavings and the scent of paint and turpentine. For a few minutes no details made themselves distinct; then I noticed separate things: a forge and bellows and anvil in the southeast corner near the big open door; a solid platform table in the center, rough built out of two-inch planks with a smooth-laid top to it of matched boarding—and on the platform a mahogany rocking chair lay on its side with clamps and cord binding its parts together. Above the long workbench were many shelves and tools and boxes and cans— I noticed a set of old-time wooden block planes ranked on a shelf between the windows. I remember a couple of wagon wheels against the wall behind the forge, and a pile of old iron somewhere, and a grindstone, and the wooden handles of a plow, and dismembered pieces of furniture all over the place— even hanging from the rafters.

Seth had the split end-piece of the saw frame in one hand and was poking and muttering along under the workbench. "It's a fact you might not believe," he said almost inaudibly, "but you can find anything in the world you need here if you just keep a-looking. I don't care what it is you want, it'll be somewhere in this shop—only you got to know it when you see it. It takes a good eye to see under some of these surfaces." He yanked a varnished half of a chair rocker from the dusty cavern, but shook his head at it. "That Grand Rapids oak— you'd split that first whack." Then a rough weathered stick came into his hands and he nodded. "There you are, son. Can you shape that to fit?"

He handed me both pieces and his small gray eyes watched me with a little glint.

"You mean me?"

"Why not?"

I looked down at the gray stake in my hand, a scarred, ax-hewn length of heavy wood shaped at one end to fit an inch-size hole. It was not more than an inch wide and two inches broad.

"I—couldn't do it."

"Couldn't, eh?"

"I suppose you want me to go ahead and make a mess of it —and any other time I guess I would. But honestly I don't know one tool from another."

"Is that a fact?"

I accepted the irony. I even welcomed it. The afternoon's work had made me humble.

"I can hammer a nail—not straight, though. I'm pretty fair at whittling. But you'll have to shape this piece—maybe I'll learn something watching you."

He thought it over carefully. "Education doesn't seem very much good on either end. I guess you'll just have to aim to be a gentleman."

I looked at him with an uncomfortable and foolish smile.

He took the wood from my hands and laid the pieces on the bench. Then he selected one of the block planes, which I had thought were relics of a dead past, adjusted the blade and began dressing down the rough stake.

I have never once since that day handled a plane or a spoke-shave or even a hand drill without that picture of Seth Kingsley as vivid as life before me, his gaunt hands wrapped lovingly over the tool and guided by the whole concentrated force of his being, the sinewed wrists and the bowed shoulders, the grave face peering down with perfect certainty. Oddly enough he looked a little like my father, with the same fine structure of face, the bony curving nose, the narrowing forehead—but the resemblance may have been simply a fancy of mine. Seth wore no silver plume, like father's; his dark hair lay flat and thin across his brow, and he seemed as dour and tough as the hickory he planed. I made a hero of him, I suppose; I elected him to be my master, but not simply because he handled tools perfectly, nor because he had ideas, to use his own phrase. I recognized that he had taken me on as a responsibility. He perceived my weaknesses and even convicted me of thorough uselessness, yet there he stood at the summit of his own mastery repairing my damage, teaching me his life's essentials.

"Was it old Mayo who said to hitch your wagon to a star? I used to work for his brother Henry—and they did seem to have great aims. I suppose most of us would get dizzy, or more likely foolish—it's not what you'd call practical advice. But any kind of idea is better than none, and as far as I can see young folks don't have any at all—except they prefer to be rich."

He muttered something about putting motors in wagons and then shook his head. "Easy enough to find fault with youngsters —that's what my father used to do. Ever see him?"

"I've heard he was the stubbornest man in the county."

"He took pride in it. He took pride in what he called doing things right—and right to him was his way and no one else's. It was a good idea, but it would have been better without so much pride to go with it."

"Sounds like grandfather," I said suddenly.

"Same pattern, that's a fact. Hard on young ones, they were, too. That's how I happened to go west. We told each other to go to hell and he wouldn't. I had to."

"What about Marvin?" I said, thinking of father and Uncle Richard.

"He's a tough one. He stuck it out."

Seth sawed the piece roughly to size, then with the ripsaw cut the slot in the end. Using the old piece for a pattern and clamping them in the bench vise together he drilled a hole for the rivet and two holes in the side where the brace fitted. Then he dressed it all down with spokeshave and rasp until it was a twin to the original. Not much need to sand it, he said; hickory came out smooth as ivory if your tools were sharp. He brushed a coat of oil over it and stuck it on a nail in the beam over one of the windows.

"Do you mind if I use it again tomorrow?"

"Sunday?"

"Well, Monday, then."

"Anyone that cuts wood gets paid for it."

"Not when he breaks tools."

Seth nodded. "Run her straight next time. You twisted when you pulled."

It all began that way. I cut and split and stacked—mostly on Saturdays when I had time and Seth stayed home. His carpentering had grown more and more specialized; he liked doing the sort of work he could bring home, and he always worked at home on Saturdays anyway—sometimes in the shop, sometimes round the place. I followed and watched and talked.

In his own domain he was as stern a boss as I have ever encountered. Whether he was fitting a leaf to a mahogany table or a hen-house door, he expected no less than precision. It would have been better, I often thought, without so much pride to go with it—but I found in time that that was his "idea"; it was the obligation God had laid upon him. In his hands he held visible truth and with each stroke of plane or saw his conscience and his sacred honor were involved. He agreed that the hens would do as well with an imperfect door, but he explained that man's happiness was more precarious than a boy could understand. "Once you acknowledge truth to yourself," he said, "then you're stuck with it. Anything less won't work."

At the time I hardly knew what any of this meant, nor did I care. I was too much concerned with managing my overgrown carcass. In the old days, as I already called them, I had been immensely but aimlessly active, and the nearest I ever came to useful work was watching Mike Doonan at the forge. By now the Madigans were all at some sort of work—Tom went to town every day, Dick worked after school in the drugstore, and Terry did odd jobs for Mike—especially automobile jobs: Mike himself never intended to be a mechanic and the business forced itself on him and in spite of himself he had to patch tires and sell gasoline and fix engines—a job that constantly puzzled and irritated him; but the more he insulted his customers and cursed their machines, the more they came to him. I went down to see Terry sometimes, but all I could do was sit on a running board while he measured gasoline in two-gallon tins or pried loose a tire. I felt an envy of him; his fore-arms already showed the muscles of a mechanic, and he wore a visored cap and blue overalls—yet I remember that he never put on airs, not to me, anyway, though he had the right to. But now I was tasting man's work too, and I began to admire my forearms, and I got a white painter's cap from Steele's (free) and cocked it on the side of my head. Whether I knew it or not, Seth was giving me an idea.

When school ended that June, he offered to hire me.

"You mean, regular man's work?" mater asked.

I knew what she meant; she meant the sort of work a "man" did. When anything had to be done at our house, carrying ashes, say, or beating rugs, or putting up screens, or moving beds up and down stairs, mater always got a "man." It used to be Patrick, but by now he grumbled at having to touch anything besides the garden—and even there he considered himself as the professional in charge—so that mater spent a lot of time getting men. Father had no objection to doing some of the things, but oddly enough mater refused to let him. His talents were better used in other ways, she said, and he wasn't the least bit mechanical anyway, and in fact she disapproved of that sort of work. It was much more suitable that a "man" should do it.

I tried to give a professional color to my job. Cabinetmaking, I said; woodworking; maybe some farming—Seth had a horse and cow, chickens, a big vegetable garden, and I thought Marvin might want me to help with the hay.

"You aren't used to work like that, Ralph."

"I certainly am!"

She had spoken with perfect justice as always, but I snapped at her angrily. It seemed to me that she had failed to recognize my character. A few months earlier I might have been a lump of idle flesh—I could hardly remember that remote past, and it didn't count anymore. "I can do a man's work," I said, flexing the muscles in my arms. "I've been doing it right along—" But I knew the words were no good.

"You'll have to see what your father thinks," she said calmly.

"He'll think it's all right."

Strange that a boy of fifteen should have to talk his parents into letting him work for pay. They knew that work was good, they believed in the natural and the simple, I think they felt a kinship with the world of the Kingsleys, yet a gentle illusion separated them from it all. They kept themselves clear of the lower order of reality and reserved themselves—and me—for higher things. I suppose the word "gentleman" was seldom spoken in our house; we were all wise enough in the ways of taste to feel the absurdity of the word itself; but nonetheless the ancient customs of gentility regulated us. We were taught to preserve ourselves from useful work and to improve our many idle hours. We drew and read and made music and played games, but if any household task needed doing, it was assumed that we would behave like clumsy but delightful amateurs. My brother Steve is still unable to drive a nail straight or to wash a teacup without conveying the suggestion that he has never done it before.

But my father, as I predicted, thought it was all right. He had an old dream of farms and the good life, and though he had never turned it into reality, he saw himself now as a patron of all country affairs. "Why, it's an opportunity," he said. "Would that I could join you just for old times' sake, but I fear my active days are behind me. Not," he added, "that I can boast of heroic activity at any time—"

"Isn't Seth Kingsley older than you are?"

He smiled—I say it now realizing the cruelty of my question.

"Why, Ralph, I am only a scholar, a mere creature of words. I often wonder if a man of tools and sinews isn't better off in the end. At least he is unaffected by thought; he is cleared of all gross humors, to use an ancient phrase."

"Thought!" I almost shouted it. "Why, Seth—he—why, I never heard anyone think as much as he does!"

My father smiled again with more assurance. "I have no doubt of it—in fact, I've heard him think a few times myself."

"Well, I mean—he thinks as much as you do, or anybody."

"More loudly, I'm sure."

I realized that I had been led into folly, and kept silent.

"Yes, indeed," he went on. "Seth Kingsley is our most notable cracker-barrel philosopher and Compton ought to be proud of him, though I'm afraid he is not genial enough for popularity. People are almost afraid of his severity. But my point, Ralph, was simply that he worked primarily with his hands—and I was expressing a certain envy of him. The contemplative life is somewhat anachronistic in these modern times."

"Anyway," I said, "he can teach me a lot."

"Oh, by all means," father agreed, and then continued with something of enthusiasm: "That craftsmanship of his is one of the ancient virtues—a peculiarly personal virtue that our world of machines is destroying. Learn what you can of it before it is too late. You say he intends to hire you?"

"Yes."

"For what rate and time?"

"Just whenever he needs a helper—sort of like odd jobs. He said he'll pay me fifteen cents an hour."

"Are you worth that?"

"Sure—I'm worth more than that."

"It makes you a professional, you know. It isn't just a game any more."

"Yes, I know."

But I didn't know, and father didn't either.

◄ CHAPTER 17 ►

THE GARRETSONS had at this time no summer place, no house
by sea or mountain lake; but they took vacation trips and
stayed at hotels. Compton grew hot and humid, and the best
people went away—and we went away too, but not all at the
same time or to the same place.

Mater took Jean and the three young ones up to Crawford
Notch, where she could talk with her peers and take rigorous
mountain walks. In her prime mater was a notable walking
lady, and after several seasons at Crawford she had achieved
a position of command. I think it must have been her life's
greatest joy to climb the steeps of Mount Webster in company
with a chosen few, to observe the phenomena of rock and rare
plant, of insect and bird, and to enjoy the whole wild northern
grandeur without ever speaking of it.

My father was not averse to Crawford, but he felt a need of
escaping his family and so devoted himself to trout fishing in
the Rangeleys in Maine. It was an acquired taste, picked up
chiefly after he sorted over his father's possessions and discovered a fine lot of rods and reels. So in half-humorous fashion
he ventured into the far country of forest and lake, and later
took Steve and me along. I found that fishing was an even more
serious and ritualistic affair than pedestrianism, and was
ashamed of father's lightmindedness and ineptitude. He pad-
dled clumsily, made noises at the wrong time, snapped off his

flies, and worst of all treated the whole matter as a childish diversion. We used to stay at a boarding camp called the Parmacheenee Club, where guides and veteran sportsmen maintained a fanatic rivalry, and we in contrast behaved like idle dilettantes. Father enjoyed the beauty of the great forests—I remember how he walked the trails with an air of sweet serenity, like a pure philosopher at large, but Steve and I were embarrassed by our inferior standing in the sporting society. I have never become a "fisherman" in that sense, and now that I look back I can better appreciate my father's humors. He made light of all professional solemnities.

But that summer when I turned sixteen I elected to remain faithful to Seth—or rather to the Kingsley family. Mater invited me to Crawford, and I felt the temptation of the wondrous mountains—but she reminded me that the society there would be very good for me and instantly a vision of the best Ladies and Gentlemen flashed upon my inward eye. Father and Steve set out on the more adventurous trip to the Parmacheenee Club, and I felt the taste of grief in my throat. But I had made the choice, and obscurely I realized that my manhood was at stake.

So it turned out. Manhood may be a variable substance, but what I have of it springs most evidently from the work of that summer.

At first I was simply a low order of odd-job boy. I cut a little wood, but summer is no time for woodcutting. I weeded and watered. I hoed long rows of beans and corn. I trimmed the grass and shrubs, and Seth taught me to swing a scythe.

I learned, first of all, the difference between active exercise and work. The scythe seemed a splendid tool, and Seth used it with a sweet and dainty ease that delighted me. I knew enough now to respect its yard-long razor edge—no more inept carving of thumbs!—and the fine long swing of body and arms came easy to me: but, oh, the labor of it! I set forth to mow the old sheep paddock behind the barn—a quarter acre of tall grass and weed, and the first few strokes were like the first strokes in a swim—liquid and flowing and powerful. Then fatigue and ache, sweat and pain; the sun like fire in that windless enclosure; the blade faltering and digging perversely into the earth; the grass ragged and bent; and the task stretching out endlessly ahead. That quarter acre seemed as big as a farm.

Seth had gone off that day and I was alone there, keeping at it with a chopping and clumsy persistence. The ease of stroke had gone entirely; the blade itself had turned sullen, like a piece of untempered iron. But under the running sweat and the heat pounding in my skull I knew that men did work like this and in the end they mastered all the hostile elements —steel, grass, heat, earth. I knew that the blade would come to life again in Seth's hands, and the grass would fall in measured ranks. It was my aim to be a man, so I kept going.

I may not have done thirty cents' worth of good that July morning, but I could have labored no harder for thirty pieces of gold.

"You'll have a stroke," Mrs. Kingsley said from the fence near the west corner. "Don't you know enough to wear a hat in sun like this?" She herself wore a white mobcap, and she carried an empty pan in her right hand. She had been taking the scraps to the hens.

I rested the scythe and moved my back slowly into an erect position. The work I had done seemed poor and ragged as I looked over it. "A terrible job," I said bitterly. "He'll fire me when he sees it."

"No doubt," she said, paying no attention to the mangled grass. "But not till I do some talking first. What's he want to make you mow out here in the midday sun for? Mow early and late and rake in the middle is what they used to say—only now they use the machines. You come in out of that heat. I wouldn't be capable of carrying your carcass."

"The sun doesn't bother me."

"No more than a bullet don't—till it hits you." She went

off still talking. "You come along in. I've got lunch made for you, and Marvin says he can use a boy on the lower meadow after noon—he's got five loads to get in."

So I put away the scythe and dipped arms and face in the spring-water trough in the old cattle yards and drank from the little round silver jet, and I felt empty and light and shaky. I wandered across the hot yard in a dream state and paused in the cool woodshed to dry. No balm of spirit, no ease after toil, has ever been like that. As a man grows older, he never escapes; he is on duty day and night. But between jobs a boy on a farm can walk on air and drink the milk of paradise.

"Spread that shirt in the sun a few minutes," she said, tossing a towel at me. "Martha's gone to visit over to Marstons, so you can take off anything you've a mind to."

I remember the deep noon silence of earth asleep under the sun, the quiet singing of the locusts and light chirp of sparrows in the shady maples. The tiredness in my muscles had already passed and a stream of sweet well-being flowed through me. I forgot the stubborn scythe and the ragged mowing, the heat and ache and bad work, and I idled there in the woodshed door like a small complacent deity surveying his private heavenly property.

"You'll have to come to lunch," Mrs. Kingsley called out after a few minutes. "I can't keep it for you."

I shall always hear that voice. It turned little words into arrows. It chided me, mocked me, bossed me—all at once; it accused me of folly and youth and innocence, yet its accent was constant laughter. If Mrs. Kingsley ever announces the first crack of doom (and who could do it better?) the wise will see the humor of it.

"Seth won't eat this green stuff, so you'll have to." New peas, picked a half hour earlier—enough for a feast. And bacon and hot biscuits and honey. All for me—she had tea for herself and a dish of peas. "Green stuff is what makes women, he says. It ought to make us strong as an ox, I suppose."

The sweet-ticking clock, the stir of country air in the windows, Mrs. Kingsley on her stool by the counter, Ralph at the end of the yellow covered table eating all he could eat. I had a notion what those biscuits were for, and sure enough—after the bacon and peas and the milk and honey came a strawberry shortcake the likes of which this modern age scarcely knows. Golden short biscuits, berries mellowed in sugar, cream too thick to whip—there I sat with enough of it for three before me.

"You think this is what makes men?" I asked with a grin.

"*He* does, sure enough. It's made him, anyhow—the amount he's eaten these thirty years. I told him he'd better stay today; the biscuits won't be so good warmed over."

I sat there stuffed and happy in the summer noon until a screen door slammed and men's voices sounded from a distance.

"They're through dinner," she said. "You can do whatever you're mind to—work or not work. I didn't tell Marvin you'd come."

We heard horse noises and creak of wheels.

"Why, sure I'll work, except I'm full of shortcake."

"Well, put a hat on you."

But I went reluctantly, like a desert traveler leaving his oasis behind.

"Martha said she might be down later. She's done considerable haying in times past—I used to myself when I didn't know any better. Take one of Seth's forks with you."

I worked five hours. The routine of pitching and loading and stowing repeated itself exactly as it did on a thousand farms that same afternoon, and all the familiar details repeated themselves—the sweat and dust, the sun heat, the creak of loaded wheels on rough stubble, the swish of the forked hay swinging up over the rick sides and high to the far top of the mound, and then the long plod back to the barn—easy and slow now, and a chance to breathe deep and wipe away sweat and pass under shade trees—and then the fiercer, hotter struggle with hay in the dust-choked mow, the pitching off and the stowing in the airless furnace heat of the barn loft. And after that the little rest in clean maple shade, the feel of breeze almost cool on the wet body, and the drink—the long bitter sweetish drink of vinegar, molasses, water, called switchel on that farm and other names on other farms; and then finally, after the drink and the talk in the shade, the whole round again —the return in the empty rick trotting over shorn meadows to the cocked hay beyond.

Marvin rode the wagon, Jim and I pitched up to him, and two of Jim's youngsters stayed with Marvin up on the load and bounced and yelled. A third raked the leavings with the big bull rake, though later on he quit and went swimming and left us to rake as well as pitch. If anyone talked, Marvin did. When Jim said anything it was to give advice: get it up there in big bundles and it'll come off better, he said; give pop a chance to load it right; watch the kids—they're all over the load. He spoke in brief grunts and worked with ponderous power like a steam-driven mechanism. But Marvin spoke from the summit of hay as though he were addressing the cattle in the north pasture, and no avalanche of forkfuls deterred him. "Last time I hired a boy," he yelled, treading his way above hay level, "he started out pretty good—pitched up in good shape—and I figgered I'd made a fair enough deal. But by thunder, next time I looked round he wa'n't there, no sign of him at all. 'Where's Elmer?' I hollers to Jim down there—him workin' along like one o' them power derricks the way he always does. 'Hey? What's that?' he says. 'Where's the boy?' I says. 'Where's Elmer?' 'Dunno,' he says. 'Ain't seen him lately, come to think of it.' So we figgers he's quit on us. 'Wouldn't think a feller'd quit like that without sayin' a word,' I says to Jim. He wasn't a stout feller at all, but he'd done plenty work before, and it seemed funny to me he'd go off like that without sayin' a word about it. I says to Jim that's what comes of gettin' a boy to do a man's work, and we kep' right on a-loadin'."

He reached for the reins and drove off to the next pair of

cocks. Jim and I were there with the first forkfuls before he turned.

"Well, we drove in to unload, same as we always did." He had to shout through flying hay. "No sign of Elmer anywhere —I thought he might have gone up for a drink or something. So I says to hell with him and commenced to pitch off. We was in a hurry that day, and I made her fly, I tell you—and about halfway down the load I drove my fork into a big bundle I had laid right center here, and by gracious it come up hard. I give it a heave—put my back into it, I tell you—and it come a-flyin'. 'Well,' Jim says—he was up in the mow—'there's Elmer.' 'Where?' I says—it was all hay and dust and I couldn't see very good. 'I don't see nothin',' I hollers. 'You just pitched him up,' Jim says. 'Well, by God,' I says, 'you must have pitched him in the first time.' 'Reckon I did,' Jim says. Jim you know, never'll use two words if one will do, but when he gets to workin' you want to stand clear."

I noticed that Jim was grinning, but I was unable to read his thoughts. He didn't pause in his work.

"What happened to Elmer?" I asked.

"That's all that happened to him, far as I know," Marvin said. "He wa'n't no good to me after that."

"How come," I said, thinking it over, "you're hiring another boy?"

"No choice," he shouted. "A man can make good wages in the mills now—better'n I can pay. Seth told me you'd work cheap, and I figgered you had sense enough not to get pitched up the way Elmer did. I believe you got weight enough so Jim could tell the difference anyhow. Think so, Jim?"

"Well, I wouldn't wonder," Jim said quietly. "The fork would get hold of him nice, though."

Marvin nodded. "Tenderer than Elmer was, that's a fact."

I remember the slow hours of that afternoon. We worked through a vast desert of time—and it was only two o'clock. Another eternity, a lifetime of toil, and it was half-past three.

Back ached, lips stuck together, hands blistered—and still the
hay had to be bundled and lifted, thrown up into the face of
the burning sun.

"Feller from the city was out watchin' us one day," Marvin
shouted. "He says why didn't we wait till fall and then burn it
all right over. He never see so much trouble just to get a piece of
grass tidy."

No lessening of heat and blaze, no change in heaven or
earth—and always more hay to get, more cocks of it standing
ready in the far corners of the farm.

"Nuther feller says why didn't we rig a big bag on the mower
and collect it right when we cut it the way folks do on their
lawns . . ."

The first long shadow took me by surprise. The wineglass elm
stood between us and the westering sun as we stopped to pick
up a half dozen cocks in a pocket of meadow made by a loop
of the brook. Time had moved. The shade was touched with
evening.

"Last load," Jim grunted, seeing my weariness.

"Like as not to get showers this weather," Marvin said, nodding at white cloud shapes far in the north. "I'll sleep sounder
if I know it's all under cover."

The two youngsters had gone home by then, and I managed
to climb up on the hay for a last ride home. I lay inert as a bag
of grain, not hot and wet anymore, but floating on a fragrant
prickly cloud. Jim trudged ahead of us; Marvin drove without
speaking much until he came up to the barn door. There he
turned the wagon and backed it in, and the horses stamped and
snorted a good deal, and Marvin yelled orders.

"Unload tomorrow," he said. "You can stay right there if
you'd rather."

So that ended the labor, and I was grateful. "I didn't suppose you'd stop till you got it all in."

"Chores to do," Marvin said sharply, implying that I should
have known. "A farmer—" He slid down to the shaft and began

unhooking the traces. "A farmer is like a man playin' a brass band all by himself, day and night. If I had six or seven more men here to work I could get a few things done."

He gave each horse a slap on the rump and they ambled off to drink. Jim had already let the cows in. I could hear the clatter of stanchions and the baritone blowings.

"You been a good worker today," he said abruptly. "Likely you're tired enough, but you got a right to be." He thrust a dollar bill at me. "That suit you? I aim to mow the west meadow tomorrow if it holds dry, so come over Thursday if you'd care to."

"Sure," I said. "Thanks. I'll be here."

He turned away and went after the horses.

I leaned over and rubbed the neck of one of the big collies and showed him the dollar. "See? That's wages." Then I wandered back toward Seth's. "I made a dollar," I said to Martha.

"That's more than he pays me," she said. "He must think you're a good man." She smiled her wide, frank smile—I felt almost as though she had put an arm round my shoulders. I loved Martha in those days—not in folly, I think, but with an almost mystic devotion. Her beauty seemed to me like country beauty, nourished on eggs and cream and wind and rain and sun.

"Why, sure," I said, not without pride. I had never felt so much like a man before. It seemed to me that she smiled with admiration. "He told me to come back on Thursday."

"I was going to help him today too," she said, "but when mom said you were doing it I knew I wouldn't have to."

Irony? I looked at her warm smile and wondered. In an instant I turned into an uncomfortable boy again, though somehow I realized that she had a right to be ironic if she chose: all beautiful women, it seemed to me, possessed that privilege. But I loved her nonetheless.

I walked over the ridge toward home rather slowly that evening. The air was still full of summer heat, but my body felt cool and dry. A heavy pulse beat against my temples—a dull ache left by the sun-glare, and I meandered a little along the roadside. Hands, I noticed, were torn, and I wondered how they'd be on Thursday. I wondered if I'd ever be fit to do such work.

On Thursday I returned to the hayfields, and Friday too, and my hands hardened and I learned to forget about time entirely and to work as though I were working forever. And after that I learned how to handle horses and cattle—what to say and where to whack them; I learned about feeding and watering, and harnessing and milking; I drove Marvin's workteam and Seth's little mare, and they knew me and accepted me as one of themselves. I learned about all the apparatus that supports life—the wood and metal, the stone and mortar, the very foundations of the earth, and I learned that a good man could control and master all those materials. I remember watching Jim cut and bore some iron straps and bolt them across a wagon floor—and I had always thought that only specialists in shops could handle iron that way; and Jim and Marvin and Ralph put a new foundation under the west end of the cow barn, with jacks and blocks and wooden forms and a lot of hard digging and long mixing of concrete; and we worked with pipes and pumps and the mysteries of running water, with solder and the white heat of blowtorch. And of course we farmed it—with hoeing and cultivating and harvesting and the ceaseless battle against pest and blight and natural evil.

I had to master the problem of getting up early enough. It took me several weeks to realize that a farm day begins in summer at four-thirty, an hour unknown to me. But as the new life got hold of me I resolved to live it right. It was Seth who had got me started, and Seth drove off to his day's work before seven; I didn't see him till late in the afternoon. I decided to get up at five, and found that the Garretson routine included no provision for such a scheme. My father smiled at my nonsense and the cook ignored it. But a new Ralph had come into being, as yet unrecognized by his family. I willed myself awake in the dawn; I tiptoed down to the silent kitchen, shoes in hand, and fixed a bowl of shredded wheat and milk, and plenty of bread and butter and jam; and long before six was on the road to the farm. Yet even so I had to overcome objections: father said I was losing sleep; Nora said it was no fit breakfast for a boy, and it was all a foolish notion anyway—but mater was off in the mountains then and I won.

It was after this that Seth began to take me with him—as his helper, he said seriously. In his building operations he sometimes worked alone, and he explained that he often wished he had another pair of hands. So he used mine—or pretended to. And I did rough sawing for him and learned to cut square; and I nailed up boarding and drove nails with the true-ringing blows of a carpenter. I perceived the geometry of building, the notches and angles and joints, and the miracle of finished work where all the parts make one natural unit. I had been looking at doors and mantels and porches and dormer windows all my life without seeing the subtle logic that made them.

I wore my painter's cap these days and a pair of overall pants and a blue work shirt, and I felt like the finest fellow in the county. I bought a hammer at Steele's—their best, a dollar thirty-five—and carried it in one of my big back pockets. I stuck a bit of carpenter's pencil in my hat or behind my ear. I used technical words: miter, quarter round, plate, stud—all new, at least to me. I patronized my old friends and hardly spoke to my brother Steve at all. It angered me that ladies looked at me with polite amusement.

"Why, Ralph, what *are* you up to?" We were putting a window in Mrs. Vane's pantry, and she came along just as I was prying off the clapboards. "You look like a regular workingman. Are you sure you know what you are doing here? It sounds to me as though you were breaking down the house." She gave me a bright social smile.

"Maybe I am," I mumbled sourly, and jabbed hard with the little crowbar.

"I suppose Lucy knows what you are up to—she has such wonderful ideas about—" Mrs. Vane stopped and glanced around. "Is Mr. Kingsley here? I just want to be sure it is all right . . ."

I knew Seth was inside and could hear all she said, but I was mad and kept quiet.

"Did Mr. Kingsley tell you to do this?" Her bright voice was strained with disapproval.

"Well, we got to make a hole here, don't we?"

"Now, Ralph, suppose you wait just a minute. I'm not sure this is all right at all—I think we ought to see Mr. Kingsley. Ralph, I said stop! I insist—my goodness, I never hired a boy like you to come and break my house to pieces."

Seth came out of the back door then and nodded gravely. "It'll be all right—it just sounds bad to hear those nails coming out like that."

"Well, if you are keeping an eye on him I won't worry, but I must say to come out here and find one of the Garretson boys simply whacking my house with a great iron bar—is he really helping you, Mr. Kingsley—I mean, is he—?"

"Right-hand man," Seth said. "Don't know how I could work without him."

Mrs. Vane was a well-trained lady. She smiled all round and said it was perfectly charming.

"No need of ripping it up like this," Seth said quietly. "Unless you need kindling wood, that is."

"What? You mean I shouldn't have done it?"

"Well, if you'll wait till I saw across the top there, you can lift the whole piece right out."

Seth went back into the house, and I appreciated the way he had handled us—but I knew I had acted like a fool.

Yet fool or not I had made a choice: come what may I was

faithful to Seth. I became from then on a Garretson renegade, and being what I was I put more emotion and prejudice and general folly into it than was decent. I even fought the opportunities my father bestowed upon me.

"Ralph, your mater and I feel that another school would be desirable. Don't you agree?"

"You mean, no more Alcott? Why, you bet I agree! What a dead dump that is—I mean, nobody really learns anything there and it's a sissy place—I mean, it isn't run right."

Father smiled. "Well, perhaps not. I've written to Mr. Hooke at Lincoln, and he is going to take both you and Steve. That was my school too, you know. Mr. Hooke is a great man."

"You mean, I've got to go away?"

"Yes, of course."

It came so suddenly I had no defense.

"I don't want to go, Father. I'd rather go here and stay home."

"You mean high school?"

"Sure—if I've got to go at all."

"Oh, no, Ralph—this school wouldn't be suitable at all."

"Well, why not, for heaven's sake? Don't Harve and Sid go there? Don't a lot of good people go?"

"That isn't quite it, Ralph. We want the best for you. This Compton School is not equipped for really good teaching— few small high schools are." He talked at length about it. In the old days of the theocracy, he said, education was very highly prized, but in these present times commercial standards prevailed. The taxpayers admired roads and drains, but they saw no good in intellectual training—nor in moral training, for that matter. Democracy, he felt, was undergoing degeneration —the nation was filling itself with strangers whose chief purpose was to make money, and unfortunately they had the power of franchise. I don't remember all his discourse; I didn't care for abstract argument, nor did I know how to answer him. But I know he spoke about my intellectual heritage, as he called

it, and he rather hoped I would elect a career of scholarship
(his words, those—and more pompous than usual with him);
he reminded me that my great-grandfather Ralph G. (for
whom I was named) had been the most distinguished moral
philosopher of his day in New England—and he explained that
moral philosophy was just another name for human wisdom
of any sort. Grandfather Ralph, he said, covered the field of
knowledge from astronomy to zoology.

"But Lincoln—" I said in despair. "Isn't it a bunch of
snobs?"

I didn't know Mr. Hooke, he explained. A regular old
Roman, a man of supreme justice, and a sportsman through
and through. One word described him and the school: *virtus,*
the word he had chosen long ago for the motto. It wasn't just
virtue, father said; it was manhood at its best.

I couldn't answer, but from then on I had bad dreams.

"Take the best schooling you can get," Seth Kingsley said.
"Many a boy would work his heart out for such a chance."

❦ CHAPTER 18 ❧

I WORKED right up to mid-September, though mater kept interrupting with preparations. Trips to dentist on Newbury Street, trips to Collins and Fairbanks to buy suits and to Jordan Marsh to buy all sorts of other stuff—and far too much of it. Steve and I were equipped as though we were about to spend two years beyond reach of Washington Street.

Steve accepted gentleman's dress gracefully, but I fought every item—one by one. The felt hat, the stiff collar (high and choking), the starched shirt, the vest, the garters for socks, the high black shoes with leather soles—I swore and stamped and grumped, I caused suffering and ill temper through all the family to no purpose whatever; mater prevailed. When we finally set off for school I remember how sleek and easy Steve looked, with creases and knots and buttons all in place, and what a rumpled and angry mess I was with tie slipping below the collar button and vest riding up above the pants and everything binding and wrinkling.

Neither father nor mater knew that I was a lost soul forever. They gave me more patience than I deserved, and concealed their distress under good advice. Father practiced his irony on me, but not cruelly. Boys, he said, were always reluctant to do themselves good; they rebelled at everything from wisdom to fine clothes. He assumed that I was passing through a difficult phase, as he called it, and mater said it was simply adolescence; but the emotions that burned inside those fine clothes of mine back there in my sixteenth autumn are still burning now—controlled, I hope, by a bit more sense than I then owned, but steadily burning nonetheless. Perhaps I still rebel at wisdom; it is a long time since I've worn what my father would call fine clothes.

I had said good-by to the Kingsleys with unmanly tears. Martha had put an arm round my shoulders and kissed me, a long solid kiss on the mouth that stopped the breath in my throat and flooded my face with blushes and very wet tears, and I hugged her for all I was worth and I hugged Mrs. Kingsley —who said she was too old to kiss anybody—and I was so full of shame and grief and love I couldn't speak. She said I probably had more stuff than I knew what to do with, but after I got there she'd send me something good to eat—she doubted if I'd get enough at meals, with the appetite I had built up that summer. Seth told me not to be foolish about school; he only wished he had had such a chance—he might not have to be pounding nails for a living now. A man by himself could learn about as much as a smart dog could learn, he said; you got real wisdom only by beginning where other men stopped—sort of like building a lookout on a mountain.

I hardly heard him, of course, but I knew that I was going away from my best friends—and it seemed like the end of a happy life. Lincoln School (still officially the Rectory) was only fifteen miles from Compton, though on a different train line—and on this solemn first journey we were going in a hired automobile, father, too, but not mater; but I felt the numb, speechless grief of a Siberian exile. We piled the luggage into what father called the tonneau, and some in a rack on the running board, and I was immensely and absurdly conscious of my fine muscles and my ability to lift small trunks. I knew that the car was a rare adventure, a Rambler with a lot of brasswork and John Hegarty in a long gray duster to drive it (father wore linen cap and duster too, as though he had always been correctly equipped for motoring) and I got the front seat as a reward for being ill tempered, and off we went with dust and waving hands. The three kids were concerned only with the car, of course, and mater expressed a kindly farewell—she always shooks hands with us, but Jean gave us a hearty kiss.

I was glad we turned right from our driveway. A trip through the center of Compton in that car and in those clothes would have caused me shame. Suppose Dick Madigan saw me—or even Terry, in his mechanic's overalls, waving an honest, grease-blackened hand. I shrank in my seat until we reached open country.

Very soon we came to the gates of Lincoln, and the lawns and the playing fields and the gabled buildings and all the solid presence of a large institution. It took us in. There were masters, official welcomers, old boys with cries of delight and manly handshaking; there were new boys, and parents and baggage—and a few motorcars like ours. There were rooms to find, and halls and long corridors, and many faces.

But until evening it all seemed unbelievable, like pictures of a distant country. Then the rector took charge. We had finished dinner in the vaulted refectory hall, and at one end the dignitaries sat at a high table on the platform, English fashion. Father was up there (he had persuaded John Hegarty to stay over until after dinner) and a few other Old Boys who had also brought their sons, and various people I didn't know—and of course Mr. Hooke at the center. Even as he sat, his presence dominated the assembly; his powerful red countenance, his hair like white spun silk round the great dome, his black clericals, his voice now and then booming above all the rest—I felt and we all felt that he had a particular eye on each one there.

"Fellows—"

That was the word, the miraculous synthesis of substance and spirit. The place became a temple.

He had walked round the table to the edge of the platform,

and he drew up his solid frame to its full six feet two and stretched an open hand toward us. The spun silk glowed in the overhead light.

"Fellows—this—this that we here feel and share, young and old together again in our beloved hall, ready for the great adventure of a new year—this is the Lincoln spirit."

The great voice ceased and let the words stand. No one breathed.

"You may travel the world round, you may live even as long as I have lived, but nowhere among men will you find loyalty such as this. We have created here, all of us together, you as well as I—indeed, you more than I, for you are the very body and blood—I say we have created together a community of spirit. I look about me, and I say from the bottom of my heart: This is Lincoln."

I had come in fear and disgust, but now the spirit of Lincoln choked my throat and moistened my eyes. All of us there felt an ecstasy of devotion. Steve sitting next to me had the face of a boy at prayer.

The rector spoke with a sort of measured power—slowly and intimately, and with immense confidence.

So it all began, and from that moment the Lincoln spirit never relaxed its vigilance. It was nothing like the soft and benevolent culture of the Bronson Alcott; rather the entire school lived as though it were a football squad training for the Big Game. If we didn't play on the First Team, or the Second, Third, or Fourth, we played on the Maroon, or the White, or Bowditch, or Endicott—and if after all that we still didn't play, we "went out for" manager, and carried water and set up the tackling dummy, or if at last we didn't even do that we backed up the rest by sitting in the stands and yelling. It was my intention to do nothing—not even yell—but after I was weighed and measured I was told to report to the Third Squad.

"What for?" I said to the young sportsman who had recorded my dimensions—Mr. Bowling, who taught history and coached football.

"Beginner, aren't you?"

"I never played much football."

"Promising build to start with. We'll turn some of that fat to muscle soon enough."

Fat, he said. His face beamed with immense and healthy superiority; his blue eyes glowed with eager sportsmanship.

"I want to see you a Second Team regular before the season is over," he said with intense good will. "You've got the weight —good legs under you. You won't know yourself after a year of Lincoln training. Why, you might win your Big L next year —have you thought of that? Eh? Have you thought of that?" He clapped me on the shoulder, moving me on toward the door. "Now jog three or four laps every day for the first couple of weeks after practice—just jog, you know. And good luck, Garretson—we're counting on you."

I think I grinned foolishly. If I had any active thoughts of my own they were ineffective against the Lincoln system. That little hint about my fat, the glittering hope of the Big L, the light application of spirit at the end—and before I knew it I was charging a dummy and grunting through scrimmage and jogging three or four laps. I suppose I must have done some studying too. For a month my body ached in every joint and muscle; at evening study hour I squirmed wearily and propped my head and watched the clock. But studying hardly seemed essential. Classes were conducted with discipline and even severity, and no one thought of enjoying them—it was still the era of classical Toryism when lessons were learned and recited, learned and recited, forever and ever. Caesar and Cicero, the kings of England, *L'Allegro* and *Il Penseroso*; Cerberus— well, he was a kind of dog with three heads who guarded the door of—of the underworld (hell was a cuss word in those days); but who Caesar was we never really found out, though we spent nine months sweating over his ablative absolutes. Algebra and French, and a kind of social geography that demonstrated that all was for the best in the best possible world, particularly in Lincoln, Massachusetts. I have to remind myself that the war in Europe had then been going on for over two years, and we Lincolnians looked upon it as an immense sporting event—not in the light sense (sport was anything but "light" to us), but in the Spartan do-or-die sense which we accepted with extreme reverence. The Allies were our team, and the opponents were a bunch of blackguards who played dirty; beyond that we knew nothing about it.

As a new boy, I remained for a time lower than the insects; but I noted that a few new boys managed to become admirable almost at once—some because of athletic brilliance, some for mysterious reasons of personality. They knew; they had words and clothes and facial expressions. Steve got on much faster than I did—before I knew it he was second assistant manager of the Maroon soccer team—in fact, I hadn't known there was a Maroon soccer team; and then somehow he became a junior assistant to the advertising staff of the Lincoln *Record*. Steve was never one of the heroes, though he prospered steadily. But in contrast I was looked upon as a slob, and was treated with insult. It was always my intention to be knowing, to have a veteran's privileges, if not a hero's, but for that first year, at least, I remained among the hunted.

"Raff," they called me, and then "Raff Ga'atson." When I first came a boy from Georgia had so spoken it—he was new too, and roomed across the hall—and a great hoot of derision swept the corridor. "Who all is this yere Raff Ga'atson we done been hea'in' about?" And for a time the Georgian was fair game for every wag in the school: "Cunnel Culpeppah, suh," we called him, though his name was McNutt. I remember his pink, babyish anger about the whole business, and how he turned against me as the author of his sorrow—though it was none of my doing; and in time they made a pet of him and he enjoyed his celebrity. But the name stuck to me: Raff Ga'atson —and then Raff, Raff, repeated forever.

My first serious sin against the code took place on the last Saturday in October, the day of the Essex game. Our Big Game with Saint Luke's was always the last of the season and this year would be played on their field; so the Essex game ranked as the major home game and was designated officially as a Big Day, with classes suspended in the morning and alumni meetings and minor events of all sorts—a soccer final, a Fourth Team game of football with Essex, a cross-country meet, the finals of the fall tennis tournament, and later a concert and dance. The one group that had nothing much to do was the remnant of the Third Team. The Second Team had the privilege of dressing and sitting on the varsity bench, with a precious chance of being sent in; but the dubs and beginners who still made up the Third Team were set adrift as part of the cheering public. The Fourth Team, I might add for clarity's sake, consisted of youngsters and lightweights.

For weeks I had plugged along as a low order of football beginner. My duty was to give opposition to the Seconds, whose duty in turn was to do the same for the Firsts. I had become simply a hole to be opened up by opposing tackles and ends and charged at by blocking backs. My universal body-aches had given way to separate bruises, and I realized that Mr. Bowling had predicted correctly. The Lincoln system was tougher than I had had any notion of. I still jogged the weary four laps, lugging the heavy armor of pads and the cleated shoes.

But those wondrous autumn days, and the woods flaming red and orange, and the cold sweetness of the air—whenever I looked up suddenly from my duties I felt a choke of breath and a pressure round my heart. Life was elsewhere than here, life was smoldering on the hills and running free with the cool west wind, life was out there on the roads and farms. I dreamed constantly of the Kingsleys, of Seth and Martha and Mrs. Kingsley, and the old house and the sanctuary beside the burning stove. I dreamed of getting back there, and of being my whole self once more.

So on that famous Saturday of the Essex game I skipped out. Right after breakfast, before eight, I left the quadrangle and the cloisters behind me, skirted the still-empty playing fields, followed the back road toward East Lincoln, and once out of sight set a furious and joyous pace for myself. I felt as though a strong spring had shot me out of bondage; I snuffed the keen air and dashed at the hills like a runaway colt; I sang and whistled and hallooed; for miles I seemed to float without touching earth, like a skimming swallow. Somewhere in the small of my back a galvanic charge of energy released itself, and nothing in me would stay quiet.

Yet—fifteen miles, not counting the ones I went astray. Earth began to strike hard against my feet; the sun grew hotter, the store of energy passed, and I walked like a mortal.

With aid of the old topographical map I had brought from home (for this very use) I came into North Compton and struck southward across country. In our part of the world there are too many thickets and swamps and steeps for practical traveling off the roads, but I knew the country well enough here and managed to come over the ridge and down through the orchards right to Seth's barn. No dogs barked till I walked into the yard, and then they knew me.

Nearly noon, just dinnertime, and they seemed almost to be expecting me.

"Here's Ralph," Martha said with a shining smile from within. They both stood looking at me as though I were the funniest thing they'd seen that day—Martha almost laughing, Mrs. Kingsley with a twist of her thin mouth that I knew well.

"He's walked it," Mrs. Kingsley said. "You'd know he'd do something crazy—like a dog that don't have any more sense than to run home."

I had been grinning at them like an idiot. "A dog," I said, "can't help his instincts, can he?"

"No more can a boy—when he's hungry. Well, come along in—we'll take you any time, day or night. We got some nice late corn for you almost boiled—I never could see why folks want their corn early when all the other garden stuff has to be et. Corn is fall food, and, Martha, if you'll pour him out some cider he'll drink it right down—I can tell he needs moistening. We got so much cider this year we'll be forced to have a party before it goes to vinegar. He'll be back pretty quick now—I believe I hear the wheels now—he says he feels sort of lonesome without anyone round to ask foolish questions. Take a kettle right over to the hand basin there—Martha'll give you a towel."

When they found that I hadn't been home and wasn't going, there was trouble.

"You ought to," Martha said.

"You'll have to," Mrs. Kingsley said.

When Seth's step sounded at the door she called to him. "You'll have to take him home after dinner—tell them you found him in a ditch somewhere."

Seth looked at me with the gravity I had expected. Then he looked at the women to read their faces, and back at me. "Playing hooky?" he asked.

"Yep. I skipped out."

He nodded with a sort of satisfaction. "Is it as bad as that?"

"I got homesick."

He waited while he thought about it.

"You plan to stay over, or go back today?"

I looked round the kitchen and out of the windows to the late green meadows. "Well—" I began.

He nodded. "We better have dinner."

And after dinner Seth and Mrs. Kingsley had a pitched battle over me: Seth said I better light out for school, she said I had to go home. Man and woman. I was on Seth's side. He said we'd just keep it quiet; she said half the town would know it no matter what we did. He said he had to go over beyond North Compton to see a man about a horse, and he'd carry me that far in the buggy. She said I ought to want to see my own folks—and what would they think when they heard about it?

Finally I said there wasn't time any more; I had to start back, and anyway it would be Thanksgiving pretty soon, and the darned old football would be over for the season and I'd go home then.

"Well," she said at last, "if he's going to North Compton in the buggy is there any reason why I can't go too? I haven't been to ride for a month, and I expect it's the last mild day of the year. Might as well get some good out of all this wicked work, but you'll have to go by the back way—I won't be seen riding through the middle o' town. Folks'll accuse us of kidnaping as it is." She blew sharply through her teeth, and I knew she was laughing.

Seth winked at me. "It's a good thing I had to see that man about a horse."

She put up some supper for me to carry, and she did many other odd jobs, and left directions with Martha about the stove and the beans and the bread, and then fixed herself up in a black coat and hat like a sort of floating island. We squeezed into the one seat and rattled off over the dirt roads, back round by way of West Compton Corners. I could have walked it more quickly, cutting through the way I came, but we had a fine ride along the empty roads in the woods. Mrs. Kingsley commented on everything and peered eagerly one side and the other to see what she could see. She liked the autumn reds and the glitter of late sun, but chiefly she watched for houses and people: she wagged her head over old farms gone to the Poles, and told who had lived there for three generations; she speculated on the parentage of everyone she saw—"Well, he's one of those Hosmer folks—you can tell by the little mouth and chin. My father knew Nathan Hosmer well. But, my land, how things change—look at this sleazy little house here; why, that property belonged to the Harts—you can see their roof right through the gap there. I never saw this house before—a mean kind of place, I must say. Who lives in it?"

I made them leave me a couple of miles beyond North Compton.

I got to school about eight, took a hot shower (the system no longer required cold tubs), ate the rest of my supper (mashed flat from being squeezed in pockets), and got into bed at the ten-o'clock signal. We had beaten Essex, dance music filled the frosty air, everyone felt the festival joy of the football holiday—even I joined it as though I had served loyally in the cheering section. And I slept well, thanks to the rigorous conditioning I had received as a Third Team tackle.

"Garretson, my lad, I didn't see you at the game." It was Lloyd Noble, at breakfast. "I hope my eyes deceived me."

I recognized the threat. Noble was a student counselor from my corridor and the smoothest man in the Sixth Form. He managed the dances and acted in some of the plays, but his great talent lay in realms of fashion and form. His suits were made by a tailor—an item of small note, perhaps; but his shirts were made by a personal shirtmaker. Another man might have suffered ridicule, but not Noble; his tailoring suited him.

The system went to work on me.

"Garretson," said Mr. Latimer, in charge of permissions and absences, "you were reported absent from midday meal on Saturday. Any reason for that?"

At least the system had slipped up on the evening meal. A football victory took precedence.

"Hey, guys, Raff wasn't at the game—did you know that?"

"Raff says he went for a walk instead of going to the game. Is that right, Raff?"

"A nice display of school spirit, if true."

I am told that in England a school game is mainly the concern of those playing it, but with us it involved the sacred honor of all. My voice in the stands was required as positively as the quarterback's in the field. Within three days Ralph Garretson had suffered contempt, scorn, official displeasure, and punishment both legal and extralegal. I accounted for myself before the Student Council, which voted in solemn session that I had failed in school spirit and recommended to the faculty that I be placed on probation for the rest of the term. The faculty on their part concurred and referred my case to the rector, who sent for me. I had grown bewildered by then and was unable to think clearly about what had taken place; possibly I had reached a point of balance between acquiescence and rebellion.

"Sit down, Garretson." A hard chair with arms beside a huge dark desk; the rector sat in a similar chair. Dark woodwork, walls of books, and light from high casements streaming down over his silk-white hair. "So you played a little hooky on Saturday. Sounds natural, I must say."

I relaxed a little. The great time-scarred face seemed genial— more than that, magnetic and even godlike. I ventured a bit of smile, and he nodded agreement.

"Yes, indeed. Boys don't change, and I've been watching them for fifty years. Your father enjoyed taking walks too." He said this last with a weight that alarmed me slightly.

"He still does," I murmured.

He shook his massive head. "There is a time to walk, I grant you. But not in the face of duty, Garretson."

It came then. And I sat and took it. I remember the planes and fissures of that face, and I studied it as one might study a rock to find what slow pressures and erosions had marked it. He talked of obligations and duties and team play. "Do you see, Garretson? Do you understand?"

He looked at me with immense conviction. It was almost as though a stone monument had spoken. I shrank under him.

"Well, Garretson, I think that is all. Kindly remember me to your father and your Uncle Richard. By jove, there's a man— we're mighty proud of Richard Garretson."

I stirred, and a voice half whispered something.

"Eh? What's that? Did you speak?"

It had been my voice. I tried again—or the voice did. "Thoreau," it said.

He heard. His face settled to cold stone. "Well?"

He had scared me, but something down inside kept on talking. "I thought he believed that the individual was the main thing—I mean he took walks sort of as though it were his duty, and right here at Walden he lived all by himself in a cabin—"

"Yes, I know, Garretson."

I lost some of my faith in Thoreau.

"And Emerson," I said, groping. "He was like that too. He said a man's main duty was to be himself—at least, I think he said that."

"How do you happen to read such things, Garretson?"

"Oh, last year, in the school I went to . . ."

"The Alcott School, I believe?"

I nodded in a sort of astonishment, not that he knew the school, but that so vague and innocent a place as the old Bronson Alcott should have armed me for rebellion. Until that moment I had known nothing about it.

The rector stroked his prominent chin. "There are many kinds of people in the world, Garretson—some are leaders, some followers, some observers. Here at Lincoln we have a very high purpose—the highest, I may say. We train leaders here. Now a good leader is a dedicated man—do you understand that, Garretson? He must know what it is to be a follower, just as the young officer first learns to obey orders; he must realize the physical and moral power that lies in co-operation—what we here know as team play; he must know how to wield that power, and what it is to dedicate himself, his own interests and personal desires, to the larger purpose. That's what makes a true leader. Have I been quite clear, Garretson?"

I sighed. "Yes," I said. "I see." I should have said "sir" also;

it was the Lincoln habit to use "sir" constantly to all faculty and gentlemen, but again my old Alcott ways interfered. I felt small and dismal.

"Your Thoreau and your Emerson," he went on, impatient now, and moving to end the interview, "were brilliant individualists and observers; they took no part in the great practical labors of mankind—in fact, like so many men of genius, they evaded much of their manifest duty."

He stood then, and I did, and he put a hand round my shoulder as we walked to the door. "Nice to have this talk, my boy. I'm sure you'll see things more clearly now, eh? I hear you are on the Third Squad—Mr. Bowling gives a good account of you. That's the spirit we like, and remember my advice, Garretson; you won't regret it."

It may be that my first conscious desire to think began with that interview. I walked the cloistered quadrangle in agitation. I had supposed that great thinkers were all more or less alike and more or less safe. The Bible and Shakespeare and Milton and Emerson all had the same sort of sound-effect and their wisdom, I thought, was tried and true; but the Reverend Codfish implied that genius was irrelevant and dangerous.

"Did you get hell?" Horace Tucker stopped me—he was turning into my best friend there.

"Tommy," I said, "did you ever read *Walden?*"

"Nope—never heard of it."

"Ever read Emerson?"

"Well, old Griggs had us read something, but it might have been Addison. Why?"

"Well," I said, "the Codfish says they didn't have any school spirit. He told me I was a poor specimen of spirit myself, and I said what about Thoreau and what about Emerson—"

"You said that to the Codfish?"

"Damn right, I said it—and I said more than that. 'Cadwallader, old boy,' I said—"

"Don't be a sap, Ralph."

"No fooling, Tommy—I said a man's duty is to be himself—"

"Don't be a damned sap, I said."

"Emerson, that is—or if it isn't Emerson I made it up. And the Codfish said we can't have anything like that around here. No, sir, we've got to play the game here whether we like it or not. We've got to be leaders, whether we like it or not. When the Codfish says cheer, we cheer; when he says hit the line, we hit the line. Some day we'll all grow up and be like him."

Tommy told me not to be a sap again, but I felt a good deal better. "You know," I said, "this is really a hell of a place. I'm just beginning to find it out."

↜ CHAPTER 19 ↝

Whᴇɴ ᴡᴇ entered the war in April, Lincoln was ready. The rector at once became a commanding general—still in his clericals, but with such military style that one could almost perceive stars on his shoulders. The old intramural divisions became companies: I was a rear-rank private in the Endicott Company, and we drilled twice a week with broom handles. For dress uniforms we wore dark suits, which meant our best, and at one command during official maneuvers—I think it was "deploy!"—we had to throw ourselves prone on whatever ground happened to be under us. But our general stopped at nothing in doing the school's duty. He had the quadrangle lawn plowed up and planted with potatoes. He sent out squads of boys to work on the neighborhood farms—a sport at which I at last won distinction, for I became a farm "corporal" and gave directions for weeding beans or young carrots, and was eventually awarded a "minor L."

"I want you to know that Lincoln is doing her part."

"In this hour of trial, we shall not be found wanting."

"The Lincoln spirit is in this crisis coming into its own."

The resounding words, the display of activity, are necessary in great enterprises. We learned that potatoes help win wars, though the Lincoln quadrangle was too shady for them. We were instructed in labor and sacrifice, and many a future leader knelt for the first time on his native earth and pulled weeds. I doubt if the sacrifice of our best blue suits in parade drill was beneficial to ourselves or the nation, but the spirit was there.

The next year at Lincoln my attitude grew worse and worse, and I was known generally as Half-baked Raff. I took delight in perversity. I sneered at the good. In that year of our war a great public persecution of radicals took place and according to the logic of respectable persecutors all radicals were pro-German, pro-peace, and pro-socialist. My attitude eventually put me in that class, and willy-nilly I became a triple-dyed villain. Lincoln, of course, abhorred irregularity of doctrine. Lincoln professed itself liberal, progressive, and immeasurably virtuous, but word got about that I had reported to my class in Social Problems on the desirability of a socialist government and from then on I was known as a socialist, a red, a Bolshevik. The abuse I received was mostly jocular, and none of us understood what we were talking about, but Half-baked Raff became a conspicuous figure. In part I enjoyed it and wore red socks in defiance of all that Lincoln stood for; and I affected a cynicism that brought attention and even, I hoped, admiration. There were jokes in the school paper about "our eccentric radical" and "that brilliant cynic and Bolshevik of West Endicott." Yet below all that remained the hard fact of social ostracism. I was supposed to be in the full flood of senior-year activity, with honors and distinctions to record in the class book, and societies and meetings and parties, but my role permitted none of that.

In this new part of cynic and eccentric I desired sin. I confess that I was poorly equipped for it, as a Garretson of Compton and inheritor of much innocence and simplicity; and of all places the sanitary Lincoln Rectory was least suitable for rank growths of evil.

It wasn't easy for me. I learned to smoke with utmost difficulty, instructed by a fellow from Texas called Musty Ellis, the most joyful sinner I ever knew. He had curly hair, a grin, a slow and heart-winning drawl, and no troubles. He followed his

heart's desire, whether it meant climbing the Endicott drain-
pipes at night or renting a goat to ride between the halves of a
game—he said he could ride anything he could get his legs
across. His father owned a ranch bigger than Middlesex County,
and Musty considered himself the world's heir apparent. He
drank hard liquor; he smoked; he read contraband books; he
spent a lot of time and ingenuity scouting the region for a girl
he could play with; yet to call his pursuits evil seems unappre-
ciative. Musty acted as leaven to the whole school, he left
ripples of laughter in his wake, and his comedy was a generous
and unstinted gift of himself. To him the school rituals were a
sort of charade—the games and functions, the letters and
honors, the Spartan rigors of training, the everlasting spirit;
but of course his kind of eccentricity led to immense popularity.

He didn't mind that I was a radical and an outcast. Politics
seemed irrelevant to him, and social hierarchies amused him.
His dad, he said, had sent him up there to get some serious
ideas, but all you got was school spirit.

So we smoked after getting the makings from Boston. And
he taught me about other fundamental things, like drink—
though we had little chance of getting hold of any; but Musty
could talk for hours about the different kinds, and he said New
England rum was no good, but the gin was fine, and he
explained about rye and Scotch and corn, and he told me the
right way and the wrong way to get drunk, and I actually
learned the sort of thing from him that most men take years to
learn at great cost. He was sorry to hear that my folks didn't
drink. "That's the trouble," he said. "You ought to learn things
at home."

I delight in the memory I have kept of Musty Ellis. I see
him sprawled on pine needles in jeans and denim shirt—his
ranch clothes: the rest of us wore suits and neckties, but Musty
did so only when ordered by the masters—many a time he
ambled out of the dining room, grinning and pert as a young
terrier, to reappear in prescribed white collar and tie; but

normally he looked more like Huck Finn. In those days ranch clothes were not fashionable, as they are now, yet Musty could be as ragged and dirty as his young heart desired. He knew he'd be fired sooner or later—he hoped it would be later for his dad's sake: I still think of him as the one mortal unbothered by care or conscience, the free spirit, the joyous adventurer.

"When they kick me out I'm going to join up in Canada." We were lying in our favorite pine grove, smoking.

"Why not here?"

"Get into action quicker that way. More fun, I figure. I'll be sore if I miss out on some part in this war—boy, it's the biggest thing that ever happened. Better than old time Texas."

Tonic for a puritan, all this—and dangerous for Ralph Garretson. I desired emancipation, and Musty seemed to be showing me how.

"You folks up around here," he drawled, "always think first about how a thing is going to look. If you think it will look right, you'll take a drink; you'd even shoot a man, you'd do anything—good or bad wouldn't matter so long as it looked all right. You're scared. You watch each other—you pick out some guy like Noble there and you watch him to see if he says it's all right. If you say anything, even if you sneeze or snort, you look sideways at Noble to find out if he allows it. And clothes—my God, what fuss about clothes. A guy with pants too short is worse off than if he had murdered his grandmother." Most of the school rules were like that, he said—just matters of form. Smoking, for instance—here we were nearly six feet tall, and all they could say was that it would stunt our growth.

Aside from my general unpopularity, I had an enemy. Why he became so I cannot say, but the pattern of our behavior is to be found in boys' books where there's always a fellow with a name like Job Haskins or Luke Trask who sneers and plots and makes premeditated trouble for all good boys. My nemesis was named Adelbert Riggs, and he may even now be composing his recollections of a sinister fellow named Garretson who continually attacked his peace of mind: but for purposes of this narrative let it be assumed that Ralph was the innocent humorist and Bertie the blackguard.

He looked the part: dark, slick-haired, sneering—I do testify soberly that his mouth curled in contempt and his voice and words expressed a grudge against ordinary folk, particularly against me. I testify also that he had a group of followers who must be called cronies—not all dark and sneering, but more or less so. I assumed that they represented the school's serious criminal element, though I have no evidence whatever except that they looked it. If they were sinners they were not joyously so, like Musty Ellis; rather they seemed world-weary and almost professional about it.

Bertie always called me Bright Boy. My concern with ideas, even half-baked ones, offended him, and he never let it alone. "Wait a minute, men," he would break in if I began to speak. "Bright Boy is about to say a few words. Silence, there—we must all hear this. Now, proceed, Bright Boy."

So I acted the fool, or I said nothing, or I muttered "shut up!" at him, and his lip curled with wicked satisfaction. My wits never mastered my emotions.

It came to a fight at last. His slick and impervious worldliness terrified me. He always carried himself like what we later came to know as a gangster; he was cool and lithe—and of course deadly. I had no desire to fight him.

The scene was the gym; the time, winter afternoon. We had played some basket ball as our required exercise and Bertie had made himself my personal opponent. He played all round me, shot baskets through my waving arms, and kept up a running comment. "Dreaming again, Bright Boy? Is it fat in the tail or fat in the head? Sorry, Bright Boy, you're a little late."

So in a fury I flung my bulk against him and received a cruel jab on the nose.

Discipline entered in the person of Mr. Wheelwright, who lectured us, made us shake hands like true sportsmen, and sent us to run six laps on the indoor track—a routine solution for hot tempers.

But after that Bertie lay in wait, not so much to fight as to curse me. He had been insulted by the discipline. He pointed out all my contemptible failings and my close resemblances to the grub, the cockroach, and the louse. We were standing alone in the "trophy room," through which one passed from the track to the stairs down to the lockers.

I felt a roaring in my head, and I suppose I sailed into him with intent to kill. The dark face and curling mouth danced before me. I flung fists at it. I charged and clutched and pummeled. My rage must have been immense, and I intended to lay on like Lancelot against all the black paynims in Christendom, but for the most part I missed, or I hit solid flesh of shoulder or bone of arm, or I clutched terribly at nothing.

Bertie hit out straight, and afterward I discovered cut lips and blackened eyes, but just then I felt nothing but the roar and frenzy.

Two accidents occurred then. First, one of my lustiest Sir Lancelot swings brought up hard on Bertie's nose—in fact, he thrust his nose into the arc of the swing, which would otherwise have missed by six inches; second, I toppled sideways and smashed my left fist right through the largest showcase window where the sacred footballs rested.

Tableau. Bertie moaning on the floor, clutching nose, with dark blood seeping through his fingers; Ralph standing in a stupor above the devastation he had wrought. Then running footsteps, and the world burst in upon us—many boys, and a janitor, and Mr. Wheelwright all pink with angry severity. But above all one thing remains in my mind—and that is the sight of the impervious and untouchable Bertie Riggs on the floor, clutching his nose with both hands and moaning. Never in the world would I have predicted such frailty, such evidence of tender flesh and blood—most of all such blood, dripping out through the fingers.

My own skinned and bleeding left hand I had hardly seen. The smashed showcase I knew to be a major sacrilege, and then and there I fired myself from Lincoln, but in view of the Riggs blood on the floor I cared nothing for a firing. I had fought with passionate stupidity, and now I stood in conspicuous shame beside the desecrated footballs, yet there also lay the ruins of my enemy, now gathering his feet for a limp stand and clapping a borrowed handkerchief against his nose. I had done it; I had socked him on the nose and all his masterful effrontery had collapsed with him. As I stared at him I felt sorry for his mortality and even for the ignominy his heavy nosebleed must cause him.

I might have said something like that—inappropriate and emotional, if Mr. Wheelwright had not taken charge with full authority. He gave us a strong prep-school dressing down, using the stunned onlookers as witnesses to our wrong and his eternal right, then ordered me to clean up every speck of broken glass and to dress and report to the rector's office. This was big-time crime.

"Why did you fight?" So the rector, with the face of Minos.

No answer.

"Come, come. I simply want to know the cause. Trouble of this sort always has roots. What was it, Garretson?"

I shrugged helplessly. "I don't know—nothing much."

"Ah—nothing much. And you, Riggs?"

"I don't know, sir." Bertie mumbled. "Nothing much, I guess."

"Did you start it, Garretson?"

"Yes, sir." Spirit of Lincoln talking.

"Is that right, Riggs?"

"Well, we just seemed to be sore at each other." Not a bad answer, that—but I hoped the rector would see that it lacked the fine manliness of mine.

He got little more out of us and swung into the lecture suitable for the occasion, with sentence of strictest probation and equal assessment for the damages. That we should brawl in hotheaded anger in the very shrine of Lincoln among the emblems of her honor and glory, that seemed to him inexcusable. Minos, did I say? Jupiter at the least, with voice of thunder and countenance harsh as Olympian rock.

"We expect self-mastery of Lincoln fellows," he said from on high. "Self-control, on or off the field. Another such exhibition and you will be separated from the school. Is that clear?"

In the corridor outside I glanced tentatively at Bertie's face —impassive again, yet vulnerable. I remembered the blood. "I'm sorry," I tried in trembling tone. "I guess I messed things up."

I wondered in a flash how Lancelot felt about all the blood and grief. Always righteous? I had thought I was right, but I apologized.

"You sure did, damn you," said my enemy, with the curl of lip I had thought was a calculated sneer. Now that I looked upon him as human, however, I realized that his mouth could shape itself no other way. He might have been sneering that way since the cradle.

"Look," I said. "I busted the glass—I ought to pay for it. I got enough—I hope, anyway—so don't worry about that part of it."

He looked almost embarrassed. "Ralph," he said, "you certainly are all kinds of a fool." Then his face settled down to the hard lines I was used to. "I'll pay my debts—you pay yours."

A threat, I knew.

But he had called me Ralph.

And from then on my social state improved. No one had ever before put a fist through the trophy showcase, and the school as a whole seemed to admire the deed. It became one of the smaller legends, and I acquired merit because of it. Further, I had given dangerous Bertie Riggs a bloody nose and he no longer called me Bright Boy.

But in early spring the penalty of probation was a heavy imprisonment: no play, no freedom, no walks in the pine woods with Tommy or Musty Ellis, no chance for pleasant lawbreaking—at least, no fair chance.

That explains my presence on the gym roof in April moonlight. The Tudor-Gothic of Lincoln provided as fancy a collection of roofs as a boy could wish for, with connections from one to another and innumerable angles and juts and parapets leading on from building to building.

It took Musty to do the pioneer work. For months he had systematically scouted the heights, and he knew the ascents and passes, even the holds for hands and feet and the bearing strength of pipes and vines. He had spoken of it in his usual epic fashion, and I hadn't been much interested; but spring and probation combined for my destruction. I followed Musty up the drains to the lovely moonlit peaks above, to the alpine slopes and the secret valleys and the long dangerous ridges.

The gym stood farthest away from the central quadrangle, a massive cluster of lonely peaks always beckoning to us in the mysterious night. We needed a rope for that enterprise and infinite cunning in the passing of some open casements on the way—one of them being where Mrs. Knapp lived, and the more dangerous for that reason. But Musty got along like a mountain cat, and with pulling and hauling he got me along too—until at last in the thin pallor of a waning moon we lay on the tar and gravel of the little flat area atop the gym—far, far above the world of sleeping men. All windows were dark except for the dim all-night lights of the main entries—and we knew each gleam and window in the whole pattern.

We talked—our last, as it turned out. He lit our cigarettes and we stretched on the black pebbles so that we could see only stars and moon and treetops, and he told me about the vast ranch like a country all by itself. "I don't care what happens, so long as I can go back," he said. "I aim to raise a little hell and

see the world, but my dad knows and I know that the ranch
is what I'm coming to. I guess he thinks I haven't got the stuff
to run it—but, boy, you wait till I start."

I remember the sound of his voice, very quiet then, rather
high pitched and youthful and happy. Yet his assurance was
mature; he did know himself and his chances, and valued them
like a man. "You can raise some hell on a big ranch, too," he
said. "That's one reason I like it. But mostly there's just too
much to do. You'd better come down, Raff; I'll give you a job
any time. And you need to get out of this—this doll's house life
up here. It's all little here, even the stars are little—you ought
to see 'em in Texas—and all the things you have to fuss about.
The guys kid me about the great open spaces, but believe me
that means something."

When we descended from the heights and prepared to cross
the vaulted passage to the roofs of Bowditch the rector himself ordered us to surrender. From his own room in his house
on the knoll south of the quadrangle he had seen the match
flame on the roof top of the gym three hundred yards away.

"Garretson! Come down at once! And you other, there—
both of you!"

But Musty was off like a squirrel. While I fumbled with vines
and pipes I heard the swift run of rubber soles, a thump, and
silence.

Then at once the roar of the great voice of the Codfish. "You,
boy! Stop! Stop at once!"

His bellow woke the whole school. He called out the watch-
man, the masters, the monitors—I never heard such roaring of
orders, such marshaling of guards and lights and dispatching of
scouting parties. Windows were flung open, bright light flashed
on, heads and shoulders leaned out, voices shouted, Mr. Stick-
ney in red dressing gown hurried aloft to the parapets of Bowditch, Mr. Bowling in black and orange dressing gown led a
posse to the high parts of Endicott, and Mr. Latimer was there,

and Mr. Wheelwright, and the rector himself rallying the forces of law and order and still calling aloft threats to the roof tops in the half light—with the fantastic night attire—with me, Ralph Garretson, sliding ignominiously down a pipe like a caught felon, the scene has grown in my imagination to Shakespearean proportions. If Brabantio had marched across the stage with a following of swords and torches looking for his stolen daughter I should have felt no surprise.

"Now, there, Garretson, who was on the roof with you? By Jove, it looked like Ellis! You, some of you there—Mr. Latimer, you see if Ellis is in his room. And smoking too—do you hear that, you fellows? Smoking in my school! I will not tolerate it —take warning from this! Was it Ellis up there with you, Garretson?"

I swallowed, flushed, grew sullen, said nothing.

The rector stood magnificently above me, like the epic protagonist of great tragedy; behind him ranged his followers and hirelings, watching the action.

"Speak up, Garretson. This is not a time for quibbling. It is a question of justice, of duty."

The stern eye fixed me. I knew I couldn't speak—it was as though I were physically unable. The rector's personality crushed me like a stone weight. Yet I stared at him, not quite in complete fear. Musty might still get away—not that it mattered deeply to him, but something of Musty's point of view had got into me. I knew that he was morally capable of looking the rector in the eye and telling him to go to hell, and though I couldn't go that far I could at least look and keep looking.

The rector knew the rest. He had talked of justice and duty, but he knew at the time it was nonsense. He had spoken in anger and frustration.

In an instant the whole scene changed.

"All right," he said in his quick leader's voice. "Get to bed everyone—all lights out in five minutes!" He didn't seem to care any more about me or Ellis; he stood long enough to see the dispersal begin, then turned away to his own house.

No evidence came out against Musty, though everyone there knew the facts.

I was fired.

It was all done calmly. My accumulation of crimes was noted, and I was reminded of the warnings and probations. Smoking, of course, always constituted grounds for expulsion—regardless of anything else. Smoking violated the true spirit of Lincoln, the *virtus* held sacred by all real Lincoln fellows.

"After your splendid family record here," the rector said to me at the end, "this failure is very nearly tragic. I assure you, Ralph, that I feel the deepest personal regret—I confess that I find it very difficult to write to your father."

He shook hands with immense kindliness, but I knew I was being cast into outer darkness.

✑ CHAPTER 20 ✑

Two YEARS later, at the end of my second year there, I was fired from Harvard too.

Not really fired in the active sense of that useful verb, rather "dropped." It was simply a matter of courses and credits, and if I had applied for readmission, and had agreed to do the required work, I could have continued. Colleges, even Harvard, are less high and mighty than the big prep schools; if a student wants to stay and will pay his bills, the college prefers to keep him. The responsibility was mine. Culturally and socially I had gone to the bad.

In a sense, that is what this book is all about. I had been born into an admirable cultural pattern. My people had achieved a sort of nobility, not by great property and power, but by plain living and high thinking, by the continued refinement of the puritan virtues—with just enough property to give freedom. Yet all the training and encouragement, the good intentions, good manners, good books, the teachers and professors and nice people, produced in me only a sort of motiveless rebellion. I failed at Lincoln, I failed at Harvard—and alas, I fear I simply failed. If I could present myself as an emerging radical, a fighter for a new order, a two-fisted renegade—like Belcher Lee Boylston, for example, the only man ever to cause riot and bloodshed in a Harvard classroom—I should write a more powerful and more simple tale. But my defections grew out of bewilderment and uncertainty.

So it has been, I believe, for many others. The truth about this era of ours is to be found not only among the warriors and crusaders but among all the folk who struggle and fail for no clear reason, who lead their lives of quiet desperation unnoticed by anyone except the recording angel.

"Mr. Garretson," said Dean Kirkland, near the close of our official interview, "please forgive me if I say something rather personal." He had an oval face and head, smooth, bald, very hard, with thin lips and small agate eyes. The only benevolent part of his expression was the horn-rimmed spectacles. He spoke out briskly, with a hurried, aggressive certainty—a lecturer's voice, quite different from the manly, sportsmen's voices of Lincoln. I didn't like Dean Kirkland, partly because he was far too busy and scholarly to like me or anyone, but I could tell that he aimed to speak the truth.

"Harvard has gone far beyond the parochial stage," he went on very rapidly, so that the words seemed almost to overlap. "Yet there's always a little pressure on us to continue as a Boston finishing school. The old families have worked with us for generations; by and large they have given us our best men —and they still continue to, not because they have special privilege, but simply because they are men of great ability. Yet more and more there's a sort of expectation on the part of the old families that we will take care of their boys, and more and more we get boys who are unwilling or unable to measure up to the standards we set. Now whether this applies to you or not I really don't know . . ."

He went on in his tight, quick-thinking tone, and I realized that he looked upon me as a degenerate offshoot of what should be a fine family. I was simply relying on my name; I was expecting Harvard—and the world—to take me along as a passenger. "In these times, Mr. Garretson, a man has to work his way."

I shook my head. "No, you don't understand—"

"Perhaps not," he agreed. "I have to judge by results—and

I'm afraid the world will always judge by results. That's the essential public measure." He stirred and forced me to rise.

It would be customary at this point to deal satirically with the great university on the score of its failure to appreciate me. True, it did discourage my little taste for learning, and it has done the same for many others; but I believe the main business of a university has been not with the confused and bewildered, not with individuals at all. Rather, it is in the business of knowledge; it both stores and issues knowledge, like a great bank, and operates with the formal routines of a bank. The small customer, name of Ralph, one of the hundreds who pop in and out of the lobby, is the least of its concerns. Not any human weal or woe officially concerns it—nothing but the knowledge it holds and increases and issues with uncorruptible integrity.

Yet I speak of old times, twenty years ago, when all business had grown greater than any human consideration. I suppose Harvard's worship of knowledge above life itself was part of the same immense materialism as Ford's love of production.

Now, I believe, humanity expects more attention. Business and sentiment must somehow be mixed. The future Ralphs will be adjusted and made happy, even at some cost to the great stores of knowledge.

The fact is that I did too little work there. I found myself in a wilderness where the old and new, the known and unknown, were crazily mixed. On the one hand a group of well-dressed stalwarts were intent on restoring every detail of old Harvard, with all social grades and exclusions; on the other hand a talkative number proclaimed that they believed in nothing whatever—least of all "old" Harvard. Nihilism, I suppose it was, but in the American manner, with a good deal of pointless humor. And though I had no occasion to be personally disillusioned about anything, except myself, I found it exciting to join this party of eager wastrels.

Yet this emancipation was never a joyous thing. The old

.sanctions loomed over the wildest of us; we embarked on freedom as on a grim voyage of duty, surrounded by ancient chimeras, constantly worried by our own innocence. If I did so simple a deed as to take a drink, I trembled at the unknown, at my own limitations in the presence of immortal evil. Logically, all was clear; the consequences of drink or sex or denial of God were all arguable, just as the contents of a forest at night are arguable, but the young men of the twenties were not as happy about any of it as they tried to pretend. It is easier to sin happily now than it was then, though sin seems far less desirable. I remember how we talked and talked, far through the night, exploring good and evil with insatiable anxiety—and how we felt it our duty to forswear all things old and familiar and to despise our national vulgarities. We began to hear of a new, still secret world of art and taste; we whispered new names: Pound (alas!), Picasso, Joyce; we praised all things French and Russian and all things bizarre and radical and remote. We looked upon the war and its aftermath with a romanticism almost mystical—all the despair it had created, all the faith it had destroyed; we reveled in bitterness and the humors of disillusionment; we hoped that our youth had somehow been blighted.

We, I say—but the college world as a whole hardly noticed us. Several years later our club, called the Left Bank, made itself notorious through its publication, *The Devil's Advocate*, which would have been suppressed had it been intelligible, but in my day the Left Bankers were too few and too silly to be widely noticed. In '19 and '20 the tides of modernism had just begun to run. The excitement came a little later, when Lawrence and Anderson began to be read, and John Dos Passos's *Three Soldiers*—I was still there when we made him an honorary member of the Left Bank.

I always remember how my friend Harvey Mayo behaved. He came to Harvard when I did, but we diverged. My fault, that—Harvey has held as steady a course in life as ever man or boy could; he even goes on looking the same year after year, and if I hadn't seen him since he was twelve, say, I should know him at once. We used to kid him then about his intellectual face—and not only because of the spectacles; thought seems to express itself in the knit of his forehead or the clamp of his rather large mouth. Although he and I have always weighed about the same, he has been the more rugged, with a square, knobby muscularity that fits the tenacity of his mind. As a youngster, he seemed older than I—wiser and steadier; he still does. He is the only person I know who has improved during life as surely as an upcurving graph: in another ten years he will be one of the nation's great men and Harvard's leading economist.

Harvey went to Compton High. His family had grown poor, but even so Harvey had decided against private school for himself, and most of his own decisions after fifteen stood. His older brother was starting medical school, an expense, of course, and Harvey took care of his mother and sister on their old farmplace a little way out beyond ours—a big house and barns forever needing something done to them. He saved what he could for college, but by then he won enough scholarships and prizes to carry him along.

"Fifteen minutes a day, Ralph, and you'd pass these courses," he used to say.

"Do you mean for each, or in all?"

"For each. That gets you a grade of C. An hour a day gets you a B; two hours, an A."

"Couldn't you get me a C without my doing anything at all?"

"You want me to make a moral weakling of you?"

"Sure."

"Well, that would cost you money. I can't afford to corrupt my friends for nothing."

But if I had asked, he would have done anything for me, even to getting me through courses. I didn't ask. He looked like what the world knows as an easygoing chap, slow of speech, deliberately kind and patient, but I knew that his own moral logic was inexorable. He never questioned my right to consort with modernistic esthetes and Left Bankers; he recognized the infinite diversities of humanity—his own mind was that of a true radical, concerning itself with roots and foundations; but he looked upon us as so many spoiled children playing on the fringes of life. He laughed at us with nice tolerance. But I knew enough not to push moral nihilism too far—in fact, it was his strong certainty of value that kept me from deeper folly.

Yet we did diverge.

"You are denying your own heritage, Ralph," he said.

"Why not?"

"Well, there's loyalty."

"Why be loyal to something silly?"

"Loyalty isn't a matter of calculation," he said, "any more than love is. And anyway, it was a pretty nice world we came out of."

But what could a Left Banker believe in?

Beauty, some said.

We proved that there is no beauty. A tree is beautiful and so is a bird, or a carved ivory box, or a phrase: in the end it is nothing.

Sensation? Yes—but not very satisfactory.

"We believe in the individuality," said Jon d'Aragon, our leader.

Each man is an original creation, he said, a wholly unprecedented arrangement of spirit and body—and that individuality is the one precious entity in the world of inert matter. Believe in yourself, he said; express yourself, no matter where it may lead you; release your true essence, your own genius. It must be released, he said; it must express itself, for only then could a man live in fulfillment.

How did it express itself? In speech, in words, in behavior, in clothes—in anything; but restraint killed it and led to death and horror and respectability.

Jon was very tall and thin, and he stooped beautifully and undulated as he moved; he carried a light cane with a sword concealed in it ("purely a symbol," he said) and wore always some tone of yellow ("for reasons too obscure to explain"), and if he had not possessed the bright, idiotic wit of a precocious original he would have been insufferable. He posed brilliantly, with professional self-knowledge.

I realize now that d'Aragon had somehow absorbed the whole new esthetic racket. Like other eminent worldlings, he came from a western farm, but all we knew of Greenwich Village and the Paris boulevards we learned from him. My own mind was then incapable of finding essential truth in Eliot and Lawrence, but he spoke of them on equal terms, as though they shared his conclusions. He wrote critical articles on Cézanne and Schönberg, and he already patronized Shaw. He must have been twenty-two then and at the peak of his abilities: only now, twenty years later, can I deal confidently with the ideas he seems to have mastered as an undergraduate.

He now manages a small bookstore on East Forty-sixth Street, New York, and writes amusing notes for his two yearly catalogues. I record a recent item following a first-edition *Sons and Lovers*. "The only really permanent value in Lawrence, worth all the rest put together. Don't be misled by the recent ballyhoo over Lady Chatterly." Occasionally I see his name in the *Saturday Review* (generally as the source of a funny story) and in lesser trade journals, but the world will never know the superb and original d'Aragon of our college days. I am told he even wears blue-serge suits with pin stripes.

Well, after two years of brilliant idling, after perceiving the pretentious folly of all scholars, all gentlemen, and all mankind prior to the year 1920, after learning to despise my native land and my forefathers, I returned to Compton and took stock of myself. Not seriously, not with manly ambition or responsibility

—rather, I conceived of myself as immune to the ordinary compulsions of life. To "get a job" in the modern, Tom Madigan manner would put me in bondage to the America of Main Street, to all that vulgar stupidity and materialism which I scorned. But as to what I might do, how I could employ my rare talents, I had no notion. I thought I'd like to "write"; I had begun to play with drawing and painting—that's one way I used up time at college; I fancied myself as a young man of rare taste in all decorative affairs—always, of course, in the Left Bank manner. Yet with all this pride and appreciation of my own superiority, I dwelt in a mist of ignorance and illusion.

"Ralph, do I understand that you are being dropped because of so many failures?"

"Yes—I'm afraid so."

Father smoothed his white plume. He sighed. "Can you account for your failure?"

I shrugged. "Not interested enough, I guess."

"So you abandon your education here?"

"Rather, I'm just beginning it."

"How do you propose to do that?"

By now our relationship was purely emotional. Father had decided that I was talking like a fool, and I realized that any opinion he might hold would be prejudiced and irrelevant.

"I want some time to read," I said disagreeably. "And I intend to do some writing."

"You've never written, have you?"

"Yes, a little. I've written poems."

"Ralph," he said quietly, "many men think they can solve their problems by writing. I'm afraid that even I once had that notion—and I did write. I was full of great hopes." He shook his head. "I still have small hopes."

I missed entirely the quality of his confession. "All that was different," I explained, making an ass of myself. "You just got smothered in Victorianism. It isn't like that now—we're just beginning a whole new era."

He considered this preposterous remark for a moment in silence. "As I understand it, you wish to abandon the best education we can offer you because it concerns itself with the dead past. Is that it?"

I knew what he meant, and I turned sullen.

"If I can't write, I'll earn my living as a carpenter. I can always do that."

"I believe good carpenters are almost as rare as good writers," he said. "But I'm glad you appreciate the necessity of a living."

He let it go for a while, not being one to force a crisis.

But before the summer was over mater went into action.

"You realize that we can't support you in idleness, Ralph. We'd be glad to make sacrifices to give you the right start in the world, but if you refuse that opportunity, then you take over the responsibility of your career. Isn't that fair?"

Her disapproval led to severity, and I perceived that she was my enemy.

"You apparently despise us and our ways," she said, "yet you expect us to support you."

She turned cold and dangerous. I had lived all those years with my family thoughtlessly, as boys do, taking it as the measure of my values, but now I saw a rift between us. I had been criticizing them severely and steadily—their habits and tastes and values—but I had expected them to accept my opinions with grateful respect. I had counted on mater's controlled reasonableness and felt that as long as she discussed matters objectively, all was well.

But now the taut lines of her face expressed hostility. "You may think you represent the new generation," she said, "but I haven't seen Steve or Jean acting like this. And the youngsters won't if I can prevent it. Ralph, I really think it's too bad, this attitude of yours toward us and everything we've tried to do." She sighed, then recovered her old patience. "I hope you have the grace to be ashamed of it some day."

⤫ CHAPTER 21 ⤫

I MARCHED out to Mrs. Kingsley's that afternoon and asked if I could come and live with them. "I'll work for board and room —I'll do anything that needs doing."

"I guess you've been making a fool of yourself," she said.

"Maybe so—maybe I naturally am a fool."

She nodded. "It seems so, sometimes."

"Everything is such a damned mess—I don't know where I am."

"Well, you're here now. Sit down and cool off."

In the five years nothing had altered, not even the Ralph who folded himself into the rocker and put a foot on the side of the stove. I had been many characters in that time—Lincoln fellow, rebel, sinner, esthete, fool—but never once had I come into that kitchen without reverting to the plain and obvious and happy Ralph I started as. Mater had said I had an "attitude" and she was right, but here in the sanctuary I had no attitude, nor any pose of scorn. I sat there grinning and watching the jutting, time-scarred face of the woman I loved.

"Been fighting?" she asked.

"I suppose so. Mater told me where I could go."

"Any reason why she shouldn't?"

I tried to tell her, and oddly enough I found myself looking back at my radical adventures from a new point of distance.

I had many times come back to the Kingsleys—I had worked there and I had come just to sit in the corner with a foot on the stove, and invariably I looked at my confusions and failures as though they concerned someone of no special importance to me. It was nothing they said, no advice or accusation. Mrs. Kingsley talked about whatever facts of life occurred to her— about weather and food and clothes and people. Her whole world was Compton, and she had traveled much in it, past and present—a world turning on Main Street and solid with the old virtues and castes I had emancipated myself from. She hated any sort of liquor and mince pies containing brandy; she hated infidelity and all pretense and nearly all innovation; she had no use for Woodrow Wilson or anything Democratic or radical or worse. She liked sentimental music and Mary Pickford, and she clipped little poems by Edgar Guest from the newspaper because she thought I'd like them too. Yet all that was part of the character I loved, and I felt always a natural kinship with her. I knew the long and honest past that spoke in her voice and showed itself in her gestures—her knee against the oven door, her frank turn of head and stare at what passed along the road, her clamp of mouth and thrust of chin to substantiate her word. It all fitted and made one thing, and when I was there I became part of that thing.

"I want to live here," I said.

"Your folks know you want to?"

"Not yet."

"Look here, Ralph, if I thought you was in need I'd say come and welcome. Land knows with Martha gone off we live in an empty house, and we had a boy once and expected to have him still. As far as I'm concerned you'd do about as well, and I guess he feels the same. But this isn't anywhere for you, Ralph— they'll tell you that, your father and Lucy Brattle; he will too, when he comes home. And they'll all be right, though I can see you think we're a pack of idiots."

"Well, it isn't forever," I began, but she broke in.

"And don't you go setting us up against your own folks. I don't want Randall Garretson over here to find out what we've done to his precious son, though I bet he's wondered often enough, with you over here at all outlandish times these last five years. What's he said about us, I'd like to know?"

"Father doesn't pay any attention to what I do."

"Well, Lucy Brattle does, I know her. And other folks— why, if you knew what that Kate Steele said to me one time, she said I must have set a pretty good trap to get you away from the Garretsons—she laughed, but she said it mean, and meant it mean. I told her to act her age, and after she thought a while she got mad."

"Couple of old cats," I said.

"Women are a sight worse than cats. I don't care a straw for that kind of yowling, but I do care about your folks—they aim to be decent, and they'd be sorry enough if anything went wrong with you."

"You think I'd go wrong here?"

"You wouldn't go right—not very far."

"What do you mean by right, I'd like to know?"

"Why, I mean lifework, that's all. You'll not get enough Garretson money to live on—there's too many of you for that. I don't know about your mother's folks, but I expect there's a lot of them too. You'll need a living, and you won't feel decent unless you do what's worth doing."

Seth refused to consider it. I argued myself almost to tears. I told him I seriously wanted to learn the woodworking trade, and I'd never have a better chance. I said he'd get a good helper for practically nothing, and next spring we could plant a much bigger garden. And I confessed my desire to write, at which he gravely nodded.

"As I see it, Ralph, this is the fork in the road. You want to get off the highway and take this other road that won't get you anywhere at all, nor will it get you back again. You'll just get lost in the brush, and folks'll wonder what ever became of that promising young Garretson feller. I don't intend to be responsible for any such business."

I had run up against an ideal. My people had done great work in Seth's world; he intended to see to it that I did too.

"But it's a different world," I said. "Just being a scholar and a gentleman doesn't get you anywhere. Look at father—he hasn't done a useful day's work in twenty years."

"You should be ashamed to say that about your father." Seth's eyes were angry and hard—more so than I had ever seen them. "The town of Compton owes more to him than you or most folks realize. If it weren't for him this would be just another way station, instead of the handsomest and cleanest town this end of the state—and it isn't only that. Folks take pride in their houses on account of him. In old times I used to say why didn't we put a dormer here or a new porch there, but not any more. I say ask Randall Garretson now—he knows how a house ought to look, and he'll take more time and trouble over one of these old houses than you'd believe possible. If I ever get round to fixing this house up I won't drive a nail without his say-so."

Mrs. Kingsley snorted at this. "Some of us will be in our graves, time that happens."

"Well, that isn't the point," Seth went on, eyeing me steadily. "If my own boy came home from college like this, I'd send him right back. And Ralph has less reason for it. I never heard any sense in a feller stopping his education because he wanted to be a writer."

"It happens often," I mumbled.

"That doesn't make it any better sense."

I walked home in emptiness and dejection. The late July afternoon lay hot on the road and fields and I lingered from shade to shade. I cared little for getting home. Normally I might have cut northward to Spring Pond and gone swimming, but uncertainty and solitude surrounded me like a substance almost visible. I felt that my perversity had barred me from the world of men, and I was fated to take the miserable byway and vanish in the underbrush. From the dean to Seth, they had all said so. And my own fine certainties were gone, my new belief in individuality and self-expression. Out here in the power of the sun, I felt lonesome. It seemed to me that the world had withdrawn itself and left me like a single foolish puppy alone in all creation.

But I went on home, had supper, slept the night. Shots may kill, prison gates shut, white turn black—but most of our crises linger like the seasons, and one moment is visibly no different from the preceding moment. I had breakfast, I read, I went swimming, I agreed to play tennis over at the Cadwalladers. Steve was off at camp, a counselor now. Jean was home—a college graduate. We were building a tennis court in part of the garden space behind the barn. The three youngsters all did the things we used to do and dragged boards up into the great maple near the barn door to build a house where they could retreat from their enemies (they never got much more than a little platform up there, but that was better than we did—and there were no riffraff and micky boys to deal with).

After a few days I went back and asked Seth if I could work for him the way I had before. In the autumn I'd do something else. He said all right, he was doing a lot of his work at home these days—furniture and small things, and there might not be so much I could do, but he'd be glad to have me there. Why didn't I write, if I wanted to?

It is embarrassing when young people talk about writing, because they and everyone assume that they are doomed to fail. The knowing ones don't speak of it at all. The modest ones reveal themselves only with laughter. Only the young and foolish speak out literally, as I did, using the word "write" with impervious innocence. My father realized my folly at once and felt helpless in the face of it; the Kingsleys accepted my announcement soberly—and their innocence in that respect was greater than mine, but like all working folk they discounted talk. They permitted me to announce my intentions, much as though I had declared for medicine or law, but they waited to see whether I knew what work meant. It would not have surprised them, as it would more worldly people, if I had succeeded as a "writer." Why shouldn't a Garretson write? If someone like me couldn't write, who could?

At Harvard I had written some verse, and several were published in *The Devil's Advocate*: free verse, following the strong stimulant of Amy Lowell—and it is safe now to describe the writing of verse at that time as pure necromancy. As a practitioner, I succeeded mainly in befuddling myself; I had a faith in cryptic syllables set end to end, and a group of exotic images embodied in oriental shorthand excited me beyond all reason. In solemn approval I created verses about the golden music of the pear tree and the passion of the plum and hearts broken by beauty.

Why didn't I write, if I was ever going to write? Seth had spoken it soberly enough, and there was no very good answer. I was trying, I said. Give me time. It came hard. I didn't say that I was too much of a fool, because I didn't quite realize it— though I had suspicions.

I worked with him irregularly—sometimes helping with some of the rough sawing or drilling, sometimes just watching. He used no machinery at all, and I learned how it felt to rip down a seven-foot length of birch or oak and how to hew hard wood with an ax or adze. I tried to learn to plane, and sorely tried both Seth's and my patience—and in the end I learned more about patience than I ever had known.

His shop at home filled itself with life that summer. His work had grown famous slowly, and the world began beating a path to his door. Heirloom pieces in need of an arm or leg came there, and new designs to be worked out for special purposes. A Waltham manufacturer named Quinn turned up with drawings for a new-fangled clothes reel and wanted Seth to make one as a pattern. A rich man from Belmont desired an oak refectory table such as feudal barons used in the fifteenth century. And many began to want colonial antiques, with worn edges and very old scratches and the patina of great age.

"What's this about making stuff look old and worn out?" he asked. Ordinarily he carried out orders as given; he followed plans or copied from a picture or actual original, and it was no concern of his what style or period he reproduced.

I explained about the growing business in antiques.

"You mean they pay me fifty dollars for a table and then pass it off as worth five hundred?"

"You ought to know the world better than I do, Seth."

He nodded. "So I ought. But a plain carpenter hasn't much chance to learn about this antique game. Are they making suckers out of us, Ralph?"

"They will if you let them—and you can't very well stop them. If a man orders a Duncan Phyfe table, and shows you the drawings, I suppose you have to make it—at your usual rates, I mean."

He nodded slowly. "Maybe so. I guess it was safer just building houses."

I can never record all the flavor and fact of this life. Just the wood smells of the shop translated me from one world to another—a cleaner and simpler world where virtue consisted of a straight edge or a dove-tail joint or a flawless surface of wood. I remember bitter oak—yet fresh and heady and potent on the air; and cedar, aromatic as spice; and white pine, soft and clean and woody; and delicate Honduras mahogany; and musty walnut—each wood familiar to the nose but indescribable otherwise; there are no true words for smells. I remember the feel of woods, the airy and velvet softness of clear pine, the fibrous, tough-grained weighty oak, the metallic denseness of hickory and maple—and the shine of their surfaces, the splintery brown walnut, and mahogany combining all the best of all the woods together—soft to the sharp tool yet hard in finish, heavy enough yet never sullen or intractable, and beautiful by itself without need of stain. I learned about quality, sour oak and white oak, the cheap varieties of mahogany and how they differed from the true thoroughbred—and how rare natural good mahogany was. I learned how to go at a raw chunk of wood—where to saw and where to hew, where to chisel or plane. Many, many things I learned: edges, for one—the burred edge of a scraper, the flat, one-way edge of a plane blade, and all the odd curving edges of gouges and molding tools, and the stones and files and hones; I think I learned the very personality of steel and when it will behave and work for you and when it won't, when it turns tired and discouraged and when it seems to do the job all on its own without push or guidance. I learned the whole weary routine of finishing, from rough to smooth, and smooth to fine, and fine to superfine, and at last to polish, and more polish, and more—but in the end the wondrous beauty like a new creation under the sun, the transfiguration into the realms of light and spirit. I used to stare and stare at the wonders we had wrought from the common substances of that shop.

I asked Seth what he thought of his work, but he wouldn't answer me. "I make a better living working for wages," he said.

"Don't you get more satisfaction out of this?"

"It's nice to have regular hot dinners," he said.

But September came, and the great migration to school and college. Everyone seemed to be going forth with certainty: Steve entered Harvard with a foreknowledge that seemed to me almost professional, and Dick Madigan and Sid Steele and Harvey Mayo were all ready to go. The world of the twenties was full of activity. While I brooded over my doubts and failures, others worked and played with immense energy. The world's goods seemed to be bought and sold continually, and new enterprises popped up in the wake of the automobiles. Terry Madigan kept right on working at the old blacksmith shop and stable, and more and more business came to him until he was hiring three or four mechanics and selling cars and making more money than any of us.

My father and Jean were going abroad for the winter. He had persuaded her that she ought to study Italian, and argued that the rate of exchange would allow them to do it without extravagance; and I could see that he really wanted to take me along too. He got together folders and guides and made many plans. But he knew mater would not let me go.

My time seemed to be mounting to a crisis. Even the cool autumn, the swift change of leaves, the ripening, the smell of dry grasses, intensified my trouble. The visible world made ready for the solemn trial of winter and every living object knew what it had to do. I thought many thoughts—of going south to Musty's ranch, of taking to the road and bumming across the country and picking fruit, of finding a garret in Greenwich Village. I suppose the innocence of my existence kept me from those adventures. I should have been thrown forcibly into the great world.

As it was, with grief in my heart, I went to Waltham and got a job.

❧ CHAPTER 22 ☙

GRIEF IS a strong word—too strong to suit a young man of twenty setting out on a career. Yet it will do to describe the heartache—not of a youth compelled to labor, but of a Garretson lost in his uncertainty and sense of failure. I played the part of a radical with a compulsion that I cannot account for. I simply disapproved of what passed for civilization in America. No foreign influences, no subversive element, had deflected me from true Republicanism; no course of knowledge and logic led me to my disaffection. Perhaps my father lent me his habit of detachment and skepticism; perhaps mater reasoned me into a state of hostility. Innocence betrayed me—and many others. We blamed our parents for their silly virtue, and our fellow men for their brute materialism.

So I got a job with a sense of martyrdom. I looked up the maker of clothes reels, who had come to Seth's shop several times, and because he thought very highly of Seth he hired me to feed rough boards into a planing machine. It was a brick mill building on the Charles called the Eastern Woodcraft Company, and many things besides clothes reels came out of its big loading door on the B & M siding: ironing boards, stepladders, towel racks, knocked-down bookcases—anything that could be milled out of spruce or western fir. The machines were usually all rigged to produce one item—ironing-board stands, for example—until a good surplus had been built up; then they were rigged for another.

I entered this life with grief, and then with growing fascination. I hated the ugly town, the brick walls of factories, the smoke and cinders and the dreariness of small industry. I saw the whole nation spread with the same makeshift mess of drab shops and shoddy houses—and no end to any of it. That's business, I thought, that's the world Uncle Richard presides over from his castle on Chestnut Hill, and his only idea is more of it, more two-family houses like upended packing crates, more dumps and cinder piles and drugstores and eating joints. And at first I hated the shop, the screech of cutting machines all day long, the dust and heat. Poor slaves there, bound to the rack. But I felt other emotions just as keenly—chiefly, I think, pride that I was there at all, that I had jumped squarely into the waters of life and could work a nine-hour day like a man.

At least, that's how it was at first. I had moved out of Compton with stubborn independence. I hired a room for five dollars a week. I faced ugliness and exile, yet a powerful satisfaction grew up in me. I worked with a Finn named Hank on the planer, and I went at it with quiet watchfulness, doing exactly what he seemed to want done. In many departments of life I have made an ass of myself, but I didn't there. I knew I was an outsider, a gentleman tainted with idle culture, but I concealed my weakness; I spoke little, listened, watched, kept working. The Eastern Woodcraft Company was a congenial place. No one at first paid me any attention at all, and my inconspicuousness seemed like a victory. Hank took me for granted and changed slowly from a stolid squarehead to a childlike enthusiast for his native land—talking at me all through lunch hour about how they handled the timber there and what they ate and what northern cold was like.

The life, I found, had some of the comfort that a sentence to a pleasant prison might be expected to have. The routine took entire charge. It prescribed steady, slow labor from eight to five; it required no initiative, no decision, no concern; mind and conscience dozed more peacefully than they ever could have under the burdens of freedom. If I had hurried or bustled or used initiative, I should have destroyed our harmony. Hank would have turned sullen and the ripple of discontent would have run through the whole chain of activity. At first I may have worked fast, and rattled the boards and raised more dust, but I felt hostility almost at once, and I lapsed passively into the routine. And I may at first have been oppressed by noise and bored by unending repetition, but all that passed. Hank was a happy man; he worked and rested and worked and rested —had done so for ten years here in the shop; he looked ahead with sweet trust to a day of freedom in a cottage in the country —but meanwhile the routine had him safe and sound.

I did get tired, but that was one element of the routine. Work, food, sleep—nothing else. Hank could go on with it forever. I remember walking home in the evening, lightheaded and heavy-boned, empty of thought, senses keen for stab of cool air and color of cloud. I remember the slow wash in the squalid bathroom, the idle change of shirt in the third-floor cell I rented, the smell of sauerkraut in the halls and then the keen air again as I sauntered down the twilight street to eat supper in a joint. If I thought of it in terms of a lifetime—if I thought at all—I was miserable enough, but if I let it all go on like the great wheel of fate, I enjoyed my helplessness.

So I faced the darkening winter with an income of fifteen dollars a week and a basic outgo of twelve. I grew less tired and consequently somewhat more reflective and unhappy—but not acutely so. I read many books in my three-hour evenings, mostly ones borrowed from the public library. I intended to write too, but for a time my soul was seized and shaken by Russian novels, and I lived night after night in a state of wonder and terror and wild laughter. There, I thought, was the door to life that Harvard never opened, never knew existed, there were the heights and depths of mankind unmeasured by scholars.

Reading Dostoevski for the first time in the even tenor of life is memorable enough, but for a speculative youth cast away alone in a hired cell in a factory town, night after night, withdrawn into the dark region of his imagination, the experience is Himalayan—even more than that, for my innocence had never dreamed human glaciers and gulfs and peaks like those. When Raskolnikov murdered the old woman in his frenzy of terror and pride, my own soul suffered equal purgations; I trembled, my breath stopped, I felt a wild, fearful laughter take hold of me, I stared at the page, the scene, the whole incredible revelation; I saw depths and follies that nothing in life up to then had prepared me for.

I had known that Russian novels were considered good by the young moderns, but I expected no such overwhelming experience. Fashion and taste were swallowed up as a garden party might be engulfed by a hurricane.

No, I couldn't write then. Too much happened—not on the outside, for events simply repeated themselves—but within the boundaries of Ralph. The very solitude reached into my character—I knew it even then. And all the little arrangements of life had fallen into my hands—from the original getting of the job to the decision what to eat in a restaurant. Father, I must acknowledge, saw to it that I had a little extra money, and I bought clothes with it, had my laundry done, and sometimes rode to Cambridge to buy books. (This confession will destroy any chance I might have to be considered an honest man of labor—but so it was. I claim no respectability whatever.)

The food was not good, and I grew thinner and somewhat pasty, and suffered colds and other troubles, but at the same time I felt tougher than I used to be—a feeling, I think, more than a fact. I had been an inch over six feet for several years, but with a soft, overgrown carcass; now at last I grew decently lean, and leveled my weight off at a hundred and eighty or so, where it still is. I stood up to other men on equal terms, not morally, perhaps—not yet—but physically, at least. I could do what the shop called good work, which meant that I followed the routines steadily, and our head man, Mr. Quinn, moved me from job to job and in December raised my pay three dollars. I thought it was still his admiration for Seth, but apparently he had real hopes for me.

"They like you, the men do—don't know why, except you grin at 'em and keep quiet. Stick with us, Ralph, and you won't regret it."

A square, wheezy, raspy man who peered fiercely through thick spectacles. "Boss is sore today"—someone said it every morning, and to see him waddling in and out of his office like an irritated and nearsighted grizzly was cause for alarm. If it hadn't been for his visits to Seth's shop I might never have perceived that his ferocious scowl came from inability to see anything clearly, and that his hoarse rasp was due to some sort of chronic laryngitis.

"Damn shop needs new blood in it. I'm too old, and these squareheads and wops never had two ideas in their life. They do what you tell 'em, all right. You ever do any designing?"

He had a drafting table in his office, and the one intense joy of his life was to design wooden things. I knew that also from his talk with Seth, for he loved his clothes reel and pointed to each detail with outspoken pride. And his scowl transformed itself into an immense baby's smile, gap toothed and glistening, and the raspy voice boomed out in a sort of Friar Tuck joviality. The beauty and efficiency of his designs intoxicated him.

"I hate managing this damn business," he said. "If I didn't have a good office staff here we'd all go broke." He had given his secretary, Miss Hagerthy, the title of sales manager and turned over the whole responsibility of marketing to her. He himself tended to the shop. And because he loved his products he supervised the buying of timber and other materials, and kept fierce watch, to see that nothing shoddy went through. He marched up and down among the machines scowling and grumbling and looking for trouble. "I wasn't cut out for business," he said to me. "This shop was wished on me after my brother died—he was the one who built it up into a real business. I was trained to be a surveyor and draftsman—but it's a good business, by God. Whatever I say about it, it's a good honest business." And he glared at me savagely, as though I had traduced both him and the business.

I said I hadn't done much designing, though I knew quite a bit about furniture, and he replied that he didn't know a better workman anywhere than Seth Kingsley. He supposed it was foolish to get a man like that to work out these cheap designs —some of the men in the shop could probably do it well enough, but he did enjoy seeing it done by a real artist.

I worked on through the darkest season and became a natural part of the machinery. It meant nothing, I realized. I had none of the ambition that drove other young men to greater successes; I saw no shining managerships and presidencies far ahead. I could simply stay there forever, like Hank the Finn or Leo Colosi or Pete Mizwa, and dream of a cottage in the country. I knew that if I played up to Quinn I'd get a better job, but I hardly aspired to it.

What did impel me? Partly a desire to do penance, I think. The long labor subdued my idle fancies and compensated for my indulgence in failure. And I also enjoyed the demonstration of independence. All along mater treated the whole affair as a piece of silly petulance—a reasonable view, but limited. Beyond these negative values something else drove me: I simply wanted to be alone with the world—not the safe and nice world of the Garretsons' Compton, but the world I had been brought up to avoid and fear. I hardly knew it at the time—I may even now be rationalizing; yet my whole nature needed the same sort of toughening my muscles were getting. I needed the ugliness of a factory town and the plain truth of how men and women actually existed. I needed the experience of human character straight, as it were, and not graded and packaged according to social habit.

There were people in Waltham "we" knew, but in spite of

mater's advice I kept away. There was my old school over on the Lexington side and I kept away from there too.

But I did get to know people. Leo Colosi lived in a swarm of Sicilians in a couple of packing-box tenements, and during October they all went into the wine business. It was illegal, but when Leo found I knew nothing of such matters he took me to see. Leo himself seemed to hate his fellow men; sometimes in the shop he argued to the pitch of frenzy, and hissed and spat out his words and brandished an invisible knife against all comers; but his own people roared with laughter at the sight of him and he grinned slyly at me and winked and moved his head in a gesture of indescribable pride. It was all right here, he said; this was home, and a man could laugh if he felt like it. And they enveloped me in mirth and universal joy.

I visited Hank too—that was his last name, by the way, or something similar. "And my wife, Mrs. Hank." Not much laughter there, no outward joy. Two stoics, they were, waiting for life to go by, living in two rooms over a grocery store—but a piece of back yard was theirs for a garden. "Without a garden," Hank said, "we are dead ones." His dream again, the bit of earth, the country—I knew it was just enough to keep them going, like a small flame, an invisible sun within. Once started, Hank talked with steady insistence, but not clearly and hardly aware of whether I followed him or not. While I was there, Mrs. Hank talked very little.

And I met Mr. Quinn one evening, not entirely by chance. After supper I circled round through his street just for curiosity, watching the numbers to find his house, and there he stood on the sidewalk with a little fat spaniel on a leash.

"Hullo," he growled, hardly looking at me. Hunched into a wrinkled raincoat, he seemed shorter and sadder, and he stared glumly down at the glum spaniel. They stood there motionless in the yellow twilight of the street lamp. I remarked on the cool weather, but he merely voiced a faint growl.

"This is my night duty," he said, and cleared his throat with a sudden roar. He peered up at me abruptly with the expression of one about to give and take blows. "What? Did you speak?"

"No, but I was wondering if the dog appreciated what you do for him."

"He demands it, if that's what you mean. He requires it."

"Your night boss, I guess."

"That's right." Then he thought of it and let out a roar. "Ha! Good for my soul, I suppose! Is that what you're trying to say?" He peered furiously at me, but before I could answer he bent down and slapped the dog on its rump. "We cannot all be masters, hey, Woody?"

The black spaniel lifted bulging eyes but said nothing.

"Ten years ago," Mr. Quinn growled, "I named him Eastern Woodcraft Company. I had just taken it over and I—well, I had a feeling." He gathered up the slack of the leash. "Come in and visit, will you?" He and Woody started up the path with a similar motion.

A slate-gray mansard house, with a central tower and a heavy load of jigsaw work and fancy cornices and lightning rods. Once a mill owner's house of splendor and ostentation, it was now pressed tight on both sides by two- and three-family tenements—all the same slate gray and as ugly a mass of nailed-up lumber as the world could show. Not much grass anywhere, not much nature except the sky and one vast elm that rose from the plot of ground to the right of the path and spread itself far up into the darkness.

A porch with whimsical scrolled columns all peeling and cracked by weather, a doorway with stained-glass panes, a hall like a tomb, like death—the air, the furniture, the very body and soul of the place were plainly dead.

"My brother's place, this," he muttered, groping back into the gloom. He opened a door at the end of a hall and switched on a brighter light. "Come into my room here. Big house kind of gloomy, I guess. The women call this my study—here, take a chair. Smoke?"

Fifty years of helpless confusion might have made the room —a big high room nearly thirty feet long, with a place for sliding doors in the middle, and two marble fireplaces, and gaslight fixtures, and ranges of household debris piled like archaeological layers.

"Used to be the dining room here," he said. "Study there— den, they called it. I overflowed. We eat in the kitchen anyway—it saves a mile of walking a day."

Books stood in piles almost anywhere, and wooden boxes full of papers, and surveyors' equipment—tripods and transit and other things, including high leather boots and a mound of outing clothes. Behind a four-foot stack of *National Geographics* stood a bulging glass cabinet full of fancy china, with a scale model of an ironing-board stand on top of it.

I can't list all the stuff, and much of it was buried anyway. The oak dining table had been pushed partly into the back bay window and was spread with drawing materials and old copies of *Popular Mechanics* and rolls of wrapping paper. A bronze statuette of Mercury weighted one edge of a drawing, a one-volume Tennyson the other. No rugs anywhere, no curtains on the high windows, though they were fitted with elaborate inside shutters that folded into recesses. The room looked as though movers had just emptied a van load into it.

"Sit down," he said again, as if he remembered an old habit. "We'll have a smoke."

The light he had turned on was a single powerful bulb hung on a long brass chain from the ceiling. He walked off to the den end of the room and switched on a green shaded student lamp on the corner of a gigantic roll-top desk that stood askew in the middle of everything. In the whole room only two chairs were available, a swivel desk chair with arms, and a morris chair near the lamp whose faded green seat sagged down close to the floor. The other chairs, part of the carved oak set, were piled up with books or papers or clothes.

One other object—a cot, rumpled with brown outing

blankets—stood right across the door leading out of the den.

I lowered myself into the morris chair and found him smiling his enormous gap-toothed baby's smile at me. "It fits my behind better than yours. The only thing about it is I can't get out of it —I'm just as apt to stay in it all night as sleep on the bed there." And his face suddenly lost all joviality; it darkened and sagged and seemed to fall apart. "I don't sleep, you know. Haven't slept for years." He settled into the creaking desk chair and breathed sorrowfully for a moment. "You probably don't realize that I'm not apt to last long—why, if I told you all the things that are wrong with me you couldn't believe it." He hunched forward in the chair. "Why, just take my kidneys alone . . ."

He couldn't eat, he never slept, he astonished his doctors by remaining alive—though in the last couple of years he had given up doctors entirely because all they ever did was shake their heads, say tut-tut, and send him a bill. Take his asthma, for instance. They said Arizona was his only chance, but he preferred to suffer at home.

What troubled him a good deal was his shop. It was called a company; his father and brother had founded it thirty years before, but now they were dead, and he really owned it, though his brother's widow owned some of it too: but if he dropped dead, as he might at any moment, who would go on with it? His wife knew nothing of it; his daughter had never set foot in it. No one in the shop could take over—Miss Hagerthy was capable, but knew nothing about making the stuff. That salesman, Eddy Rose, was a damn fool. Old Shelly, who kept the accounts, had been there longer than anybody, but he couldn't manage anything.

A telephone bell rang somewhere in the hall, and to my astonishment steps went to it and a voice answered. I had felt that we must be abandoned by humanity.

"Dad, for you!" A cool, high, annoyed voice.

He grunted himself out of his chair.

A knock, and the door at the other end opened. "Dad?"

"Yah" (a growling noise), "I'm here."

"Well, why don't you yell? It's the telephone."

He started toward the girl in the door, then stopped and growled again. "Oh, Marilyn, this is Mr. uh—uh—"

Silence an instant.

"Garretson," I said.

"Garretson!" he bellowed.

She gave me a cold appraisal. "Oh?" And she turned away and preceded him out into the hall.

I heard him shouting fiercely that he never saw anybody on business at home, and he didn't care if the man was leaving for the west coast or not. He banged down the receiver, muttering.

Then more mutterings, and a tense feminine whine. "I will not! You're such a *fool!*" Then the grunt and shuffle of steps and he reappeared. He shut the door.

"That girl—" He waved me back into the morris chair, offered me another cigarette from a crumpled package, took one himself, and began groping for matches. "She has the worst set of friends you ever saw. I shouldn't talk like this, I know, but she exasperates me. We made the mistake of sending her to a high-class school—Hemlock Hall or something fancy like that, and now she's too good to associate with us any more. Her mother's idea—probably a good one, but it just didn't work. You notice she wouldn't hardly say hello to you—thinks you're one of those common workmen from dad's shop. Her idea of a man is one that never does a damn thing except ride around in a roadster."

He shook off the idea like a bear shaking off flies.

"I suppose I shouldn't say this either, but when I feel something I usually say it. Like my health—I know nobody gives a damn about my symptoms—why should they? I don't give very much of a damn about other peoples'. But I get to talking and can't stop— Well, about the shop—what I need to do is to get somebody who can keep it going when I give out. I believe you could—" He groped for my name a moment, then gave up and went on. "You're young, you don't know much yet, maybe you have other ideas—I don't know, but the fact is I've been looking for the right kind of man for quite a while. You may not think so, but I'm a good judge of men—I pride myself on that." He paused to glare at me. I nodded. "Now, the kind of feller who thinks he can run a business doesn't know a damn thing about wood—all he thinks about is selling and all that hoop-la." For a moment he muttered something about the salesmen who gave him a pain. "And the kind of feller who can handle the wood is no good at running a business. What I need is a man who can do both."

I said I knew nothing of business.

"That's what I'm telling you: I'll teach you." He waved an arm with a bearlike gesture. "Everything. In the end you'll be a better man than I am."

Yet I listened to all this without real belief. The dead house, the fantastic room full of two generations of junk, the tragic bearish figure slumped in the squeaking desk chair—none of it belonged to any life I had ever imagined. A nervous sort of laughter welled up in me, and I felt a keen ache of suppression in my chest; it took conscious restraint to keep back the impulse to cry out foolishly. If I had been alone, I should have cut a caper and whacked the side of a box with a newspaper.

Not for levity. Mr. Quinn had touched me deeply, almost to the point of tears. His grizzled face folded itself into lines of heaviest sorrow—I hardly knew why. He personified the tragedy of all flesh. Yet I wanted to escape, to release myself from what seemed like a dreadful allegory, a masque of pathetic mortality.

The "business"—what did it have to do with my dream, with the world of sun and space and freedom which Ralph Garretson had made up for himself? A life of towel racks and trellises and ironing boards, of buying and selling.

"You can think it over—no use committing yourself yet."

"Why don't you make furniture too?"

"Hardwood stuff?"

"Yes."

The idea—suggested simply to fill in—cast him into gloom again. He shook his head and stared at the floor. "Well, I couldn't. Maybe someone like you—" His voice sank to a grumble. "Need a larger plant, different machines—too damn complicated for an old man like me."

"There's no decent furniture in the stores," I said. "I'll bet you can't buy one simple, well-designed chair in Waltham."

"Maybe not." But I realized he cared nothing about a well-designed chair. He came back with tenacity to his own idea. "All I want is to keep the shop going the best I know how."

Before he allowed me to go he leaned toward me and muttered very secretly that he wished he could invite me there more often. Mrs. Quinn seldom saw people any more: as a matter of fact, their only son had died in the war—just at the end, in that influenza epidemic, and Mrs. Quinn had never recovered from the shock. She stayed in her room most of the time. He guessed she hadn't been down here in the study for three or four years. It made it a little awkward, but he wanted me to understand how it was. He peered at me very closely and fiercely to be sure I did understand.

Then at last we groped our way along the dark hall again to the front door and he let me out. "Glad you stopped by—it's a long time since I've had a caller."

The black spaniel, I noted, had slept all the time on an old coat in a corner; but he came to the door, and both of them watched me down the path.

My thoughts that evening were long, long thoughts, but not quite happy. Conscience and reason teamed up against me— whatever "me" might be—and informed me clearly of my opportunities. Mr. Quinn was not a creature of allegory and dream, nor even a sad and lonely grizzly; rather, he owned and managed a successful manufacturing plant and was inviting me to be his heir apparent. It all seemed naïve; business, I supposed, didn't operate on terms so simple—even if Mr. Quinn did. But there was the fact: he did. I saw him every day. He was both effective and realistic—more than that, trustworthy.

A good business, reason said. Clean lumber, sharp tools, forthright products. It might have been—well, chewing gum, mouthwash, painkiller, kewpie dolls. A hustling young man of vision like Ralph Garretson could build it up into something big and turn out beautiful simple tables and chairs and beds; he could revolutionize American taste, do away forever with the Grand Rapids funeral-parlor school and the pink bawdy-house lamps. He could be in the end a financial and social power, and his Uncle Richard would retract his hasty accusations and admit his error.

No, it all seemed like dismal folly. Conscience and reason made no headway against the current of my romantic individuality. Only Babbitts, said Ralph to himself, using a new term in American speech, think in terms of money and position.

A couple of weeks later Mr. Quinn took me aside one morning and after glancing furtively in every direction invited me to dinner that evening. Things might be somewhat rough and ready. But it would give him much pleasure, and Marilyn too.

I accepted.

✦§   CHAPTER 23   §✦

CONFESSIONALS in these times have dealt mainly with early love. Before the nineteen-twenties the subject was treated by implication only, except, I suppose, in France. Then came the hysterical orgy of revelation, a this-side-of-Paradise time when the young shouted out their secrets in competition. I was young then too; I knew the compulsion that was on us.

We had little race knowledge of passion. In our childhood it was a whisper of evil. Then war, new times, and release— but with the release a deadly ignorance, an inherited fear, a stampede into emancipation. Youth flung itself into experience with the reckless and terrified compulsion of young soldiers going to their first battle. Every small detail grew big with significance; each recruit felt that the facts of his own passion were utterly new on earth and must at once be recorded and revealed to all men.

After the hysteria came the clinical restatements, the "new naturalism." After that the whole subject began to be a bore— as a subject, that is. Young men discovering in public their physiological resources are not popular any more. Perhaps we are at last getting the necessary race knowledge.

I was brought up to be nice to little girls. I was taught that they were pure and untouchable. I learned that they lived apart and that it was best for a boy up to the time of marriage to have nothing whatever to do with them. The experiences

273

at Bronson Alcott and the dancing class confirmed this knowledge.

But an age of emancipation makes other demands. My pal Musty Ellis spoke of women as though they were a marketable and pleasant variety of cattle, though I learned in time that his talk was very artistic. At college the lads were eagerly striving to free themselves from moral bondage, and a few succeeded.

I failed.

I talked of the folly of innocence. I dreamed of splendid indulgences. I felt lust like an electric charge, numbing my mind and burning through my blood. I lived that absurd and secret and terrible life of desire that all men live. I thought everlastingly of fair women and imagined satisfactions beyond the bounds of sin. All my cussed independence, my impulse to be separate and alone and peculiar, was obscurely a part of my secret passion.

Yet no record embodies that life. Some quality of taste, old habit, cowardice, kept me from experience. No link seemed to exist between dream and fact. I lived outwardly among the forms and manners and words, in the watertight compartment of respectability, and discovered no way out of it.

Many, I think, will scarcely credit a tale so naïve. The broad, broad road runs fair and straight to wickedness—so they say, and men discover it too easily. But not Ralph, and not others like him. I envied some of those travelers, I admired their bold confidence and wished I were with them, but I seemed to be stuck willy-nilly to my own path. It may be that I was also a moral snob and considered drunkenness and commercial fornication too vulgar. It may be that I was bound by certain esthetic habits and had no taste for common sin. In part I was afraid, like Mr. Prufrock.

So my passions remained suppressed and secret. I attended a few intellectual dances at Radcliffe. I appeared at the debutante parties, but not among the ones supposed to carry hip flasks. I had been to dinner and tea, and discovered many cousins near and far. And always I looked for my true partner in romance, my own complaisant queen of elfland. I searched hopefully among Hollisters and Hardings, in and about Marlborough Street and the Chilton Club, but all I found were the nice ones, the cool, admirable ones who had read *Little Women* when they were younger and were now reading *Women in Love* (with distaste, I acknowledge). Little Lucys, little Carolines, as well trained as thoroughbreds.

At home there were little Cadwalladers, who grew up without much blood in their bodies.

Truc, I loved Martha Kingsley. She had long been my pioneer bride, my woman for mountain or forest or uncharted seas—though of course she never knew it. It wasn't quite passion at all, hungry as I used to be to kiss her sweet big mouth and feel the assurance of her strong body against mine. She had been gone a long time now—had trained to be a nurse and was in a hospital in Pennsylvania, but I kept on thinking of her as my own woman. I knew now that she had once been in love, had traveled to Florida expecting to be married, had been deserted there—they never said exactly why or how, but I realized the savage evil of a man who could do that to my Martha.

There alone in Waltham I thought of her a great deal, and often wished we were together, married, safe, in the grim little room I lived in.

When I went to dinner at the Quinns, Marilyn opened the door, took my coat (I never wore a hat), asked me to come into the sitting room at the right side of the entrance hall. A pale, reserved, gracious hostess, yet curiously ill at ease. I had thought of her first as cold and selfish, but now she smiled a little and seemed to suffer from repression. She stood when she should have sat, and eyed me with a flickering, furtive look.

"Dad will be down—he wanted me to tell you that mother isn't feeling well enough. She—I—I'm sorry—"

I said he had told me already.

She eyed me again.

"You know," she said in louder tones, "we eat in the kitchen here."

The words came out harshly, like a challenge.

I nodded and said I had seen the dining room. I hoped she would smile at least, or express some little recognition of our comedy; but she stood there like an anxious martyr. Pale, she was, and blond and slim—no visible resemblance to her father: in fact, she expressed a literal contrast, and I stared at her with too evident curiosity. Her ash-gold hair was bobbed in style, short behind and longer on the sides; her face, naturally colorless and almost transparent, as the saying goes, had been very slightly painted—and even then artificial color on a woman suggested harlotry: color was permissible only when undetected. Yet she was uncommonly pretty with a waxen, fashion-book sort of distinction.

I said I lived in a room eight feet square and ate in the one-arm lunchrooms, and would like nothing better than to dine in their kitchen.

"You went to Harvard, didn't you?"

The question seemed to shoot itself at me.

"For a couple of years," I said.

"I know a lot of boys there. I know Bill Marvin and Bertie Riggs and Don Hoffstetter—his father owns the Samoset Textile Mills—and Ed Styles—you know, Styles' Hats—"

"Be in style with a Styles hat," I quoted.

She nodded with a smile. "Do you know Ed?"

"No, I'm afraid I don't."

"Oh—well, let's see: I know George—George—oh, dear, I forget, but I meet so many boys at the country club. Don't you ever go out to the club? We have a lot of dances there."

"Did you say Bertie Riggs?"

"Yes, he comes often—he has the slickest new Stutz. Do you mean you know him?"

"Well, sure—I went to school with him."

"Why, he went to Lincoln."

All this time we had been standing near the empty marble fireplace, Marilyn with hands clasped in front of her and one foot coyly behind the other in an arrangement made popular by one of the Gish sisters on the screen. Her steady, fixed stare was part of the same pose.

Now she smiled. "Did *you* go to Lincoln?"

The smile changed her into a beauty—very briefly. Then she reverted to pale anxiety.

We heard a heavy body on the stairs, and Mr. Quinn came in, panting from the exertion of descent. He regretted again that Mrs. Quinn wasn't able to come down, and explained the circumstances, as he had done twice before. He should have been down earlier himself—had planned to be, but his collar button had popped off and completely disappeared. It took him ten minutes to find it—way back under the bathtub. By then he had got his shirt dirty crawling round the floor, but there were no clean ones in the drawer, so he finally wore the dirty one anyway—he pulled back his left coat sleeve to show us how it was. Then he invited us all to sit down.

Marilyn turned abruptly and walked out through a door toward the kitchen, her face set almost to the point of tears.

"See if supper's ready," he called to her. Then he turned to me. "She doesn't think I ought to talk about collar buttons." He stared at me grimly, as though he expected me to challenge him. "I always seem to have trouble with them, I must say. I rather think I'll try to get some shirts like that soft one of yours where the buttons are all sewed on. I have a hard time getting anything to fit, though—built like a meal sack the way I am. If I weren't so darn stingy I'd have them made."

Marilyn told us to come, and we walked out through a back hall to a pantry and through that to an enormous kitchen, where a white-clothed table was set for three.

I was introduced to the cook, Mrs. Eckstrom, who stood by the coal range twenty feet across the room and stared somberly at us with military severity. The kitchen, I perceived instantly, was not like the rest of the house—not cold and dead; rather it seemed bright with life in spite of its burden of Victorian equipment. The bare wood floor had been scoured like a ship's deck; the stove glistened with heat and polish; the shelves and tables were tidy and shiny.

"Mrs. Eck," he was saying, "is queen out here. We have to do whatever she orders."

"Well, sit down to your soup before it's any colder."

We sat under Mrs. Eck's commanding eye. Mr. Quinn had adopted a manner of joviality and his voice boomed out at us. "I'd urge her to join us here, but I know she won't. She's afraid she might lose some of her authority." He grinned and looked all round—at her and me and her again. "Now, I hope you're hungry—er—your name *is* Ralph, isn't it? I even forget Marilyn's sometimes—I'm poor at names, though I know faces. If I can see them, that is. My eyes don't focus, you know." He urged more soup on me, more crackers, more celery, and kept shouting across to Mrs. Eck, who never replied.

Marilyn remained pale and silent.

A fine dinner of steak and mushrooms. Under constant urging I ate enough for two. Marilyn's only remark during the meal was to ask me if I knew Barry Higgins, whose father owned the B. B. Higgins clothing stores; she thought Barry had gone to Lincoln.

"What's Lincoln?" asked Mr. Quinn cheerily.

Marilyn compressed her lips and rolled her eyes ceilingward.

When I explained, Mr. Quinn turned gloomy. "Another one of those rich country clubs. That Hemlock Hill place was enough for me—there's no excuse for such places in a democratic country. Now take a fellow like Ralph, here—what's the sense of his wasting his time playing round with rich boys in roadsters?"

I tried to explain more justly, and described the Spartan ideals of Lincoln, but he heard little of what I said. A boy ought to learn to work, the way he had. His father had run a small lumber yard, and the boys had gone to work in it right from the start. Of course, you had to have training—he realized it when he got through high school and took night courses at Middlesex Institute, but that was different from this leisure-time culture stuff. He said that culture was all right, but you could pick it up as you went along. He peered angrily at me and asked if I had read all of Shakespeare, and when I said not all he nodded in triumph. "Well, I have—some of it two or three times too; and I didn't have to go to an expensive school to do it, either." He stared at me, then at Marilyn, then at Mrs. Eck, then at me again; he broke into his eager baby grin and nodded. "I really enjoy Shakespeare, though you may not believe it." Suddenly he lifted his fork and swept an arc with it; his voice boomed out powerfully. "I am as hot as molten lead, and as heavy too. God keep lead out of me! I need no more weight than mine own bowels." He glared from right to left as he hurled the words at the corners of the room; then he grinned again. "That's Falstaff, you know. He was supposed to be fatter than I am, but I understand how he felt." He looked at me shrewdly then and asked how I happened to go to a place like Lincoln, and when I said my father and uncle and brother had all been there he nodded very seriously several times and kept glancing at me. "Maybe I spoke with too much prejudice," he said finally. "I sometimes think I have very strong prejudices."

After dinner he insisted that Marilyn play the piano. She resisted passionately for several minutes, then did it like a pale martyr—a medley of songs and practice pieces very lightly and coldly performed.

Mr. Quinn had shut the door to the hall. Any kind of music, he said, seemed to make Mrs. Quinn unhappy. Marilyn had had to give up most of her practicing. He used to like to sing, himself, but he seldom did any more.

We talked a little, and I made some effort to take an early leave. But they held me. I felt almost like a captive. Marilyn sat near me and watched me with a curious eager intentness, and when I spoke she listened and smiled and answered in ways that led me to speak more.

"Dad," she said once on a quick impulse, "I wish we could have a party here—I mean a real big party for my friends, and we could dance and have fun. I've never had a party—never once."

But at the word his face had fallen into its mold of despair. "Well, we can't." He turned to me with a stiff sort of formality and explained that Mrs. Quinn was far from well; he regretted that she wasn't able to join us. As for a party, it was of course out of the question.

Marilyn's eyes filled and she turned away and said nothing.

I broke away finally, and they both came to the door and watched me off into the dark.

Thereafter I found myself attached to the Quinn household, but somewhat secretly.

"I probably shouldn't say this," Mr. Quinn explained to me later on, "but Mrs. Quinn really doesn't want us to enjoy ourselves. You may have noticed that we have very little company —in fact, aside from you, we have none at all. Now, she has had a serious shock and is far from well—you must understand that very clearly; but it does make it difficult for us, especially for Marilyn."

So I came to dinner very quietly, and grew friendly with the stern Mrs. Eckstrom, and we sat and talked in the kitchen. And Mr. Quinn took me into his study and we looked at drawings and discussed new ideas.

I never got used to the sepulchral air of the house. It remained always lifeless, never fresh or bright; the old veneered and plushy furnishings stood neglected in the gloom—in fact, the front rooms were never used at all and might as well have been shut up entirely. The study was always the same mass of haphazard junk and bad air.

But I began to feel a sort of responsibility for them in there, as though I were an appointed missionary to a place of darkness. Mr. Quinn, I found, was a man of many little projects which had withered from lack of encouragement. Even his Shakespeare needed an audience, and as he grew more used to my presence he remembered more and more Falstaffian lines and rapped them out with immense growls and bellows. And he showed me his collection of watches and clocks, and a set of tools he had once used to repair them with—he said he had grown too blind and clumsy to do such work now, but several times I found him tinkering with little clocks, with pieces all over his desk. And his *National Geographics* had meant a lot to him for thirty years—he had them all there, piled up in corners and against the furniture; no one but him had ever cared for them, he said, and he showed me his favorites from long ago.

Except for his long days of work at the shop, he lived almost entirely within the walls of his "study," as solitary as a hermit. And Marilyn, as far as I could tell, spent most of her time in her room upstairs—and what she did there no one ever knew.

But now when I came she always appeared. She opened the door before I rang—her mother, she said, grew restless when the bell jangled and wanted to know what was going on. Later I used the side door, whose bell buzzed quietly in the kitchen, but her room must have been near the head of the back stairs, for she was always down in an instant. Mrs. Eck, she said, never liked to answer doors—in fact, Mrs. Eck did not work outside of the kitchen. If I were visiting with Mr. Quinn in the study, Marilyn would come in to have her watch regulated, or to borrow the newspaper, or to ask if it were time for Woody to go out.

I began taking her to the movies once or twice a week. I took her to the theater in Boston. I used up the remainder of my pay on her, and when the pay was raised I used that up too. I even cast about for a Ford, and was offered the use of the empty carriage house in the Quinn's back yard.

In no time at all, Marilyn was my girl.

Her talk always flowed round the people we knew. Lincoln had been a magic name at Hemlock Hill. Lincoln boys had come to their dances; Harvard boys came; Bertie Riggs came in his Stutz, and fellows named Eddie and Barry and Don, with lots of money. There had been a dance at the Hoffstetters' once, and a couple of dances at a country club—but now they seemed to have forgotten her. Yet she lived in expectation of them. She waved and smiled when they went by, and said that Eddie was the wildest driver and didn't Barry look ducky with his hair cut short that way. She wished I knew them all better —and somehow I found myself taking her to a benefit dance (exclusive) at a place called Riverview Pavilion. I don't know what it benefited.

The first Marilyn I had seen was a cold and petulant creature, and I disliked her. Then I realized how she seemed to be caught there in that catacomb of a house, and how she suffered from lack of sun and air, and yet craved it. She was nothing there but an inmate, and her anxious little efforts to be a hostess were carried on without any sort of backing, and with heavy troubles stacked against her.

Then Childe Ralph came to the dark tower, and the princess flung herself upon him. I try to record these truths fairly. I believe that Mr. Quinn matched me with his daughter, not in malicious scheming, but with intent most benevolent. As a matter of principle he hated the social set his daughter preferred, and so looked about for what he thought was an honest, industrious apprentice, like me. He fancied himself on his human perspicacity—but I fear he greatly overrated it. The speculative Ralph was a poor bet for any man's daughter.

But the name of Lincoln did wonders, of course, and the Quinn plan flourished.

What I hadn't forseen in all this was the transformation of the princess. Her pale and droopy petulance gave place after a while to radiance, to beauty itself. I suppose I must go on and say that a kiss did it. I fear there's no doubt; it did.

It did something to me too. The creature I had at first inspected so coolly had become as lovely and feminine and desirable as any damsel I had ever imagined. She grew soft and sweet. She smiled a little familiar smile she must have been saving for this occasion. She moved under my protection, body and soul, with all the Evelike innocence of a woman who knows her troubles are ended forever.

An old campaigner would have known all these things, though I think no one ever fully knows them until after they are all over.

I was not a campaigner at all, though at the time I assumed that I knew everything worth knowing. I had always wanted a golden princess (so it now appeared, at least); I had always resented the social arrangements that my family had made for me; and now at last I had found this lovely creature—in fact, I was rescuing her, creating her as Pygmalion created Galatea. Eagerly I thought of all I could do for her, the wondrous ideas I would put in her pretty head, the books, the art. Even now I had wrought a miracle.

The kiss had been put off a long time. I knew at first that it would lead to many consequences, but as days went by I grew more and more fascinated by her charms—her clothes, her skin, her gold hair, everything about her, and naturally the thought of consequences grew dim. As a matter of fact, a young man is no more master of his fate than a spider in a high wind. When I picked her up to kiss her I had no notion what I was doing; it simply happened, and there I was on a Victorian divan with a bundle of sweetness in my arms—I, at least, being blown far and wide in a gale of hurricane force.

"Oh, Ralph—do you—do you really? I mean, you shouldn't —if—if—"

Yes, really. As real as fire, as cataracts and hurricanes.

In a torrent of first love nothing else exists. Her voice had marriage in its tones, but why not? Marriage was a passing detail, a trifle, a small and obvious necessity one had to accept on the same terms as food and lodging and job. Compared with this magnificent passion all those minor essentials diminished almost to nothing. I suppose a man riding out a gale at sea cares not for his exact social status back home.

Like everyone else, I had been taught that marriage was the corollary to passion, and any other arrangement was a breach of sportsmanship (I almost wrote "sin," but I had emancipated myself from that word—so I thought). At any rate, here was a girl in my arms craving love, and here was I ready and willing, and full of disastrous good intentions. Perhaps a stern caddishness on my part would have led to better results.

I loved her with the sort of delirium for which no youth is responsible—any more than dry grass is responsible for what happens when a flame is touched to it. We were both too innocent to be safe, and we clutched at each other with a wild and desperate fumbling. We blushed and trembled and laughed foolishly and sighed in ecstasy; we pretended, we acted, and mostly we evaded any admission of what was happening.

Other evenings, more kisses. And more, and more. No end to it—always a little more.

She grew incredibly lovely. Her transparent skin flushed with rose and amber tints, her gray eyes glowed with mysterious starlight, her thin mouth softened, curved tenderly and smiled in ways it never had before. Even her body became conscious of itself, as though it recognized its womanliness for the first time.

"Why, Marilyn, you're more beautiful every day. You've been sleeping like the princess in the fairy tale, and now you're coming into your own again."

I wanted to talk like poetry to her, but it didn't come the way I hoped. I wanted to make love in rare terms, but beyond the squeezing and kissing there wasn't much to say. Instead she talked to me.

She told me about her loneliness. She had no friends, nothing to do. Her mother kept people away, kept her at home idle. She wanted to take a business course and get a job—but no, she had to stay home. Not that she cared much for business, but it would be better than this doing nothing. And dad was so—well, queer. He didn't try to understand her at all, and was all wrapped up in his own interests, though of course he worried a lot about mother. She did too. They all worried. The house was more like an asylum than a real home. Neither dad nor mother would have anything to do with doctors.

So far, she said, her mother hardly knew about me at all. Goodness knows what would happen when she found out—but of course she'd have to know sometime.

Yes, I agreed. Maybe her dad could break the news.

Well, maybe, but mostly dad made her furious—her mother, that is. The only way he could keep things peaceful was by acting like a little boy in school—tiptoeing round and talking in polite whispers. When I chuckled at the picture, she looked accusingly at me, then smiled a little for love's sake.

And by the way, didn't I think it was time we told dad?

In the midst of active love, telling dad seemed like a remote and minor duty. But on a cool working morning, when I saw him churning his way grimly down the line of machines, peering right and left for trouble, I began to recognize consequences.

In the end, it was he who told me.

My visits to his study had grown less and less frequent.

After dinner, Marilyn and I usually walked off into the darkness, or went to a movie, or sometimes to a dance; but one evening she disappeared abruptly upstairs and I was invited—in portentous tones—to the study.

He furnished us with cigarettes, asked me formally to take a chair, cleared his throat with a roaring cough and remarked that by now I probably realized he was a blunt man.

"I want you to forgive me for speaking this way," he went on, peering at me hard. "I just don't know how to go at it in a gentlemanly manner. As a matter of fact, I don't consider myself a gentleman at all." This time he glared at me as though he expected me to try to punch him in the jaw. Then he harrumphed hoarsely and went on. "The question is, are you and my daughter going to get married, or aren't you?"

It was as though a thundercloud had spoken.

I searched for a few small words, but he raised a heavy finger and pointed me to silence.

"Now, I want you to understand—I want to make this very clear: whether you do or don't is mainly your business. I'm not trying to railroad you into it, or out of it. But there are certain issues that have to be faced. You see that, don't you? You realize yourself that we can't dodge issues?"

I struggled again to utter words, but he waved a hand and went on.

"I want to tell you now, before you speak, that I think very well of you. I invited you here for that reason. I thought you and Marilyn might be friends." He stopped and breathed hard a few moments. "I haven't spoken to her about it, but I know she likes you." He stopped again, as though he had collided with something.

Now was the time. Silence covered us. He puffed his cigarette and looked closely at the end of it. The words literally choked in my throat.

"Why—" I said, and coughed.

He eyed his smoke with an expression of grimmest melancholy.

The consequence rose before me like a wall.

"Yes," I said strongly, with sudden energy. "Yes, as a matter of fact we do want to get married. We have been planning to tell you."

He eyed me for a second suspiciously, as though waiting for

added truth to trickle through, then suddenly he smiled. His face broke into its widest grin, gap-toothed and wrinkled in pure delight. "Well," he said, and surprise pitched his voice high, "well, this is certainly fine. You and Marilyn." He stood up and I stood up and we shook hands. "I can't rise very far to the occasion, but I want you to know that I am certainly pleased."

Then slowly the cloud came down over his face and figure. He shrank, drooped, sank heavily into his chair, and once more his face folded into its lines of despair.

"There'll be trouble," he said. "Lots of it, I'm afraid." He cleared his throat sorrowfully. "Sit down again," he said. "That's what we have to talk about."

✌§ CHAPTER 24 ᠊ᡠ᠊

THE FACTS of this Waltham love story were probably more sordid than I pretend. Facts nearly always are. I am tempted to get on with my tale quickly, to jump ahead to better times; but the many human characteristics of the story keep coming back to me. I aimed at the honorable estate of true love; I aimed at freedom and adventure and originality; I was conscious of striking out into manhood, of discovering my own resources of strength and competence. I set forth on my conquest of love with the high heart of a scout challenging the Oregon territory.

Yet I knew almost at once that I had been betrayed into failure. I had to carry on in secrecy and darkness without any splendor, with no joyous fanfares, nor any blessings by Apollo and the other gods of light. I realized uneasily that something had gone wrong.

Any bystander could have told me—or could now tell me. I know it all too, now that I am more than two and twenty. I suppose I've paid with sighs enough also, but bystanders are not exempt either.

It was all a confusion of good intentions. Mr. Quinn did me the honor of holding a high opinion of my abilities and character (still, I think, under the influence of Seth and the old shop), and with rare benevolence he elected me to inherit his business and rescue his daughter. And I accepted my new duties at first out of respect for an honest and desperate man, and then

out of compassion and pity (and condescension, if you like)
for the slowly languishing heroine. After that came passion.
The heroine turned out to be a creature of lovely flesh (what
other kind is there?); the hero seized her in unaccustomed arms
(how else do heroes rescue?) and from there on nature permitted no retreat.

Result: an engagement of marriage.

If I had been possessed of a bystander's wisdom and virtue, I
would have left the lady to languish in perfect innocence and
safety. If I had been intelligently unscrupulous, I could have
avoided consequences without increasing grief—not very much,
anyway. It was simply my fate to stumble along in the dangerous half-light of my good intentions. And again I should put
the whole thing down to the damned romantic innocence of
puritanism. It may be that sex and social harmony are forever
at tragic odds, no matter who makes the codes; possibly blind
virtue and evasion achieve illusions as comfortable as the
results of brutal fact-facing. But at this point, at least, I
feel justified in my course. I had been badly prepared for passion.

For several days I kept the great consequence a secret almost
from myself. No man could have been less prepared for
marriage; in fact, I simply did not believe in marriage, or
recognize its existence. I revolved on my cycle of work, as
before.

But not so Marilyn. Another great transformation took place.
First, sleeping beauty; then rescued princess and enthusiastic
heroine; now, bride. Everything she did seemed to be primarily
the act of a woman, secondarily the act of a reasoning character
named Marilyn Quinn. The dangerous problem of mother was
put off—we seemed to agree to that without discussion—and
instead a whole secret movement of preparation got under way.
She still looked upon me with affection, but her gaze more and
more fixed itself on a world of sheets and towels and new
clothes; she brooded on announcements, and cards and social

amenities reaching far into the future. She engaged in wide-ranging shopping reconnaissance.

And again, all this had no real existence for me. I continued uneasily to keep my head well buried in the sand. What really shocked me into recognition was the need of a ring.

"Ralph, when you do get the ring, dad says to see him about it first. He knows where you can get one—I mean a wholesaler or dealer or something, I don't quite know who it is, but he says it might save you a little, and I do think saving is important even in getting a ring. Of course, it would be nice to have one from a place like Tiffany's—that's where Clarice Martin's came from, and she always reminds you of it, but after all, that's a name—they say Bigelow and Stoddard is a very good place too, in on Winter Street, isn't it? But you better talk to dad anyway. He meets a lot of people in business."

"Oh," I said. "Yes, that's a good idea." Luckily Marilyn never noticed my emotions closely. I felt the warm blood in my face, and my words were muttered shakily. The thought of a ring had simply not entered my head. It is reasonable to say that up to then practically nothing had entered my head.

But now suddenly I began perceiving the facts of life. A suitable modest engagement ring would cost me a month's pay, and in my opinion its human value amounted to nothing.

"You—you'd really like a ring, then?"

"Why, Ralph! What a question to ask a girl!"

In a state of dejection I began figuring out other things. Marriage, I found, took more money than I had ever had to reckon with, and the thought of money foolishly irritated me. My sentimental liberalism caused me to despise it as a thing beneath the notice of a proper idealist; in some vague fashion I believed it possible to live without it, like the saints and philosophers, like Diogenes and Thoreau, whom I admired. But now the price of diamond rings confronted me, as well as of rent and food and clothes and monogrammed silver.

All in all, it is too easy now to forget that Marilyn Quinn was lovely to look at and sweet and fresh and blond and naturally feminine. When we walked in the dark, close pressed to each other, the problem of life grew as simple as that. We talked of nothing much, and the blood sang happily in our bodies, and time went like a dream.

Through all our loving and planning, Mr. Quinn watched with fierce and benevolent intentness. He seemed to take me with supreme faith. He never asked for credentials, inquired who I was, questioned my purposes. He was a good judge of character, he said, and having once accepted me he assumed that all doubts were at an end. He promoted me through various positions to a sort of assistant manager at fifty dollars a week, and such was his faith that my conscience drove me to extraordinary zeal. He addressed me now in the shop as Mister Garretson—often the name roared out over the humming machinery, and the men looked at me with dark resentment.

"I want you to understand, Ralph," he said one evening, "that I am personally very pleased. You believe that, don't you?"

"Well, if you say it, I do."

"You see, I may not have told you—but I am liable to drop dead almost any day. I'm in poor shape—couldn't really be much worse; I think you'd be amazed if I described all my symptoms to you." His voice had a jocular note, and he grinned. Then grim solemnity again. "I don't mind telling you I've been pretty badly worried. I had a feeling Marilyn was too much interested in those damn country-club fools—forgive me if any of 'em are friends of yours, but I just don't like 'em."

I said they weren't my friends.

"I didn't believe they were. You're a different type of person entirely. And if you can keep the works going, and look after Marilyn, why, I'll feel a lot better about dropping dead." He peered at me unwaveringly for several seconds. "There's something else," he growled. "I shouldn't tell you, but I'm going to. I intend to make a will leaving my right in the business to you—"

I felt as though a sandbag had hit me.

"No!" I yelled.

He stared at me in anxious surprise.

"Well," he began, "that's my intention—"

"No!" I said it with a choke of terror. "Don't do it. I don't want the business. I don't know anything about property—I don't like property—"

His stare settled into lines of bewilderment and pain. "I knew I shouldn't have said anything," he muttered. "Trouble is, you're young. Twenty-two, is it? I didn't know much at that age either." He shook himself and spoke out with a sudden loud rasp. "Now, you just forget about it. For all anybody knows, I may be running the shebang for years."

He may have said more, but I felt as though a prison house had closed over me—in the form of a red-brick mill building. I perceived that I had got myself committed to a future I never in the world would have elected if I had known—if I had used any intelligence in directing myself. The whole iron chain of compulsions began with my natural desire to own a woman. I was inevitably going the way, not of all flesh, but of the free and enlightened Anglo-Saxon. A paying business, solid property, solid respectability, all the typical features of suburban success —just marry the boss's daughter and everything follows in order.

After almost a year in Waltham, I knew enough to be scared. And I had the advantage of good honest activity too, of creating solid objects for people to sit on, or stand on, or hang clothes on. But a young fellow running a saw or planer was one thing; taking on a wife, a family, a state of mind, a business, a town like Waltham—all that was an immensely different thing, and, as I said, terrifying.

I was young, he said. There was nothing fearsome about

property. Even the stupidest people learn how to handle it. But I couldn't explain that it wasn't the property itself I feared, but the life it required of its servants, the life he, John Quinn, was leading, and the house he lived in and the grim mask of despair that covered his face.

I went off alone and walked in the night. I rushed out to where I could see the stars plain, and where I could hear sounds and silence of the open—wind in many leaves, peepers and buzzers of a spring night. I solved my doubts by getting so tired I had to sleep, and being so late I had to run to work.

I needed to talk, but except for the Quinns I had spent the winter pretty much alone. My father and Jean were staying in Italy and would go on to Greece in early spring. Steve made a complete life for himself at Harvard—without unkindness I often think he should be allowed to go to college forever. In all the years since, his taste, his pleasures, even his appearance, have remained those of a Harvard senior—and as long as the world leaves him alone his is a happy illusion.

I used to go home for an occasional Sunday; took a trolley to the end of its line and walked the remaining seven miles along a highway streaming with motorcars and more and more littered with the debris of city culture. A bicycle would have done well on the road, but in that particular time of automobile dominance no one rode bicycles and I never thought of trying to get one. And I liked to walk, and took pride in my pace. In spite of the highway litter, the country out there remained fresh and open, with the lovely design that centuries of cultivation give to rolling northern land.

Mater had organized our household to her own specifications. The three young ones there seemed to me a subdued and earnest lot, like three rather slim owls, with very keen but literal intelligences. It isn't fair to sum up three personalities in the same phrase, but they had been shaped by mater toward the same end—and mater was a very effective shaper. And now with everyone else away she could operate freely. The air seemed almost antiseptic and time was measured out in even lengths, and all good things were carefully admired and cherished. I remember little Ellen at the piano doing scales to a metronome, her straight brown hair cut short as a boy's, her back erect and stiff, her stubby fingers working systematically up and down the keyboard, and her eyes focused through round-lensed spectacles to the open page of notes. And Ted, thirteen, reading *Ivanhoe* and expressing doubts as to the authenticity of the treatment of King Richard. And the youngest, Franklin, was directed into the footsteps of his great namesake, and studied birds and beasts.

It was my duty to tell mater of my engagement, but once I came into the house there I seemed to be incapable of speaking of it. The Ralph who dwelt in Waltham became quite separate from the Ralph who sat down to Sunday dinner with his family, and that one should speak for the other was out of the question. The quiet ancient certainty of that life at home, the serene simplicity of taste, the pure virtue and pure reason, had no connection whatever with the grubby commerce of my other life. And mater, of course, would disapprove; with calm precision she would probe and lay bare my folly and would demonstrate that I was abandoning my heritage, not simply for a mess of necessary potage, but for a way of life I had no taste for.

But life, I said, is what the mind makes it; nothing human is alien to the philosopher, and this world of commerce, of brick mills and matchbox tenements, of dumps and dusty streets and cindery vacant lots, of John Q. Public and the house and family of John F. Quinn—all this is more nearly human than the sanitary virtues of the Compton Garretsons. Man's task—so I rationalized—is not to accept the pleasant inheritance but rather to go forth and make.

Not that I ever put this in fine phrases. My old incommunicative habit still kept me from any candid talk with mater. I mumbled a few misleading remarks about my job and erected a blockade against the anxious questions I saw unexpressed in her face. No use to talk to me, I said in all but words; I'm running my own show now.

In these years, the Garretsons aimed more deliberately at a New England classicism. Grandfather Theodore, like his generation, had grown baroque and almost polyglot. His taste was an emotional confusion of moral dogma, indiscriminate European culture, and self-importance; in short it was Victorian. But father, in his retreat from confusion and his search for justification, had already begun to reach further and further back, through transcendentalism to a vision of a colonial golden age. The old house had clearly reflected his thought, and gradually the Victorian adulteration disappeared—the fringes and veneers and carved walnut, the marble tops and Dresden ornaments, the cultural souvenirs, and in their place came colonial purity, the hooked and braided rug, the amber glow of native pine and maple, the white-painted panels, the black of hand-wrought iron. All father's talents had focused on this task. With learning, with love, with eternal vigilance, he had re-created his house to match his vision.

Mater's vision too, for her own taste approved the plain symmetries of that colonial age of reason. She lacked the ecstasy, the enduring emotional satisfaction that turned father's later life into a sort of dream; but she consciously devoted herself to early American virtues. She aimed at purity and self-sufficiency and the man-made domestic economy of the pioneer; she hardly seemed aware of chain stores and electrical marvels, any more than she was aware of the other Babylonian weaknesses of mankind; rather, she permitted only the natural and authentic, simple coal and ice, storage bins and cold cellars, pickle jars and bean pots, and preserves all ranged rank upon rank on cool shelves, labeled and dated. We lived on native foods, prepared in ancestral fashion, and now that I am old enough to know about such things I realize that we lived in rare luxury. Where now are home-baked beans like those, and Indian puddings and cornbread—and all the other breads, brown and white and golden, and the cakes and cookies and brambles and brownies, and a yearly cycle of pies from spring rhubarb through all the fruits and berries to winter mince? And handmade sausage, and wondrous varieties of pickles and relishes and jellies and jams—I suppose my memories of it all are turning rosier with passing time; but whether or not it achieved a flavor unknown to a world of chain stores, I am sure it created a rare spiritual pleasure. The Garretsons, and least of all mater, never ate in the grand manner; excepting only me, their flesh tends to be undernourished and unsatisfied; but they do take delight in a plate of authentic beans and brownbread, and ancestral mince pie, and genuine colonial piccalilli.

No, it was all too remote from the life I led in Waltham. Infinity stood between.

Because I had to talk to someone, I told the Kingsleys what had happened and girded myself for defense. I could hear Mrs. Kingsley blasting me for a fool.

But they simply accepted it.

"It'll be a good business," Seth said. "It's what a smart fellow ought to do, instead of staying home like me and using a handsaw."

"Well, it's the first time I ever knew him to do a smart thing." So Mrs. Kingsley's asperity. "You marry the head man's girl and you'll be pretty well fixed. I just hope she's fit to marry, that's all."

"She's pretty," I said, and waited for the retort.

"A man engaged to a tattooed marvel would say the same. What else is she?"

Neither then nor now can I feel sure of what Marilyn was. The task of bringing her to life is greater than I ever expected. Even her infinite (to me) physical charm has somehow slipped away, and I can only go on remarking that she was essentially a woman, with the suddenly blossoming flowers of youth and feminine beauty. I couldn't tell Mrs. Kingsley that my whole body was thrilled by the way Marilyn's skirts swirled round her legs, or by the fact that she lacked a sense of humor and smiled only on rare and special provocation—and if that last confession seems to make no sense then it makes no sense. As far as I was concerned, Marilyn was a pure mystery, concealed by pretty and rather flimsy clothes, and my chief desire was to get at its root.

All this leads to ribaldry in comedy, or to the ironic smiles of the knowing, but I record that a young man's desires are like flood waters that bear him off—not only for an hour or a night but for months and years.

But Mrs. Kingsley hoped for the best. Like most country women, she felt that marriage was a tough but practical necessity, involving any normal man and any normal woman. As long as my girl possessed the customary set of faculties, we could make out well enough. Of course, a girl like that was probably spoiled, but if we had money it wouldn't matter. When a Kingsley married, he had to get hold of a tough old hen, but with a Garretson it was different.

I was relieved, but in a way disappointed at this acceptance. I had looked for a fight; perhaps I wanted one.

"When's the wedding? Do we get invited?"

I explained about Mrs. Quinn.

"Woman like that ought to be shot," Mrs. Kingsley said. "What you going to do about her?"

"Leave it to them to handle."

She thought that over, then shook her head. "I believe you'll have trouble. Such a woman aims to make everyone else as miserable as she thinks she is."

IN ALL that time I had not once heard Mrs. Quinn's voice—
and for all I ever knew, she might have been a figment. She was
supposed to live in a corner bedroom, with closed door and
rather dim light. Yet whether flesh or fantasy, she pervaded the
house. No decision could be made without an upward cast
of the eye as a sort of propitiation to her dread power; no voice
could be raised in natural speech without a sudden muffling and
a self-conscious whisper to follow. All the household peculiari-
ties, from the utter confusion of the "study" to the airless
and deathlike chill of the halls, were in some way related to
her presence above.

I saw old photographs of her—two framed portraits—and
a number of snapshots; in fact, many more of her than of anyone else in the family. She posed herself with charm, tipped
her head, flashed her eyes, smiled in her role of sweet wife or
tender mother, and I could see that she had been dainty and
pretty and always young—a child to her husband and almost a
sister to her children. She played a happy part in those pictures,
with many frills and flounces and curls and an eager delight in
her miraculous feminine self; she lived always in a play, in a
dream, I suppose in a house of pretty cards that one day collapsed and left her to perish from exposure.

"Everyone," said Mr. Quinn in a voice of tragedy, "always
told her how lovely she was. I have to admit she no longer

seems like the same person—even to me. Of course, she found me a very disappointing sort of husband—as you can imagine. I'm not the Prince Charming type, exactly." He forced his jocular expression for a moment, and then as quickly relapsed into sorrow.

But we would have to face this question of our marriage, he said. No use in just putting it off all the time. And he supposed it was up to him. He usually considered himself a man of decision; if something needed settling, he settled it and took the consequences—and as he said this, he glared at me as though he expected some consequences then and there.

In this matter, he went on, he had been weak, but I must admit that the circumstances were puzzling.

Yes, I admitted it. And I said why didn't Marilyn and I simply go and get married without any fuss at all.

We'd better, he muttered. If Marilyn would agree, that is— he was afraid she had notions about a wedding, like most girls. Then he looked at the floor and muttered something I couldn't make out. "Yes," he said abruptly, "get her off and marry her. It's the best way. In fact, I'll be present—if you'll allow me." He stirred with a sort of resolute enthusiasm, as though motion were needed to scatter doubt.

But then he paused, glanced at me, at the floor, and at me again. About our plans for the future, he said—he didn't know what I had in mind, but he'd been thinking about it a good deal and wanted to make a suggestion. If we agreed to it, he would have the rooms above the kitchen made over into an apartment, with a bathroom and possibly a kitchenette, if we wanted one. It would work out very nicely there—plenty of privacy, side entrance and stairs, of course. The big house was pretty much going to waste as it was, and he had often thought an apartment could easily be put in.

I saw his point. It would certainly make things easy.

But then, he said, he'd really have to explain to Mrs. Quinn. Yes, he'd do it. He'd do it tonight, or tomorrow.

Mr. Quinn did finally break the news to his wife, and carpenters came to remodel the rooms, and we set a date in November and Marilyn agreed to the simplest of ceremonies at the Methodist Church they used to attend.

Mrs. Quinn at once declared that if we went through with it, she would die. She put it frankly as a threat. She demonstrated (I report this only from hearsay) exactly how she would die, with fits and agonies. She caused Marilyn to cry intermittently for a week and reduced Mr. Quinn to a bag of grief. But he stuck to his resolution. He spoke to her more frankly than he ever had before—as he explained to me afterward. She refused to believe that Marilyn was anything more than a child and denounced me for a scoundrel, and Mr. Quinn said he had to be pretty brutal.

I found myself involved deeply in these emotions. Marilyn's sorrows seemed pitiful to me, and it was pleasant to comfort her and bring back little flushes and smiles of happiness. Mr. Quinn confided in me more and more, with the candor of one who has saved his confessions too long. I became a sort of focus for family problems, and grew intimate with all sorts of dreary matters, such as the property itself and its management, and the repairs and taxes, and the job of running the monstrous old coal furnace down in the cavern below. I heard a lot about insurance and inheritance and the other Mrs. Quinn, "my sister-in-law," and about many cousins here and there. And the more I found out the more dreary and bewildering it all seemed.

And it all happened with an almost tidal certainty. In a little more than a year I had been picked up and carried out into a life I had no notion of.

"Ralph," said Mr. Quinn, "we need stepladders, ten thousand of 'em. Now clean up these other things as quick as you can and we'll get the whole shop going on ladders. We've got the patterns here, and I'll see to the hardware . . ."

"Ralph," said Marilyn, "there's a benefit dance—you know,

the festival party out at Riverview, and it's more fun—some of them come in costume . . ."

And even Mrs. Eck, the cook: "Now, just see, Ralph, we've had this piece of linoleum here for six months and no one to lay it—and it's only for the pantry. You could have it fitted and laid in an hour . . ."

It is hardly a heroic role, though many a success story has no better justification. As a reflective liberal, I had failed; now, through no effort of my own, I was being swept along into a career. But at the time I hardly considered myself as a test case in the current argument on will and fate; I was certainly unaware of the powers of earth that had me in charge, and if anyone had challenged me I should have justified myself as a free agent.

Yet two more acts of fate must be recorded before I can resume anything like heroic dignity.

Marilyn did love a party—any sort of party, but especially those of a certain social quality. She admired the younger manufacturing set, with their roadsters by Stutz and Wills St. Clair, and she suffered from their neglect of her. She loved to jump in and out of rumble seats with pretty flying skirts, and to dash from here to there and there to here again, and to be offered drinks from a silver flask, and above all she loved to know everything—what Brad had whispered to Sally, what the kids in the front seat were giggling about, and who were in or out of love, and who had or hadn't committed sin. And though I made a poor showing in this game, I played it for her sake, and because she had captured and tamed a full-sized man she sparkled with triumph and grew more confident and pretty. For the first time the admired younger set paid attention to her and sent out summonses to their affairs, and they included me without further thought—even my sworn enemy, Bertie Riggs, treated me as though I were a necessary evil, like unpopular royalty. And after a while, several young men discovered that Marilyn was worth investigating.

The first act of fate, trifling as it may seem, occurred at the autumn dance which celebrated the end of the period of white trousers and summer frocks and the beginning of the serious formalities of winter—though it was far from serious as yet. And in the middle of the dance, Marilyn disappeared. I strolled about casually, then systematically, then angrily. Porches, lounges, lawns, no Marilyn. Steps down to a canoe landing and boathouse—I felt ashamed to be a snoop and went back up to sit on the porch. Too cold for girls and boys to be out in the dark, anyway. I smoked—a man-about-town habit I had picked up lately.

"Are you lost too?" A voice in the dark spoke near me.

Now that I look back, I can say that those words make up volume one.

I started, turned, saw nothing. It was a young woman's voice, but not pitched to any note of romance; rather, it was level and a little chilly.

"A man alone," it went on, "doesn't usually think he's lost. He keeps on as though he knew where he was." I heard something else in the voice, but I wasn't quite sure.

"You mean, even when he is lost, he doesn't think so?"

"Well, no. Lostness is only a thought, isn't it?"

"Were you reading my thought when you asked me?"

"I was guessing at your thought."

I remembered how she had phrased it. "You confessed, didn't you? Why did you do that?"

"Just for companionship. I watched you go down to the landing and come back, and I thought I knew what was going on."

I could see shapes more clearly now, and I moved to a chair next to hers.

"Think how much harder it is on a girl," she said. "I can't even go hunting round. I just have to disappear."

I waited a moment to be sure she wasn't crying. The voice had gone along quietly, but its self-control seemed unnatural,

as though it were under great tension. If she had cried, I should
have retreated and escaped—at least, so I now suppose. At the
time I had no notion of what I might do.

"I've been doing this sort of thing for ten years," she went
on. "You'd think I'd have learned—but there's always a subtle
difference. I must be one of those appointed to get caught, like
the ones who keep buying gold mines and electric reducing
machines."

"Who brought you?"

"Ah—his name! You make me feel abandoned, like Hester
Prynne. No, really, let's not do it that way. There isn't any
betrayer. If anybody is to blame, I am. And you'd better run
along and find your girl."

Unlikely as it may sound, we talked on for an hour. I shivered
in the cold; she had a coat, and said she liked the cold, but
after a while she shivered too. But we talked.

We were cold as ice. It was one o'clock, the orchestra was
beginning its last piece; we stretched, stirred. I asked her to
dance, and she asked me if I were six feet tall and then stood up
to show me how tall she was. Five feet ten and a half—and if
it weren't for us idiotic men, she'd love it; but most of us acted
as though she were a sort of side show.

She turned in the light of the dance floor and we looked at
each other.

Her voice had already created a being to go with it. At first
I had heard something cold and reserved in it, or thought I had,
but by now I realized that she simply liked to think. Except for
mater, who had apparently done all her thinking years before,
I had never talked with a thinking woman—at least, with a
young one. My aunt May, in Boston, enjoyed using her mind.
I don't doubt that there are a number of other women in the
world who think, but I never met one who went at it quite as
sweetly and joyously as this tall stranger I met on the dark
porch. She liked being female, she liked the mystery of our
meeting and the personal equation we made—I could tell by

tone and laugh and the way she moved, but her method was quadratics, or higher, rather than simple identities.

Neither had she been bedeviled by the histrionics of youth. It may not be so at present, but in the twenties young people had achieved an agonizing self-consciousness, and no act or word seemed quite trustworthy. We were like beginners thrust into the roles of *The Way of the World,* uncertain of our memories and of what the lines meant, but forced to play it through. Sin and the knowledge of evil were expected of us, even though we had been trained for other ways.

Well, there she was, as tall as she said—but for a moment I saw only eyes and mouth and sand-colored hair: eyes hazel brown at the center, spreading out to green, and very bright and watchful and full of delight at the humor of my appearance; mouth wide and cut rather straight across, but finely carved in simple sweeping curves to the delicate corners—a good mouth for marble or even ivory. Her whole face was like that, actually: rather grim underneath with high cheekbones and angled jaw and chin, yet sweetly modeled and balanced and clean of line. Her hair, part sand yellow and part light brown —like the streaked shades in molasses candy—was coiled heavily over each ear in the common fashion of the time.

She struck me at once as a girl unsuited for this particular kind of party, and I almost asked her why she had ever come. Her greenish eyes were still brightly watching me, and slowly her face broke into what I can only describe as a grin—a delighted and somewhat diabolic grin, full of knowledge and friendly malice.

"You *are* Ralph Garretson, aren't you?"

"Yes. Who are you?"

"Well, fancy that!" The humor of it gave her face intensest delight. I grinned back at her, and we stood staring at each other enthusiastically.

"Let's dance while we can," she said.

"All right, but what's so funny?"

"You'll see in a minute."

We did dance, and it went well. At first her motion seemed awkward, like mine; but she had a free, wide, long-limbed rhythm to her and we got to swinging round the uncrowded floor with a lot of enthusiasm. The blood ran warm in our cold bodies and everything felt fine. "Dardanella" it must have been; does anyone still remember that happy tune?

"Well, who are you?"

"I'm surprised at you, Ralph."

I studied her sculptured face, but as long as she grinned I didn't know. Then once I saw her mouth in repose, the straight line of it, and out of the past the little dream began to materialize. I looked again.

"Good lord," I said.

"Yes, you've got it."

I could hardly bring myself to say it. I took a breath. "Beanpole?"

We stopped in the music, and I suppose my face expressed ludicrous surprise. She didn't laugh aloud, but she couldn't stop smiling.

"Damned old hatrack," she managed to say.

"Well, gosh if it isn't!"

The recognition had filled us with intense joy; in fact, our lives suddenly became miraculous—not only because we had met so humorously, but because we had lived and grown through all those eight years and yet remained what we were destined to be.

"People do usually live and grow," I said, stumbling among the words. "I mean, it is customary—but aren't you surprised too? Aren't you astonished? I simply wouldn't have believed you were alive any more; you belonged forever back in the old Prune's dancing class—poor old Beanpole, she never had much fun there and she never liked me at all. You see—past tense for you. And now here you are, all grown and beautiful. Do you believe it, really?"

She was smiling too much to speak for a minute. "I don't know why it's so funny, Ralph—but really it is. I—I wish I could stop grinning; it seems like the funniest thing that ever happened."

We still gazed at each other. The music fell sadly into "Good Night, Ladies."

"That dancing class," she said. "I could have murdered the whole lot of you."

"Specially me."

"Yes, you too. It shows the fiend in me—I knew you were being nice and the nicer you were the madder I got. Every time you said Beanpole—why, I'd have shot you dead. I tell you, my character is blighted."

"Well, it doesn't show," I said, and meant it for she looked as cheerful and confident as a young Diana.

We walked vaguely round the emptying hall and talked. The excitement had swept us into a world of our own, and the foolish days of our childhood had to be re-created. Did I know that the Prune still had dancing classes? A fact almost beyond belief; she must surely be one with the dead past. Did I know that Gladys (the peaches-and-cream girl of our dreams) was married—and divorced? And Otis Weatherby had already made a fortune out of stocks, and as for Myrtle . . .

A car whirled up to the door then and young voices shrieked and brayed. Marilyn and the others poured in and screamed with laughter when they saw the empty floor.

"Oh, Ralph—you should have come! We had the wildest time—and Brad was actually arrested. We nearly died, honestly! He kept saying, 'Yes, Officer. No, Officer. Yes, Officer.' And the rest of us just—well, honestly—we just—"

And the whole crowd began yelling "Yes, Officer! No, Officer!" They pounded Brad on the shoulder and doubled up with laughter.

I glanced furtively at Beanpole and was startled when she winked at me. Her smile had a twist of sweet irony in it. A very tall man whom I knew slightly as Wally was speaking to her, and I took him to be her deserter—a young lawyer, he was, with spectacles and one of those loose, flexible faces that are constantly talking and twisting and grinning. Just now he was grinning with a moist sort of self-satisfaction and I wondered how she could stand him.

But Marilyn was in a state of radiance, like an *ingénue* who has suddenly run away with the show. Her laughter rang above the others, her smile dazzled more brightly, and she squealed and chattered at the very center of the little stage. It was Marilyn who pacified the cop, they said. She just smiled at him —smile like that again, Marilyn; show us how you did it— show Ralph, here—he doesn't half appreciate what you can do . . .

She smiled at me, and tucked a hand under my arm, and told them to stop their kidding. I could feel the tremor of delight in her hand and body, and I knew that her possessive gesture was part of her triumph.

When we went out to the cars she whispered that the gang was going to Don Hoffstetter's, all but Wally and his girl; he was all right enough but she seemed a little weird—and anyway they didn't want too much of a mob; Don's folks were nice about it, but you never could tell . . . She went on with intense incoherence. She hadn't meant to run away, but they'd just started down for a soda, and I knew how Brad was—and then next thing they were in Lexington, and that's where the cop was, and all that about her smiling was just talk; it was really Ed Styles—honestly, he knows all the right people— you'd think his dad was the governor himself.

I had a Model T then, a touring car open to the winds. Marilyn would rather have crowded into one of the others, but she was happy enough to go along with me—after a lot of cheering and laughing across the parking space.

It occurred to me quite literally at that moment that I was frightened. Marilyn was prettier than ever, and more confidently feminine, and full of unscrupulous sincerity; in the last months she had developed a ruthless "personality" suitable to the life she desired. My connection with her now seemed accidental, and almost any man with money and youth could have played my part better.

"That Christina Ross," she was saying, "they say she's some kind of genius. Can you imagine that? She's certainly no fun at a party—just a stick, I guess."

"What kind of a genius?"

"Goodness, I don't know. She does a lot of things, like art and poetry—I really don't know; I'm not that highbrow. She used to play at recitals—you know, Miss Ross will now render the Moonlight Whatsis."

"Piano?"

"Well, it must have been. I guess I was jealous—but I'm not any more. I feel sort of sorry for anyone like that—she's so serious all the time, and when a girl is tall and—do you know what the boys call her? Beanpole! Poor thing, it must be terrible. I bet Wally won't get tangled up with her again, though goodness knows he's enough of a beanpole himself."

"We used to call her Beanpole ten years ago."

But Marilyn was hardly curious at all. "Well, you must know all about her, then," she said, and a moment later added that she hadn't any call to be stuck-up—her father owned a drugstore which certainly wasn't much to boast about.

I said I liked her, and Marilyn snuggled close and smiled up at me, as though she were emphasizing the difference between them.

I said I hadn't thought Christina was stuck-up at all.

Marilyn laughed happily. "You're pretty highbrow, too. Ralph. The gang all thinks you're a regular intellectual—did you know that?" Then she added thoughtfully, "It's sort of nice in a man, specially if he's big and strong too. It makes me proud of you, Ralph. And then of course it comes natural to you. But with a girl like the Beanpole—goodness!"

"You don't think a girl should have brains?"

"Don't be silly! But after all, a man doesn't want a girl to go round looking like a schoolmarm."

"Schoolmarms aren't really human, I suppose."

"Well, no—not the way I mean. But Ralph, let's talk about something else." She squeezed my arm. "Do you know what Don said? He said if we all chipped in a little we could get a good orchestra and have a Halloween dance at his house. Wouldn't that be wonderful, Ralph?"

"No highbrows invited, I suppose."

In the silence I heard my own disagreeable voice repeat itself.

She shot a swift glance, then stirred uneasily.

But a fire of irritation burned in me. "As long as we act like empty-headed idiots we'll be welcomed in the best houses. As for intellectuals and highbrows and ordinary adults—to hell with 'em. They aren't fit to associate with."

She laughed nervously. "Don't be silly, Ralph."

"All we need is a couple of tin horns and a bottle of gin."

We said nothing more until we got there. She smiled then, and I could feel her determination to stay happy whatever happened. "You're funny, Ralph. I guess you don't realize how much everybody really admires you—I mean *really!*"

So I kissed her, and we went into the Hoffstetters' and had fun.

❧ CHAPTER 26 ❧

My FRIEND Tommy Tucker was a senior at Harvard. I used to go to some of the football games with him, and one day we made a plan to go off together with Tommy's roommate, John Somes, to climb Mount Washington. Tommy had never been there, but I had, and John Somes was a veteran mountaineer, rock climber, and cross-country runner, just back from a summer in the Canadian Rockies. He had been up Washington several years before and said that out west they'd hardly call it a mountain.

Both John and Tommy were enthusiasts, and with a little mutual encouragement would as readily have headed for Pike's Peak; and as it was they tried to talk me into going to Katahdin instead of Washington—an easy all-night drive each way. Washington, they said, was almost too suburban, especially on a holiday weekend in October. I said that eight hundred miles in an open Model T might be a nice weekend for college students who had nothing else to do—and so we compromised on Washington and Pinkham Notch, three hundred and thirty or so, round trip.

We loaded sweaters and windbreakers and knapsacks into the Ford and started north on a bright October afternoon. Motoring twenty years ago was a more rugged adventure than it is now: we had to force a passage through cobbled streets and jammed-up traffic and then jounce everlastingly over the

high-crowned washboard roads in the open country, determined to maintain a twenty-five-mile-an-hour average. To
achieve a hundred miles in four hours in a Model T was fine
work, but exhausting. Yet on this day the air lay sweetly over
the golden countryside, full of balm and peace and the faint
taste of leaf smoke. We sang and laughed and drank the rare
and mellow distillations of Indian summer; our hearts grew
light, our heads giddy with joy: the flames of the northern
maples made great chords of splendid music in our spirit. We
hailed the northward adventure, the lifting of each higher hill,
the spreading miles of forest, the coming of dark spruce, the
first glint of rock peaks in the silvery blue, and then the long
slow waning of the sun, the golden flow of light from the south-
west level across the colored land, the intensity of it, deepening and brightening toward night, the palpable gold on the
leaves and grasses, the blue wells of shadows, valleys lost now
in dusk and high hills still glowing in smokeless mantles of fire.
We turned silent and watched the slow evening climb the
slopes of brightness. In the far north a peak gleamed like a
luminescent spearhead of pearl, purer than white itself.

Snow, we said.

Snow already? Winter up there in that far point in the sky?

Several peaks—a range of shining pearl like a shimmer of
unearthly light. The land below, ourselves, everything, fell
away and vanished in the dark.

The White Hills, John said.

We plunged into forest and the headlights made a small
tunnel in the night ahead.

The day and evening remained as warm as summertime. We
stopped at Conway for supper in a restaurant, continued on
to a place John knew of beyond Jackson where we got rooms
for the night.

Warm in the morning too; but at first foggy and sunless,
even drizzly. We drove to the Notch without much hope. The
forests were wet, the sky dark and low.

John Somes, the mountaineer, said he thought it would clear; he had a pocket barometer, and though the changing elevations confused the readings, it seemed to be rising. Anyway, he said, unless it really poured we might as well try it.

Then, as we stood waiting and gazing, a vast piece of mountain pageantry occurred. In the overhead darkness a ragged blue hole showed itself, then a drizzle of rolling white cloud all bunched and broken, then splashes of pale sun. Mountain shoulders suddenly took shape high among the curtains of light and cloud. The west wind came down over Tuckerman's Ravine and moved the whole cloud-mass before it.

We jumped and scurried like starters in a gold rush. Knapsacks were stuffed with food and sweaters and cameras. Matches? Pocket knives? Compass? Yes, all those in spite of a certain disdain on the part of John Somes, who was accustomed to Canadian Rockies. Light of foot, tireless, happy as puppies, we started at midmorning up the Tuckerman trail.

Of the three who stepped so lightly up the steep trail that brightening October morning, one would not return. We went in innocence and immense confidence. The sun came out and filled the glades with yellow warmth. Blood ran joyfully in our veins, and we could have climbed to the moon. Innocence, I used to say in my precocious days, leads to more evil than good —and over and over this picture has flashed with terrible clarity in my mind's eye: Tommy and John and Ralph stepping joyously westward toward the summit of Washington. The cool breeze lifted our damp hair and refreshed the skin under our open shirts. Clouds rolled up over the mountain wall and fanned out into the high blue. That must be Lion's Head, and Boott Spur beyond—the high wall of Huntington Ravine up there to the right . . . The mountain torrents sang through the forests.

John Somes wore boots with nails and led the way as though he were master of ceremonies; he was fashioned like a runner, deep chested yet lean and whiplike. Tommy and I wore sneakers—mine high sided and fairly heavy, his simply tennis shoes. We carried small packs of sweaters and jackets and food enough to last till the next day—a grubby assortment of sand-wiches, cheese, chocolate, doughnuts, and a can of beans. John had done all the inquiring and planning, and he talked eagerly about trails and routes and cabins and huts— Lake of the Clouds, Lonesome Lake, Madison Gulf, Gulf of Slides—I hear his voice calling in the sharp air, sounding through the forest song of wind and water, and I still feel the wild joy we took in the mountain adventure. He said we could stay in a cabin at the summit—there'd be a stove to keep us warm—and tomorrow we could follow the range north to the peak of Adams and down by the Madison Springs Hut; this north-wester meant clear weather coming—and cold, he said: it might freeze at night; it might snow a little in the squalls.

Up out of the woods we came, to the rocks of the Little Head-wall, and stood in a lee in the noon sun to look eastward across the bottomless valley to Carter Dome and Wildcat. All earth and air rang with clear autumn brilliance. White cumulus marched away through the blue to the pale southeastward rim of the world, but the sun kept its warm blaze against us, partly drying our wet skin. In the thin air the white vapor of our breathing took shape.

"Colder than you'd think," John said.

I remember how Tommy Tucker danced on the rocky ledge, grinning and making happy whooping sounds. "I bet that's where God lives," he said, waving up to where the crags of the great headwall dissolved into the silver edge of a rolling cloud. "He sits up on one of those pinnacles and feels like the boss of all creation." Then he cocked his head at John. "Just a dinky little foothill—I realize that. Out west God does things up much bigger—but of course he's a much bigger guy out there than he is here."

"Well, you do get the effect of high mountains, I must admit." Like so many enthusiasts, John was profoundly literal

and earnest, and he looked bewildered when Tommy broke
into howls of laughter.

"The *effect*, he says!" He scrutinized the vastness round
about us. "Damn clever effect, if I do say so."

We ate some of our lunch there where it was warm. Once
a cloud-mass obscured the sun, and the shroud of winter settled
over us—the harsh and purple cold; I remember how the chill
touched my heart and sent a tremor through me of something
deeper than cold.

But the sun blazed again, and we pushed up against the
funneled wind to the ravine and began the long climb to the
top of the vast wall. And wondrous climbing it was, with sun
still on our shoulders and small whirls and gusts of mountain
wind, and the ocean of space deepening and spreading below
us. John's boots clashed on the rock, but he went up powerfully,
muttering a chant of joy to himself and watching for the turns
of the trail.

Ice appeared in shaded hollows. Some of the north rock faces
were enameled with it.

"Maybe you guys shouldn't have sneakers," John said.
"They're no good on ice." He laughed.

So on up over the rim to the sloping fields of rock.

"Clouds are lifting!" we shouted. Far ahead through a rift
appeared a small dark nub that might have been the top itself.

But the wind had us. Not the gusty autumnal air, nor the
tree-bending, whirling blasts of earth—not anything known to
men or the world of men; rather, it was the released power of
all creation, the one irresistible force, a nothing so intensified
and materialized and charged that up there on the high cone
of the mountain it became the all. In wind like that, no other
life existed.

We tried to duck back out of it and prepare. Caps, sweaters,
jackets—we fumbled them on, feeling the touch of ice on our
skin, in fingers and toes.

Turn back? No one said it. Give it a try, anyway. There's the top, right ahead—a straight and easy slope.

We crouched, waiting and beginning to shiver. The wind blast would have to relent, we thought; nothing like that could keep on and on. Sun still shone and the sight of it warmed us. We couldn't feel it.

So, the plunge across the rock fields. Tommy shouted, and from the hiss of syllables I decided he was trying to say "excelsior!" Blood and sinews responded, pushed us buoyantly against the wall of wind. We had to bend low and breathe in quick gulps, turning our mouths under the lee of our shoulders. Our lungs felt the raw cold.

The old notion that it was a cold autumn day still persisted; the gust, we felt, would pass, and our working muscles would spread warmth and life through our bodies. We kept pushing upward with slow and fumbling steps, stooping over our shadows, slipping on ice surfaces like old men. It took a half hour or so for the thought to settle in my mind that we ought not to be there, that the windwall was coming at us more relentlessly, that we were stooping lower and fighting to stay on our feet, and especially that all warmth had withdrawn from feet and legs and hands.

I tried to speak, then to yell, but made no sound. John Somes went on ahead, pointing his hood into the wind like a twisted gnome. His boots and parka were a better sort of armor than ours, and we knew he was tireless. Tommy had dropped behind and seemed hardly to be moving. I crouched and waited.

When he came close he put his mouth to my ear and shouted, "I think we're damn fools." The words came faintly and stiffly, but I heard them and nodded. Back to the wind, we looked down the rough slope. My watery eyes were closed slits, and a fine spindrift of snow blew like white smoke over the rocks, but I could still see where the headwall fell away into cold space.

"We better get back down there," I yelled.

John had not turned. We saw him dimly in the smoke, a hundred yards above us.

"Can't feel my feet any more," Tommy said—still shouting.

The truth broke suddenly, shooting downward from brain to bowels. We were in deadly danger. The illusion of "October" vanished forever and I faced the facts of arctic winter and the ice-created hurricane.

But there was still John Somes—we ought to stick together. Tommy, I thought, could start back, and I could still keep on and get hold of John. I leaned to yell in his ear, glancing up once more to see if John had turned yet. What happened from that point on is so mingled with my fear and increasing desperation that I can re-create it only as a terrible dream, without logic or human landmarks.

The mountain slope had glistened remotely above us in the cold sun—not clear to our half-blinded eyes, but palpably there, a visible part of earth's substance. The smoke of snow revealed gray rock and even the cairns set by human hands to mark the trail; and beyond those outposts of earth the blue of sky had given us comfort. But now white and gray masses of cloud came like a cataract, solid, vast, silent in the gale. The sun flashed against it with cold and terrible brightness, but in the hollows and rifts it deepened to dark gray and black. Tatters of it came first like flying arrows, and I saw them flash past the dim, hunched figure of John Somes; then the mass came down like a solid avalanche of death itself, silver above and black in its caverns, riding the wind. A few seconds of terrifying beauty, and I saw John Somes fade, go under, vanish; and then before I could draw breath or warn Tommy it happened to us too.

No beauty then. Nothing but wind and our hunched selves. The very rock we stood on lost substance. Air, earth, all reality, was turned into this gray force. I had felt fear like a blade when the cloud charged against us with solid, sun-touched front; now in the gray my feelings like my body grew numb.

"Time to move!" Tommy yelled. He punched me savagely on the rump, then began beating my back and shoulders, but with slow and stiff motions. All the time up to then I had kept my hands in my trouser pockets, close pressed against my thighs, and when we started to move downward I slipped and fell full length on a ledge of rock. I felt no bruises, but the shock seemed to loosen me up a little and I was able to step along more nimbly. Tommy had pulled sweater sleeves over his hands, but he said he hadn't had any news from his feet in quite a while. We kept close together, though we agreed that if we lost each other we'd go on anyway.

In ten steps we had lost the trail, so we had to work cautiously over unknown ledges. Visibility, we figured, was ten feet, though it was hard to get our eyes open enough to see at all. We kept the wind square on our backs.

I speak of wind, but the word alone means nothing. Whatever it may be called—force, or elemental substance—it pummeled our bodies and spirits with solid blows, and I felt the life slowly going out of me as a man might who is being beaten by rubber truncheons.

"Can't seem to think," Tommy yelled in my ear. "When we get down to the wall, I'm going to let go and roll."

A whiplash of snow struck us, and then the air seemed solid with it. We moved in a single gray-white element.

We crouched backward against the wind and shuffled downward, unwilling to lift foot from earth lest it never return. Somewhere close below, the slope broke abruptly down the thousand-foot wall to the ravine floor. The wind, I thought, could whirl us like flakes out into space.

Tommy went ahead, groping and crawling along, but I came so close that we could touch each other. I remember the comfort of the closeness. We yelled at each other when we paused, and Tommy's stiff face still managed a grin.

But before we quite knew it, the slope dipped steeply downward. Tommy took a little sliding step, then both feet went together. He sprawled out on his side and slid off feet first, flashing his grin at me and saying something I couldn't hear. At once he vanished in the white below.

I crawled from rock to rock after him, and realized that I was holding now to a steep wall. Tommy had gone.

If I had come to that point alone, I might easily have lost courage and slipped down into the ravine. But the desire to find Tommy put me in a frenzy of action. I moved clumsily along the ledges—not with any conscious thought, but with a sort of galvanic recklessness, jumping and sliding and clutching. I hoped to get down to a point near where he might have landed and I worked among the slippery rocks with furious speed. But in all that thickness of snow and mist and wind I lost bearings. The steep wall made enough of a lee so that the wind no longer came in solid mass, but instead it whirled and exploded, and the gusts struck in from one side and the other with abrupt concussive force. The air remained opaque with stinging flakes.

From then on my memory grows less clear. There are isolated pictures, such as my sudden awareness of the torn whitened flesh of my hands—hardly mine any more, for all feeling had gone from them. And I remember finally the first vague sense of darkness coming on, then piercing my outer fears and stabbing into my vitals. I had felt forever lost up there among the gray rock shapes, as though my small human mechanism had been locked in everlasting ice; but the fear had grown numb and cold like my body. Now suddenly night meant death itself, as sure as the eastward roll of the mountain.

I started downward at last. I gave up Tommy—abandoned him to wind and night.

The dusk came fast. Whether wind blew harder and colder I couldn't tell, but I remember groping down into the dark stone crevices. And then after a while a new wave of light seemed to roll up from below and shone against the curtains of mist and roof of dark—an effect so incredible that a new sort of terror rippled along my backbone and I gave way to superstitious dread. I suppose my head was full of apocalyptic notions. I stopped in a tremble and stared up and around and then far down to a clump of perfectly clear trees and bushes, all silent and small as though seen through a reversed telescope but nonetheless a part of midearth. And at once I rushed downward into the visible world and saw it stretched out clear and free in the evening light, with dark-green forests rolling down to the deep valley and up again to the heights far beyond still wine-bright in the sunny sky.

But up above and behind, the cloud-masses rolled and broke over Washington and fanned and scattered in the wind, with silver edges far up, but black as night underneath—right up where I could still nearly reach.

Below the snow level I tried to move faster, but made only shambling progress. Some parts of me were frozen, and there were more bruises and wrenched joints than I had any notion of. I got down over the Little Headwall and into the woods, chafing hands and ears and chin as I went along. The soft bed of the trail had frozen now into rough corrugations, but no feeling had yet come into my feet.

By then I was convinced that Tommy must be ahead of me. No one could still be up there in that blast of death—no one I knew. As for John Somes, he was surely snug in a cabin on top. The trickle of warm blood in my veins convinced me of the inevitable triumph of life.

Then a figure appeared in the trail below, and a voice called sharply. John Somes came up in a steady lope, his glistening face all tense and eager.

"Ralph? Is Tommy there?"

They found him on the mountain next morning. He had fallen about fifty feet, had broken both legs and perished from cold. Men from the Pinkham Notch camp brought him down. John Somes said he had turned back from his climb when we did and followed us down expecting to overtake us— we were only a few yards ahead of him, he said. But he saw nothing till he got below the clouds, and then he climbed back up again to search, and finally decided to run down to camp for help. When I met him on the trail he was running up again in advance of the search party, but by the time he got up into the ravine night had come.

Meanwhile I had been bundled into a closed car and driven a hundred miles to a hospital, where I was kept for three days.

⋙ CHAPTER 27 ⋘

THOUGH my father came to the hospital at once and stayed in the neighborhood until I was ready to go home, we had little to say to each other. He kept resolutely away from the subject that filled our thoughts and we talked instead of his trip abroad, and of leaves falling and books and colonial doorways. He studied the houses of Hanover, and the Dartmouth buildings, and spent several hours in the library where he was welcomed as a visiting scholar.

"Really, a very congenial place," he said—and made further remarks about provincial Bostonians, like himself. "Why don't you come to Dartmouth, Ralph? I've been observing the boys closely, and I find that they lead the ideal earthly existence, with all the delights and none of the realities of the frontier. You can be a sportsman without troubling yourself about being a gentleman."

"You do sound provincial," I said grumpily.

"Yes, indeed. I even feel a twinge of jealousy. I was chatting with a learned gentleman I met in the library—a professor of literature, with a gray Vandyke, nose glasses with black ribbon, cane, tweeds from London—a superb sight, Ralph; and feeling the need of offering credentials I remarked that I lived in Compton. 'Ah,' said he, 'Compton—Compton—surely you don't mean Chipping Compton in Warwickshire?' I assumed, of course, that he was English and asked him—he spoke in choicest Oxford; but no—alas, he was merely a devoted admirer. I said Compton was near Boston, not far from Concord—and as I said it I tried to recollect if I had ever before been obliged to offer that explanation. And do you know what he replied then? 'Ah, yes,' he said, very brightly, of course, like one who speaks only in epigrams, 'poor old Boston—a melancholy spot, I'm told.' I looked him up in the records afterward and found he was graduated from Skaneateles College—"

"There's no such place," I grunted.

"Tut, tut, Ralph. The man was a mountebank. But he did enjoy his role, and he bowed and stepped off with a flourish of stick, and—like Richard Cory—he glittered when he walked. I believe I really envied him."

"All you need is a Vandyke," I replied, hating myself for my ill temper.

But in the train on the way home we got to talking rationally. I had been irritated that he had glossed over my tragic folly on the mountain, that he had come patiently and loyally to my bedside as though my own precious body needed his ministrations, even as though the catastrophe had somehow lent me distinction. The pain of thawing flesh, the unmentioned threat of amputation, the recollection of death, the whole nightmare of impotence and failure—all occupied me so vastly that I looked upon my father as a trifling alien; and his polite and tactful graces offended me. He had no right, I felt, to the sort of realities that I now perceived. But through all my stupid, unhappy savagery he remained his even self, with chat of foreign lands and minor arts and letters and his boyish surprise at finding so much "culture" so far north of Boston, and when I was able to hobble off homeward I confessed my debt.

Back in Compton we talked too, with more ease than either of us expected. He said he troubled a good deal about me and felt himself to blame for not seeing me through to a profession. He appreciated my independence, but he pointed out that modern life gave less and less scope for independence. In the past, society allowed a man time to be a philosopher—time, in fact, to be eccentric, if he so desired; witness the original thinkers of Concord—not the bats and owls, as Hawthorne called them, but the true and faithful individualists living in a mountain atmosphere of lofty thought. Now you had to make connections like a party on a Cook's tour. It is quantity, Ralph —the age of quantity; you are expected to go through your training the way cars go down a production line.

I hadn't seen much of my father for a long time, and it came as a surprise that my mind ran along with his.

"Tell me," I said, "was grandfather as much of a stuffed shirt as I seem to remember?"

An old picture had taken shape in my head: the quiet pastoral of Charles Edward Mayo, the time of beauty and peace, of mowing and reaping under the eye of God.

Seeing father's startled brow, I went on: "He seemed so choked up with dignity. Didn't he wear black clothes and starch and didn't he tell my friends to go to hell? How did he get that way in old Compton?"

My father's eye remained cold and he pressed his lips tight for a moment. I thought again how like a prince of scholars he looked—how the fine clear bones of his face seemed to have been molded by thought itself and the high forehead and the silk-white hair sweeping back from it represented the very peak and crown of intellectual beauty. Then he nodded, not to agree, but to grant amnesty.

New England, he said, was a microcosm, with its own middle ages, its renaissance, its reformation. Our theocratic days were medieval and fundamental, and his father simply represented that heritage—an admirable one, he added respectfully, but stern. It surprised me to detect none of his habitual irony as he spoke. The Harvard scholars, he went on, revived learning, created a new classic age, and opened the way to religious liberalism and a new art and literature; then at once came industrialism and science. In one century we took a five-hundred-year stride, and in the one town of Compton you found all the historic types of humanity living together. As he said this, his twinkle returned. "Between you and your grandfather lie at least three centuries."

"And what age of mankind do you represent?"

"I? Oh, I partake of all but the present. I'm simply an anachronism."

It pleased me that he had said it, and I grinned—the first in several days.

He shook his head, responding to my thought. "Don't you fall into the same error, Ralph. After thirty years of thought, I conclude that it is better to keep facing ahead, however little one likes the prospect."

I began to tell him about my life in Waltham, realizing as I spoke how little I had ever confessed to anyone. Secrecy, I began to feel, undermines judgment—at least of youth which holds stubbornly to its small illusions. My thought moved along several levels, as it had done with feverish intensity for days; I saw the mountain continually, not as a special and temporary arrangement, but as the very arrowhead of reality, the lethal edge of nature itself, a sort of inlander's Moby Dick, white as all eternity and beautiful as heavenly truth and far beyond good and evil—beyond any range of mortal value; and I felt inclined to worship that power, not in love and hope, but simply in recognition of it as the inescapable weapon of destiny. Mine was no Ahab spirit, to hurl myself singlehanded against infinity; I had no desire to tilt with cosmic windmills: I accepted the mountain, humbly and with awe, as the sort of fact that my limited will had to make the best of. Just then I had no fight left in me, though I've since realized that the will is by nature a fighter and sallies forth again and again to test the immortal enemy: Ahab and Quixote must be the brackets in which all men are enclosed. Well, so much for my metaphysics—which do actually make up a little part of my reality. Quite aside from them I experienced an increasing emotion of remorse that weighed on my chest like a stone, and as I recovered from shock and injury I found a physical difficulty in eating and sleeping. It seemed incredible that my reflective and self-centered nature could generate such a choking mass of feeling, wholly apart from thought or desire. I had even wondered in earlier times if I could muster up an appropriate grief in the event of a death, but I found out now that nature takes charge of such matters; I grew ashamed of my weakness, and I spoke as dryly and coldly as I could—and when mater told me I had to go and see Tommy's family in Cambridge I snapped back rudely at her. But as for my life in Waltham, which I described in part to my father, it had retreated so far to the edges of my thought that it seemed like a story in a book. I had sent Marilyn a message from Hanover, had written, had telephoned from home and said I'd be back in a couple of days.

For those few days that I remained at home I managed to antagonize the whole family. Mater took me aside and told me I had a right to my own ideas and my own career, but couldn't I manage to be a little kinder? And I resented the criticism and turned away in a huff—though at the same instant I saw her point. Her sober face had grown more sober with the passing years and had begun to droop under the constant responsibilities, so that the fine lines of it all turned downward and seemed set there like marks in rock. The fact that she was a lady irritated me—and it seemed to me that she was conspiring to make Jean one too, and I even found myself angry with Jean because she was now engaged to a man of distinguished social connections and was preparing for her wedding with an inexcusable regard for tradition and formality. Jean did laugh at my scorn as though I were a small boy, and retained her wondrous good temper through most of my lectures on the follies of gentility, but she kept me outside the boundaries of her affairs, and I was jealous. As for Steve, who came home for Sunday, he presented so bland and glasslike a front that we barely spoke to each other.

The underlying fact is that I suffered from a sense of my own futility. In body and mind I was prepared for that state of life which young people call "happiness"—that is, I wanted a career and a woman and the comforts of peace and beauty; yet fulfillment had somehow gone astray. I felt like a graceless alien at home and an imposter in Waltham. The world which had seemed to lie before me like a land of dreams had now grown hostile and cold—more so than I had ever been prepared for, and more vain and ugly. I might still look far ahead beyond the darkling plain and see some sort of dim glimmer of beauty, but it had no part in this compelling present.

John Somes brought the Ford back on Thursday and stayed for supper, but his presence filled me with uneasiness and a sense of guilt. He behaved with careful gravity and informed me didactically, in prepared phrases, that he had called on the Tuckers. I could see that he took great comfort in doing the right thing and speaking the right words, and I noted the formal integrity of his actions: it was primarly his fault, he told them; he had had more experience as a climber than Tommy or Ralph, and his misjudgment of the dangers of Mount Washington was unforgivable. That failure of judgment bothered him deeply, for he was essentially a methodical and professional-minded person.

He advised me to call on Tommy's family as soon as I could get about—they counted on seeing me, they had told him. They worried a lot about how Tommy had suffered, and he had tried to assure them that cold minimized all pain. I thought it would be better if I wrote instead of called—just yet, at least; and I did so with as much detail as I could reasonably give. It was a letter written in uncertainty and blindness, and more emotion than I knew what to do with.

I can recall the details of that week very clearly, almost as though I were under sentence and waiting for the end with acute sensibilities. The weather—perfect: pure, translucent October, each sunlit hour like a clear amethyst; brightness still

in the leaves, in the yellow chrysanthemums and the orange
dazzle of the marigolds. The village life had settled to autumnal
quiet, and the air was scented day and night with sweet leaf
smoke. The morning I first walked out—down the leaf-matted
path and along the street—I remember the cool and crystalline
silence: no breeze, no motion of leaves—except only those
that fluttered one by one down through the golden canopy
of high elms and maples; no people either, not just then—
nothing but the quiet brightness of immortal Indian summer.

I walked down by the green—and noted the morning routines of the bread truck, a baby carriage in the sun by Steele's
steps, Mr. Kane raking dry leaves into a smoldering pile in the
road in front of the church; I walked on across the tracks to the
old Madigan stable. A red gasoline pump stood near the door
now, and the ground between there and the road was black
and hardened with oil.

"Busy, Terry?"

"Why, sure, Ralph—always busy." His smile gave him away,
an open, almost helpless smile—not withholding anything, yet
not foolish. Terry was sharp with strangers, but allowed his
friends to take advantage of him.

He came and stood in the sun beside me, just within the wide
open doorway. It surprised me that he was a man, with adult
modeling in his features—cheeks slightly hollow, jaw set and
thrust forward, mouth marked with strength. It seemed to me
that we must still be boys, as I felt myself to be long after that
particular time.

"How busy?"

He shrugged, looked at the jacked-up Chevrolet in the
middle of the floor. "Busy as I want to be, I guess. If I do it, I do
it. If I don't—well, folks get sore."

"Who's working for you."

"Greasy Gus—when he works." He grinned—and his
smudgy face seemed to drop ten years. He had a short Irish
nose and a squarish face with high cheekbones that might have

been a fighter's face except for the gentleness behind it. I wondered in a sudden irrelevant flash why he seemed to have no trouble with women.

"Terry," I said, "what about dropping all this for a while and going out west with me?"

His grin returned; he almost winked, and then his eyes flickered away toward the valley and distant edge of colored forest. I think we both saw ourselves trudging over those hills with Daisy air guns.

"Sure," he said.

"When do we start?"

This time a longer silence followed. He still looked at the distant forest—through the gap between some houses and the box factory—and I began to wonder if he had heard me.

"Any time," he said.

"Go in my flivver," I added.

That's how it was. The idea took shape as mysteriously as a crystal does, almost as though that hushed Indian-summer morning had provided the perfect chemical solution.

"Tell you, Ralph—"

"Huh?"

"Keep it quiet a couple of days."

"Sure. What about your ma?"

"I'll tell her."

"What'll she say?"

He shrugged.

"Don't back out, Terry."

Silence again for five seconds.

"Not me," he said.

When I walked back I felt an electric charge running through my nerves—not from joy, not yet; from fright, rather—mixed with immense expectation.

◄§ CHAPTER 28 §►

I WROTE to Marilyn and then to Mr. Quinn. I tore up the letters, rewrote them, left them unsealed on my table, and walked out to see the Kingsleys.

It was late on a Friday afternoon, and the still autumn light lay like amber on the land. A small boy seldom has a thought for beauty—not by that name, or anything like it; his state is good, or not good—that's all he needs to know. And the old ones, like me now (aged forty-four), perceive only that it is a piece of staging, a temporary composition of line, color, tone —in other words, a work of art, which arrests for a moment our habitual disbelief and gives us a few breaths of divine illusion; if we think, we know the curtain will soon fall, the dream world of bronze-green meadows, of flaming woods in the cold blue air, will pass into night and death—we know that we and all things are one with remorseless time; we are grateful for any beguilement, however brief. But youth, aged twenty-three (more or less), believes and has faith; more than that, he lives completely and steadily within the composition, like one in love, like a mystic, like one essentially involved in a great and beautiful design. So, at least, I felt that early evening as I walked over the little hill and breathed and tasted the air and saw how the light surrounded each leaf and blade like a casing of precious stone.

When I came into the kitchen without knocking, Mrs.

329

Kingsley was sitting on her high stool cutting up boiled potatoes. Because I was there again, and because a natural afflatus had occupied me, I did something I had never yet done: I put an arm around her bent shoulders and kissed her.

"So you want to make up, do you? I don't know but you're too late."

"Make up for what?"

"Desertion, I'd call it. It's a great thing when I have to find what you're up to by reading the newspaper." She looked me over. "I didn't know as I'd ever see you again. The paper had you off in a hospital and left you there."

"Listen," I said. "I'm going out west. Don't tell anyone yet."

I sat in the rocker, put my feet on the stove, drew a long breath, looked all round.

"And when I get back—if ever, that is—I'm going to move in here."

"Well, you'll have to talk to him about that."

She asked me no more questions and went on with her potatoes. My tensions eased, and in the stove heat and steam-soft air I grew drowsy—but I talked about almost everything. I talked reminiscently, as though yesterday were ages gone, almost as though I had for the moment been released from the world's web. I suppose it was a sort of gentle intoxication, brought on by love and peace and the heady fumes of the teakettle.

Seth came in with the set habits of his lifetime—bowed under the lintel of the door, nodding toward us in the same motion, turned and hung his short coat on a peg at the far wall, came round and back toward the stove with hand ready to take the kettle—making a beaten trail on the wide-boarded floor, but then he paused and gravely nodded again toward me.

"I heard you were still alive," he said.

Mrs. Kingsley lighted the lamps then, and the room closed

in round us entirely, made us a safe and sovereign unit against night and space.

"They've got the electric power over at the other house," she said. "Jim's going to put wires in here—so he says."

"If you wait till I get back from out west, I'll do it."

I didn't expect them to believe me, of course.

"Jim knows how to do it," Mrs. Kingsley said, watching to see how it struck me.

I grinned. "Tell him to put plenty of power in the shop. We're going to need it there."

She looked at Seth. "He's full of crazy ideas again."

I looked at Seth too. "Will you tell me what a man lives for?"

Seth had the kettle in his hand. "He lives to do what he can," he said.

"Well, that doesn't mean much."

"It means all anything means."

He washed himself with so much concentration that for a while there was no more talk.

After supper Seth said he thought I made a lot of fuss about life. I apparently had a notion that a man could be happy the way a youngster is happy, just by doing the things he liked to do. There was nothing sadder in the world than the sight of people chasing after happiness—pursuing it, as they said.

I told him he was a grim old puritan, but he said he didn't know anything about that—and neither did I. "If you ever went to church, Ralph, you'd find out a few things. You'd find it's the heathen who can't see any use in what they do—they're the ones make the complaints all the time."

"You think it's better to be a Christian martyr and keep quiet?"

It was better, he said, to forget about your precious self entirely.

I talked a good deal, off and on, and when I left them I felt that the current of my existence had turned into a new channel. Not that much of anything actually happened. They accepted my notion of going "out west" as the most natural thing in the world. Mrs. Kingsley said she'd go too if we'd ask her—and in a way she meant it; she had a deep desire to "go" (I hear her own resonant sounding of that little word). And Seth said it would do me good to get lost in a desert, but I better watch out for rattlesnakes and poker players.

One thing they couldn't understand: the last they knew (it was Mrs. Kingsley who brought this up) I was arranging to be married. What happened about that?

In actual fact, I have been dodging this issue in hopes that some sort of justification will occur to me. None does, and the actualities grow more rather than less sordid. A wise youth would have known what he was about from the start, and a hero would go through with it, but this particular specimen of a Ralph Garretson simply stumbled into trouble and then made it worse by disgracefully stumbling out again.

I drove into Waltham on Saturday morning. And when Marilyn opened the side door she had a pad of paper in her left hand. "Ralph, we have to order these announcements today. I intended to have it done a week ago, but then you suddenly went off."

"Well, I didn't plan to be away a week."

"I hope you're all right." She glanced at me with a preoccupied sort of anxiety. "I've been awfully worried all week, with everything to do and you not here." Then suddenly she smiled in a wondrous dazzle of blond girlishness and flung herself upon me, and what I began to say had to be changed.

Whatever it is that grows heavy in the breast turned to lead. Her smile and shining eyes appalled me; it seemed to me that I had never before recognized her identity as a human creature, as a fair and innocent target for sorrow. Everything about her conspired—the crisp print dress of white and lavender checks, the curls of gold above the clean satin of her neck, the motion of her breathing and the beat of her heart.

She drew back quickly and eyed me almost as though she

read the evil muddle of my thoughts. The smile had gone, the flush faded, and a pale intentness looked out at me.

"Well, come in," she said. "Wait here in the kitchen till I get the lists and things—Mrs. Eck has gone to the store." She backed toward the stairs.

"No," I said. "Wait . . ."

A sort of trembling had taken my voice. She watched me, one foot reaching back to find the first rise.

"I—I want to talk," I half mumbled.

She poised herself a moment, and no other words took shape. She turned and ran up lightly.

"I'll be down in a second," she called.

I remember staring at the brown cellar door. It seemed to me that everything up to that moment had been a part of my childhood, an innocent and sheltered life where nothing happened for keeps, where work and love were games without mortal stakes, and I felt suddenly and strongly that there was nothing for it but to go on just that way, playing it through to its insignificant end. It was as though I were choosing between familiar and protected waters and the dark ocean of danger out beyond the barrier; and in those two or three minutes of waiting I agreed to remain in the little waters.

Choices are seldom truly like that, but as long as they seem so the values remain the same. Those dark oceans actually lie all about, whatever we pretend to choose.

She tripped lightly down with hands full of papers.

"Now go over this list, and then add the names you want . . ." She laid things on the kitchen table.

I took a pencil and began looking at the jumble of papers. "Jenks," I said. "Who's that?"

"Oh, father's friends. I never heard of lots of them."

"These Tuckers," she said after a moment. "What's their name—oh!" Her eyes lifted quickly. "Why that's your friend. You called him Tommy, didn't you? Do you want to put his people down here—or—or what?"

I found myself walking to the window, and I heard a voice say, "Look, Marilyn—" Then silence.

"Ralph, I'm sorry—you must feel terribly." Her voice was very thin in the quiet. In a moment I heard the scratch of a pencil.

"Marilyn, we can't be married. We just—can't be." It seemed to me like a voice speaking on its own initiative. "There's no sense in it." My thoughts, such as they were, had fixed themselves on the last glimpse of Tommy on the mountain, but the voice continued from some source of its own. "It's much better to recognize it now than to pretend it's all right and then—well, it would be terrible." The little words were swallowed in the darkness of the humiliating nightmare. For a moment nothing more was said.

I glanced furtively and saw how white and watchful her face was. It seemed remote and almost lifeless, like a bit of cotton cloth.

"You—you mean—" Another silence. "I guess I don't know what you mean."

I tried to assume some control of my voice. "Why," I shouted —at least the abrupt loudness seemed like a shout in that stillness—"why, since this trip I've been thinking—" Then I stopped in the middle of it and looked at her. "It's just what I said," I mumbled. "I don't think we ought to go through with all this." I must have hoped that she would simply agree with me, as though I had proposed that we abandon a plan to walk in the park.

But she was staring at me with a sort of terror. "Ralph, something has happened to you—"

"I'll speak to your father," I said. "He'll think it's a terrible thing—I hate to do it, but it has been my fault all along and I'll have to go through with breaking the news to him."

"Ralph, do you feel awful about what happened up there? I mean it wasn't really your fault, was it? You shouldn't blame yourself like this—honestly, it doesn't do any good."

She looked at me strangely, as though I were half mad.

"It isn't that—" I began, then stopped. She thought something terrible had happened to me on the mountain, something beyond the limits of her comprehension and she was afraid. Her white face watched me with unwavering dread.

"I can't help it," I said fiercely. "I'm going away—I've got to go away." I paced the floor. I said I had seen my best friend die—I had contributed to his death. I was no fit person to marry—not now, anyway.

I talked like a damned hypocrite—or like a third-rate Hamlet trying to scare the wits out of Ophelia. And it all came that way without any plan or apparent volition. I seized the opportunity with a kind of desperation.

Marilyn's whiteness grew mottled as she continued to stare at me, tears slid from her brimming eyes, and suddenly she flung her head down on the scattered papers on the kitchen table and broke into enormous sobs.

I changed my tune at once. I stroked her hair and patted her shoulder and said she'd be better off without me; she needed another sort of man anyway, and as soon as I was out of the way there'd be plenty of men in her train—a lovely and popular girl like her. And though all that happened to be true, I almost choked with the shame of having to say it.

The scene at last moved toward its close, and I fear I hurried it. She never did seem quite to understand what had happened; I left her in a state of bewildered dissolution. In retrospect there may be overtones of comedy in such affairs, but as I drove away into the October morning I felt self-disgust and shame. I confronted my own failures and was appalled at what I saw.

Yet worse followed, for a grim sort of backbite of conscience sent me down to the shop to see Mr. Quinn. I felt a need of scourging and conceived it my duty to go through with the worst. That I could do cruel damage to other lives than my own had never before occurred to me, any more than I had ever pictured myself stealing or committing a felony. And as

I brooded in the high front seat of my Ford I recognized my kinship with all evil—not that it was a piece of orderly or durable thinking; rather, a swift revelation, a dark chasm like something in a dream, a crack into inferno opening at my very feet.

Conscience, did I say? More likely vanity. The vision of myself I most admired had no place in it for such goings on. I confronted Mr. Quinn with abject determination to restore my romantic opinion of myself. It would have been as well to write to him, but I required a more active satisfaction. He might say he understood, he sympathized, he knew of course that I was an honorable fellow who acted from the highest motives.

But for a few seconds he only glared at me. It was lunch hour, and he held an apple in his left hand and a pint bottle of milk in his right hand. Then he asked me what I was talking about.

After I repeated it in stumbling words, he set his apple and bottle down on the desk and stared at them. His seated figure crumpled a little and seemed to shrink.

"Going away, you say?"

"Yes."

"Giving it all up?" The words were hardly more than a mumble.

"Yes."

"No use talking it over, I suppose?" He roused himself and shot a glance at me. "What does she say?"

It was my turn to mumble, but he hardly tried to listen. In the silence that followed he stared down as though he were slowly immersing himself in a profound and familiar darkness.

"I misjudged you, I guess. I used to think I was a good student of character—prided myself, I suppose; went ahead and planned . . ."

"Marilyn's a very popular girl," I recited.

"I learned all this long ago," he muttered. Then he walked back to the desk and stood there hunched and solid with head lowered. "I can tell you this: you don't know anything about what life can do—not a single damned thing. It isn't your fault; you grew up innocent, the way most people do; you learned nice manners and how to play games." He stopped and glared up at me for a moment. "Do you know we could sue you in court? It would do you good—give you a look at the sort of reality you don't know anything about." He continued to glare, then swung his head in a slow, bearish shake. When he spoke again, his voice quieted almost to a whisper. "I beg your pardon, Ralph. I don't seem to have learned to avoid the risk of disappointment, though I've had more opportunity than most people. I used to be foolishly hopeful—I suppose you could call me a sentimentalist, or simply a damned fool. I have no right to accuse you or anyone else."

He extended a broad hand and we shook. His face remained ruefully grim. "Maybe you think this business, this life, is just a trap; you want to get away from it, get out where you can be free. I know how that is, Ralph, but I think you'll find this is as good a trap as the next one—better, maybe. When you get back, come and see me."

I thanked him in a voice grown husky. We both stared at the floor a few moments. Then I walked out.

Again the cool, still October afternoon: even down there among the mills and freight cars the autumn air washed over all things like an assurance of immortal freedom and beauty. I breathed deep, not just of air, but of the great arch of blue and the steady golden light and the sweet northern cold. I walked over the cinders and shavings to my car with the self-conscious step of one released from prison—apprehensive, half-reluctant, trembling on the threshold of dangerous freedom.

The troubles I had made were nothing to this sudden ecstasy of escape that now ran like a new chemistry in my veins. I fired up the motor with a roar, slammed down the low-gear pedal, and charged out to the street in a racket of explosions and crashing metal.

I bowled merrily out into the sparkling countryside, humming a song above the rattles and snorts. And then suddenly in the full flight of my freedom a new thought struck me. I slowed, looked back, whipped the Ford round in the road, and made for Waltham again.

The cynic, if he ever gets this far, may make what he pleases of this record. In my new joy, my release, my passionate flight into freedom, I recollected that I was in love. Up to then some force of puritanic propriety had kept the fact well smothered, though it existed as steadily as a banked fire. My good-mannered brain simply ignored it. Now as I hooked down the throttle with eager forefinger I realized that much of my activity in the last few days had resulted from that well-smothered emotion. I wanted no part of the Quinn business or family simply because I overwhelmingly wanted something else. The brain seemed to have nothing to do with the affair; it followed along, exactly as it followed the flight of my Ford back to town.

No thought about planetary traps disturbed me. It was still a day for the gods, and I lifted my voice in song.

CHAPTER 29

Terry Madigan and I went west in a Model T at that moment in history when it was most desirable to do so. We co-operated with destiny; we rode the floodtide up to its highest mark. In a time of innocence and cheerful stupidity, our own youth flourished; we racketed away into unknown regions without care or forethought, observing all men, all places, all poverty, greed, waste, the whole immense show, as though it were a state fair on a perpetual holiday. I had been taught even then by some of our writing men—like Dreiser—that the nation was blighted by materialism and tragic injustice, but Terry had never heard of all that and I was glad to forget about it. Prophets of evil meant nothing to us or to millions of others. Main Street struck us as funny, and the devil-take-the-hindmost economy all seemed part of the day's sport.

The Ford was part of our mood, of course. It came to seem like a homemade contrivance, and we almost felt that we had invented it ourselves. If we needed parts for it, we simply browsed among the dumps until we found something suitable; in a day's work or so I think Terry could have reconstructed a whole new car out of what we found here and there. We never bought a tire, though we had to change and patch them two or three times a day. In the end our best tire was one we found in a dump near Baltimore on our way south.

Other adventures go with other times, but that careless,

buoyant vagabondage belongs to the year 1925. The nation was still hidden in mystery; no man quite knew where the roads went, or what lay across the plain or beyond the pass. Main Street may by then have run from coast to coast, but all the side roads, the back roads, the hill and forest roads, were as capricious as Indian trails. Floods, snow, ice, bogs, mud, wet clay—all had to be faced in their natural state and overcome by active skill, guile, or force—and many times Terry and I lifted our Ford to firm ground by main strength.

And we made many friends, and worked at whatever jobs there were—often Terry mended machinery while I sawed wood or shoveled manure; and often we slept cramped in the seats of the car, or spread out on grassy soil; and sometimes we grew sick with hunger or vile food, and then renewed our lives again with a big farm meal with pies and melons at the end.

We hardly bothered to count the passing days. Mountains and plains absorbed us, the infinite space and variety of a continent we had known nothing about, the strange ways of survival, of work and speech and behavior, the fears and hatreds and intense affections. We lost touch with past and future, with our very selves, and floated along on the ever-moving present like the charmed figures in a vision.

We went to Texas and visited Musty Ellis, and the wonder is we ever left again. He gave us outright his house, his ranch, his share of Texas itself, with all our hearts desired of horses, cattle, cars, food, drink, friends. We stayed there four months.

Then at last the westward journey again, the deserts vast and mountains in the sky. We turned rugged and leathery, talked cattle talk and horse talk, slept under stars, and Terry grew a set of golden whiskers. No foretaste of the grapes of wrath—we felt merely a romantic resentment at the ugliness of an age of motors which we ourselves were the apostles of.

In California my mother lived.

Our meeting was not quite happy. She lived then in Santa Barbara, in a world of rich and emotional flattery. She and her well-to-do friends—nearly all feminine—made an eager, warm-hearted, very safe society for mutual admiration, and though she welcomed me with tears and cries—even with transports of affection—we had no ground in common. In an excess of pig-headedness I elected to behave in a tough, hairy, unwashed fashion, like a combination ranch hand and Death Valley prospector, and while she tried to accept that as part of the romance, it was an awkward problem among the club ladies. Terry Madigan, with necktie and jacket, fitted the scene better. For no discernible reason, I resented their happy complacence, their money and comfort, their luxurious innocence, and felt it my duty to insult them with the grim fact of my own existence.

I behaved without wisdom—as I half realized; but a demon had charge of me. It may have been disappointment.

I felt a strong desire for home, for the ones I loved. I yearned; at night I could have cried with the thought of home, and the vast distance to it.

Terry felt it too, though he never spoke about himself. He had grown mournful. His watchdog faithfulness and durability continued unchanged, but I could see that he was just waiting for me to move. Then and later our partnership held up well, through weariness and hunger, and now through idleness and plenty, and finally through the long voyage home; for the most part I did the talking and he did the doing, and we got on together the way we always had. He accepted my effusive and bountiful parent with the same patience he had always had for my privileged relatives. But he wanted to get away, and so did I.

All these things and more I wrote to Christina—daily and nightly, as I had been doing ever since we left home. Terry had made sport of me at first as I scribbled through the twilight or in the cold dawn, cramped and shivering: use it for a book, he said; don't throw it all away on a girl I hardly knew. But then he came to accept my folly as one of the conditions of our adventure. He allowed me the right to be in love, though I had to explain to him that, as far as I knew, the lady had no particular interest in me at all—a fact which he refused to believe.

"If you want a girl badly enough, you can have her," he said.

"You mean that goes for anyone?"

"No, I mean you. You've got the words—you can talk; you can make anything sound good." He grinned at me. "You better be careful what you write."

It was Christina I chiefly wanted to get back to, yet in all that time I had not heard from her—not once.

That October afternoon when I had dashed back to find her—without thought, with nothing but an eager heart—she had looked upon me with extraordinary merriment. I had probably known for days that I would do just that—on a Saturday when she would be home from college: call her from a drugstore somewhere, ask if I might drop in, take her for a ride . . . with no awareness of anything else, no sense of what it might mean in fact.

I called, and the strange, severe voice came as a little shock —her mother, of course: then Christina—Beanpole, I still called her—amused and cool. A shock of delight rippled up and down my bones; her voice was like a spring of mountain water, cold and open and clear all the way to the bottom. Ross's Pharmacy, she said—Prescriptions, Hospital Supplies, and Sodas—corner of Linden and State—side door on Linden.

A second-floor apartment of a two-story brick building, built for stores—an almost invisible dwelling, she said when I came, since no one ever looked higher than the shop windows. She had to run down a flight of dark stairs to let me in and lead me up again.

It was her voice—and words—that had stuck with me in the few weeks since we had met at the dance—that adventurous experimental voice, and the world of clear and humorous perceptions it seemed to create for itself. Now as she led me up the stairs, half turning to watch me, I admired her long legs and the coltlike bounce of her step. I felt very happy.

"Will you come for a ride with me?" I asked her.

"Not until mother inspects you," she said, loud enough for mother to hear.

The living room was suddenly large and light, with white painted woodwork, a big blue broadloom rug, white curtains, and a lot of small oils and pastels on the walls—hers, as I found later.

Mrs. Ross was waiting there, standing like a fate in the center of the carpet, a gaunt, gray, somber woman, almost as tall as Christina, bony, with deep features. She shook hands suspiciously, without a smile or nod, watching me from deep, steady eyes.

"You almost died up on a mountain, I believe," she said—and her speech was clearly Scotch, and rang out with that strong, harsh music.

"Yes—we were very foolish. Up there they call people like us goofers."

She nodded slightly. "When I was a girl my grandfather lived in Fort William—he made harness and kept a shop, and I used to visit him there. I climbed to the top of Ben Nevis seven times. That's more than this girl ever did."

"It's a nice thing to reproach me for living in Waltham." Christina put an arm across her mother's gaunt shoulders and shook her hard. "Whose doing is that, I'd like to know?"

"We'll just see what you're good for next summer. Your cousins will be ready for you—we're going back for a visit, Mr. Garretson. I promised her when she graduated from college—"

"You mean I promised *you*. She's crazy to go—for my sake, she says."

Mrs. Ross looked as somber and stony as a monument, and then suddenly turned and smiled at her daughter. It was a complete and helpless confession of love, an almost frightening surrender; if the stern old warrior had knelt with bowed head at her daughter's feet her submission could not have been more plainly revealed. I knew that Scottish character and its core of

steel, and this immense love seemed to me almost tragic—
though I couldn't have told why. The smile was somehow fatal.

We sat down formally, and Mrs. Ross asked me if I knew
Walter Scott. He happened to be her great-grandmother's
second cousin, though her people for the most part were
more humble; Sir Walter was balanced between plain folk
on one side and gentry on the other, though he fancied the
gentry and set himself up as a great squire. Did I know *The
Legend of Montrose?* It was her favorite of them all: those
bloodthirsty old highlanders—no one had ever understood
them as he did; blackguards and heroes they were, fools and
men together, like children with the power of strong men.
They hadn't changed much, she said, except the law found
them out quicker. And the covenanters—did I know *Old
Mortality?* Did I remember Habbakuk Mucklewrath? The
warped, bitter soul of Scotland was in it, but what a storm of
eloquence, what poetry; the man could write like a demon,
as though the ink he used was the very blood of his people.
You found nothing in Shakespeare like that—nothing anywhere in all creation. Shakespeare was all right in his way, but
he worked in a sort of vacuum, and there's no hard ground
under his feet; but take Davie Deans—he's got more true grief
in him than ever a King Lear with his fairy-tale troubles, or
take Lucy Lammermoor . . .

"It isn't fair to throw Scott at him right at the start, Mother.
He's still just an innocent visitor, you know."

Mrs. Ross did not smile. Her dark eyes were glowing, and
she had drawn breath for a long plunge into her memories, but
she nodded rationally.

"Forgive me, Mr. Garretson. When I meet anyone who
reads Walter Scott, I can't hold back."

It occurred to me that my teachers had all looked upon Scott
as not much more than the author of *Ivanhoe.* I hardly knew
that he wrote about his own people—much less dipped pen in
their blood. When I said that, she did smile a little. "In a

thousand years," she said, "the teachers and all such gentry will begin to see the stature of the man."

I don't know how it happened, but Mrs. Ross wholly confirmed my love for Christina. The two characters rang against each other like true metal. I wondered how there could be an effective third in such a partnership, and I couldn't recollect that Christina had ever spoken of her father. I knew nothing of him except that he owned and managed the prosperous-looking drugstore underneath their apartment.

Christina was more fair and open than her mother, and not simply because of youth. Her hair and eyes attracted the light, and her smile quirked into a grin at the corners; her thoughts moved lightly and fast; but in repose her face showed the strong bones that shaped it—chin a bit pointed, cheeks high and flat and perhaps slighly hollow; a sure, clean-lined face. I suppose her mouth was too wide, and when it didn't smile it set itself too firmly—the same set as her mother's. I think it wasn't only love that kept me watching the fine harmony of her features, though the more I looked at it the more beautiful it seemed. Yet I recollect that other men saw no beauty in her.

We talked a little more of Scotland, and Mrs. Ross questioned me on Robert Burns, Stevenson, and someone named Crockett whom I knew nothing of. I realized that she was willing to favor me simply because I read books. She spoke of Christina's work at college as though she had shared it all herself. "They belittle Carlyle in these times, Mr. Garretson. We are supposed to be beyond the need of moral teaching, as though we had outgrown it all. I'm not one of your old-time hell-fire Presbyterians prophesying damnation, but I know there will be a reckoning. I know what human nature is, which is more than some of your great scholars know."

Well, we did go riding together, with an anxious, half-jealous blessing from Mrs. Ross.

Two hours of it. I think we walked round Walden Pond—

on a path of cushioned gold. To me each breath, each slow step, each half word, was a pure crystal of esctasy. I don't know about Christina—she laughed a good deal, and color flooded her clear skin. Hadn't anyone, I said, ever told her she was beautiful—like a northern fir, like snow and ice, like the cool sky? No, she answered, she had always been given to understand that she resembled the beanpole and the hatrack —which were useful items, at least. But why, she asked, this sudden attention, this onslaught of fine language; what had she done to deserve this flood of metaphor?

"Suppose," I said, "you wanted to paint that winding bit of water and bushes and trees, how would you do it? What kind of shape and color would you make?"

"Why—" She looked at it a long time. "I guess I'd try to paint light. It's a sort of thick brightness lying along the sunny side there—it isn't really bushes and water any more, it's just light; you can see it flowing down the center like—well, honey or white shellac; I'd make that stump there the brightest white splash, and then all along on the right it's dark as dark— blue dark with reflections sort of disappearing away into a lot of shadow—"

"And why," I broke in, "is it good to change bushes and things into light? After all, a bush is just a bush."

She glanced at me a little suspiciously. "I'm just a young girl, Mr. Garretson. I believe in the nice illusions, like Santa Claus and God—and the bright radiance of eternity."

"Effulgence of bright essence increate," I spouted.

We got to laughing then, not in loud guffaws, but in grins that wouldn't stay quiet.

"You only have to paint a little bit," she said after we walked on, "to find that light is the only truth that matters."

"Will you show me how to paint?"

"I'll show you how to begin, which is about all I know." We were arm in arm then, and swinging along, with slow, aimless strides. "It isn't all fun, though," she added. "A painter gets to realizing what a little, little soul he has—I mean me, of course, but I guess it goes for a lot of others."

"Are souls made of light too?"

"Sure. Bright essence—what was it you said?"

Aimless talk, too; but to me it turned into wondrous two-part harmony, supported by all the golden afternoon, the colored leaves on the path, the shine of arched trees overhead and the thin blue beyond. Our voices joined and rested with spontaneity—not as though it had all been said before, but as though nothing else could be said. I suppose we went on foolishly and represented ourselves as brighter, wiser, purer, more miraculous than all the rest of creation—I'm sure I did. Christina, I recollect, made greater efforts at candor. She had the flush and brightness of one beloved—her words and laughter, the joyous swing of her long legs expressed her awareness; but at the same time she watched me with a detached and amused gravity.

When I told her I loved her, she shook off my words as though they were light drops of a shower. It was almost a hardness in her, I thought; an uncalled-for skepticism.

"Ralph," she said—this was some time later, as we drove homeward, "what are you doing in the world? Are you just a young man with a job?"

A little dart of resentment touched me that she, my beloved, should think fit to question my intentions—not toward her, but toward life. I said bluntly that just now I was a young man without a job. The flash of concern in her eyes made me realize instantly that I was a fool, and in the agony of love I turned humble to a childlike extreme.

I told her about everything—we sat in the Ford somewhere while I talked: perhaps it was the middle of Main Street. I told her about my wholly unpromising career, about the Kingsleys, about Mr. Quinn and Marilyn—and I think I put it decently. It is hard for one to speak truth about himself. A twist of phrase, and no one knows—no one will ever know . . .

She fathomed me as I spoke—a steady moral scrutiny. Did she have any idea, I wondered to myself, how lovely her plainness was, with the clean hair pulled back from the white forehead, and the almost marble fineness of her wide mouth. I recollected the starched frills and sashes she used to be decorated with at dancing class, emblems of her mother's fierce pride: now she wore the plainest gray flannel jacket and sweater and tweed skirt—heathery color, and to my eyes extraordinarily graceful and harmonious. An orange marigold was pinned to her jacket. I realized that she took delight in being a woman.

My aim in life, I said as a sort of final defense, was to live in terms of its real materials—like the folk of old who believed that all truth began with air, earth, and water. It was not my intention to evade duty and labor—so I said, at least; I was willing to immerse myself in the destructive element and acquire strength and merit by mastering it—I said that, too. But I couldn't act without belief. A year here in the mill had made that evident; no sense in plunging into any element if your only aim is survival. In the infinite and hostile waters, a solitary swimmer—or even any number of swimmers, however skilled and strong—lost all human significance. Nothing could happen but death.

She listened with a woman's patience—that is, half not listening, half amused at my rhetoric. What I said about mastering the elements seemed to her a bit confusing. Suppose my swimmers did have belief—suppose they swam in full faith, like the martyrs of old: wouldn't they be mastering their materials?

Each to his own belief, I said. Mine simply wasn't that strong.

And then, she went on, the question of what the real materials were—wasn't I being old fashioned? In college she learned that substance was nothing but a mass of electricity . . .

By then I knew she was making fun of me.

Would she marry me, I asked.

No, certainly not.

Would she be my girl?

By no means.

Was she anyone else's girl?

None of my business.

For an instant I almost shed tears. A wave of grief and frustration seized me without the slightest warning: I had been talking with a lot of boyish pleasure, and the last remarks were wholly impulsive—and I knew what she'd say. But just then the whole sweetness of her being occurred to me; it turned into a physical emotion, and vibrated all through me as though I had been shocked.

"Why?" I whispered it helplessly. "Why won't you?"

"Ralph, don't—well—"

"Don't be a fool, you mean." I started the motor and we drove on home. An intense misery had got hold of me, and I said nothing. I planned to go west—it was ordained; she was going back to Scotland. Ages would pass—a lifetime lost . . .

She smiled and shook hands the way girls do.

"Can I write to you?"

"Why, yes—of course you can."

"Can I come back—next year?"

She nodded. I suppose her smile would have seemed transparent enough to an onlooker, but to me it meant a year of study.

I fished in my pockets and came out with the only treasure I carried, a small jackknife with three blades of the best Sheffield steel.

"A parting gift," I said. "To enable you to master your materials."

Her smile changed a little—I can't say how.

"Thank you," she said.

I suppose I was blind.

CHAPTER 30

"You mean this seriously, Ralph?"

My father paced the length of the mantel, back and forth.

"Yes."

"You meant that your whole ambition is now to be a village carpenter?"

"I don't know about whole ambition—but that's part of it."

"Ah—what else, if I may ask?"

He had grown smaller in that year; the lean head bowed forward more than it used to, the shoulders sloped somewhat—or so it seemed to me when I first saw him. But the white hair waved back from his scholar's brow more strikingly than ever. He spoke just now with severe correctness, and I admired the fine distinction of his speech. In all the voices I had heard over the length and breadth of the land, none could match that exact, quiet clarity.

"Well," I said, "there's marriage—I suppose that's a sort of ambition. And I might make things rare and beautiful—you can't tell. I've been designing stuff for quite a while. And I used to say I wanted to write—I still do, though it's silly to talk about it. And I'm going to paint—you ought to see my sketches: well, perhaps you ought not to see them; but I'm improving anyway. And, God willing, I shall some day raise a few eggs and some milk and the best butter—"

"Ralph," he said, "I tell you this earnestly, and I beg you to listen: it is a young man's dream—a dream of sweet meadows and pure hearts and peace, of the horns of elfland faintly playing, of enchantment and love and everlasting youth. It is the oldest and deadliest of all dreams, more beguiling than the wines of forgetfulness or all the drugs of Circe. Once you accept it, the illusion builds up in you overwhelmingly: your heart and mind collaborate to reject the senseless bondage of the actual. On one side you see the harsh and bitter pain of a world at work—men and women struggling to do what they hate and in the end achieving weariness and death; and then on the other side you see your enchanted land like a benediction, where beauty dwells forever."

"Well," I began, "I've thought of that too—"

"It was my dream, Ralph. I'm not speaking out of books, but I do confirm them—I testify to their truth. You will wake up alone on the bare hillside, without virtue or hope—"

"Would you have those if you had braved the harsh world?"

He flashed a look almost of anger, then spoke quietly. "Yes, you'd have those. I don't mean comfort, Ralph; I mean simply virtue, which is manhood."

"That's the old rector's theme."

"Yes. I used to hope you'd understand it."

"You think it's impossible for a man to live his own life, as we say."

"I think men—especially men like you—have obligations, manifest destinies. I know that evasion means living death. Within the terms of his destiny, a man may shape his own life, but only within those terms."

"Queer to hear you talking of destiny," I said. "I thought you transcendentalists were superior to that."

He turned on me with almost passionate intensity. "Don't get caught up in names and theory—don't fool yourself with abstraction. Life happens, Ralph. It hits you—it breaks bones and hearts. You can't turn it away by putting up signs."

It was his face more than his actual words that touched me

most deeply. I had been sitting in his desk chair while he patrolled the hearth, and I had never seen him so earnest in speech, so forgetful of all but his thought.

"Ralph, take my advice now and go back to college. The year is just beginning—there's no reason in the world why you shouldn't."

"And then what?"

"Why, whatever you choose. You have mind enough, goodness knows." He looked at me with anxiety. "It could hardly be called a painful duty—not yet, anyway."

"Well—give me a day or two. I'll think hard—though it seems to me I've been doing nothing else for years. I do see what you mean. I honestly agree with you, and I admire the way you put it: but I believe the conditions of my decision are different from what you think—in a way they are almost opposite. Actuality, as I see it, is here where the visible materials of life are—even duty—" I stopped abruptly, then took breath and said, "I want to get married, Father."

He made a gesture of helplessness. "So you told us."

"Well, this is different."

When I told him about Christina he looked at me in utter dejection. I hadn't seen her for nearly a year, I didn't even know where she was, her father owned a drugstore—the whole thing was manifestly idiotic. "There's really no use talking rationally to you, Ralph. I don't know why I try."

Almost instantly he reverted to his familiar manner of ironic whimsey. "You'll be one of the village eccentrics, I foresee—an appropriate position for a Garretson, we must acknowledge." But he spoke with a steely coldness, and walked out of the room.

Yet I accepted his disapproval almost with complacence. My heart and mind collaborated to justify my own desires and to discount his. Whether for good or ill, my illusion had established itself. The freedom and space of the west had given me greater self-esteem, and I walked and talked with the air of a pioneer who no longer concerned himself with the vanities of eastern townsfolk. I had even adopted the costume of free men, the corduroy pants and flannel shirt. It may be that I behaved obnoxiously, though my intentions were kindly and full of good hope.

But—no Christina. I felt that the absence was temporary, of course; I expected a happy ending; yet thoughts of evil haunted me. She had not come back.

When I walked out to the Kingsleys on the day after Terry and I got home from the west, the land seemed small to me, like a miniature laid out on a rug; and it seemed to be touched with the neglect and sorrow of summer's end, with yellowing leaves and drying grass. I walked along with acute perceptions, smelling the weeds and dust, the faint smoke, the juniper and cedar on the ridge, and hearing the jays and far-off crows, the puff and toot of a B and M train across the small hills from West Compton. I saw all the green colors, the light emerald of swamp grass, the rust and bronze and gold of many leaves, the metal evergreens, distant mowings like rolled lawns, the sunny mass of maple and elm that covered up Compton Village like a summer flood. I thought of the bold words I had spoken to my father: actuality is here, I had said. He must have said that to his father, and had since regretted it; now I thought I knew better. I had the grace to grin at the passing glimpse of my conceit, and then I came over the ridge and down to the little spread of valley, and stopped to wink back the sudden tears.

In the stillness of sun and shade it lay like the very secret place of the heart. The white walls and plain low angles of the old house were fixed there forever, outlasting all time and trouble, exerting a power of harmony and persistent truth against the wastes of sad mortality. I walked down the curve to the level in a dream, and without further awareness I floated over the dust and weedy grass to the big open door of Seth's shop.

But the shop was empty. A beech timber lay along two

horses beside the bench, partly shaped into a wagon tongue. I walked through to the woodshed and knocked at the kitchen door, thinking that this time she wouldn't have seen me coming.

No one there, either. I walked in with a stab of concern at the emptiness and stillness, and some impulse led me to feel the stove. It was hot, and I saw with surprise that a bucket of coal stood in front of the closed woodbox; I moved a lid and looked in at the banked coal in the stove. Then I prowled back to the pantry and looked in cooky jar and cake box, found a piece of ginger bread, wandered over to the front windows and peered out while I munched. My heart was pounding in fear, though I couldn't have explained why—except that a year had passed and I knew nothing. They burned coal instead of wood, and even that change troubled me.

A small shelf was fixed at eye-level between the windows, with pins and buttons and an ink bottle and a stubby pencil and a postcard picture (colored) of the Fall River Line Steamer *Priscilla*—and a white envelope with a foreign stamp and postmark and my name on it. Care of Seth Kingsley, in strong, sure hand. Christina, of course—the grace and rhythm of a woman, the assurance of an artist. I reached for it, took it, and seemed to be floating suddenly in a far space with no body but a thudding heart. I held it a moment as though it might be a few square inches of her soul: Glasgow, it said; Sept. 3—her hand had been on it two weeks ago. Had she mailed it in lighthearted disdain, in farewell, in loving memory, in dutiful friendship? Not thin or slight—she must have put an hour, two hours, of her life into it. That much was mine. I slid a table knife under the flap and cut.

"Dear Ralph, My native city, I have learned, has neither beauty nor charm, but I wish I were there . . ."

My hands trembled, my brain buzzed; I gulped the letter down, took a long breath, and began it again. I hardly knew what she said; her words strangely danced and faded and loomed. When she said her father had died suddenly just after they had arrived, I felt a rush of tears. Heart attack—no warning. I had never seen him. Her mother, she said, wanted to stay there in Scotland; but the store and property in Waltham had to be dealt with, and they didn't know what to do. Their cousin Wingate Ross from Saugus had taken charge of things, but he owned a milk business and didn't know much about drugstores. Neither did her mother, for that matter. It would have to be sold.

"Mother wants me to stay here—we seem to have relatives in every town in Scotland; she says she'll go back to Waltham, sell everything as quickly as possible, and return here with the proceeds—and she's a good bargainer too. She wants to keep me here forever, and I don't want to be kept. I might as well confess that she wants to marry me here too—she has dug up every eligible man in the country, from a Lord (so she says) Glenconnor, without a cent—penny, I should have said, to Cousin Fergus McFergus who is heir apparent to a public house in Glasgow and wants a hostess. I haven't met the Laird yet—I think he's just a talking point anyway; but I have met a lot of boys by name of Sandy, Alan, Jock, not to mention Fergus, and have even been seriously questioned on the state of my soul and my standing in the eyes of God. I find that mother is reputed to be rich, which explains a good deal (my mother is an amazing woman—I hope you realize it). Scotland is a very serious place on Sundays, and my soul is in a state of embarrassment: but other days it is nice, and beautiful as a ballad, and I did climb some high mountains—at last, at last, though I shocked my cousins by bursting into tears in full view of everyone—just because it was so beautiful, and I hadn't the least idea; it was like getting hit by an arrow. They all said what a pity, I must be a poor weak female not used to the rugged ways of highlanders. I suppose you do get used to it—the beauty, I mean. I suppose you can even get so you can look right at Rockies and Grand Canyons without beginning to blubber, though I hope I won't have ever to do it in the presence of my Scottish cousins, much as I admire them. I really feel like a sort of Jekyll and Hyde creature—I have led a whole secret life just reading your letters: it is as though half the summer I had spent in the wild west, and the other half here being verra respectable. Mother nearly exploded with curiosity, so I let her see some of the more scenic parts of the letters and she said they were as good as Stevenson—and whether you think that's funny or not, it is wonderful coming from her. Be sure you laugh the right way."

Christina, I said to myself, is what I must have. Her voice came through the words, her tone and laugh. She asked if I had found my materials yet: in parables, she said, the seeker after truth always found it back home where he had started —which was one reason why she wanted to get back to her home in Waltham; truth was probably sitting right on the corner of Linden and Main waiting for her. But her mother was a fierce and unscrupulous woman; there'd be a lot of hard fighting—maybe even a real clan war if the cousins got into it, with pibroch and claymores. Yet she did like it there, the people and the country and even the oatmeal, and it was beautiful for sketches and water colors—in fact, she had sold a picture for a guinea (that's a pound with a title, she explained) and she sold a poem to a magazine in Edinburgh— a guinea for that too. She sold another poem to a paper in Glasgow—five shillings (clipping enclosed).

She said my letters were more than she deserved, but would I write some more: she needed something to laugh about, and she'd like to hear of my travels in Compton—and so signed herself my humble beanpole Christina.

A postscript: "Mother is plotting terribly against me. What shall I do?"

Steps in the woodshed. I looked up from my dream and saw the door open.

"Martha—hello!"

"Why, Ralph—"

We stood in a stare for a long moment. She shook her head a little smiling. "You're a man, aren't you? How does it feel—all big and old like that? But I'm so glad you're back—you don't know how they miss you." She shut the door. "I miss you too—I miss all of this. I don't have any self when I'm not here: I'm just Miss Kingsley."

"Martha," I said aloud, and waited for her smile. The old gentle softness had almost gone from her, the full curve of the mouth I had remembered. She had grown more set and square; the cut of her chin resembled her mother's. "Why don't you stay home a while—why don't you live here?"

"Because it's a better thing not to have any self." She smiled again as though she were practicing. "No you won't catch me feeling sorry for myself—not while I can do my work."

"Well," I said, "how are they?"

She stepped to the stove, looked in, opened a draft.

"Dad's got himself banged up. He fell off a scaffold."

So. I took a breath.

"It won't be very bad, I guess. He broke his left wrist and twisted his back—that's the worst because you can't tell about a back till you try to use it. The rest of him will be all right."

He shouldn't, she said, be climbing round scaffolds at his age—but it wasn't his fault, really: the man who worked with him was an idiot; he hadn't nailed the scaffold into anything and one end of it collapsed. It's a wonder they weren't killed.

How would it be, I said after we talked a good deal, if I became a sort of junior partner to Seth? What did she think of that? I'd nail up the scaffolding tight and strong; I'd keep him on the ground—I'd keep him here at home in the shop.

Her look was grim and skeptical.

"You're just playing round, Ralph—the way you used to go haying with Uncle Marvin."

"Miss Kingsley," I said. "I bet you scare hell out of your patients."

She wouldn't smile. "I hope I do," she snapped. I remembered how soft her mouth used to be, and the full sweet curve of her face.

I told her I wasn't just playing round, and I tried to go ahead and account for my existence. It wasn't easy. Her cold eyes studied me. As I spoke I watched the lines of mouth and chin, firm, durable, not quite humorous—yet full of human concern. She smiled slightly, almost as though she too remembered, and she brushed the hair back above her temples with a familiar stroke of her right hand.

But I couldn't stay. I grew impatient, and turned and hurried back to Compton, and started the Ford and headed for town to see Seth in the hospital. On the way I worked on the words for a cable. Please return at once: position waiting; urgent, take first ship; if broke will cable funds; reply collect . . .

CHAPTER 31

WHEN SETH came home, I went to work in earnest. I took over his car, his tools, his jobs—and instead of watching with a fierce and grudging suspicion he seemed to enjoy the experience as though he had grown young himself.

"I stand to profit whatever happens," he said. "If folks complain that my new man's no good, they'll appreciate me when I get back. If it's the other way about, they'll say the old Kingsley firm is getting new blood in it at last. I tell you, I never expected to enjoy loafing round here like this. You'll have a hard time getting me to do a day's work again."

I lived there now, in the room over the kitchen—low ceilinged, small windowed, warmed by a vent hole in the floor. Each evening Seth and I went over the day's work and planned the next. Each morning I was up in the half light, washing in the kitchen, tending the horse (an ancient survival now) and milking the cow (she barely tolerated me). Marvin and Jim had been doing those chores, but I took over under Seth's direction—though in a few days he could do most of it one-handed.

So the routine—autumn dawn to autumn dusk with rain and wind, frost and sun, and a strange day-long, night-long peace. I was always aware of the quietness lying like mist over the country, quietness of trees and grass and the road in morning, of barnyards where a rooster cried, or of crows calling above the forest on the ridge, and the quietness of buildings, of roofs and gables lying still against the sky. I felt myself merge with a slow-going river of life, as though Compton itself, and the Kingsleys and Garretsons, the roads, farms, stores, mills, trains, and the cocks and crows and earth and sky, had become one fluid substance making its sluggish, rolling way toward destiny. I drove Seth's pickup with the pride of one appointed to a junior partnership with mankind; I earned a membership in the fraternity of storekeepers, lumber dealers, freight handlers, mechanics, craftsmen, and farmers. I took carnal delight in my hunger, my muscles, my sleeping and waking; the very air of ease and freedom came over me like an ecstasy. At the end of a raw, iron-dark autumn day when I came home cold, stiff-jointed, numb in feet and hands, it was like returning to the heart and arms of a lover.

Indian pudding, Mrs. Kingsley said, was hardly worth making just for two, but she liked it and Seth liked it. She made it on Monday, when the stove kept hot for wash water; we had all the cream we needed, beaten stiff and piled on just when the pudding was cool enough to taste. Corn—she kept it coming almost every day through October (it's meant for October, she said). Apples, sugared and baked, with unbeaten cream, and pies and crisps and deep-dish puddings. Cider from Marvin's press: no need to drink water unless you like it. Baked beans, of course, nutlike and sweet, with onions in them; brown bread without raisins; pickles and relishes. Cakes, biscuits, muffins, breads—nut bread, corn bread, spice bread, honey bread; pancakes and waffles; upside-down cakes, tarts, turnovers.

She laid out projects like a commanding general. Saturday, if I got home in good season, I could drive them right into the Faneuil Hall markets, and on Sunday we'd better make the most of the weather and start up toward Townsend, and we could look in on her cousin Clara—they had apple orchards up there, and nice country it was in the fall—golden-delicious is what they were so proud of, a nice-eating apple but not tart enough for pie . . . Yet all this vital force made a sort of peace, a resultant of accord and pleasure. She pushed on into each day like a scout into new country with eyes keen for whatever was there. "I manage to lead him round a good deal," she said with faint accent on the him, "but he likes it—he intended me to when he married me."

Autumn rains renewed the springs, filled the wells; after the light frosts came the last harvesting, potato digging and days and days of apple picking over at Marvin's; Seth took advantage of his leisure and began painting the house—a task he kept at without end (having one hand was no drawback except for itches and flies); he got to work on the new plumbing—he had already ripped out and enlarged part of the pantry under the low part of the roof. Jim Kingsley had wired the house and shop, and I put in more outlets and ran a cable to the barn. We kept on using coal in the kitchen range, but I laid in wood for the other stoves, especially chunks for the potbelly in the shop.

He had some small jobs in there—some of Marvin's farm tools and a fancy seaman's chest Mr. Cadwallader had ordered for one of his girls who was engaged to a yachting enthusiast. We had to have power tools, I said—and knew I'd have to do a lot of persuading and figuring. Not mail-order stuff, either— but the best and stoutest. He shook his head and said he'd spent all he had on bathroom fixtures and the hospital—and he declined to buy goods without money, the way some folks did. I said we'd have to—and I'd do it myself; I still had some savings, and I could earn six dollars a day, and good machine tools would pay for themselves.

There's not much drama in the slow shaping of a life, but to me that was the time of crisis and decision. Past and future met in a balance, a turning. All that had ever happened to me reasserted itself and called out for a verdict, all the gleams and shadows from the well of memory, the old ways of heart and mind leading back beyond any recollection, beyond the

limits of one life—perhaps to the grave marked Beatrice
Randall Garretson, 1839-1887, or to the long-ago festivities in
the Hollisters' house, and the sisters Alice and May and beautiful Caroline, or to the long, transcendental dreams of Randall
Garretson in the Compton spring, to the age of poetry and
grace when God took care of all good things, or to the greatness
of Theodore, and the carriage and the stiff black hats and
Patrick with reins and whip, and the kids in the yard—yes, sir,
we'll put it all away, sir—we'll fix it clean as a wistle, sir—
and Dick Madigan with the white face of hatred, and grandfather at the mantel flipping his black tails and chuckling—
chagrined, he used to say, chuckling—very much chagrined.
Now in this autumn of peace, when the nation made much
money and played with the wondrous new toys of science, the
automobile, moving picture, and radio, Ralph Garretson, sig-
nificant only by virtue of his membership in the human race,
committed himself to hope—to more than that, but mainly
to the dream of work and love in Compton. Perhaps in this
simple life record it may be seen how commitments take shape,
the trifles planted in memory, the whims of small passion, the
hurt of failure, the unlooked-for comforts like the warm blaze
of old Mike Doonan's forge, Tom Madigan's hands moving
my shoulders to teach me how to bat, Musty Ellis on the sunny
hillside beyond the bounds of school, a pool of burnished
mahogany in Seth's shop. And fear, too—how much I can't
tell: the rector commanding virtue, the brick factories and
machines slatting all day, the big money, the multitudes, the
far challenge of ambition like the white peak wreathed in mist
and deadly cold—no man knows the springs and sources,
except that he sees the region from where they come, the huge
terrain of the past.

In the course of a few weeks I received five separate Garretson emissaries. My father seemed to resign himself to my folly;
when he saw me he simply inquired whether I had learned not
to hammer my thumb: but not so my stepmother and my

brother Steve, who prepared and delivered speeches of indignation. Mater's point of view had been clear for a long time, though she surprised me by walking out to the Kingsleys' to make a formal request that I come to my senses.

Steve came entirely on his own hook. He drove a maroon Buick roadster—had come down from Andover where he was beginning his second year of teaching. When I saw him I felt a stab of pride: bronze from his summer camp, graceful in gray-flannel suit, easy, quiet, wholly sure, he had achieved perfection. "Ralph, old brew, how are you?" He gave his clasp of fellowship and smiled. "What a junket you must have had—you and Terry!"

"Steve," I said, "you look like one of those Harvard men I read about. How do you do it?"

He had grace enough to grin then, a quick and charming grin that at once became a natural part of his design. "I trained for it: four years of steady application and a good tailor."

His hair grew in varsity pattern, low on his forehead, springing back cleanly—it had a natural sleekness independent of artifice: if he had plunged into water he would have emerged a well-designed gentleman and athlete, with hair, clothes, accent, and expression all in their natural place.

"Come to talk to the black sheep?"

"Well, partly that." He smiled again. "Haven't seen you in a year, you know."

We talked in the shop, and he wandered about with ironic curiosity, poking into drawers and shelves and tool kits. He said he'd keep on at Andover for another year, then take a year to get his master's degree. He spoke of his tennis, and when I asked if he were taking his degree in that he laughed aloud— a quick break of laughter, followed by a silence.

But he went on to say that mater felt pretty badly, and of course Uncle Richard did. We kept our tempers, drifted off to minor formalities, and Steve departed. His smile was the one he used after losing a match to a wholly unorthodox tennis player: a charming smile, implying that his defeat hardly counted among the right sort.

Uncle Richard called me a few days later on the telephone and invited me for Sunday dinner—he lived on a hill in Brookline.

Jean came to see me, bringing her first child. But she made no mention of how badly people felt. She said I looked fine, wondered if we could make a trestle table and benches for their summer cottage, and settled down for an hour's gossip with Mrs. Kingsley in the kitchen while the child crawled round and round the shop floor.

"Do you mind if I drum up some business for you, Ralph?" She spoke hesitantly. "You may have principles—no family interference, no favors? But I keep meeting people who want things, and the stores—you know how they are."

"Aren't you going to talk to me seriously, Jean?"

She smiled with sudden anxiety. "I thought I was." But after a bit she went on. "If I were a man I'd like to do what you are doing—live out here, work with my hands—only I'd raise animals too. Did I tell you we're going to buy a place in Lincoln? It's just ten miles from Dana's office. It's a dull little house, but lovely land and a pond and a whole big hill—and some day we'll do wonderful things to the house." She paused. "I don't know why you and Mr. Kingsley shouldn't do them—or would you rather not get mixed up with your sister in a business way?"

"You're very tender about my principles," I said.

"You know, Ralph, you look very healthy and strong, but you look sort of anxious too, as though you were on the defensive. Is it too much family?" she hesitated. "Mrs. Kingsley said you were worried about—" She picked Teddy out of a corner, wiped and dusted him off, and set him in a clean place.

So I told her all about Christina, and she nodded soberly, and suddenly I grew enthusiastic and pictured the two together, friends, sisters . . .

"I'll be your confederate—if you need one, Ralph." She tucked Teddy under her arm. "We've got to go. I don't know how you're fixed, but if you need any money I've got some— if you think you have to rush over there like Lochinvar, I mean. Or for anything: a honeymoon, for instance, or a pair of wedding pants." She smiled. "Come on, Teddy—we're late for your supper. He's a marvel, isn't he? People think he ought to howl more. Ralph, will you promise to let me know what happens? And take me to see her, will you? I mean, whenever you can." She walked out to her car. "It's so quiet and lovely here, and the old house, and those two just belong in it."

When she had gone I turned back to close the shop doors, but I had to reckon with a sudden heat of tears in my eyes, and waited a few minutes in the dusk to let them cool. I could hear a clink of Seth's pail in the barn, and I went to see if he needed a hand.

That ended the first series of visitations. Uncle Richard, I might add, offered me my choice of two jobs: one, a clerk in a copper mine in Arizona, the other a clerk in a bank in Paris. Either, he said, would give me essential business experience.

All these events are the separate pieces of the mosaic of that autumn. Because of the suspense, the patience to which I had been commanded, I lived in dreamlike incompleteness, without reasonable sequence.

I drove about a great deal—very often through Waltham in quest of supplies, very often along State Street, glancing up at the lifeless windows. The drugstore had fallen into the hands of a surly and indifferent manager who, I thought, managed it badly. He expected Mrs. Ross sometime in October.

Yet it was only the sixth of October when I saw the open window.

I rang, waited, rang again. I seemed to be standing several inches above the actual wood of the entry door, suspended there and beaten by my own heart.

Sounds came, heavy feet, a figure on the stairs, the dark face of Christina's mother.

"So," she said, "it's you." She confronted me.

I had prepared a smile, but quickly concealed it.

She stood in the posture of one holding a sword.

"Well," I said, "hello. You're back at last—is Christina with you? Could I see her?"

"You've made things very difficult, Mr. Garretson." She hadn't budged.

A silence followed. She seemed to be waiting for me to vanish.

"My intentions," I mumbled, "are good—at least, they're as good as I know how to make them." I summoned up the concealed smile. "I wish you'd tell me what's wrong."

Her sword glinted as she stirred menacingly against me. I continued to speak. "Wanting to marry Christina is not a fault, is it? If you think I'm not good enough, you're right—I agree to that—but after all, a man has to do his best, and that's what I'm doing."

She glanced beyond me, as though suddenly aware of being in a public place, then stepped back with lowered guard. "Come in, Mr. Garretson."

She led me upstairs. The place had a barren look, but western sun warmed the sitting room.

An awkwardness came upon us. I wondered if I had understood the nature of her hostility.

"I must speak frankly or not at all," she said suddenly. "Marriage, in my opinion, is not a private affair. The past and the future are in it, as well as family, and property, and public decency." She looked at me as though I would dissent. "Good folk are not accidental, Mr. Garretson. They have to be planned for and made, and not only by church and schools; it's mostly family, and family tradition." She fathomed me with gleaming deep eyes. "It's more than decency and goodness in the end—it's happiness, it's belonging to God's world." She nodded to the room, the windows, the street beyond. "Now this place is nothing—it has no future that I can see, no part in any good scheme of things, nothing that I could call either decency or happiness. My husband found it necessary to live here—naturally I made the best of it. But there's no more need of going on with it; we can go back to the real place we belong and live decently—and I believe happily too."

"And Christina," I went on, "can be the sort of wife and mother you didn't have a chance to be."

She almost glared at me. "Well, and is that a harm? I don't know why I discuss this with you, Mr. Garretson. After all, my plans are none of your concern."

A power of anger ran all through me, but I had enough sense to quiet it. I didn't know for sure that Christina had come back, yet neither did I really doubt it, and I kept listening and watching for her. I remained in a state of tension.

As the anger receded I heard Mrs. Ross's voice again. "I'm sorry for speaking hastily that way. It has been a great worry; I feel the responsibility like a weight on me. I can't tell you what it meant to be back among my people—my sister in Glasgow is very close to me, and they took Christina in like their own daughter."

"You think I'm not good enough for her."

"We don't know very much about you."

"After all, I've known Christina for ten years."

Her glance flickered to my clothes. "Can you support a wife?"

Suddenly I realized a lot of things I had been taking for granted. "Why," I said, "I'm—I'm—that is—"

Then the sound came, the click of the door, then the steps, the rustle. I stood up—and she was there at the door of the room.

We didn't move. "Hello," she said, very quietly, as though she knew I'd be there; her smile spread to her eyes and the corners of her cheeks. I said hello. Her bright, clear color surprised me. I noticed her breathing, the quickness of her eyes and smile, the motion of her tall figure, and I felt almost alarmed at the miracle of her life; it seemed like a sort of divinity, a grace and youth beyond my mortal limits.

She smiled again and looked at her mother. "You'd better ask him to supper. I bought enough chops." She turned with the big bag of groceries and went into the hall.

Mrs. Ross sat for a moment like a bronze image.

"I'm afraid I can't stay—" I began.

"You'd better," she said suddenly. "Of course you'll stay. Christina would be disappointed."

"All right, then." Her face still frightened me, but I spoke lightly. "Please forgive my work clothes."

She stood up. "Do you think I mind a man's honest work clothes? I'm not that kind of woman, whatever else I may be." She came to me, put a strong hand on my arm just below the shoulder and gave a fierce little squeeze. Then she walked on to the door, saying as she went out, "We have no telephone connected; you'll have to use one down in the store."

But I couldn't move until Christina came back and we stood looking at each other in a long moment of tension.

She spoke first. "You used to be a little chubby."

"Chubby? Me?"

"Well, yes—sort of like a kid. Years ago, it seems. You have very distinguished cheekbones."

I hardly heard. "Remember what we said about light—the divinity of light?"

"Did we say 'divinity'?"

"It's what you are, Christina. If I painted you, I'd paint light. That's something I just discovered now—when you came in with the groceries. It's there in the way you smile and stand—"

"Yes? Can you go on?"

"When you go to a store to buy chops, are there riots and disturbances? Do young men and clerks and bystanders follow you in a rout, and do you—?"

"No, Ralph, I always buy chops in disguise. Tell me, how did you know we were here?"

"Don't change the subject, Christina. You are beautiful—more than my brightest dreams; and that's what astonishes me, because I thought all along I was overdoing it. The actuality almost frightens me; my old beanpole has turned into an angel of all light—"

"A sort of celestial lamppost?"

All the time we had been talking we had been floating strangely in a far space without any walls or floor or physical substances. We came together, close, touching, arms, bodies, lips—yet hardly feeling or even knowing.

"Is it you, Christina?"

"Yes."

"Real?"

"Yes."

"Mine?"

A silence of space pouring round us.

"Did you say mine, Christina?"

"Yes."

"Forever?"

"Yes."

Still no substance to us, though we were together. A lifetime, it might have been.

"I'll have to fight for you, Christina."

She stirred, smiled as though the smile were answer.

"Won't I have to fight, darling?"

The smile shook into laughter against me. "What do you suppose I've been doing all summer?"

"But—she isn't licked yet."

She kissed me. "We're here, aren't we? I'm here—or am I?"

"Well," I said, "you're where I am."

"That's all there is to it," she said.

❦ CHAPTER 32 ❧

Love should rightly be the end, since there is no other except death. But chronicles go on without benefit of end. It was soon after this that my father invited me to supper; in time, after that, he died.

One evening Seth looked at me with a curious look. I could read the smile in his eyes, though his mouth expressed nothing.

"What you been doing?" I asked.

"Visiting," he said. "I been to see Mr. Garretson."

"Father?"

He nodded in a sort of relish of my surprise. " 'Twasn't about you—chiefly, that is." He waited again, and I waited, knowing his timing. "He did ask how you were."

"And you said I was doing middling well."

"It might be."

After a bit he explained that someone had bought the Dwight place and wanted it fixed up. What did I think about tackling it?

It fronted a country road that turned east from the highway about a mile northwest of Compton. Most travelers never saw it; even from the little road the house lay half hidden behind a forest of lilac trees. But Compton people knew it because it had once been the most beautiful of all our gentle farms, to use a term appropriate to its eighteenth-century fashion. House, barns, stables, gardens, fences, all belonged

together in white symmetry, designed and built as a unit—
about 1802, my father said—and intended to embody forever
the clear certainty of family and social good. Now in the twenties of another century it stood among wild-growing bushes
and grass with dreamlike loveliness. The Dwights who still
owned it—second cousins of the old Mrs. Townsend Dwight
whom mater used to call on—had employed a neighbor to take
a little care of it, so the roof was tight and the windows un-
broken. My father made it the objective of many a walk, and
kept a loving eye on it; he poked at clogged gutters and fastened
loose blinds and reported serious wrongs to Mr. Webb the
caretaker.

It was a man named Krueger. He wanted Seth to throw the
two west rooms downstairs into one big living room, with a
plate-glass window facing the old formal garden.

"It's a good idea," Seth said. "He'd have space and light and
a fine view. He's got enough rooms down there—there's a
small sitting room in back and a dining room, not counting
the kitchen ell."

"Did you tell him that?"

"I thought I'd drop in and see your father."

I almost asked why, but suddenly checked myself.

"Stayed an hour," Seth went on simply. "First talk we ever
had together; first time I was ever in his study there. He did
most of the talking."

I walked across the room twice. "Did you—did you decide
about Mr. Krueger?"

"Well, we agreed."

"Did father agree with you, or you with him?"

"There's going to be a meeting tomorrow—out at Dwight's.
You better come too." Seth's eyes narrowed in a smile. "I
presume I agreed with him. That's what I aimed to do when I
went there." He was looking at me shrewdly. "I've always
aimed to agree with him."

"That's one of your fancies," I said too sharply. But he

merely nodded with the sort of smile I could not then counter.

The "meeting" next day came in the late afternoon. We wore coats and hats and walked about in the chill rooms, staring dumbly at walls and ceilings and doors. I was not introduced to Mr. Krueger, but trailed along as the lesser member of the Kingsley firm.

"Mr. Garretson," Seth said in a voice unexpectedly loud, "is an architect we think pretty highly of. You'll find he knows more about these old houses than any man alive."

Father had been staring at the little carved pineapple in the pediment above the doorway between the rooms. He had seemed somewhat pinched and wispy to me, and his mantle was pulled up to his neck and chest against the close autumn damp of the unused house. But he turned, smiled, and a sort of radiance surrounded him. "Mr. Kingsley speaks as an old friend." He drew himself up as though many were watching him.

Mr. Krueger was a stocky man who moved about with vigor. He looked sharply at father, a level, somewhat hostile look, quite detached from personality. "An architect?" The word alone carried his whole thought.

"Well," father said, "I happen to be an old admirer of the house. I think Mr. Kingsley felt that you might enjoy hearing a bit about it, though you may already know what little I can tell you. That door between the rooms, for example, is beautifully sketched in Rockwell's *Colonial Interiors*—do you know it? Rockwell did the drawings himself. But this house is almost unique in the completeness of its interior design. The paneling over the mantel carries the carved motif of the fireplace—the little leaves there and the classic moldings—right up to the frieze and round to the doors and windows. Each room was designed as a small whole. I think much of what we call colonial—an unfortunate word—was rather accidental in its design—merely a collection of habits, perhaps; but here you have a conscious plan."

His face shone as he looked about him. He lifted a hand. "The motif of the other room is slightly different—see, you have a sort of formalized oak-leaf-and-acorn pattern . . ."

He walked through, talking. We followed.

"I didn't plan to consult an architect," Mr. Krueger said.

Father smiled again. "Oh, I'm just an officious neighbor. Mr. Kingsley shouldn't have used the word—I don't practice as an architect. I love the old houses—I'd like to show you my own house in the village. It isn't quite as fine as this, but it is very similar. Parts of it are a good deal older, and it has a somewhat conglomerate effect."

The hostile Mr. Krueger readjusted his gray-felt hat. His small eyes were steely blue as he measured us once again. Then abruptly, like an act of magic, he transformed himself from a man of business into a good fellow. "Well," he said in a higher pitched voice, "it's mighty nice of you to come over, Mr. Garrison. My wife would certainly like to talk with you—she picked out the house, you know. I said it's pretty far from town, it's pretty much run down—cheaper in the end to build, I claim. But, by George, it's beautiful. You feel it too—I can see that."

A strong sense of kinship grew among us. Mr. Krueger, correct in costume and business method, took us into his confidence. They would keep horses. And two cars—you'd have to have at least two in the country. And fix up the gardens. No cows or chickens—no sense in that—but plenty of fruit, and stuff like asparagus and peas and corn. He had come from a farm himself—Minnesota—and knew enough not to be sentimental about farming. But a couple of horses were different— he had two girls who were crazy about horses.

But the rooms, Seth said. It would be a shame to spoil that old woodwork. He nodded at the white pattern of the door frame.

Mr. Krueger glanced at us narrowly. "Got to have a good big living room," he said. Take out that wall—put a steel beam across. He had the steel—that was his business; he'd send it out in one of his trucks—send out men enough to handle it. There wouldn't be any trouble. He showed where the new window would be, facing right down the garden to a white gate at the end.

Seth looked pretty grim.

I spoke suddenly. "It would make a fine room." A sort of perversity made me say it, though actually I inclined to agree with Mr. Krueger.

"Two fireplaces?" father said with faint asperity.

"Why not?"

Father hardly glanced at me. He turned to Mr. Krueger. "It would destroy one of the essential values of the house. As it is, you have a perfect original. Time will increase its worth. In twenty years, I venture to say, it may be worth twice what you paid for it. But once you tear out that wall, put in steel and plate glass, you no longer have the genuine Dwight house. It would be like trying to improve the title page of a first edition, or perhaps resketching the features of a Reynolds portrait. However interesting the effect, you do destroy the original."

The words sound didactic, but father spoke with intense belief and a sort of grace that made one want to listen. He went on, even though Mr. Krueger had begun to answer. He had put the matter of value first because Mr. Krueger was a businessman. But beyond that were other considerations—both esthetic and sentimental. Mr. Kingsley agreed with him in feeling that a house like that was a sort of sacred trust—like all works of classic art. The age of reason was now simply a lifeless phrase, but once it was a vision of order and grace.

To me his discourse was beautiful. In that chill and empty house he created a living ideal. One felt a divine rightness in the endangered doorway. The pineapple in the pediment grew infinitely precious, and the clean little designs in wood and white paint attained a life and spirit of their own. It wasn't an abstract piece of esthetics, he said—a rarity for a museum, rather it was a way of living, a statement of faith, a creation of pure good, a happiness made everlasting.

Logically I understood Mr. Krueger's desire for a big room with light and view. I had expected him to be a sort of vandal come to trample down our old ways, but he represented nothing more sinister than a simplehearted man with a family to settle and a taste for country life. He knew nothing of sacred trusts, and I half thought he was better off for not knowing. But father's talk moved me—not because of its matter and logic, but because of a fiber in it, a strain. I remembered dimly how I had visited my grandfather at his death, and how the man I had feared, even hated, had seemed to be transformed into a character of austere beauty. Perhaps no one ever truly perceives his own kin, but here in the Dwight house I had the curious experience of seeing plainly a Randall Garretson I had never quite distinguished before. He spoke out with love, with wisdom, with an alert and easy mastery of all his elements. "Henry Miller designed this house," he was saying. "Rockwell had the bad luck to attribute it to Peter Banner, and now has to stick to it. Like potentates and politicians, an art expert never admits error. But that oak-leaf pattern is Miller's alone. You can see the McIntire influence in every line of this interior, and of course Miller was one of McIntire's later pupils. He nearly starved, I believe—architects in those times were luxuries. A good carpenter could turn out a very pretty house by consulting *The Country Builder's Assistant*. Have you ever seen that, Mr. Kingsley?"

Seth's grave face had concealed all expression and he had stood without motion except for a shift of his hooded eyes from one speaker to another. Now he shook his head, and something in his carved features softened almost to a smile. "It would do me good, I expect."

Father paused to relish the remark. "Books do harm, too. An architect has to be better than the book he learns from. Miller was, and that's why his house is unique." He spoke lightly, and the words carried no rebuke. I had never seen so much vitality in him. His face shone brightly and his words danced. "I've tried to find out who actually built the house—who cut and planed and nailed the wood. Henry Miller would have got nowhere without his craftsmen. Was it one of your grandfathers, Mr. Kingsley?"

"Might have been. It's nice work, no doubt of it. There's still plenty carpenters who could do just as good, but mostly now they don't get a chance."

Mr. Krueger spoke then from a slight distance, as though he were detaching himself from us. "I'll talk with my wife about it—she likes the old things. But I don't figure on living in a museum. The way you put it, I'd be running a sort of show place, like something in a guidebook. I don't mean to say I haven't appreciated what you've been telling me; I guess I didn't know much about the old place—had no idea it was written up in books and all that. My wife'll certainly want to know about it. But my idea is just a comfortable home, a place to use and enjoy . . ."

I expected father to argue, but he nodded affably. He said he hoped to meet Mrs. Krueger; if she were interested he would enjoy showing her the material he had collected on the history. We moved toward the door. Mr. Krueger said they'd be coming again on Saturday afternoon, and father said they must stop at his house in Compton Village. So we stood in the fresh November air, feeling the presence of the silent house, the old gardens, the fences, walls, shadows. A luminous dusk surrounded us. Father courteously declined an offer of a ride; he counted on his walk home. Mr. Krueger drove off in a long black touring car and Seth drove off in the pickup. Father had invited me to supper and we set off together.

The question was, I said, whether preserving the exact features of the past was a good idea. We had to live here and now.

It was some time before he answered. His words, when they

came, were filled with a sort of placid good humor. "You are perfectly right, Ralph. My position is anti-human."

"Well," I said.

We turned into a small road that wound up through pines and red-leaved oaks. A shimmer of late sunlight filled the haze-blue air above us, but the ground lay under shadow. Father's stick played among the dry leaves as we walked.

"But only, it seems to me, in one sense. You probably feel that Mr. Krueger represents life; he counts, whereas the house is dead. Yet to me the house is not dead, nor is the existence of Mr. Krueger's family of primary importance. We don't change a law to suit the convenience of the individual."

"The house is not the same as a law," I said.

He turned on me and his stick flourished. "But it is, Ralph! That's my whole truth. The house is a statement of principle— an embodiment, an example of it. You would modify it to meet our temporary desires—make beauty less beautiful so that the Krueger girls can give bigger parties. Well, I haven't the least objection to the Kruegers living in ease and pleasure, and if they built a house for that purpose, I should consider it very sensible. But the Dwight house was not designed for their desires—"

"Or for anyone's?"

"Now, come, Ralph! You know as well as I do that certain expressions are immortal, and this house happens to be one of them. It is certainly not anti-human—quite the reverse: it embodies hopes, it sums up mind and spirit—every line of it represents a lofty human vision. And as between that embodiment and the passing desires of a temporary family named Krueger there's really no valid issue. They'd be just as well suited by a hundred houses, but once you destroy this house you destroy an irreplaceable human value."

I pointed out that he was not being consistent.

"You remind me a little of your Aunt May Hollister. She

used to take me to task." He smiled fleetingly. "After all these years I have no great desire to defend my position—in fact, I don't know that I have a position. I make what I can of things."

I said nothing.

"It may be," he went on, "that I have merely lived out a dream. From the way you look at me I assume you think so. Your reality is flesh and blood—or hammer and nails: Mr. Krueger and Seth Kingsley."

"And yours," I said, "is a vision."

"Tut, tut, Ralph."

"Well, idealism is a weak word. You live in terms of absolutes."

He smiled with a serenity that matched the cold autumn dusk. "Pretty big words you use, Ralph."

"In another age you'd have been a monk."

"In which event I shouldn't have had a son to put me in my place."

We left it at that. But from then on we walked with a close fellow feeling. The time of year was peculiarly right for our communion. Coming from the old Dwight house into a November afternoon, raw and shadowy, yet filled with fading radiance, was like discovering the very heart of our life together. The place had given up all its temporary tricks of charm—its decorative leaves and blossoms, its beguiling warmth and fragrance; nothing remained now but the austere facts, the earth and stones, bare branches, hard curves of field and hill. The early night brought winter frost; the road hardened under our feet, and a deeper silence got hold of us. Yet above these realities existed an immense freshness of air and light, a fragrance and spirit together that kept our heads high and our steps quick. Whoever lived here had to face up to these conditions, the plain earth, naked trees, frost, darkness.

"You don't," I said, "seem really worried as to the fate of the house."

"Well, I may be a monk, as you say, but I'm not a fanatic.

I'm ready to compromise with the inevitable. But the game isn't over, Ralph; there's a lady in it."

"So that's how it is," I said.

Later as we turned into Compton Street together he slowed his step. I saw that he was trying to find words for something. Presently he asked about my plans.

"Forgive my questions—I—" He hesitated. "As a matter of fact I should have spoken of this some time ago. You must realize that our property is no more mine than it is yours—that is, all the family's. I've been setting aside some funds for just such an event as this—and I'm going to turn them over to you now. I can think of no more desirable use for them—"

At this point we came to the front path of our house. Father almost ran up to the door. "Perhaps I might be permitted to call. I've been very slow, Ralph—very." He opened the white door and stood back with a humorous little bow and scrape. "Come in, come in," he said, gesturing with his walking stick. Blinking a little, I stepped into the yellow light of the hall.

I was taught to accept or reject men according to label, and when I began to think about life in Compton I naturally thought in those terms. I learned certain responses, mostly bitter and contemptuous. My people were puritanical, and genteel, and reactionary, and decadent. I saw my father, not as a man breathing, but as a sort of object lesson arranged by the Left Bank Society of Harvard. The habit continues among us even now and represents, in spite of its intellectual sanctions, a fanaticism. In recent town meetings I have been called an intellectual, a half-baked red, an impotent liberal, and a futilitarian—all in connection with spending tax money to make Spring Pond a town park.

The Garretsons are not offered here as object lessons, but as men and women living. Uncle Richard has amassed enormous property and power, not because he inherited a family habit, but because his personal energy and ambition drove him. Steve, my brother, has followed a conservative pattern which I deplore —yet he went to war, distinguished himself in battle, became a colonel, received decorations and honor. Whatever his label may read, he is a man. And as for Jean, she would do honor to any generation, though I once overheard someone accuse her of having the accent of a damned Bostonian snob.

I should like to chronicle other Garretson destinies—Aunt Liddie living in her little cloud with a few family relics; Aunt

May, more and more profiled like an early statesman, fighting for playgrounds and better schools; my half brothers—one killed by a German bullet on Anzio beach; even my cousins, particularly Oliver, Uncle Richard's eldest, who was expelled forcibly from Greece and now writes a syndicated column in the liberal press—but all these lead away from Compton into the infinite of life and time.

It is fair to say that love triumphed over all. We lived happily in a three-room tenement above the town clerk's office, then in a one-storied farmhouse all alone in the country a mile and a half along the back road to West Compton, then in a four-room cottage designed and built by Garretson and Kingsley and in part paid for by unearned Garretson money. It stands about a hundred feet from the road on the east slope of the ridge above the valley of the Kingsleys, looking down toward the elms and maples of Compton.

I often feel that I am taking an unfair advantage over life. When I read Thoreau I have an uneasy sense of his stacking the cards before he plays them; his truths are too convenient —for him. But my own are that way. I took things without earning them—Mrs. Kingsley's heart, Seth's mastery of materials, many other things. When we equipped the old shop with power tools and hung a small sign over the door (my project) I found that we began to be known far and wide. People drove in with precious objects, or with ideas and desires. Everyone knew that Seth Kingsley did good work—everyone knew it better than Seth himself did. The business flourished and all we did was to work to our hearts' content.

But we made only meager profits, and for several years after the great depression we lived in poverty. Yet it hardly mattered. We had more of what we most needed—time. Perhaps that is unfair too, but so it actually happened. Since then there have been many fluctuations, and many deaths and victories; the business has been at times extinct, at times absurdly profitable—as when I made a set of scale working models of a dynamic modern house to be produced in quantity by a former airplane factory.

But the unfairest advantage of all I am forced to mention somewhat hurriedly and secretly. Christina has read most of this—she laughs at what I take seriously and ponders over the items I present too lightly. Women, she says, will not see the humor of it, nor men the seriousness. One thing no one will ever truly see is Christina herself. We live with a surrounding of beauty, the small, quiet, durable beauty of this familiar bit of earth, the woods and metals we use, the tools, the ideas and purposes—and the essential spirit of the whole is Christina. She took charge of all these things, not with vague sentiment, but with intense Scotch realism, with an austerity matching the place itself, with the fierce creative energy of a born artist. She astonished Seth by coming to work in the shop, and keeping at it week after week through the most humble jobs, doing each trifling task with devotion, learning and watching like an acolyte. She was a woman in love, not simply with her partner, but with her way of life and her dream of how it should be. She grew beautiful and strong, and kept herself so.

In the end—for this is it, at last—one may only indicate a direction, an opening into possibility. Each man has to do his traveling on his own. My discoveries in life are here for whatever they are worth—and the worth may seem slight in this age of power. A lone man is a small thing and the simple life seems out of place, just as air and earth and fire and water are out of place among the elements. Before he died my father often walked out to see us; he said he had lived most of his life wrong end to, beginning far back with a full-grown ideal yet with no warrant of experience; now in his age he was getting acquainted with the roots of things. I remember him the last time he came, very thin and white and almost transparent— my children called him the good ghost; he wandered about the place poking into things with an eager humor, like a clever child himself, and finally sat in the sun on the doorstep with an ax in his hands. He weighed it, felt the steel, stroked the handle. "I suppose I'm a little too old to learn to use it. If there were time, you could teach me a good deal, Ralph." He glanced at his grandsons and smiled happily.